DISCARDED

Praise for Lara Donnelly's *Amberlough*

"An astonishing first novel!" —Ellen Kushner,
World Fantasy Award–winning author

"*Amberlough* grabbed me from the first page. It is beautiful, all too real, and full of pain. Read it. It will change you."
—Mary Robinette Kowal,
Hugo Award–winning author

"Sparkling with slang, full of riotous characters, and dripping with intrigue, *Amberlough* is a dazzling romp through a tumultuous, ravishing world."
—Robert Jackson Bennett, winner of the Shirley
Jackson Award and the Edgar Award

"Terrific! Very Evelyn Waugh meets *The Sandbaggers*."
—John Chu, Hugo Award–winning author

"What a rich and melancholy book; so tragic, so gay!"
—Kai Ashante Wilson, Nebula and World
Fantasy Awards finalist

"James Bond by way of Oscar Wilde." —Holly Black

"This is the book we need right now. *Amberlough* is a gorgeous, crucial reminder that even when the fascists take over, people will fight back—no matter how flawed or frightened or damaged they might be, or how much they risk by doing so."
—Sam J. Miller, finalist for the Nebula,
World Fantasy, and Theodore Sturgeon
Awards and winner of the Shirley
Jackson Award

"*Amberlough* offers a sharp, lush, sensual espionage cabaret, a Weimar world of lovers, criminals, and spies all floating toward the fire."　　　　　—Max Gladstone, Hugo and LAMBDA
Literary Award finalist

"Be careful or you too will be lost in the whirl of the kind of glamour familiar in 1930s Shanghai or Weimar-era Berlin. Powerfully seductive and wrenching."
　　　　　—Fran Wilde, author of *Horizon*

"A glittering cabaret of a novel, with show-stopping language on every page."　　　　　—Lev AC Rosen, author of *Depth*

"Sexy and suspenseful, with characters who play for keeps, Donnelly's debut novel mixes secrets, spying, and outlawed love like a perfectly made cocktail . . . one that seduces before hitting you with an unforgettable kick."　　　　　—A. M. Dellamonica,
LAMBDA Literary Award finalist

"Lust and betrayal, intrigue and treachery, feints within feints within feints—*Amberlough* will keep readers up late into the night."
　　　　　—D. B. Jackson, author of the Thieftaker Chronicles

"Weirdly elegant, wholly engaging. I couldn't put it down."
　　　　　—Josh Lanyon, USA Book News Award for GLBT
Fiction and an Eppie Award winner

"If you put David Bowie, China Miéville, and *Shakespeare in Love* into a blender, you might get something as rich and frothy as *Amberlough*. An intricate tale of society where nothing is as it seems, and where the political is all too personal."
　　　　　—Cecilia Tan, author of the Struck by
Lightning series

"Donnelly blends romance and tragedy, evoking gilded-age glamour and the thrill of a spy adventure, in this impressive debut. As heartbreaking as it is satisfying."

—*Publishers Weekly* (starred review)

"Striking debut brings a complex world of politics, espionage, and cabaret life to full vision."

—*Library Journal* (starred review, Debut of the Month)

"A sense of inevitable loss and futility permeates this rich drama. The fascists may never be defeated but only escaped—if the characters are willing to abandon the people they love. That dilemma will haunt them, as it haunts the reader." —*Kirkus Reviews*

"A timely novel exploring the roots of hatred, nationalism, and fascism, while at the same time celebrating the diversity, love, romance, fashion, and joy the world is capable of producing, Donnelly's *Amberlough* is a thrill and a wonder from start to finish." —*Book Riot*

"Immensely compelling. Full of color and verve and poor life decisions on the part of the characters—full of humanity. If this is how Donnelly is running out of the debut gate, I want to read many more novels from her pen." —Liz Bourke, *Tor.com*

"A hefty novel full of fascinating characters exploring oversized topics such as sexuality, music, culture, fascism, nationalism, class wars, revolution, and love. Donnelly's exuberant and complicated espionage thriller is a delicious adventure that smoothly addresses timely topics such as diversity, nationalism, corruption, and repression." —*Shelf Awareness*

"If you want reminder of a forgotten era of history overshadowed by the horrors that came afterward, give *Amberlough* a try."

—*Amazing Stories*

ALSO BY LARA ELENA DONNELLY

Amberlough

LARA ELENA DONNELLY

ARMISTICE

TOR

A TOM DOHERTY ASSOCIATES BOOK · NEW YORK

This is a work of fiction. All of the characters, organizations, and events portrayed in this novel are either products of the author's imagination or are used fictitiously.

ARMISTICE

Copyright © 2018 by Lara Elena Donnelly

All rights reserved.

A Tor Book
Published by Tom Doherty Associates
175 Fifth Avenue
New York, NY 10010

www.tor-forge.com

Tor® is a registered trademark of Macmillan Publishing Group, LLC.

The Library of Congress Cataloging-in-Publication Data is available upon request.

ISBN 978-1-250-17356-0 (trade paperback)
ISBN 978-1-250-17355-3 (ebook)

Our books may be purchased in bulk for promotional, educational, or business use. Please contact your local bookseller or the Macmillan Corporate and Premium Sales Department at 1-800-221-7945, extension 5442, or by email at MacmillanSpecialMarkets@macmillan.com.

First Edition: May 2018

Printed in the United States of America

0 9 8 7 6 5 4 3 2 1

To the Alphans and the Awkward Robots, who helped me along the way.

ACKNOWLEDGMENTS

This book wouldn't have been possible without my agent, Connor Goldsmith, and my editor, Diana M. Pho. Thank you both for bringing another one of my twisted, shrieking book children into the world.

Thanks to my mom, of course, who is always there in a plot emergency. To my dad, who endured my frantic revising when we ought to have been doing fun things in the Big Apple. And to Eliot, who met me at the peak of pre-debut release anxiety and has patiently endured—possibly even enjoyed—being in close proximity to the high-speed creation, revision, and finalization of book two. I think he might even stick around for book three!

My friends in the pub were instrumental to my finishing this book, especially Jay Wolf for plot bouncing, and Gabrielle Squalia, who gave me an amazing title. Alyx Dellamonica and Kelly Robson smuggled Voltaren in from Canada, and gave me permission to just Write A Draft Already, and Stop Fussing. Stay hydrated, friends!

The students of the 2017 Alpha SF/F/H Workshop put up with my frantic revising, and in fact helped me with my writing while I should have been teaching them. Keep an eye on those kids; they're going to amaze us all someday soon.

Alphans of the past also put in their bit: Sarah Brand very helpfully pointed out that everything bad is always Cyril's fault somehow, which resolved one of my biggest logistical frustrations early in the game. Seth Dickinson's commiseration on the difficulties of writing a sequel assured me I wasn't alone in despair. Maya Chhabra linked to Urdu poetry in an emergency. Alina Sichevaya provided memes and enthusiasm, and Ana Curtis waved pompoms every time I sent her a snippet, so I knew I was doing okay.

Many thanks to the Awkward Robots, of course. There wasn't time this go-round for a full critique from all of you, but Sarah Mack read snippets at the inception of this book, so many years ago, and told me it was worth working on. And anyhow, would I even be writing these if not for all of you? I think not.

Shout out to all the people on Twitter who helped with incidental research. Shockingly helpful! Thanks a bunch. And to the good folks at Infinity Sports Medicine and Rehabilitation—I'm typing these acknowledgments by the grace of your physical therapy skills.

Thanks again to Sunshine, for letting me use her last name for my villain. She's a much better, nicer person than Flagg. He brings shame to the family.

I'm sure I am forgetting scads of people. If you had a hand in this book and feel slighted, go ahead and throw down a gauntlet. Pistols at dawn, or maybe drinks at the bar next time we're in the same town.

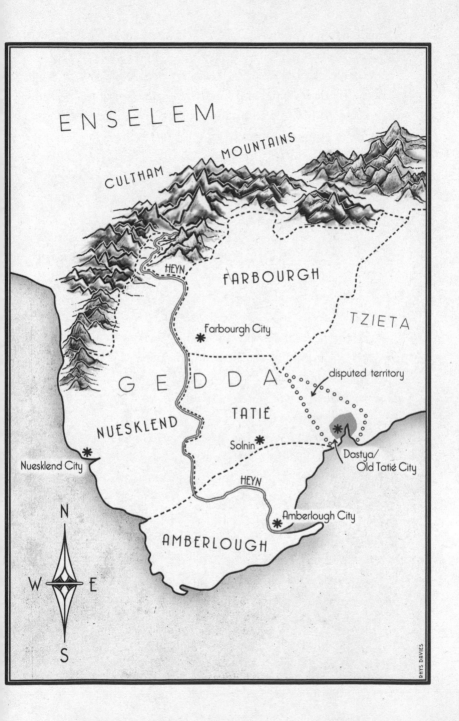

What he needed to do from now on, if there was going to be a now on, was abandon his morbid quest for order and treat himself to a little chaos, on the grounds that while order was demonstrably no substitute for happiness, chaos might open the way to it.

—John le Carré, *The Night Manager*

"Louis, I think this is the beginning of a beautiful friendship."

—Rick Blaine, *Casablanca*

PART

1

CHAPTER

ONE

Cordelia sat through the customs inspection nailed inside a crate, breathing into her bunched-up shirt to muffle the sound. She couldn't understand the words—blood pounded in her ears, and besides, they weren't speaking Geddan.

It went on for hours, felt like, and then there was a long stretch of silence, broken by bangs and curses and the groan and scrape of metal against metal. Unloading the real cargo. By the time Josippa took a pry bar to Cordelia's hidey-hole she'd soaked through her clothes, fear-sweating.

"Stinks like a sauna in here." Josippa tossed the length of metal to the floor of the newly empty hold. The clang echoed. "Come on, out. Sun's down and there's some women that won't go away. I think they're yours."

"You sure they ain't hounds? Foxes?"

"They're neither of them a beast of any description. If I'd a guess to venture I'd say they're the other end of your line, but I'm not in the business of guessing things I'm not supposed to know. Helps me to speak honest with the harbormaster about my cargo."

Cordelia stood and twisted her spine until it popped. "Yeah, what were you, working out a marriage contract with your customs folk?"

"You haven't whined a teaspoon since we took you onboard. Don't start now." Josippa opened up the hatch on an evening sky, purple turning black, burnished by city-glow.

It had been hot inside the hold, sure, but it kept right on being hot on deck. A breath-warm wind off the ocean swept over her skin, leaving behind a salty film. Factory reek mixed with harbor dross, all of it cooking into a putrid stew.

Josippa took a deep breath through her prominent nose. "Ah, Berer. Almost as good as Dastya in the summer, and here it lasts all year 'round."

"Where are these women?" Cordelia peered cautiously over the side, down at the dock, but didn't see anyone. At this late hour, most everybody seemed to have gone home.

"Down the street," said Josippa. "I told them I'd bring what they were looking for later. Made it sound very mysterious. I just needed them out of my underclothes long enough to unload. And the harbormaster was starting to look leery."

"You're a treasure," said Cordelia.

"Maybe I can pawn myself. You paid me spit on tin for this and told me it was silver." But she smiled when she said it, and led Cordelia down the gangway.

Smoke from half a dozen hookahs hung in veils from the low ceiling of the coffeehouse. There were other folk around, sucking on the ends of hoses, but the low light made it tough to pick out details. Cordelia was grateful for that—it meant nobody would get a close look at her.

Not that she was so recognizable, anymore. She'd hacked away most of her scarlet hair early in the game, leaving a tumble of curls longer on the top, styled in a ragged high-and-tight. Easy to cover with a cap, colored red with whatever she could get ahold of— sometimes just watery paint. It gave her scrappers a little bit of hope, a little bit of the home they remembered. Since she'd blown up the Bee sometimes it felt like her six-inch square of bright red curls was all that remained of old Amberlough. In three years, the Ospies had managed most of what they set out to do, and Cordelia—lagging behind a little bit—had gone from opportunistic arsonist to organizer. Joachim, Zelda's man, had been hers for a while, and he brought along some useful friends. In turn, they brought some of their people. Word spread in whispers, mostly through theatre folk and black-market scullers with greasy palms. It was Opal, who used to work as gaffer for the Diadem, who said *Let's call ourselves the Catwalk; we get things done unseen, and then light it all up when we please.*

It was her idea to hit the trains, too. All the grain and fruit and fabric and coal coming down from the north. The goods shipped into Amberlough's harbor meant for the rest of the country. Kill the railroads and you killed commerce. Kill commerce and you killed the country.

When they started to need code names—when their pictures went up after they blew the tracks at Lindenbarr and one of Joachim's old sparks tried to collect some scratch by singing about them—they called Opal "Gaffer" and laughed about it. Joachim was "Stagehand." Cordelia, with her bright red patch of curls, was "Spotlight."

Now, she wasn't anybody except her new fake name—Nellie Hanes—and the red hair was long gone. She'd dyed it brown in Dastya, in the sink of a public washroom.

"Ladies," said Josippa, opening her arms to two women in a

shadowy corner of the coffeehouse. Their table was bare: no hookah, no coffee, no food. "My apologies for the delay."

"Captain Bozhic." One of them stood. "We have been here for *three hours*. What *is* going on?" She talked like a swell, though this close Cordelia could see well enough to clock her dusty clothes and her hair coming out of its pins. Stood straight, though, and had that gimme-what-I-want attitude.

It had been a long time, and they'd only met the once. She wouldn't have known the woman in the street. Didn't really know her now, except to know she *should*. Only knew her name because Luca'd told her: Sofie Cattayim.

"You asked about your package," said Josippa. "I brought you your package. Here she is, and I'm glad to be done with her." The captain clapped Cordelia on the shoulder, hard enough she almost staggered. "She's a nice sort but not worth so much worrying."

"What on earth?" said Sofie, but Josippa had already turned away and headed for the door. Robbed of that avenue, she rounded on Cordelia. "Who are *you*?"

So she didn't recognize Cordelia, either, and hadn't had someone like Luca to give her memory a shake. Cordelia wondered if she even remembered handing off those earrings, if she knew who all she'd scratched.

"It's hard to explain," she said. "Maybe somewhere . . . well. Not here."

The swell's companion, who so far had kept her peace, clicked her tongue slow against her teeth three times. "Oh, Luca, ye've visited a proper trial upon me this time, haven't ye?"

The swell jerked her head around, losing a pin. "What?"

"She's right, Fee. We'd better hie back home before we ret this out. Come away." She unfolded from her seat and ushered Sofie out of the booth.

"Mab," said Cordelia. "Right? Mab Cattayim."

"And at the moment wishing I was anyone but, and Luca not my nephew after all."

"What's going on?" snapped Sofie.

"Home," Mab insisted, and gently pushed her toward the door.

Cordelia had landed in Berer because one of the boys helping to hide their cell in the Culthams had an aunt, he said. Dead to him, on account of marrying outside the people, but she wrote to him every now and again on the sly, and she was hale and hearty enough for Cordelia's purposes. Which were, as Opal put it, "get as far from Gedda as quickly and quietly as possible, or they'll put you away somewhere there ain't no sun."

Luca's aunt had an old marriage, he had said, to a Nuesklen girl and a foreign boy, who'd been arrested when they ran off together but then slipped the hounds with the help of some runner in Amberlough City. Aunt Mab had paid the man all she had and half again to get out with her husband and wife before the Ospies got a good grip on the country.

After comparing some dates and descriptions, Cordelia realized she knew who he meant. She'd helped Ari ferry a few people out of Amberlough—moving money, doing deals down at the docks—and this one she remembered. Zelda's attic, the police in the street, and those stupid earrings she should have pawned straight off.

She'd let Luca think she was going. Let him send the letter, and let Opal bundle her into the back of Luca's father's truck, but she'd planned all along to lie low in the eastern foothills of the Culthams, just over the Tzietan border, until things cooled down and she could creep back.

But things didn't cool down. They blew up, and then they burned, and there was no safe way back in. So in the end, she did what Opal and Luca had been expecting her to do all along.

"How is he? How is Luca?" The street was quiet—it was late, and the neighborhood was mostly warehouses. Mab still kept her voice low.

"I don't know," said Cordelia. "They sent me out before the . . . before it happened."

"Massacre," spat Mab. "Call it like it is. Be nice if somebody would, since they won't say on the wireless. 'Successful raid' my right tit."

"But they *were* harboring members of the Catwalk," said Sofie. "The CIS thought the Chuli were—" Then she stopped, in the middle of the footpath, and stared at Cordelia. "Mother and sons. Now we are too. Aren't we?"

Cordelia didn't answer. That didn't mean it wasn't true.

The Catwalk had hit a few rail lines in and out of Amberlough in their first year, and word spread the way word like that always did—quiet but quick, always with a fat dollop of *Who, me? Just making conversation*. They ended up with radio operators in a couple of different cities, cells of scrappers here and there. And then a free agent—a Chuli woman—blew the depot in Farbourgh and the Catwalk got credit for it. Suddenly Cordelia's people were linked in the press with the small but fierce resistance in the Culthams, where Geddan farmers were seizing ancestral grazing grounds for their own, unhindered by pro-Ospie police.

So when Amberlough got too hot for Cordelia, that was where she went, Opal and some others with her. To make that newspaper alliance real.

It lasted a good long while, and drew a fair crowd of people ready to fight, before the CIS caught on (the Central Intelligence

Services—the Ospies had dropped "Federal" from the acronym as soon as they had a firm hold on the reins) and sent some terriers down the hole after them.

"Mab," said Sofie. "Aren't we?"

"I dinnae know," said Mab, tone flat. "And I dinnae plan to ask, either. She's a friend of my family, in a tight spot."

"Your *family*," hissed Sofie. "*I'm* your family. Nadia is your family. *They* tossed you out on your rear. And now they send you *her*?"

"*Home*, Fee."

Sofie pointed at Cordelia, finger shaking. "I won't bring her into the house with our daughter."

"The Ospies killed Chuli kids, Fee." Mab held her hands open, pleading. "Three of 'em, under the age of ten. It doesnae matter who's hiding under the wagon or in amongst the flock, nor how poorly you aim. Ye dinnae shoot a kid and call it plumb."

That had been the day after Cordelia went into the back of the truck. She'd been bumping over the border, probably, when the militia went in to ask a few questions about the Catwalk, prompted by the CIS. Got sass back from the wrong person, they said. Said they were afraid for their lives. Who knew what had really happened—the militia claimed the Chuli had showed their weapons first, which likely meant a crook or an antique rifle to keep off wolves. None of the Chuli from the camp had been given any column inches.

"I'm not saying it was *right*," Sofie went on. "I'm saying they had reason enough to go in, and now they've got a reason to *keep* going in, again and again." Sofie's lips were thin, her face white. "You heard on the wireless. So many arrests they haven't got room in the jails; they're keeping them penned like sheep, in the open."

Cordelia hadn't heard *that* bit of news.

"You talk as if I dinnae know," said Mab.

"More than you've let on, I think. How often has Luca written you? Is that where the petty cash has been going?"

Mab's jaw flexed, and Cordelia could see the tendons standing out in her neck. Rough living in the Tzietan foothills, foxes on her tail, might have been preferable to this.

"*Home*," said Mab again, this time in a voice that brooked no argument.

They fought all night. Cordelia slept through most of it. She was used to shouting by now, and to anger, and any number of loud noises in the dark.

Their rooms weren't large—a bedroom and a dine-in kitchen with a sofa, above a shop that had been shuttered when they arrived. Given the oily stench in the air, the downstairs neighbors likely served a good fry-up. Cordelia had the bed; the women stayed in the kitchen so they could tear each other up and down in a kind of privacy.

When she woke in the wee hours, it was to a small, warm pressure and the sound of muffled weeping. Mab and Sofie's little girl, Nadia, had left her cot in the corner and climbed into bed with Cordelia. Snot shone on her upper lip. She clutched a doll made out of a stocking, with yarn for hair and a ribbon tied around its neck. Snot shone on that, too.

Cordelia, the younger sister, had never been good with kids. She'd been the one getting her rear wiped and raggies changed, not the other way around. Awkwardly, she petted Nadia's dark tangles of hair.

"They fight like this a lot?" she asked.

Nadia shook her head. Then, after a pause, nodded once.

"Where's your dad, huh?" Cordelia asked. The bed was too small for three, and she'd seen no sign of the husband.

Nadia shook her head again.

Cordelia sighed and scooted over, making more room for the snuffling kid, then dropped back into a dead sleep.

In the morning, when she staggered out of the stifling bedroom, Mab sat at the table, smoking a pipe behind a newspaper. Her back was turned to Sofie, busy with a knife at the counter.

"Mornin'," said Mab, flicking the top half of her paper down.

Cordelia nodded, and lowered herself into the chair opposite, keeping a wary eye on Sofie. There was tension in her shoulders, in the line of her neck below her gathered hair.

"Nadia still sleeping?"

Cordelia nodded again.

Mab sighed and set her paper flat on the table. "Sofie and I've talked and we cannae keep ye."

She was starting to feel like a jack-in-the-box, head bobbing back and forth at the end of a spring.

"It's hard enough in Porachis right now for us," she went on. "We haven't got the right papers to stay and work, and there's little enough love for Geddans these days. I do better than Sofie most of the time, thanks to my coloring, and with folk who're up on the news from abroad. The massacre at Tannover dinnae play well here, not for the Ospies. Porachis already had half a wad saved up in her cheek to spit at Gedda on account of the Spice War. Just waiting for a reason to let it fly, now."

"You saying it's gonna be hard for me too?" asked Cordelia.

"We know some folk around; if we hint at what you've done, where your sympathies lie, might be we could help you find some work. There's the queen's hostel you can stay at: three nights free by royal mandate, and not too dear after that. Though your skin and talk might get you some rough treatment there."

Cordelia stopped listening. Not because she didn't care, but because she'd seen Mab's paper, open to the roto. She stabbed one picture with her finger. "What's this?"

Cut off mid-sentence, Mab took a moment to catch her balance. "Sorry, the roto?" Then, following Cordelia's stiff finger to the page, she said, "Ah, Makricosta? Do you know 'im?"

Cordelia pulled her finger away, leaving a smudge on the glossy page. "He's why I'm here, if you go at it the long way." They really didn't recognize her. Good.

"Showed up not long after we did." Mab tapped her pipe out on the edge of the table. "Funny, it was. We paid him so much to get us out, and 'ere he comes running after."

A bowl of yogurt landed on the table hard, splattering. Sofie followed it with a plate of bruised, roughly chopped figs. "Sometimes, Mab Cattayim, I wonder your jaw doesn't fall off from all the loose talk you let fly."

"It's not as if they can arrest him for it now."

"It isn't him I'm worried about." Sofie flung a pair of spoons onto the table.

Mab picked one up, looking amused. "Anyway, who's she gwine to tell?"

For the first time since Cordelia came into the kitchen, Sofie really looked at her, mouth screwed into a one-sided frown.

"I'm going out," she said finally, and snatched a handbag from the back of the third, empty chair.

After the door slammed, Mab sighed and sat back, chair creaking. "That's a break that'll take some time to knit."

"Sorry," said Cordelia.

Mab waved her off. "Don't you take my blame." She scrubbed her hands across her face. "I just meant to help."

"If you sent Luca money," Cordelia said, "you did. Helped

him and us. Might have gone to pay off a hound, or fed us for a night or two."

"Nights that we went hungry, most like. Blessed stones, I should've told her."

"Should've *asked*," said Cordelia. Then, "Sorry. Not my place."

Mab shrugged and let her head drop. The paper was under her nose, and she soon found a change of subject. "Makricosta, though. You recognized his face."

Cordelia slid the roto closer for a better look at the picture.

He'd changed. Cut all that curly hair off, first of all, and there was silver in it now, thick at his temples. In the photo, he had a short Porachin woman with big hips hanging on his arm. Cordelia wondered what *that* was, but couldn't tell from the caption. Porashtu script was all curling lines and dots and dashes, nothing she could read. "You understand this?"

"Getting better," said Mab. "Reading the paper helps."

"Overgrown blush boy always did put his big nose where it didn't belong." She touched the ink of Ari's face and wondered if this was a hex or a blessing. "What's he doing here?"

"Working in the pictures, down in Anadh."

"Pictures, huh?" She hadn't thought about that. Hadn't thought far beyond landing in Mab and Sofie's nest. But the pictures were big in Anadh—much bigger than they were back home, where they'd never quite caught on—and now she was being pushed out and had to trust her own wings. "It's easy to get work like that?"

"In Anadh it's hard to find work doing anything else, even if you are Geddan. See Phoebe Francis here?" Mab tapped the face of an older woman, pale, with white or blond hair wrapped in a neat bun above a stern face. "Born abroad, but her parents were Nuesklen straight through." Mab picked up a fig. "Anyway, that's what I glean about Anadh. Fee and I don't travel much. But it's a big town, bigger even than Myazbah—that's the capital. Lots of folk from all over the world."

"Is it far?"

Mab shrugged, ate the fig. "Couple of hours down the coast, by car. It might be I know someone who could take ye, if ye want."

She wasn't sure she did, but where else was she supposed to go?

CHAPTER

TWO

Lillian stood in the antechamber of Regional Affairs for five full minutes, telegram pinched between cramping fingers. She knew if she held it in her hand she'd make a fist, and crumple it. Smoothing the paper would add an indignity these proceedings wouldn't bear. Or which she, at least, refused to.

The door finally swung open, and Lillian jumped.

"Counselor Flagg will see you now," said the secretary, smoothing her skirt. "So sorry for the delay." She gestured Lillian across the threshold, then shut the door behind her. It closed with a firm, metallic clank. Other offices in the chancery had locks; none of them were quite so formidable, and most of them had keys instead of combinations. Lillian wondered how often they changed the series of numbers. Wondered if anyone had ever been locked in.

"Ah, Ms. DePaul." At his desk, Flagg's aide stretched his arms above his head. "We do not see you down our long, dark hallway often."

"I'm the press attaché, Mr. Memmediv. I conduct most of my sabotage from behind a podium."

He had a nice laugh: deep and soft, accompanied by a smile that made his eyes crinkle up. She almost mistook it for genuine.

Vasily Memmediv had arrived later than the rest of the Ospie staff, which made Lillian trust him less. Not that she trusted the Ospies all that far—she just knew where she stood with them. They'd cleaned out all her old colleagues when Acherby took power; those that hadn't abandoned their posts when they heard the news. Replaced every single one of them with someone who would toe Gedda's new line.

They'd even fired her, until they figured out she had a useful secret. She had been off the job for all of three days, which she spent trying to get her brother on the telephone, trying to determine if she should go home or stay put. Then she had a knock at the door.

That was the first time she met Maddox Flagg. He'd handed her the thick dossier with Cyril's photograph clipped inside the cover, a shocking red stamp across his face: *deceased*. Most of the names and dates were blacked out, but he'd left her enough information to frighten her. The next file he took from his briefcase was her son's. Refusing her reinstatement as press attaché had not been an option.

Six months ago, Memmediv had shown up, already snug in Flagg's good graces. Lillian wasn't privy to much that went on in Flagg's office, but she had an imagination.

Acherby's interventions on the border between the Kingdom of Liso and the North Lisoan Republic had stirred the pot of international relations, especially longtime royalist ally Porachis. The counselor needed more foxes on his staff. He and Memmediv must have shared some bond of clandestine professional association, because Memmediv's area of expertise was purely domestic, and he spoke Porashtu like a primary school student.

Lillian was good at narratives, which was why she was good at her job. Though that wasn't why the Ospies had kept her when they ousted everyone else. She was very good at what the old guard had paid her to do, and the Ospies—neck-deep in ill will at the time over the expulsion of several dozen Porachin immigrant families from Gedda—needed her touch.

"And," Flagg had said, seated across from her at her own coffee table, "there is the small matter of Stephen. You're sending him to school this fall, correct? Cantrell? His tuition will be paid in full by the government. As a token of our thanks for your hard work."

This was not what he really meant, which was something more along the lines of *Your son is a jess to hold you, and we will keep it punishingly short to see that you do as you are told.* Or, she thought as much, until she learned it was not about her role in the corps, but about Stephen's father's family.

"He is being recalcitrant," Flagg told her. "We would like you to provide a good example."

More like, *We would like to keep you close so we can hold a knife to your throat if he balks.* Putting her back behind the press podium was just the hard sauce on the pudding.

Memmediv pulled her from the mire of her past. "Is that for us?" he asked, inclining his head toward the telegram.

"Oh, no," said Lillian, shaking off her old anxiety to more easily bear the new. "I do need to speak to Flagg about it, though. The secretary said that he was—"

"Ready for you, yes." Maddox Flagg emerged from his office, which was a locked fortress within a fortress. Gray-haired and gray-eyed, with a pallor that tended toward gray in the wrong light, the only thing that saved him from utter monochrome was the red rim around his eyes: the consequence of a lifetime spent sleeping in three-hour increments. High, hollow cheekbones and an aquiline nose lent his entire expression a drawn, disapproving cast. Lines seamed his narrow face, ironed in by a calculating squint under a perpetually furrowed brow.

"Can I offer you coffee, Ms. DePaul?"

"No, thank you," she said. Flagg took the strongest coffee in the foreign service. If she drank it now her heart would probably explode. "I need to show you something."

He took the telegram with an air of bemusement that only increased as he read. "Is she serious?"

"How would I know? I've never spoken to her in my life."

"Really?" Flagg's bloodshot gaze caught her over the edge of the paper. "You're quite cozy with some of the royal family."

"Not that branch," said Lillian crisply, hating him.

"And she sent this to your home?"

"She did. This morning. Well, around half three. So perhaps she stayed up late last night. Maybe she was drinking?"

Flagg snorted. "No doubt. But I imagine it didn't affect her judgment in this particular matter."

"Would someone mind explaining?" Memmediv kicked his feet up on his desk and crossed his arms behind his head.

"You know Satri's film," said Flagg. "That swipe at us she's dressed up as a historical drama?"

Memmediv grinned. "I like the pictures. I think it looks good."

"Ms. DePaul has apparently merited a last-minute invitation to the premiere. Which is—"

"Tomorrow," said Memmediv, and whistled. "What did I tell you, huh? Satri's smarter than she looks."

Lillian nodded agreement. "She wants one of two things from us, sending this at such late notice. If I say no, she can accuse us of cowardice. Worse, she can claim I've been *prevented* from attending. Gedda's public image takes a blow. Who would stop me seeing a picture about my own grandmother?"

Grimacing, Flagg asked, "And the second option?"

"If I say yes and scramble to prepare, she hopes that we'll embarrass ourselves somehow."

"After Moorehead's gaffe last month," said Flagg, handing back the telegram, "you must endeavor to be faultless. We can't lick any more of our own boot leather in front of the Porachins."

The Geddan defense minister had recently expressed his support for troops in Northern Liso in their endeavor to spread democracy south of the partition. His defense—which would have come too late even if he'd led with it—was that his support was merely personal and moral, rather than official, military, or financial. Lillian had been holystoning the deck behind him, trying to smooth the splintered diplomatic relations his idiocy had left behind. The Porachin press had not been receptive; pundits were convinced Gedda was preparing to fight a proxy war in Liso. Lillian was fairly certain of the same thing, but it wouldn't do to say so.

"So I'm going to the premiere?" she said.

"Unless you can write an ironclad statement excusing your absence."

"I'm very good, Counselor, but I still do use language to make my points." Lillian bent the telegram in half and ran a sharp crease along the fold: a concession to nerves that was neater than balling it up in her fist. "I've found it's a tool that will work just as easily for others as it does for me. No matter what I say, she'll twist it."

"The invitation says 'and guest.'" Flagg tapped his chin. "Mr. Memmediv, have we got any good-looking fellows to send along with her? No one *too* exotic. Not one of those playboy foxes we run, nobody who shows up in the tabloids too often. Someone respectable, who will keep an eye on her."

"Counselor," said Memmediv, with an ironic tinge, "what kind of operation do you think this is?"

But Flagg let his aide handle all the humor in Regional Affairs. "A functional one. Find somebody."

"Why don't I go?" He took a cigarette from his case and lit a match. A habit not endorsed by the OSP, but behind that locked steel door, who would know? "I'm due a little holiday."

Lillian expected Flagg to strike that down out of hand, but instead he cocked his head and considered the prospect. Intensity narrowed his eyes like iron filings following a magnet.

Lounging behind the desk, cigarette dangling from a languid hand, Memmediv didn't look like a chancery drudge. He didn't even look particularly like a fox. He was suave, in an innocuous kind of way: middle-aged, sallow-skinned and bleakly handsome. Flagg must have seen the same thing, because eventually he shrugged. "You did say you like the pictures. Ms. DePaul, what do you think?"

"My professional opinion?"

"It's the only one that matters."

Which meant Memmediv was going whether she liked it or not, as long as it wouldn't cause problems for Flagg. "Most people who know anything about the diplomatic corps will know a little bit about what he does and who he works for. That will make them wary, which might be good. It's also a very subtle threat, to me and to Porachis, but one you can make without causing a scene. Besides, you know you can trust him."

When Lillian left the chancery that evening, there was a car waiting at the bottom of the steps. Pedestrians and other motorists gave it a wide berth, wary of the diplomatic plates. Lillian suspected there was an extra several inches of deference—or disgust—added for the gray-and-white Ospie flags on the bonnet. As she approached, the driver opened the rear door. Its sweep revealed a pair of knees in pin-striped, steel-blue trousers.

Her stride only faltered for a moment, easily attributable to an uneven flagstone or a rock in her shoe. She recovered almost instantly, and slid into the backseat.

"Counselor," she said, cool and even. "Are we going somewhere?"

"It's hot. You've had a long day. I'm giving you a lift home." He said it in a curious monotone that meant it was not true, or not wholly.

"Is this about the film premiere?" she asked, once they had pulled away from the curb.

"In a manner of speaking." He paused, considering the street as it slipped by outside the window. "How well do you know Vasily?"

"Not well, sir. In fact, given his background I was rather curious that you brought him on at all." It was more than she would have dared, if he hadn't been the one to bring it up. "I understand the mandate of your office isn't exactly the same as the rest of the mission's, but . . ."

Another man would have done something to hide his reluctance: smoothed his trousers or examined his nails. Done something besides stare with raptor-like intensity at nothing in particular. "He requested the post," said Flagg at last.

"Why? He doesn't seem to have an abiding interest in Porachin politics, or even rudimentary knowledge of the culture."

"New cultures, new countries: that can all be learned. But Memmediv and I have some history together; we worked under the same supervisor during the election, three years back. He was instrumental in the party's success in Amberlough."

She'd used the euphemisms so many times in press conferences that they no longer grated.

"I knew he'd be good at the job I hired him to do," said Flagg. There was a caveat hanging on the end of that, unspoken. She could feel it in the air like an electric charge, the smell of smoke. All was not well in Regional Affairs.

"But," she said, because he clearly wasn't going to.

Regret passed across Flagg's face: the shadow of a fast-moving cloud. Lillian was amazed to see him express any kind of emotion; it drove home the gravity of the situation.

"He *requested the post*," Flagg repeated. "I was flattered, which in retrospect was stupid. His motivation has always been domestic; his family lost everything in the Dastyan Solstice riots thirty-odd years ago. Their business, their home, social cachet. His father was an alderman, and ended up serving time in prison. Memmediv was just old enough to understand the ramifications, but too young yet to fight. His affiliation with the Ospies during the election was based purely on Acherby's campaign promise of returning Dastya to Tatié."

"And Acherby's moved very slowly on that."

"You needn't pander to *me*. This business about an armistice with Tzieta is a slap in the face to people like Memmediv. To them, that border, that port are the most important issues of any politician's platform. Tatié's been fighting for its own harbor for decades. Acherby promised to end their struggle, and he did: by making it unnecessary."

Tatié had gone Ospie on the strength of Acherby's allusions to military strength, to state solidarity, to ending Amberlough and Nuesklend's shipping monopolies. He kept that promise by dropping the state border tariffs. But there was no push to reclaim the old capital of Tatié, granted to Tzieta in a fifty-year-old treaty many Tatiens still refused to acknowledge.

But why expend the effort of reclaiming that port, reasoned Acherby, when goods could flow freely throughout Unified Gedda? Dealing with domestic terrorism and a proxy war was probably more than enough to keep Acherby busy. So there were peace talks now with Tzieta, to the chagrin of many Tatiens who'd spilled blood into the cracked dry soil, hoping it would yield them a harbor. To the chagrin, she supposed, of Memmediv.

"When Vasily felt the regionalist government had failed him, he betrayed them and threw in his lot with us. Now that the OSP is slacking in the yoke . . ."

"You're worried he'll throw in with someone else. But who is there?"

"Tatien separatists," said Flagg. "There have been some murmurs of secession."

"He'd be a fool. The militia has gone federal."

"On paper. Do you really think he volunteered for this trip to Anadh because he likes the pictures? You can't be entirely ignorant of Pulan Satri's past."

"'Past' being the operative word. It was my understanding that once her father died she put all his assets into the studio."

"That doesn't mean she isn't meddling. It just means she's learned to keep secrets. Or that others keep them for her."

"I assume you have eyes on her."

He closed his own. "It's largely fallen under Memmediv's purview. Another job he volunteered to take. And now you're invited to her film premiere, last minute, and he raises his hand again."

It had been slowly dawning on Lillian, during this conversation, that they were not headed for her neighborhood, but out of the city. Equatorial evening had faded fully into night. They wound along the water, passing rice fields ready for the winter flood. Darkness pressed against the windows of the car.

Lillian sank more deeply into her seat to hide the stiffness of her posture. Her hands she folded demurely in her lap, letting tension gather in her forearms instead of in her fists.

"Are we taking the long way around?" she asked lightly.

Flagg didn't match her jocularity. "If what I suspect is true, I can't trust my networks, or anyone in the office. No one who works in proximity to Memmediv."

"Which is why we're having this conversation on the move, and not at the chancery."

"Yes."

"And the driver?" she asked, to delay what she knew must be coming.

"Doesn't speak Geddan."

"But you trust me," she said.

"I know exactly what you have at stake."

It took everything she had not to growl, tear at her hair. She bit the inside of her lower lip, catching the raw spot she resorted to when unwise words or actions threatened. "I'm afraid I'm not particularly close to your target."

"That can be changed," said Flagg. "Beginning tomorrow night."

The bottom went out of Lillian's stomach. "I'm a journalist," she said, "a press secretary. Not a prostitute."

"You are whatever I need you to be!" Flagg rarely raised his voice, and the sound rooted Lillian to her seat. "He has given me an opportunity and I *will not waste it*."

"How can you suggest this?" she demanded. He went to temple every week. She'd seen him with a streak of ash on the back of each hand at high holidays, when he attended small-hours services in order not to miss work. He didn't drink or smoke. As far as she knew—and she certainly didn't want to know farther—he was faithful to his wife. "You're a good Hearther."

"Yes, but you aren't," he said. "You should have no qualms. And, even if you do . . ." He reached into his jacket and produced an envelope, already opened.

Lillian stared at the glued-down edges of the flap, the raw edge where the paper had met a blade.

"It's almost Solstice holidays," said Flagg. "I assume you'd like to see him. And he's heartily sick of Gedda."

Lillian removed a few folded sheets of letter paper. Stephen's handwriting had improved since the beginning of the year. He despised practicing his penmanship, but here every serif and stem stood out crisp and straight against the grain of the paper. It was the written version of his best behavior, and it pled for a reward.

The line of Flagg's mouth shifted subtly. In someone with a stronger affect it would have been a smile, though not a kind one. "Negotiations with Tzieta are due to wrap up around Solstice if everything goes according to plan. I'd like to put a stop to this interference before then. If Memmediv succeeds in supplying weapons to the separatists, it will put paid to any possibility of an armistice. Gedda cannot sustain conflict on three fronts. We can't mop up the Catwalk, grapple with Liso, and fight a civil war."

"So it's on my shoulders," she said. "Keep the peace, see my son?"

"If you have something for me by the end of Cantrell's autumn term, I might have something for you."

She put the letter into the inner pocket of her jacket, where it crackled against her breast.

"Oh, and Ms. DePaul," said Flagg. "It would be . . . deeply embarrassing if your assignment came to light. I'd like to clean up everything quietly, and keep an appearance of order. As far as my superiors at home are concerned, you're still just the press attaché, and Memmediv still my loyal deputy."

"Of course," she said, and wished that it were true.

Flagg dropped her by the front steps of her house. Though other parts of Myazbah were probably bustling with markets and nightlife, her street was silent but for locusts and the occasional trill of a nightingale.

She hoped her majordomo, Waleeda, hadn't waited up for her, especially after the long detour. Lillian had kept her awake late into the night too often by necessity; she would have hated to do it for nothing, too. In all likelihood, Waleeda was on *someone's* payroll, along with the rest of Lillian's staff, but that was all the more reason to treat her with respect. Sour milk didn't make cats smile.

Instead of letting herself in through the front door, she unlocked the gate at the side of the house and slipped down a cool, narrow passageway into the courtyard. Fountain echoes plashed from the archways, rippling through the night-thick scent of jasmine.

Exhaling, she sank onto one of the benches under a curtain of ornamental oregano. In recent years, the courtyard had become her favorite part of the house. It gave her hope that somewhere, deep behind the walls she'd erected, underneath the urgency and fear, was something quiet and beautiful.

She took Stephen's letter from her pocket and smoothed the paper over one knee.

Dear Mummy, he began, and immediately launched into a blow-by-blow of the end-of-term bowling match, which his team had won in no small part due to his own keen eye and devastating hooks.

Lillian snorted. He had certainly inherited his father's modesty—meaning, exactly none. The thought sobered her. She went on reading with a heavier heart, a less steady hand.

Stephen's letters in his first year—small missives scrawled in block letters—had been straightforward begging: *Mummy, I miss you. When can I come home?* Now his tactics had evolved to include bargaining and manipulation.

Must I stay with Mrs. Hallerlight again at Solstice? he wrote. *She serves potatoes and burnt mutton every night and the house is very damp and cold. At the end of summer I asked her did I have to come again and she said it was up to you and that you are very busy and I would be in the way.*

It was a skillful play—he was the son of a diplomat and a courtier after all, and strategy was in his blood. But he needn't have made it. She wanted him back on this shore, even just for Solstice holidays.

Given the choice, Lillian would have sent him to school at Cantrell anyway; DePaul children had always gone. Her own name was engraved onto a debate society plaque in the trophy hall. On the wall of the head's office, she and Cyril both appeared in group photographs of graduating students gowned in black. Her father had gone, as had her famous grandmother (there was a beautiful oil portrait of the latter in the library, where she had endowed a history collection).

But Lillian had not been given a choice. Flagg's first move, upon arrival, was to pluck Stephen from Lillian's home and deposit him behind the high brick walls of Gedda's most prestigious school. Since then, she'd seen him a handful of times, always with the unspoken reminder that those visits were by the grace of the OSP, and if she desired them to continue she would smile and nod and occasionally pay a call on his father, to jerk the reins and let him know he didn't have his head.

She worried about how the other children at Cantrell might treat her son. She and Cyril had both been bullied some about the Spice War. Their grandmother had made strong allies with her decisive actions, but bitter enemies as well. And Cyril had made an ass of himself at university; tongues had wagged. Thankfully he'd plunged into such obscurity afterward that most of the scandal dissipated. She hated to be grateful for that: If he'd continued to stumble in public spheres, she might still have some family left.

And if Cyril hadn't operated in the shadows, she wouldn't be in this situation to begin with. His copy of her will had a sealed letter appended to it, addressed to Stephen. Even her brother hadn't known what it contained. But the seal had not been sacred to the foxes who went through his things after he died, and the contents of the letter skyrocketed through several security clearances to land on the desk of Maddox Flagg, the new CIS station chief in Myazbah.

Children were tactless, and his classmates would ask Stephen awkward questions. *If your mummy is Geddan why are you so dark? Why did she send you so far away? Where's your daddy? Is he Porachin?*

Only some of his answers would be lies, and he wouldn't know the difference because she had never told him. Because she lived, he would never see the letter. Because Cyril died, Flagg had. And now, because she'd loved the wrong man once and he had given her a child, she would pretend to love another and hope he told her secrets she could exchange for her son.

THREE

From his post in the dormer window of Pulan's boudoir, Aristide puffed out an irritated breath. "We need to *go*, Pulan, or we won't get to the city in time to change or eat. If you take much longer, you'll miss your own rotten film." Below, in the turnaround, Daoud was directing a chauffeur twice his size in the loading of baggage. Aristide saw his own set of heliotrope leather on the gravel, and Daoud's smaller, plainer cases stacked on top of it. He hoped he'd remembered everything, but if he hadn't, toothbrushes and underthings could always be acquired in Anadh.

"My film is not *rotten*. Every early review has called *Katunjaan* a resounding success." Pulan uncapped a tube of lipstick, examined it, and then swapped it for a different shade.

Aristide rolled his eyes. He had finished dressing twenty minutes ago and been packed since last night. Pulan's dawdling and lengthy preparations left him partly gratified, but faintly vexed. Was this what other people felt like when he made them wait?

"Idiom," he said. "I apologize." Pulan was fluent in Geddan, but sometimes missed the subtleties. "Please, can we leave? The sooner this day is over, the sooner I can hang myself from the closet rail." Not that he would—it was such an ignominious end. Pills or a revolver, *please*.

"While that would certainly excite the tabloids and garner excellent press coverage," she said, "I would really prefer you sink yourself into a morass of sex, drugs, and drink."

"Is that your way of saying that you'd miss me?"

She rose from her vanity in a rustle of silk. "It is my way of saying I would rather not find out."

"Well, you'll have to do without me for a week or so, at least. I've made a slew of reservations in Anadh. I'm very much looking forward to my holiday once this hideous ordeal is over."

"Honestly," she said, picking up her small valise. "You are not the greater loss. The boys the agency sends are never as good as Daoud."

"The services that he provides to me," said Aristide, "will render me far less peevish upon my return."

"And that is the only reason I gave him leave to go. You have been an absolute . . ." She pursed her lips. "Monstrosity?"

"Monstrosity," he agreed.

"Working on this film."

"I told you I never wanted to be in charge of it," he spat. If he counted up how often he'd said these same words, in exactly this tone . . . "I don't know *why* you insisted."

"Because you're *Geddan*," she said, also for the thousandth time. "An expatriate, forced from your home. It's *romantic*. People *love* it."

"I know," he said, not happily. Production and the ensuing tabloid scramble had been an utter trial, which he endured like a hair-shirted Hearther penitent streaked in ashes, starving on a cold stone floor. Eating well and sleeping on silk sheets, yes, but agony of the mind and soul could spoil even the richest luxuries. "Why the Spice War? Why not a love story, or a musical comedy? I could have been working on *anything*."

"I know you do not read the news," she said, "and have an unhealthy aversion to the wireless, but the current political situation cannot have evaded you entirely. Liso is nearly ready to go to war again; there is fighting on the border every day. It's topical. Besides, Inaz needed to do something dramatic; people were starting to think she could only play insipid and sexy. But she is *excellent* as General Ojo."

She was that. And a stunning contrast to grande dame Phoebe Francis, cast opposite as Geddan strategist Margaretta DePaul.

Three-odd years into his tenure as a director at Hadhariti Studios, Aristide had thought he had his feet under him. But Pulan yanked the runner from beneath him on this one. A special project for him, she said. Only he could do it justice. He wanted to do *her* some justice, when he found out. The rough kind.

Pulan didn't know much about what had chased him out of Gedda. She *certainly* didn't know about Cyril. And he wasn't going to invite her pity any more than he had, showing up on her doorstep unemployed and stateless. So he clenched his jaw and made the film. And he made it *well*.

The Ospies, of course, were seething mad but had to hide it for diplomacy's sake. Pulan was just making *pictures*, which was not against the law in any reasonable country. And while Caleb Acherby's government in Gedda might have tightened its fist on artistic expression and political criticism, in Porachis, a film about the Spice War was just exotic historical entertainment.

Except that it very much wasn't. Plausible deniability was a grand disguise for pointed commentary. Acherby had abandoned several of his campaign promises in favor of expanding interference on the border between the Kingdom of Liso and the ostensible democracy in the north. On the face of it, a crackdown on the narcotics trade, but Aristide smelled retribution in the wind. There had been some kind of hairy situation in the news last month that nearly led to blows, but he'd kept well away from it. Suffice to say, a popular Porachin film painting antique royalists in a romantic light was the last thing the Ospies wanted with tensions running high.

The alliance between Liso and Porachis was centuries old, bound by marriages and soaked in blood. Modernity had transformed this into treaties and carefully neutral statements, but deep down, if you crossed Porachis, you crossed Liso, and vice versa. Nowadays, that meant the monarchy—Gedda had been in the Porachin black books since it first bungled its way into the Spice War, and especially after it brokered the partition of Liso into two halves, wresting the north from the royal family's control and helping it build what passed for a democracy on good days.

In a funny way, Aristide had Cyril's family to thank for his asylum.

Daoud was waiting for them on the steps, his linen trousers rumpled, a smear of dust on the knitted yellow cotton of his vest. Aristide rarely saw him in Porachin clothes, and suspected it had something to do with his stature, his looks, and his place in society. As a slender young man with camel lashes and a mouth like a ripe fig, who had aspirations toward other people's respect, Daoud seemed to have landed on masculine, foreign tailoring as a device for demanding what so few people gave him.

It flattered his figure, at any rate.

His rolled-back sleeves revealed delicate forearms lined with the tendons of a practiced typist, and a utilitarian wristwatch of leather and steel. This he checked, ostentatiously, as Aristide and Pulan stepped into the stifling heat of the afternoon.

"I thought you were never coming," he said, in Geddan rather than Porashtu. That meant he was livid, and wanted to make sure Aristide understood. "Pramit has been burning petrol for nearly twenty minutes, idling out here."

"Terribly sorry." Aristide tapped Daoud's horrible timepiece with a fingernail. They'd have to do some shopping in Anadh, if he survived this night. "Someone had to powder her nose, and for once, it wasn't me."

Daoud shot a poisonous look at Pulan, whose innocent shrug belonged on a doe-eyed ingénue rather than a forty-year-old executive. "The pair of you!" He threw up his hands and ushered them to the car.

"You ought to slow down," said Daoud, putting his hand on the base of Aristide's cocktail glass. He kept his voice low, pitched to slide beneath the laughter and conversation of their dinner companions, and spoke in Geddan against the sibilance of their Porashtu. "I will not be on the red carpet to catch you if you stumble."

Irritated, Aristide slipped the glass free of his grip. "Prince Asiyah isn't exactly demonstrating restraint."

"His Royal Highness has Inaz to lean on." Daoud plucked the martini from Aristide's grip and swapped it with his own glass of water.

At the other end of the table Prince Asiyah Sekibou, two-bit scion many heirs removed from the Lisoan throne, threw back another shot of sorghum whiskey and settled his mistress more snugly against his side.

Inaz Iligba had risen astronomically far from her origins. Asiyah had found her a few years ago during one of his frequent business trips to Anadh, dancing in a down-market nightclub with a string of pearls around her waist. Smitten, he'd arranged a meeting with his old friend in the film industry. It was unlikely Inaz knew what Asiyah's real business with Pulan had been.

She was certainly beautiful. Porachin mother, Lisoan father, plush lips and waves of thick dark hair. And by some miracle, she could act. Otherwise Aristide would have suspected a political maneuver on Pulan's part, casting her in so many films. But act she could, and other studios had been trying to poach her since her very first film with Pulan. Inaz stayed loyal to Hadhariti Studios, though, even when better contracts came along.

«What *are* you boys whispering about down there?» demanded Pulan. «And in Geddan too. Such an appalling lack of courtesy toward Ms. Iligba.»

«Apologies,» said Daoud, and ducked his head.

«What about courtesy for me?» Aristide took advantage of Daoud's averted eyes to bring his martini back from exile. «My Porashtu is . . . very bad. As bad as Inaz's Geddan. Worse.»

«She's prettier,» said Asiyah.

Inaz's laugh rolled out like a banner unfurling, big and bright. Aristide noticed heads turn at other tables. So far they'd been lucky—no one had approached their party for autographs. «Sisi, don't make him angry. Do you want me playing bit parts for the next five years? Aristide can be—»

He didn't catch the last word and wondered what it meant. Vindictive? Horrid? Vengeful? An absolute beast? He drained the last of his drink, though alcohol wouldn't make it easier to move between languages.

«We need to go,» he said, checking his watch, which he still wore on a fob. Unable to formulate the sentence he wanted in Porashtu, he said, "Any longer and we won't be fashionably late; we'll just look foolish."

Pulan sighed and rose from her seat in a rustle of crêpe and clattering bangles. «You're hopeless. Inaz, Asiyah, ride with me? Daoud, don't let Makricosta get any drunker on the way over. If he's got a flask, take it off him. He'll let *you* rummage around in his clothes.»

Daoud's smile tightened. Guilt painted the back of Aristide's throat with acid.

"I'm sorry," he said, as soon as the driver shut the door on them. "I know you hate it when she does that."

"You always are." Daoud neatened the folds of Aristide's scarf, straightened the sprig of jasmine in his lapel. "*Do* you have a flask?"

"Don't be ridiculous."

"I never am." Daoud gave him a stern look. For such a small boy, with such bowed lips and luxurious lashes, he could be positively terrifying when he had a need.

"I don't have one," said Aristide. "Primrose promise." The vowels in the childhood saying got a little bungled up.

"I hope you are not planning to spend our entire holiday this intoxicated." The stern look graduated to irritation.

Aristide squeezed closer to him and put on a theatrical purr dug out of his old box of burlesque tricks. "Only with *love*."

Daoud rolled his eyes.

"Oh, all right. After tonight, I'll be good."

"You will be good *tonight*, or Pulan will have my skin."

"Too late for that," said Aristide, and pulled Daoud into his lap.

"You are a filthy old drunk," he said, but let himself be kissed.

Lillian's hotel suite adjoined Memmediv's; no doubt an arrange-ment of Flagg's. The presence of the closed, locked door pressed on her as she slipped into her gown. Bias-cut silk in unadorned storm gray, it left her back bare from the nape of her neck to the edge of her lowest rib. The dramatic cut and delicate fabric did not admit of undergarments. Porachis was hot. One only covered what one needed to.

Normally she loved the freedom of loose, minimal clothing. Normally, she was vain about her body, which she kept in very fine trim. But tonight was not normal, and she wished the brutal heat and the dictates of fashion allowed for something more sub-stantial.

She ran a brush over her hair, smoothing travel-muss from her sharp blond shingle. Black pearls for her ears, and a rope around her neck. She preferred to go without maquillage but, in acqui-escence to the occasion, applied dark shadow and a muted red lipstick.

It did not take her long to dress and paint her face. By then, the early tropical dark had descended and the casino and cinema marquees blazed. She took a tentative step toward the balcony, and fresh air, but the weight of the unopened door pulled her back across the room like a dragging anchor.

Her knuckles hovered over the studded panels for half a breath before she steeled herself and snapped them down once, twice. It took Memmediv a long moment to answer, in which time she experienced the entire emotional range of the heroine in a three-volume novel.

"Stunning," he said, when he opened the door.

The sweep of his eyes made her angry, but she pressed it down beneath what she hoped was a flirtatious smile. "You don't exactly look like a bootblack, yourself."

He wasn't quite finished dressing—an ivory shawl-collared jacket hung on the valet stand behind him—but a cummerbund hugged his waist over pleated trousers of summer-weight black wool. Warm light caught in the facets of his cuff links: cushion-cut smoky quartz set in white gold.

She caught his fingers—her chest tight, breath short, a parody of lust—and raised his hand, angling it so the gem flashed. "These are beautiful."

"Thank you," he said, bemused. He didn't pull away, and there was an awkward pause before she released him.

"Are you nervous?" he asked, turning to the clotheshorse and lifting his jacket free.

She noticed a deep burgundy orchid set on a handkerchief amidst his toilette, waiting for its buttonhole. Picking it delicately from the folds of linen, she put her free hand against his chest, to stop him moving and stop her shaking. With unwarranted care, she placed the flower in his lapel. "Why?" she asked, raising her eyes to his. "Should I be?"

He did not flush, and there was no hunger in his smile; this raised him several grudging rungs in her estimation. It also terrified her. She had hoped—and hated to hope—this would be easy.

He took her hand from his chest, ran his thumb over her freshly varnished nails. "Flagg did say faultless. I would be quaking in my pumps."

"You're not planning to behave badly, are you?" She plucked her hand away. "Please don't make my job any harder than it is."

It was good that she was used to flashbulbs. Standing on the red carpet was like entering a packed press conference. Blindly, she maneuvered through the gathered paparazzi by sound and touch and aching smile, arm in arm with Memmediv.

It was a different type of press corps than the one she usually addressed—Society columnists, feature writers for the glossies—but some of the usual suspects were in attendance as well: front-page reporters, political pundits, a few of the foreign press. She wondered who had put out the word that she'd be here. Between packing and briefing, she hadn't had time to write a release, much less liaise with her contacts. But it was a good story; she wasn't surprised it had gotten out.

At the end of a long, glamorous gauntlet, the Ocean Star picture palace raised its illuminated blade into the night sky. Date palms cast delicate shadows onto the pavement, silhouetted by the blazing marquee. Behind velvet ropes, fans jostled with reporters. The prevailing style of dress was very little, and brightly colored. Geddan-style formalwear was thin on the ground. Women mostly wore fishtailed skirts, heavily beaded, and intricately embroidered abi. The crêpe silk garments wrapped tightly around the ribs and tied between the breasts, ending in a cascade of fabric over one shoulder that fell in a train to the floor. Men wore long tunics and dhoti with gilded hems. Elaborate sandals mixed with pumps and velvet slippers.

«It's a very great honor,» Lillian said, again and again, answering questions thrown at her by the pen-toting throng. «Yes, I'm thrilled to be here.»

«Your grandmother is a major character in the film,» said one reporter. «Were you consulted at all during production?»

She laughed, sparkling. «I'm afraid this is the first I'll see of it. I'm sure it's very well done.»

«Are you close to Ms. Satri? Are you two friends?»

«I've never met her,» Lillian said. «I look forward to it.»

«Ms. DePaul, can you comment on Gedda's attitude toward Ms. Satri's film? Was there any resistance to your attending tonight?»

She let that one slide by with a smile, turning to answer the next.

«Ms. DePaul.» A low, familiar voice cut through the din. «How very good to see you after far too long.»

«That isn't a question, Mr. Addas.»

Jinadh Addas could have passed for a leading man, if he hadn't been holding a pen and steno pad. Passably tall and very broad-shouldered, he kept his waves of hair swept back, and long enough to brush his collar. His opium-dark skin was shadowed with earthy green, glowing rich red wherever light struck. In profile, he looked like a demigod from a bas-relief: a long, straight nose curved softly downward over a sensual mouth and close-clipped beard. Incongruously, he wore a fiercely tailored Geddan tuxedo, so dark blue it passed for black. Incongruously, but *very* well.

She met his gaze, and saw nothing there but jocularity and journalistic interest. Jinadh was wasted in the tabloids. Anyone who could hide their inner thoughts so well should have gone into politics.

«I didn't expect to see you here,» she said. «Are you down for the premiere?»

«Yes, just for the evening. I'm going back to Myazbah tomorrow, but I couldn't miss Pulan's masterpiece.»

She wondered if he knew she had been coming. Satri might have told him, though she wasn't sure how close they were, as cousins.

«Who is your handsome escort?» asked Jinadh, with an edge so keen Lillian didn't think Memmediv had felt it.

«This is Vasily Memmediv.» She stepped back so they could shake hands. «He's in Regional Affairs, under Maddox Flagg.»

«Ah,» said Jinadh, and smiled blandly. Even Lillian, who knew his expressions more intimately than most people, couldn't parse this one. Did he know he was talking to a fox? Or was he simply jealous?

"Mr. Memmediv," she said, abandoning Porashtu to be sure he understood, "this is Jinadh Addas. He's a cousin of Ms. Satri's, and he writes a society column for *Gelari*."

"Yes," said Memmediv, equally bland. "I've heard of him."

Jinadh's lips did something strange that almost betrayed an emotion. In lyrically accented Geddan, he said, "Only good things, I hope."

Lillian wondered exactly how *much* Memmediv had heard. His security clearance was certainly higher than hers, but then, it would have been hard to keep this particular secret from her, and she didn't imagine Flagg would have shared it widely.

«Ms. DePaul!» Farther up the carpet, people were shouting for her attention. She glanced toward the theatre, tingling with a flash of nerves.

«Pulan is due to arrive any moment,» said Jinadh, with admirable urbanity given their situation. But Lillian noted the switch back to Porashtu. «She's very eager to meet you. Did she really only send your invitation yesterday?»

«Really,» she said, keeping an eye on Memmediv to see if he was following. His smile held, but his eyes had gone narrow and intent.

«Well, I, for one, am glad you could make it.» Jinadh put a hand on her arm: casual enough to look like a friendly gesture. The warm ghost of his touch lingered on her skin as she turned away, in time to see two shining black cars draw up at the end of the carpet. Attendants rushed to open the doors. Cameras turned away from her, away from the other luminaries heading into the theatre, and refocused on the new arrivals.

The first car disgorged a headache. If she had been less distracted by Flagg's orders, she would have foreseen a Lisoan contingent. Inaz Iligba had Prince Asiyah Sekibou on her arm.

"Oh good," she said to Memmediv. "I had begun to wonder if the evening wasn't going a little too smoothly."

He chuckled, and she felt it through their linked arms. "I would not worry about Asiyah. He's barely royal, and the work he does for their intelligence organization is minimal. A courtesy appointment. He's friends with the defense minister."

"So why do you think he's here?"

"Iligba. Nothing beyond that. This would be an awful place to do the kind of business you're imagining."

"Satri looks pleased, though." She stepped out of the car after Sekibou, wearing a black abi, beaded slippers, and satisfied smile. Her hair—extremely short by Porachin standards—was glued to her head with a bucket of pomade. An elaborate kiss curl crossed her forehead, pasted flat above her eyebrows. Gold dust made her russet skin shine.

"It's her film premiere," said Memmediv. "Were you expecting her to sulk?"

Satri waved, queenly, then cast her kohl-rimmed eyes at the second car. An almost-hush fell over the seething crowd. Lillian fancied she could hear the mechanism of the door click in the moment before it opened.

Preceded by one highly shined white-and-walnut wingtip, the man who unfolded from the car struck the red carpet with an attitude that implied the rest of them would never match up, and might as well go home.

His white linen suit blazed in the battery of photo flashes. Around his neck and trailing down his back, a scarlet silk scarf stirred in the breeze. As he greeted the crowd, light flashed on his rings. Silver pooled thickly at his temples and thinned to threads amidst finger waves of chestnut purple-brown.

Aristide Makricosta, the notorious Geddan refugee. He shouldn't have been so famous. But his story was compelling, and once the tabloids got ahold of it he became too popular to mysteriously disappear. Either very lucky, or perfectly calculated. The Porachin government certainly wouldn't extradite him. He was the royal family's new crown jewel, to flaunt in front of Gedda. He was everything the Ospies hated: brown-skinned, boy-loving, and crooked as a kinked zipper. Queen Yaima was happy to give him a home, casually displaying her stance against Gedda like someone newly affianced might let their ringed hand rest, just so, in a patch of sun.

"Ah," said Memmediv. "He's looking well for a man on the run."

"I thought we weren't chasing him." Makricosta had once worked, onstage and off, with Gedda's most dangerous anti-Ospie resistance leader: the woman behind the Catwalk's terrifying bombing campaign. But as far as she knew, that was all in the past.

"We have eyes on him," said Memmediv, mocking her. "Didn't you know? It isn't unreasonable to assume he's still in contact with his old networks."

But, as Flagg had said, those eyes might not be trustworthy. And Makricosta had plenty of reason to support Lehane, to fight the OSP with every resource at his disposal. Lillian had read her brother's file cover to cover, or at least the parts that weren't redacted.

"Oh?" she said, hoping Memmediv was the kind of man who liked to impress a woman, rather than to be impressed.

"You think he would settle for an expatriate life and a career in the pictures?" Memmediv jostled her arm a little, showed one dogtooth in a crooked smile. "People with that kind of dossier don't slow down or stop. They gather momentum until they crash."

The cheers gave Aristide a moment of gratification, swiftly supplanted by a familiar acid burn below his sternum. He would be utterly unsurprised if making this film had given him an ulcer.

Pulan caught him around the waist as he approached, pulling him away from Daoud. It would look carefree and flirtatious for the cameras, but her grip pinched.

"You look ill," she said between her teeth. "Rearrange your face."

Aristide closed his eyes, took a deep breath, and affixed his most indulgent smile. The one that made him appear gracious while inciting the paparazzi to guilty soul-searching.

"That is better," she said, and waved to the public. The cheering redoubled. People strained at the velvet ropes as they passed, holding out postcards and magazines for autographs, waving flowers and bangled wrists. Pulan sailed serenely through it all, nodding her head and gently clasping outstretched hands.

She was, perhaps, more greatly admired than many of her stars. Certainly more than other studio executives. As glamorous as any actress, birth and circumstance had granted her the manifold blessings of nobility, beauty, and a whiff of international scandal. Her mother, a wealthy shipping magnate, had married a penniless aristocrat much younger than herself. She died when Pulan was very young. Rumors circulated that widowed Nadar Satri—prone to gambling, and not good at it—had maintained his lavish lifestyle through unsavory means. Aristide was in a good position to confirm those rumors, having early in his own career brokered a lucrative arms deal between Nadar and a shadowy branch of the Tatien militia.

Not that he had blackmailed Pulan for his current position. That would have been an egregious breach of faith between friends. Decades of chatty letters and business dealings had built between them a bond that did not necessitate extortion.

After her father died, Pulan gracefully exited the business of imports and exports. She had done it so well, Aristide wouldn't dream of muddying her success. Besides, he'd gone straight now, too. He had knocked the last traces of nighttime dock sludge from his shoes when he left Gedda. He was practically respectable.

The thought made him laugh. A flashbulb burst in his eyes. When his vision cleared, a giddy-looking emcee was beckoning him to a microphone beneath the theatre marquee. Pulan already stood there, beaming at him, one arm held out in invitation.

«And here's Mr. Makricosta,» said the emcee, as Aristide stepped up. «Ms. Satri's foreign muse and our most glamorous refugee.»

Pulan smirked. Her eyes slipped sideways, catching his. He had never seen someone so good at silently saying *I told you so*.

«But not the only Geddan here tonight,» the emcee went on, peering over the crowd with a theatrical hand shading his eyes. «Ms. Satri invited a special guest to this premiere, if I'm correct.»

Aristide's smile faltered. He glanced down at Pulan, trying to make it look admiring, and not anxious. She hadn't said a word about this to him.

«Ah!» exclaimed the emcee, and Aristide jumped. «There you are! Come up here and smile for the cameras.»

Aristide followed the line of the emcee's outstretched hand and felt his breath snag in his throat.

The shifting illumination of searchlights and palm shadows

slid over the specter's golden hair. Cut in a neat shingle, yes, but hair grew. It could be cut. Aristide knew all about that.

The impossible apparition had Cyril's face, Cyril's sharp nose and bold, open-mouthed smile. It laughed as it slipped past ushers and actors and the general throng, amused by a trite joke from the emcee. An expansive, theatrical sound—almost mocking— bright and warm as electric lights. Aristide knew that laugh. Like a catchy tune he had not heard for years, even now he could identify the opening chords.

But when the ghost left the crowd behind, light from the marquee burned through the illusion. Aristide saw the shape of small breasts beneath gray satin, the curve of narrow hips. With that, like dominos, each difference fell neatly into place, revealing itself. Jaw too wide, slightly too tall. Short dogteeth. Longer, leaner hands. She had a kinder brow, and softer, tired eyes. Eyes that regarded Aristide now with concern, tinged with amusement.

"Are you all right?" she asked, stepping up to join him. "You look as though you've seen—"

"Don't say it." Aristide held up a hand, as if to ward off a blow. The amusement vanished from her expression, and he knew he would lose his audience if he didn't get a grip on himself. "I just *abhor* cliché."

«A warm welcome,» said the emcee, «to Lillian DePaul!»

Around them, dozens of flashbulbs burst at once.

CHAPTER

FOUR

Cordelia passed the long ride south reading a newspaper Mab had gotten for her in Berer—in Geddan, so she could read it. The *Call*. It was printed on poor-quality paper and the ink smeared if she touched it, but Mab had sworn it was run by a friend and the information was good.

Well, accurate, more like. She wouldn't call it *good*.

Now the Ospies had figured out there were Catwalk operatives up in the mountains, they were diving in like terriers to a rat's hole. Sofie'd been right about the camps. Outdoors, in the rain. Cordelia wondered if they'd keep that up through the winter, when it started to get cold.

The stories gave some names, of Catwalk folk who'd got drug in. So far no Opal Saeger, no Luca Cattayim. That was good. Opal had been with her since early days and knew too much about everything. Luca knew almost nothing, except where they'd sent

Cordelia. She wondered how long they'd hold out, if either of them got scratched, and hoped they'd keep from singing a little longer than she had last time the Ospies had ahold of her.

She'd fallen asleep by the time they arrived in Anadh. The slap of thrown-back canvas startled her awake.

"Hurry," said Siyad, who'd driven her. "Put this on." He gave her a cheap pair of slippers and a dark cotton robe cut high and tight in the collar and loose everywhere else. "From my sister."

Sofie and Mab hadn't been able to spare clothes, so Cordelia had been stuck with what she came over in. She stripped down right there in front of Siyad, peeling sweat-stiff, stinking clothes from her body and tossing them in a heap on the ground. She left her knife and money belt strapped against her skin.

Siyad stared at the rafters, which was more courtesy than she expected, and far more than she needed.

When she was done with that, he handed her a scarf. "For hair. Porachin women no wear it short. People will see. We go through the night market, and is crowded."

He opened the small door to the side of the much larger truck bay, which was closed and padlocked for the night.

It turned out the warehouse was on a wharf, so that when Cordelia stepped out she saw searchlights flash on the water before zipping up into the sky. She flinched and snapped, "What's going on?"

Siyad glanced over his shoulder. Two more bright white beams split the night. "A film is starting. The first night."

"A premiere," she echoed, imagining the furs and jewelry, white spats and flashbulbs. They all seemed made-up, hallucinations or half-remembered dreams.

"Come." Siyad waved her toward the gangway. "I take you where you can stay. Then you are alone. You are dangerous to me and my family."

"I clock you." She wiped her mouth with her hand, the lamb pastry settling uneasily in her stomach. "Let's stroll."

It was close to midnight, but the city was still living. Even the narrower streets and shabbier neighborhoods were lined with fruit stalls and ice-cream vendors. Cafés had put their tables and chairs out onto the footpath, and did a busy trade. Folk were out shopping and running errands. Kids played between groups of chatting parents, running after dogs and little siblings and the occasional monkey. Trucks and carts rolled by, laden with people, rugs, melting ice, fruit and spices, bales of cotton, cords of wood . . . and it was *loud*.

Moving freely in the street had become an impossibility for most of the Catwalk. When they did, they traveled with the weight of fear, eyes cutting side to side at each corner, with each step. Even in the mountains she had hunched and scuttled, wary of shepherds and tinkers and travelers, of children by the road.

It was hard to shed that weight. She walked with her shoulders crunched up to her ears, trying to talk herself down. Distracted, she bumped into folk left and right, and realized she didn't know the Porashtu word for "sorry."

She knew "please," "thank you," "no," and "yes." She knew "where is," and "How do you say . . . ?" and "My name is . . ." not that she could tell the truth. And she knew none of it would be enough. She had to find some people who spoke her tongue.

She was leery about picking up the lead Sofie and Mab had dropped for her. It wouldn't be safe to look up Ari. He'd have eyes on him: punters and secret police, most like. But it wouldn't exactly be safe or easy to live on the street in a country where she couldn't speak the language. She could make it work if she had to, but . . .'Tits, she was tired. She'd been willing to go without, grub for money, sleep rough, when she was building bombs and plotting. When it felt like she was fighting something. But if she'd been forced out of her fight, if the Ospies had come down hard as she heard they had, she didn't want to struggle for nothing.

But she didn't want to be found out, either.

"I can't believe you didn't tell me," Aristide growled, when the lights came up for intermission. He'd spent the remainder of the press barrage, and the first half of the film, silently seething. Judging by her crystalline smile and magnesium-bright manner, Pulan could clearly tell he was furious. There hadn't been a chance to discuss things. It wasn't as if they could slip away from their own film.

And, it seemed, there would be no chance now. Pulan was already out of her seat, gathering the folds of her skirt in one hand. "I did not tell you because I knew you would not like it."

"No one at the studio mentioned it. Did you put a gag order on them?"

"It was a last-minute lark. I only cabled her yesterday."

He didn't believe her. Well, he believed she'd cabled at short notice. But she'd planned this; it was too perfectly uproarious not to be one of her publicity plots.

Daoud would know, but he had slipped out of the theatre five minutes before the intermission title screen, presumably to put Pulan's order in at the bar. And anyway, he'd be pinch-lipped in Pulan's presence.

"Shall we go greet the vultures?" asked Pulan. "Jinadh is here and you know how testy he becomes when he thinks that I have slighted him. He asked for some quotes from you."

"Too bad; I don't want to give them."

Pulan's theatrical flightiness evaporated. She spoke forcefully, but kept her voice low and her expression placid. "Aristide," she said, "you work for me. Please do not forget."

After a moment spent mastering his rage, Aristide closed his eyes and took a deep breath, banishing tension from his shoulders.

It sprang back the moment they entered the lobby. Lillian, a horrible, beautiful vision in silk satin the color of blue smoke, stood poised at the foot of a marble pillar with a beaky escort at her side. They made an odd but handsome couple. She, somewhat taller, fair and starkly elegant. He, compact and clever-eyed, a badger streak of silver through dark hair swept back from a high forehead.

Pulan's unctuous cousin marked the third point in their triangle, no doubt assaulting them with frivolous banter.

Jinadh was related to Pulan in the complex manner common to all Porachin nobility, and therefore her "cousin" for convenience's sake. He certainly had the manner of a born courtier: carelessness and condescension tempered with a slight strain of simpering. Public opinion dubbed him debonair. Aristide found him to be tacky, and a cad.

Lillian's escort noticed them first, and lifted his glass in greeting. Aristide envied him his drink. Lillian, following his gaze, raised her arm halfway as though manacled by restraint.

When Jinadh saw them, his flirtatious smile turned ferocious and the steno pad came out. Aristide bypassed him, extending a hand to the other man. "I don't believe we've met."

"Vasily Memmediv." Tatien, by the name and accent. "Regional Affairs, with the Geddan embassy."

Coworkers then, not lovers, though Lillian was standing awfully close; it could be both. Aristide wondered what they got up to in Regional Affairs. Boring name. Just boring enough to pique

his interest, if he had let it. "Aristide Makricosta. It's a pleasure."
It wasn't.

"I should have done that," said Jinadh. "Please excuse me."
There wasn't even venom in it, though he wouldn't have missed
Aristide's snub. Jinadh could divest himself of all sense of irony
when it suited his purposes. "Ms. DePaul, I know that you met
Mr. Makricosta onstage in front of a thousand people, but per-
haps you'd like a more intimate introduction?"

She laughed: Cyril's laugh again, but not quite. This time,
Aristide could detect the disingenuous note at its heart. Cyril's
laughter had to be surprised out of him, by a particularly apt
piece of bitchiness, or Aristide's tongue pressed against the high
arch of his foot. Aristide had the sense that Lillian's laugh got
marching orders, and followed them or faced a court-martial.

"And of course," said Jinadh, "my cousin Pulan Satri, the
genius behind this evening's entertainments."

«It's such a pleasure to meet you in person,» said Lillian. Her
Porashtu was almost unaccented, smooth as velvet. How long
had she been speaking it? Living here? How had he not known?

Because he hadn't asked, or looked, or lifted up his head, most
likely. And now he wanted to plunge twice as deeply into oblivion.

"Would anyone like anything from the bar?" he asked, and
promptly forgot every request that was made of him. That was all
right, though: He didn't plan on returning once he had a drink
in his hand.

«I suppose my quotes just walked away for good.» Jinadh slipped
his steno pad into his pocket. «Unless you'd care to give me a line
or two, Ms. DePaul?»

«It depends on the line.» Lillian's cheeks were beginning to ache from smiling. Switching back to Geddan for Memmediv's benefit, she said, "I may be here as Ms. Satri's personal guest, but I *am* a member of Gedda's foreign service. You won't get a very candid interview."

"You underestimate my wiles," said Jinadh, and Lillian's heart twisted. "May I take you someplace quiet to talk? The balcony perhaps?"

"Go on," said Memmediv. "Go with him. You've got ten minutes until intermission ends, and I have every confidence in you as the face of Gedda."

She would have said no; should have. She needed to stay with him, flirt with him, put warm weight on his arm. The least useful thing she could do right now would be to abandon him for another man, *especially* Jinadh. If Flagg found out—

But then Jinadh had his arm through hers and refusing would make a scene, which was the last thing she wanted.

He took her up the curving stairs, chattering about something neither of them would remember later. She laughed in all the right places. Eventually, he picked a spot at the railing with clear lines of sight in all directions. At least from there she would be able to keep an eye on Memmediv; she could tell Flagg, truthfully, she hadn't let him out of her sight.

It wasn't, in fact, much quieter than the mêlée below, but they were less likely to be interrupted or eavesdropped upon. Still, when she asked, "What do you want?" she kept her voice low, kept smiling, and kept a careful space between them. And she spoke in Geddan, because on the balance there would be fewer people fluent in that language, if they did overhear something.

"Lillian, I . . ."

He didn't touch her, but his voice, when he said her name . . . She crossed her arms, pulling farther away from him. "Don't."

"I apologize." He dropped his head, flipping through his steno pad. She didn't think he was actually reading his notes.

"I'm flattered that it's still so hard for you, after so long." Dangerous, to say things like that in a public space; but it was cruel, as well, and she needed cruelty now to cool Jinadh's ardor. This had always been more difficult for him. He had not been raised to school his passions with the rigor instilled in her by His Excellency Stewart DePaul, known to diplomatic colleagues as the Cipher. In Porachis men were expected to be volatile, free with their emotions; weeping and expressions of anger were par for the course. Growing up in the middle of court intrigue had taught him craftiness and the importance of masking what he truly felt, but it had not taught him to kill the fire, only to lie about the fuel.

Jinadh shifted, taking half a step away, and she was satisfied to see her tactics had achieved the desired effect. "You are right," he said. "It should not be. It is not, usually. Or if it is, I am better at ignoring it."

"So why did you bring me up here?"

She saw his cheek dimple, knew he'd caught the inside with his teeth. It marred the lush bow of his lips. "Do you know who that man is?"

"Vasily Memmediv, deputy counselor of—"

"Regional Affairs, I know." He snapped the steno pad shut and tapped it against the railing. "And why is he here with you?"

She turned her head enough to catch his pained expression from the corner of her eye. Despite herself—they shouldn't talk about this here—she said, "Are you jealous?"

"Would you blame me?"

"Yes. We agreed long ago—"

"I know." He sighed. "But that isn't why I ask."

"Jinadh," she said, a steel shank of warning sliding into her tone. If she'd wondered, before, whether he was leveraged . . . "Don't tell me something you'll regret. Don't tell me anything *I'll* regret."

"Tell me why he's here with you, and maybe I won't have to."

"I know what he is," she said. "What he does."

Jinadh leaned heavily on the railing. Below him, gowns swirled in eddies of gossip. "That isn't an answer to my question."

"Satri said I could bring a guest, and he volunteered."

Jinadh shook his head. «My butter-headed cousin,» he said, lapsing back into Porashtu. «She's up to something. And I would give good odds your guest is mixed up in it. Look.»

Lillian had gotten caught up in conversation, and missed the arrival of Inaz Iligba and Prince Sekibou into Pulan's circle. Sekibou was shaking Memmediv's hand, his smile a bright arc destined to draw the eyes of photographers.

It was not a picture she wanted to explain in her next press conference.

"Excuse me," she said to Jinadh, and tried to bolt. But he put a hand on her arm—too much a Porachin gentleman to close his fingers around her wrist, but firmly enough that she stopped to listen.

"Let him talk," said Jinadh. "If you frighten him now, you frighten her, and then there will be nothing to tell. And they've asked you to tell them something, haven't they?"

She swallowed against the constriction of her throat. "If I can catch him at treason," she said, "Stephen comes home for the Solstice holidays. If not . . . I don't know when I'll see him again."

He didn't flinch at the name, though the pressure of his hand on her wrist briefly increased.

"It's the first time they've really . . ." she started over, reframing. "Is this what it's like for you, every day?"

"Yes," he said. "Except I will never see my son, no matter how faithfully I report."

Not this argument again. "You knew how it would be, when I decided to keep the baby."

He withdrew his touch from her arm. "I always wanted children. A big family." Bitterness coated the words.

"I loved you very much." Now she was angry that she hadn't stopped him earlier, and it was making her imprudent. He had *always* made her imprudent. "I would have married you and you know it. But it wasn't a possibility."

"It *was*," he said, forcing the word between clenched teeth. "You know that it was. All we had to do was leave Porachis. And I would have, for you."

"And what would that have gotten us? My brother is *dead*, Jinadh. If I had forfeited my position with the embassy here, and we had gone to Gedda, who knows what would have happened to us?"

"Don't pretend it was about them. Regime change wasn't a threat then!"

"That didn't stop it from happening. And I don't imagine Acherby would have treated our family with kindness."

"But I would have been able to raise my son. He does not even know who I am. He is *eight years old* and he does not know who I am." He turned his back on the railing and the lobby, to hide his pained face, and pressed the flat of his palm across his mouth.

Lillian had always been able to turn her own guilt into strategy against the thing that caused it. If something hurt her, she picked it apart to find the critical thread, and then pulled.

"Maybe," she said, a plan assembling in the theatre of her mind. "Maybe it's time he learned."

"What?"

"Help me," she said. "Flagg wants me to . . . to inform on Memmediv. If he and Satri are working together, we double our odds. I know you aren't intimate, necessarily, but you're family. She likes you well enough, doesn't she?"

He shrugged. "She tolerates me."

"Well, get as close as her tolerance will allow. You visit her estate sometimes, correct? If you get anything good and I can use it, I'll . . . you can see Stephen."

"For five minutes at a cocktail party, politely saying goodnight to all his mother's guests before he goes to bed?" Jinadh sneered, but it was the anger of animal pain: defensive, terrified. "I won't do that again."

She hadn't been proud of that, but she had needed something to cement his cooperation. Flagg had agreed to bring Stephen home during last spring's Equinox, for just that purpose.

"No," she said. "I don't know how we'll manage it. I don't think . . . eight is too young to keep that kind of secret. But we'll make you a part of his life. Somehow."

He was quiet too long, and she began to worry she had erred in telling him anything. But finally, he looked into her eyes. Her breath didn't catch, but it was a very near thing. "This means that we will be a part of each other's lives as well."

This time, the terror was hers. "Like I said: we'll manage."

The multitude of cocktails Aristide had consumed during intermission struck him full force about twenty minutes from the end of the film. He knew he was laughing at inappropriate moments, and the smart remarks he insisted on making to Pulan were most likely asinine and far too loud. But it all seemed very far away, at a further remove from reality than the scenes played through the projector.

The festivities following the film were catered. Aristide filled a plate then promptly forgot where he had set it down, so replaced it with another cocktail. The room—he thought they might be in a hotel ballroom, or perhaps some civic building, though he did not remember how he had arrived—spun dizzily, and the various faces of actors, critics, investors, and hangers-on blurred together into a collage of bright white smiles and banal chatter. Except for Lillian—she stood out like a beacon in the throng.

He tucked himself into an alcove behind a fountain and watched her through the falling water as she talked with Phoebe Francis, the actress who had played Margaretta DePaul. They looked nothing alike. He laughed at that. A photographer waved her arm for them to smile and pose. Silk and crystal beading hissed as they arranged the trains of their gowns and linked their arms. The photographer made a flirtatious remark and everyone laughed. Flash spots haunted Aristide's field of vision, skating across the swirling surface of the world.

Daoud found him some time later, wedged into a corner he didn't remember retreating to.

"I will take you to your car," he said. "But I must stay with Pulan for a while. Business. I will come see you before I go to bed."

"You're not my dolly bear," said Aristide. "I can fall asleep without you as long as I've got pills."

But he didn't. And Daoud arrived at his hotel suite an hour or so later, heralded by a soft knock on the door. He did not wait for Aristide to answer. «I have bad news about our holiday,» he said, slipping out of his shoes. «Pulan needs me back at Hadhariti tomorrow.»

"That lying skink." Aristide raised his glass of brandy, only to find it empty. "I'll tear her forked tongue out of her face."

"I will not tell her you said that." Daoud crossed the room, padding over the thick carpet.

"I don't care if you do. I made some very tricky reservations for us, you know."

"I am sorry." Daoud moved Aristide's abandoned book and empty glass and took a seat beside him. "I was looking forward to it."

Aristide was silent a moment, working out a translation. It felt more honest to say what came next in Porashtu. «You were going to be bored stiff.»

«*I* was going to be bored.» Daoud pulled the tails of Aristide's shirt from his waistband. «*You* were going to be stiff.»

«Because I am old?» asked Aristide, taking over his own unbuttoning.

"*Nuance*," said Daoud, guessing rightly Aristide wouldn't know the word in Porashtu.

Aristide sighed. "Oh, I *hate* not to get a joke. I really am clever in my mother tongue, you know."

"I believe it," said Daoud. "Since you are so clever with your own." His fingertips skimmed the sweat-damp seam of linen between Aristide's legs.

Aristide twisted free of his shirt and turned Daoud's strategy back against him. Once the boy's breath began to hitch, Aristide said, "Why didn't Pulan tell me about Ms. DePaul?"

"She knew you would be upset." Daoud's fist caught at Aristide's hair, but he couldn't get a grip. It didn't feel strange anymore, the featherweight of his short crop, but tonight it sent a lance of nostalgia through him, and regret.

"She was planning it all along, I assume, even if she only sent the cable yesterday."

"Hells, Aristide, she has cost me my holiday and it is to be business all weekend. I do not want to start early."

"Well, I wish anyone had ever started with me at all."

"The premiere is finished," said Daoud. "Let it be." He unhooked the tab of Aristide's trousers and reached for the zipper, but Aristide snatched his hand away.

"And next time?" he asked. "And after that? Will she keep dropping these little surprises into my lap indefinitely?"

Daoud flung his arms up. "Talk to her! She is the woman in command. I am just her little secretary!"

"Didi—"

But Daoud had scrambled from his lap and was tugging his clothing straight. "I will see you back at Hadhariti, when you are done drinking your way through the week." He shut the door softly when he went, out of deference to the hour, but the decisive click of the latch echoed in the quiet.

Repetition should have made the task easier, but knocking on the door between their rooms cost Lillian even more dearly than before.

When he answered, Memmediv had shed every item of clothing he could spare without complete indecency—still not used to the heat—and went barefoot with his shirt open at the collar.

"Nightcap?" asked Lillian. She'd ordered a bottle of fig brandy to her room, and a healthy portion of it had gone to prepare her for this. "If you're done packing. We have an early train tomorrow and I don't want to distract you."

"I had a call this evening," he said. "I won't be going back to Myazbah with you. There's a small crisis down the coast; I need to liaise with one of my contacts. I've already let Flagg know."

"Oh," said Lillian. "Well. Will you still take a drink?"

He cocked an eyebrow, but ceded space so she could step into his room.

Tomorrow's suit was laid out on the valet stand, conservative tie hanging between gray linen lapels. Every other personal effect had been carefully packed away into the open black leather valise at the foot of his bed, which remained unrumpled beneath a canopy of delicate mosquito netting. There were no pyjamas in evidence on top of the coverlet, or in his open valise.

Porachis was hot. One only covered what one needed to.

"I'll just . . ." Lillian waved the two tumblers she'd brought in, then set them on the vanity to pour. "Don't tell Flagg? I wouldn't want word to get around that the public face of the OSP in Porachis is a lush behind closed doors."

Memmediv took a glass. "Of course not." Lifting it, he offered, "To closed mouths and closed doors. And the secrets safe behind them."

"Eloquent," said Lillian, and settled onto his sofa with her drink. Already tipsy, she landed more heavily than she meant to. Patting the cushions, she said, "Come sit?"

He did, though the crooked line of his mouth showed more humor than desire. His bemusement wasn't ideal, but it was better than refusal. Why did she have to be yoked with this burden? She had never been a skilled seductress.

"I hope you're not upsetting anyone's expectations in Myazbah with this last-minute trip," she said. "Wife, mistress? Maybe a boy? I wouldn't tell."

"No," he said, uninflected, and drank his brandy.

Lillian clenched her jaw hard enough that her teeth squeaked. "Good," she said. And then, because stress had turned her into a veritable teakettle and alcohol had loosened her control, a little burst of steam squeaked out. "Because you certainly upset a few of the administration's. I saw you talking with Sekibou."

"Please." He snorted. "It was a film premiere, not a battlefield. Not even a negotiation table."

"Everything is a negotiation." It came out more sharply than she meant it to.

That got his attention. He finally met her gaze and his bemusement was gone, replaced by surprise. She wasn't sure if that was worse or better.

Getting a grip, she amended her outburst with an apology. "The OSP hasn't made my job very easy lately, approving foreign aid packages that go straight to the republican army in North Liso." Inspiration caught her, and she resented it but let it drag her along. "I'm sorry for my temper," she said, and put her hand on his thigh.

He looked down at it, and she saw the edge of a smile in the shadow of his collar. "What's this?"

"I'm under a lot of strain," she said, and pressed softly into the wool of his trousers, the give of his flesh. "You're not hard to look at. And it's been some time since . . . well. I can't afford to be caught at something like this, and I don't have time for it anyway." All truth, bent in service of a lie.

"You're not afraid I'll mention it to Flagg?"

Her laugh, too, was genuine. "Speaking of closed doors, Regional Affairs has a formidable lock. Even if you do say something, Flagg won't mind it if it stays in the chancery."

"No," said Memmediv. Amusement deepened the cadence of his accent, made it purl like a stream. "I am certain he would not."

That turned her cold with apprehension. He might simply be agreeing with her sentiment, but he might also be alluding to a plot he wasn't supposed to be aware of. She pleaded with whatever powers might be listening—the heavens, the holy stones, the Wandering Queen, and any form of divinity or providence as yet unknown to her—that it was only a subordinate's humor of solidarity, and nothing more sinister.

"I have to admit," Memmediv went on, "this is not what I was expecting when I volunteered to come along."

"No?" she asked, proud of how smoothly she slid into the opening. "What *were* you expecting?"

He looked at her strangely then, and her hand on his leg felt so painfully obvious, so contrived. His dark eyes, deeply set beneath skeptical brows, were too keen for comfort.

"A show," he said. "And I'm certainly getting that."

He wasn't going to give her a better entrée, so she leaned in and kissed him.

She caught his mouth and held it long enough to taste a trace of the brandy she had poured for him, and the lingering acrid breath of cigarette smoke. His smooth face spoke of the recent pass of a razor, and his bitter aftershave filled her nose with vetiver and hyrax.

After waiting slightly too long for him to reciprocate, she pulled away. He was already watching her, inscrutable.

"Thank you for the drink," he said. "As you said, you have an early train."

Summarily dismissed, she collected her glass from the table, her bottle from the vanity, and wished him a good night.

"I hope your meeting down the coast is productive," she said, retreating into the formal cordiality that was her true professional strength.

"Thank you," he said. Then, just before she shut the door between their rooms, "Perhaps we might see one another again?"

It surprised her, so much so that she might have said yes even without Flagg's demands hanging over her. "Of course," she said. And then, gathering her wits enough to make a play at sultry, she added, "I look forward to it."

For a long time that night, she lay awake under the canopy of mosquito netting, watching for the faint breeze in the folds, the shifting moiré patterns of warp over weft. She had failed in the task that Flagg had set for her, but still, she had forged some tenuous connection with Memmediv. Where that might lead her, and why in the Lady's name he had asked to see her again, she had no idea.

Her hopes lay mostly, ironically, with Jinadh. And while they were no longer lovers, her intentions toward Memmediv felt uncomfortably like betrayal.

She bit the raw inside of her lip. She had never cried over Jinadh. Not then, and not once over the long years in between as Stephen's face lost its baby roundness and lengthened into a narrow-jawed likeness of his father. But seeing him again, without warning, on this night of all nights? Blood salted her teeth and tongue.

Familiar dead-end "what if" scenarios began to play in her head like one of Satri's silver nitrate dramas. She was a foreign diplomat from a state whose relationship with Porachis was less than friendly. He was the favorite nephew of Her Resplendent Majesty Queen Yaima. That was one strike against each of them. And Porachin taboo was very strict about widowers remarrying. Tradition had grown lax in recent decades, and women in Porachis picked up widowers all the time. Sometimes even married them. But Jinadh was noble, and the sin would be one of hypocrisy if it could be tied—even tenuously—to the queen.

Years ago they could have been together back in Gedda, but Lillian refused to leave Myazbah for him, not when she was doing a job she loved, excelled at. Besides, she didn't know *how* to have a family, or a marriage. Her own parents had spent almost all their time apart, working themselves to death for the foreign service and the courts of law. And her brother hadn't exactly been a model of familial virtue.

Even if she and Jinadh had left together, her home country

would not have remained welcoming for long. If only she could pretend it had been prescience that kept her in Porachis, instead of pride.

She had very little left now, and knew he would forgive her, because he'd never had any to begin with. But Flagg had told her early on, in no uncertain terms, she must stay far away. He wouldn't risk his eyes and ears in the Porachin court blinded and made deaf by scandal.

CHAPTER

FIVE

Aristide woke late the morning after the premiere, sore and cotton-mouthed. Daoud was gone; the sheets were rumpled, but cool. Aristide wondered if he'd left late last night or early in the morning. Neither fire nor earthquake nor flood could rouse Aristide from the dreamless coma of his sleeping pills, let alone a feather-weight boy slipping out of his bed.

Then he remembered that they'd quarreled, and levered himself up to face the day alone, wincing as a piece of his spine popped into place.

In rumpled, candy-striped red seersucker, with a silk parasol over one elbow and Kuravic's collected critical essays in his hand, he descended to the hotel mezzanine, the restaurant, and a break-fast of lamb confit and poached eggs with sumac, which he hoped would subdue his hangover.

At the next table, a woman in a yoked tunic and narrow trousers sipped coffee, reading her morning paper. Over the tops of his reading spectacles, which softened everything at a distance of six feet or greater into illegibility, Aristide caught a glimpse of the photograph above the fold:

Lillian DePaul, behind a podium, rather more soberly dressed than she had been last night. Opposite, a delegation of Lisoans inspecting troops at stiff attention. Royalist or republican, he couldn't tell.

When the woman set aside the front pages in favor of lighter fare, he caught a different photograph entirely: last night's emcee, arms open to cede the floor, and then Pulan, Aristide, and Lillian again, this time in her revealing satin gown.

The women were both smiling. Pulan as though she had just eaten something particularly indulgent, and Lillian like visiting royalty: distant, kind, and unimpeachable. By comparison, Aristide's expression looked blank. Some people might mistake it for pained arrogance, but he knew his own face. Here, it had been rendered affectless by shock.

Disgusted with himself, he left the restaurant and went down to the lobby, where the concierge informed him that Ms. Satri had left a car for his convenience. He discovered it was not the one they had driven up in, and wondered where it had come from before deciding that he truly, deeply didn't care. She had five; she could spare this one.

His watch read half eleven. There were hours to dispose of between now and dinner—in a private room at the decadent Najaloor—followed by Srai Sin's performance of Maihu's new art song cycle.

Aristide had heard the acclaimed Asunan contralto perform once in his life, and she was so exceptional that he had put aside painful doubts born of past circumstances to hear her again. He did not have *many* misgivings, and had convinced himself this meant that he had *none*. Facing the prospect of the concert on his own, abandoned by another lover—albeit in less dire circumstances—he wished he had given his doubts more credence.

Cyril had been late to that particular party; he had missed the music. Still, it would be hard to listen to Srai Sin with Lillian's laughter haunting him, harmonizing with art songs and arias to conjure more deeply buried ghosts.

He regretted the box seats now. At least he'd be alone; no one to see him wince. Or, plague it all, to see him weep.

Since he didn't have a companion to help fill his time, he could, he supposed, go by the office. Or maybe the soundstage the studio rented in the city. Most of the real work they did on Pulan's estate, where she'd built everything a film might need. But Chitra was auditioning dancers today for *Galatar ul Walibi*, which was due to start shooting on location two weeks from now, in the windy steppes of Tzieta. Roughly translated, the title meant *Song of the Sky*, and there would be plenty of both in the fantastical romance.

The audition might be amusing. At any rate, it would give him something to do besides drink.

Traffic was abhorrent on Charaplati—the Silver Street, where all the film folk worked. Vans and wagons jostled for position on the curb, unloading catering, props, and equipment. Bicycle messengers wove between cars and buses. A man strolled by with a tiger on a lead. The cat's tongue lolled, its ears flat with the heat. Anywhere else he would have done a double take, but on the Silver Street, Aristide had seen stranger things than a tiger at heel.

When he slipped into the soundstage, Chitra had her troops drilling a nasty piece of footwork. The way these things went, she'd probably shown it to them once and would cull the ones who couldn't pick it up. It worked the same way for the stage. Ruthless, but no one wanted to waste precious production time on a straggler.

A few of those stood out, from where Aristide had parked himself. They wore a defeated look under their glaze of sweat, even as they strove to keep time.

One other dancer stood out, though she was following the choreography doggedly. Her gait was a bit stiff, and her expression cutthroat. But what drew his eye was her complexion. The other dancers were mostly Porachin, with a sprinkling of Lisoan, Yashtani, and the children of Anadh's melting pot. Brown and black and gold skin, barely covered by jersey sport clothes. This woman was pale, with short dark hair badly dyed, her face burnt bright pink across the nose and heavily freckled. She didn't wear dancing gear, but a cambric robe tied up at her waist and a pair of wrinkled narrow trousers. Something about her scratched at the back of his brain, but he couldn't place the feeling of recognition, couldn't summon up a face to hang it on.

When the accompanist banged out the last chord of the final eight count, the hopefuls hit their marks if they were on the beat, held them for an agonized moment, then dropped their heads and arms and sucked in desperate breaths of stinking hot air. The fans hanging from the ceiling did nothing to cool the place down.

Chitra started barking instructions for the next step, but cut herself off when she saw Aristide lounging against the wall.

«Ah,» she said. «Our esteemed director. I wasn't expecting you.»

A few of the dancers craned their necks to look at him, but most of them were too tired to do more than pant. The pale woman was one of these, which frustrated him—he would have liked a better look at her face.

«My holiday is canceled,» he said to Chitra. «Can I stay to watch?»

«Of course. Would you like a chair?»

He shook his head. «I am well. Go dance.»

She shrugged and turned back to the dancers, shouting technical terms in Porashtu and demonstrating the next setup steps. Aristide watched the pale woman copy her, eyes narrow, until the dancer next to her stuck out a foot and sent her sprawling.

A torrent of Geddan curses—specifically slum swears straight out of Amberlough City—burst forth from the woman on the ground.

"You better watch it, you bandy-legged whore," she snapped, "or I'll give the tricks another hole to knock you in."

It was, he realized with a shock that stole his breath, Cordelia Lehane.

He couldn't believe he hadn't clocked her. But she had changed, quite starkly. At the Bee, she had always had an ageless quality—not beauty, necessarily, but an inscrutable bearing. When anyone dared ask how old she was, she told them she didn't know, and left it at that.

In the dusty light of the soundstage, he could see lines pinching the corners of her eyes. She seemed smaller, too, and sharper, as if she had gone hungry. Her breasts had never been large, but she'd made a lot of them. Now, they were disguised by folds of loose cambric, if there was much left to hide.

He wondered if she would recognize him. He could have passed for a local, and did sometimes; his complexion had darkened here, under the merciless sun, and that wasn't the only thing that had changed.

"They teach you moves like that in the lockup, or the meat house?" Cordelia scrambled up from the floor and advanced on the target of her rage. "I left cheap swineshit like that behind when I stopped taking three bits a jockey."

She'd always been careful to keep the slum whine of Kipler's Mew tamped down when she spoke, and it was softer now than it had ever been. But Aristide had been listening to Porashtu's lush vowels and soft dental consonants for nearly three years, and her voice rang out like a brassy horn.

«Ladies,» said Chitra, advancing on the two. The guilty party had gone from looking smug to looking scared, and Aristide didn't blame her.

"It's 'cause I'm Geddan, ain't it?" Cordelia said. "Mother's tit, third time today."

It would be the rankest sort of stupidity to reveal himself to her, like pocketing a grenade without a pin. He was in the Porachin queen's good graces thanks to Pulan and a tense political situation, and he had no desire to test the strength of those conditions. As long as his associations with Gedda remained in his tragic past, they were glamorous. He didn't imagine they would remain so, if dragged into the present.

«I have no time for scenes like these,» said Chitra. «Both of you can go.» And though she said it in Porashtu, Aristide could tell Cordelia clocked her. Her head fell back and she closed her eyes. In the moment that her face hung slack, she looked immeasurably tired. That was what broke him: her exhaustion. He knew that look. He had worn it, on his worst days.

«I want to speak to our respected sister,» said Aristide, proud he could remember the honorific for an unknown woman in this mental state. «Chitra, please?»

«You can take our *respected sister* outside,» said Chitra. «And don't bother bringing her back when you're finished.»

"Come along," he said to Cordelia, and offered his arm. She didn't take it, but instead stormed out ahead of him so that he had to rush after.

"Cordelia," he said, as he caught her elbow just outside the door. "It's me." He had to grab her arm to get her to look up; she was fighting him, trying to shake off his grip. Even when he finally raised her face to his, she squinted at him like an invalid forced into the sun. "It's Aristide. Ari. From the Bee."

She had gone stiff all over, though she had stopped struggling. "Mother's tit," she said, and swallowed. Her skin had a terrible green tinge to it, under the freckles. "You scared me two steps into the grave."

"If I climbed out," he said, "then so can you. Let's bend our knees and talk."

When Cordelia hit the passenger's seat of the car, she hit it hard. It was one thing to know Ari was in the city. It was another to encounter him entirely by chance.

"So, what are you *doing* here?" he asked, sliding in behind the wheel.

"Looking for picture work," she said. Her voice sounded funny in her ears: thin, with a nervous wobble. She swallowed against it, and went on: "I didn't know it was your show. Somebody just told me there was a Geddan director and I might have better luck."

"I meant in Porachis."

"I know what you rotten meant." She leaned against the hot leather upholstery and closed her eyes. It made her queasy to look at him.

"Well?"

"Same thing you are, I'd wager. Scurrying, far and fast."

"You waited a little while." There was half a laugh in it.

"Yeah, well. We didn't all jump on the first boat." The anger spat out of her like sparks from a foundry. It came on suddenly, unexpected, and it sobered her. "Some of us couldn't afford to. Some of us didn't *want* to."

He didn't seem to know what to do with his face, and the expression he landed on made him look like he'd smelled something rancid but was still trying to smile. "So what *have* you been doing?"

Like she could tell him. "This and that. Odd jobs. A girl like me can get all kinds of work, even in a place like that."

"It can't have been very pleasant," he said. That little dent between his eyebrows, the drawn-down corners of his mouth . . . he thought she'd been whoring, maybe, or cozied up to some hypocritical Ospie clerk.

He pitied her. She wasn't sure how she felt about that. "What about you?"

"Funnily enough, picture work," he said. "I have an old friend in the business I thought could help me. I was right."

"Now you're in the slops, huh? Look at those rings."

His fingers squeezed the steering wheel harder, as if he could hide the gems like a pill bug curling tight. If it had been anyone but Ari, she'd have thought he was ashamed.

"You don't look like you've had the same luck."

"I didn't have a lot of time to plan this, did I? And what do I know about Porachis? I lived in Amberlough my whole life."

His face went funny when she said the city's name. Not quite a wince; more like he'd swallowed his soup too hot, and it burned on the way down. Something small and mean in her was pleased at that.

"Why did you leave?" he asked, and she should've seen it coming. But her wits were still catching up with her spinning skull.

"Same reason as you?" she ventured.

He still had that smile: the one that made you want to lick your thumb and scrub it off his face with spit. "I doubt that very much."

The anger came back, hotter than before, and burnt out what

sense was left in her. She yanked her hands from her lap and let them fall heavy on the dashboard, though the shock of the impact sent a stab of pain sizzling up her left arm.

She'd gotten good at hiding them. The left was easier, in some ways. As long as she was holding something, most people didn't notice the kink in her wrist or the painful curl of her fingers. The left hand hurt worse, but she was good at hiding the pain, too.

It was the right hand that really got people, if they noticed. What made it so bad was the way her hand looked fine until she reached out, or laid it flat. It was just the last joints, on her pinky and her fourth finger, but it was startling to see the smooth pink caps of scar tissue where you expected a nail and a fingertip.

"Lady's name." They were stopped in a snarl of traffic, and Aristide leaned across the gearshift for a closer look. "What happened?"

"Somebody wanted some questions answered," she said. "Questions about you."

He closed his eyes, just a little too long for a casual blink. She'd called the shot right, and sunk the ball.

"I got banged up, running your race. Made some enemies."

"You stayed, though." She watched him scramble back to the top of the log, steady himself. "You didn't run right away. You said you didn't want to. So why now?"

There wasn't a good way out of this. Even if she turned tail now, he'd seen her face and knew she was here.

So maybe the only way out was farther in. They'd trusted each other after a fashion before, with lives at stake and a big kitty in the center of the table. And she might have something to gain here, if she was willing to take on the risk.

"Listen, Ari," she went on, letting her vowels sag with the weight of her exhaustion. She'd always hated how she slipped into a slum whine when she was tired, but it would work on him if he missed home. And from his face, when she'd said "Amberlough" . . . "I maybe got into something, after you left. After this." She tapped the edge of one crooked fist on the glove box. "Not anything the Ospies popped a cork about, y'know? You keep up with the news?" It was a test, a sounding. If he said yes, she could give him some half truths and let him write a story for her.

But he surprised her. "Not if I can help it."

"Really?"

"Cordelia, I left Gedda because it wanted nothing to do with me anymore. So now, *I* want nothing to do with *it*."

Oh, he missed home all right. Lucky her. "Well, sorry to bust in on you like this. If I'd known, I wouldna come." Now she'd let the whine out, it was taking over.

"That's not what I meant. It's certainly a surprise to see you. And I wish it were under easier circumstances, but . . ."

He was trying to say he was happy she was here, but the lie wasn't coming to him. She wondered what that meant, and was suddenly worried he wouldn't fall the way she wanted on her next roll. But she'd come this far and might as well ask.

"Listen," she said, "you always seem to weasel your way into the right crowd, and you sure look like you done it now. I just need a name, maybe two. Or can you point some people my way? Give me a lead and I'll get off your chain."

"As a matter of fact," he said, then stopped.

"What?" The word cracked against the silence between them, harder than she'd meant it to. She might be tired as a soggy rag but she hadn't let her nerves loose yet. Didn't know if she ever would.

He flinched. She almost felt bad. "I know a very reputable studio that's looking for an assistant choreographer."

Her shoulders sagged. "Thank you. You got no idea what it means to me."

"I think I do," he said. "A little, anyway."

"Listen, though." This part made her breath come tight. "It ain't safe for me to be Cordelia right now." If she had a shred of luck left, he wouldn't ask why.

He spun the wheel and put the car in reverse, slipping them into a parking spot beneath a drooping tree heavy with sweet white flowers. The dappled shade hid his expression, keeping her on edge until he said, "What serendipity."

"Talk a little plainer, why don't you?"

"It's only safe for me to be Aristide Makricosta if I don't dig up any old friends." He cased her long and hard, lip caught in his teeth. "With that in mind, it's a pleasure to meet you, Miz . . ." The sentence hung in the air, like his extended, open palm.

Cordelia stared at him for several seconds before she realized what he was waiting for. She shook, and the pressure of his hand made the scars on her fingers itch.

"Hanes," she said. "Nellie Hanes."

He took her to a café a few blocks down the street. They sat under a striped awning, and Aristide ordered, in Porashtu. Of course he'd picked up the language. She wondered how long he'd been here, and what exactly he'd done to earn his rings and his expensive watch. Next to his clean suit, slick hair, and little blue sunglasses, Cordelia felt shabby and wrung out.

Olives and coffee arrived. Cordelia drank her cup in one swallow, wincing less at the flavor than at the memory it stirred up. Porachin coffee, black and sweet over fine grounds, reminded her of the stuff they served at Antinou's. *Had* served.

Antinou and his wife went back to Hyrosia six months into Ospie rule, leaving the restaurant shuttered, the stoves and ovens cold. He gave Cordelia the key, and the beginnings of the Cat-walk were born in the brick kitchen, over coffee not too different from this.

To cut the taste, she turned to the olives. She didn't realize Aristide was watching her eat until he said, "My, my. You never looked particularly well fed, but have you eaten at *all* since we last saw one another?"

She'd left a pile of clean pits soaking in oil, next to a single curl of orange peel. "Not a lot. And don't ask me why; I can't tell you."

"I wouldn't want to know."

She'd never thought somebody's disinterest could make her feel so safe.

A long pause. Then, "What was it like?" he asked. "After I left."

"How bad do you think it was?"

When he said nothing, she went on: "It was worse than that. Not that you'd have noticed, maybe, if you were the right kind of people." She poked her pile of olive pits with her finger, then hacked up a bit of laughter. "Well. You'd have noticed eventually."

"Where are you staying now?" asked Ari, as the waiter arrived with plates of lamb shank and rolled grape leaves. The smell of garlic and lemon made spit pool in Cordelia's mouth, equal parts queasy and starving.

"Hostel," she said, shoveling down a grape leaf. "I got three nights free. There's two more left on that; I only been in town a day. Berer, before that." She wouldn't have given him details, if she didn't know he didn't care.

"Not to belittle the queen's charity," he said, words starting slow then speeding up like he was warming to the idea, "but I have a suite at the Abna Bhangri and I'm bouncing around like a pea in a barrel. There's plenty of room. I'd offer to take the chaise but I'm old and I have a bad back."

"Old my rear," she said. "My great-gran lived to ninety-six. You're maybe half that."

"Your dubiety," he said, "has little bearing on the state of my spine. If you mind the chaise so terribly, I'm sure the hostel won't object to your continued presence. Especially if you stay longer than three nights and start paying. Though with what money, I can't imagine."

"Sweet mother's tits, you ain't changed one bit."

"I think you'll find that isn't true."

She snorted into her lamb, and choked on her rice so it caught at the back of her throat, got up her nose.

"Sorry," she said. "I know it ain't funny."

"Laugh or else you weep."

That got her in the guts. She hadn't expected him to quote Tory's old northern nursery sayings at her. And from the look on his face, he hadn't expected to do it, either.

"You don't stutter anymore," she said, glad she had the coughing fit as a cover for the sudden tightness of her throat.

"No," he said, eyes dropping to his plate. "I don't."

"And you cut your hair."

"You too."

They stared at each other for too long in silence, surrounded by lunchtime laughter and sun so bright it stabbed. Aristide broke first, and this time when he smiled it fell on her heart like a weight.

"We got a lot of catching up to do," she said.

"Luckily, I have lots of time." He sipped his coffee two-handed, pinkies delicately splayed. "I'm meant to be on a little lovers' holiday; a slew of plans all week, set up for two. But my companion has been called away."

"Oh, so now I'm *your* female company." The sudden pressure behind her ribs wasn't hope, exactly. It bore a likeness to anger, and to fear. If he was here, what would she say to him? Cyril, who'd as good as kicked her country in the rear on its stumbling way to ruin. Sock him in the teeth, first. Spit in his face. Then maybe haul him close and cry on him, because he'd ruined everything and now he was one of the last scraps of her old life left. "You think your *companion*'s gonna be jealous?"

It took Ari a moment too long to clock her. When he did he faltered, and that not-quite-hopeful pressure popped like she was sinking into deep water.

"Yes," he said, too cheery. "A lot of catching up to do."

In the event, they didn't attend the concert. Cordelia couldn't face the crowds, and Aristide couldn't face Srai Sin with her at his side. It would have been worse than going alone.

They passed the afternoon on his hotel balcony, ordering up a long series of bottles. "You drink harder than you used to," she said, bare feet propped on the elaborate railing.

"I've got every reason." He topped up her glass, then his own. Porachin terroir produced delicious young wines, crisp and vegetal, alive with tiny bubbles. Very easy to consume in quantity.

"About that," she said, and he wished she hadn't been keeping pace so handily. The wine had eroded her reserve, and now she was asking questions. "What happened? To you, and . . . After I got drug in, and then let go, I never saw either of you again."

"I killed myself," he said, ignoring her "and" and "either of." "Or rather, made it appear as if I were dead. It worked for long enough that I got out of the city. I spent several hideous weeks up-country, hiked through the mountains, grew a rotten *beard*, and showed up in Erlsbord looking like a *tramp*. I ran a shell game to pay for a third-class ticket to Berer, by way of Hyrosia. Not the escape I'd planned."

"What *was* the plan?"

"There was money here and there, which I would have been able to get my hands on if I hadn't been dining left-handed by the Geddan border and worried about drawing attention. I meant to get much further much faster, but that isn't quite how things worked out."

After he left Amberlough, his alias accounts and shell corporations went on making trades and earning interest without him. There was even still property in Asu: a neat little apartment in the capital, and a bungalow off the red-sand beach of Ishin Sao.

He hadn't bothered to retrieve most of his wealth; not once Pulan took him in and started paying him. When he'd landed at Hadhariti he couldn't scrape himself off the tarmac. It was too much effort, too much commitment to a new life he'd never wanted.

Every now and then, when he thought of breaking with the studio and doing something with his money, he always shied away. Dissolving the companies and selling the land felt like an admission he refused to make. He tried, mostly, not to think about his assets at all, or the plans that he had made for them.

Cordelia didn't have those scruples. "And Cyril?"

He felt the delicate stem of his wineglass press into the edge of his finger, and took a deep breath to steady himself. No call to smash the crystal.

Blunt as a hammer, she asked, "What happened to him?"

Aristide shook his head. "I don't know."

"And you never tried to find out?"

"How successful do you think my inquiries would have been?" He let acid drip through the words, to discourage her from touching any further on the topic.

She shrugged, small enough he could tell she was chastened.

Awkward silence persisted. Then, because he felt he owed it to her, and when else would he say it? "I met his sister last night. Lillian."

"What? How? What's she doing in Porachis?"

"At a film premiere. She's the press attaché with the Geddan embassy. Been here for years, apparently."

Cordelia cast her gaze upward, as though she were searching for a particular slide or file in the library of her mind. "He told me," she said at last, and it hit him in the gut as squarely as a prize fighter's blow. "Told me he had a sister, in Porachis. I just forgot."

Aristide closed his eyes, as if it would stop him from seeing the truth of his words. "I never knew in the first place."

"Yeah, well, you two were cagey as harbor cats," said Cordelia. "And probably screamed about as loud when you—"

"What shall we do for dinner?" he asked. "It's getting to be about that time."

"Ah," she said. "So that's how it is."

This was why he had rebuffed every effort his old life made to creep up on him in Porachis, sent every Geddan expatriate who sought him out back the way they had come, with a swift kick in the rear if they dawdled in their leaving. To avoid this conversation.

"We could order something up," he said, and knew he was talking too fast. "Or there's a very nice place down the street that cooks the most delicate savory almond custard. We could even have someone from the hotel pick up the custard and bring it here. I've been very generous with my tips to the staff, so I should hope they're well disposed toward me by this point."

Cordelia eyed him narrowly for a long moment, like she wanted to push him on the subject. Eventually, she just shook her head. "Were you always such a rotten swell?"

"It's insidiously easy to get used to luxury," he told her, grateful for her disgust. "And appalling to be deprived once you've acquired the taste."

"My heart's breaking." She thumped her chest. "Hear that jangle? Shards."

Her callousness made honesty easier. "I *have* missed you, Cordelia."

"Sure you have. You'll lose your edge without something to grind it on."

Raising one lewd eyebrow, he asked, "Are you volunteering?"

"Queen's sake." She emptied the last of their latest bottle into her glass. "You're wasted off the stage."

The small, sharp sound he made surprised him. Cordelia's grin brightened, then wavered when she caught his eye and realized it hadn't been laughter.

He took a deep breath against the ache of memory's bullet wound, gave her his showiest wink, and said: "I know."

CHAPTER

SIX

Lillian had hardly been back at her desk an hour when Flagg's secretary rang her up. "Ma'am, Counselor Flagg would like to see you in his office at your earliest convenience."

Which meant *now*. Tidying the drift of news dispatches that had spread across her blotter, she took a deep breath and rose to make her report.

The girl who'd called Lillian from her work also let her into Flagg's office. He smiled at them both, all paternal graciousness. But as soon as the door shut, the pleasant mask fell from his face like a sheet of ice shearing from a glacier. "Sit."

She took the chair facing his desk, sitting halfway back on the cushion. Neither comfortable nor wary; merely attentive.

"Coffee?" A fresh carafe steamed on the sideboard.

"Please." She was making do with an hour's poor nap on the

train. And if Flagg's coffee *did* cause her a heart attack or aneurysm, it might be a welcome relief.

He placed the cup in front of her and settled into his chair without the slightest creak of wood or whisper of upholstery. Steam rose between them like a scrim, behind which Flagg's keen eyes shone.

"Well?" he said.

"He's gone down the coast. To liaise with—"

"One of his contacts, yes. He told me that willingly. Satri's estate and studio are just south of Anadh. The safe wager is he'll claim it's one of our agents in her household. None of them are reliable, though; she's too careful for that. Give me something I don't know already."

"He did spend some time speaking with Asiyah Sekibou and Satri, at the premiere."

"What did they say?"

Damnation. "I was out of earshot."

"A curious strategy. I wonder if you're taking this as seriously as I'd hoped you would."

"I tried to get him into bed," she said bluntly. "He didn't jump for the lure."

Flagg's lip curled with distaste.

"He wants to meet again," she said. "But I don't think it's a good idea. I had a keen sense he knew what I was about."

"Take him up on it," said Flagg. "These things require time and repetition, in my experience. Build his trust."

"I'm sure you saw everything that came in yesterday's pouch. Negotiations in Dastya are hanging by a bit of tinsel. A sneeze would send them toppling, let alone a well-armed separatist movement. I imagine you'd like to wrap this operation up in as little time as possible."

"And I imagine you would prefer fewer repetitions. But we all make sacrifices for the foreign service mission."

"This is hardly what I expected when I took the exam," she said. "It's certainly not my area of expertise. But I think I've found someone who can help."

If there had been any blood in Flagg's face, it would have drained away. As it was, he turned a paler shade of gray, and his expression exchanged its habitual cast of exhaustion for something verging on terror. "Ms. DePaul, this is a covert operation of highest—"

"Someone trustworthy."

"It is my job to judge these things."

"I believe you already have," she said. "Not that he's ever said, outright. Not that anyone in this office has ever told me as much. But I can extrapolate from the facts I do know."

Flagg verged on blustering. "But if my networks have been compromised—"

"Not him. Because no matter what Memmediv may have offered him, you hold him by a stronger, shorter jess. The same one that holds me. Unless you've told Memmediv what you know about my son?"

Comprehension brought a faint sparkle back to Flagg's eyes, like light playing over antimony. "Ah. Of course. And you approached him?"

"It was a chance meeting," she said, unwilling to admit Jinadh's motives. He had been ready to expose himself, and Memmediv, for her. Such a romantic, and a fool. He shouldn't be playing this kind of game. "I admit I took liberties, but it seemed he could be useful. He's Satri's family, and from what I understand visits her estate quite regularly. If Memmediv is there now . . ."

Flagg nodded. "Well done. Out of line, but when has this profession ever been in the habit of orthodoxy? And given the cable I received this morning, it will be especially important to keep trustworthy eyes on Satri in the near future."

"Why?" she asked, wariness threatening.

"How closely do you follow the Catwalk's activities?" Other Ospie officials would have found a way around the name. Favored terms included "anti-Nationalists," "terrorists," "troublemakers," and "our little problem with the trains." Not Flagg. When he meant a thing, he said it.

"Closely enough to answer questions from the press." And to make convincing condemnations.

"You know about the raids on Chuli encampments, then. The arrests."

"Yes." The alliance between the Catwalk and the Chuli had never been a formal thing, but Lillian had done her best to weave it into one when the Porachin press questioned Gedda's police and military action against its own citizens.

She imagined many Chuli would have been amused at the idea they were anyone's citizens.

"I've received a cable from Farbourgh with some interesting news. A Chuli boy named Luca Cattayim and a woman named Opal Saeger were among those arrested outside Tannover. The press hasn't printed their names yet, and we're keeping it that way. Cattayim said his family had been harboring a Catwalk operative named Spotlight, but that he never knew her real name. Our intelligence says Spotlight is the code name for a high-level operative of the organization, possibly its founder."

Flagg picked up a folder from his desk, flipped it open, and removed a photograph. With a deft motion of his wrist, he turned it and placed it in front of her, revealing two scantily clad people buried in feather boas. A tall, dark-skinned man with a head of sumptuous curls held a smaller, paler woman in a deep dip over his knee. Her arm trailed elegantly behind, wrapped in a long rope of pearls.

She knew the man; had stood beside him last night in front of a hundred cameras. He had cut his hair, and his face had lost the taut, satin-finished haughtiness here leant—she suspected—by copious application of cosmetics. She recognized him more by his carriage than anything, and by his eyes, which caught the camera in a gaze that both invited and incensed.

"The woman?" asked Lillian, because she couldn't feature Makricosta living rough in the Culthams, or scrounging matches and fertilizer to build bombs.

"Her name is Cordelia Lehane. They worked together." Flagg tilted his head slightly to the side, regarding the photo from an angle. "Strippers."

"And now?"

"Saeger eventually admitted Lehane was smuggled out of the country into Tzieta, supposed to catch a cargo ship bound for Porachis. It seems she didn't know the ship's name, or the intended port of call. I'll say this for the Catwalk." Flagg's eyebrows puckered. "They know just how far to trust their people, and won't trust them an inch farther."

Lillian kept her face pleasantly bland, and breathed through her nose—the kind of shallow, unsatisfying breaths one took when nauseated. She wondered how long it had taken to extract that information from Saeger, and how many times she had to tell them *I don't know* before they believed her.

"The Cattayim boy has an aunt in Porachis—shunned by the family, but he said she'd been sending money on the sly to fund terrorist activities. That's a place to start, but . . ."

Lillian pressed her fingertips to the lip of her coffee cup. "You think she'll look up Makricosta."

"Wouldn't you?"

"Not if I was smart."

"But if you were desperate?"

"Those two things aren't mutually exclusive," she said, and hoped for her own sake it was true.

She called Jinadh from her desk, because the cover story she had created would stand up to eavesdroppers. She didn't need the operator to connect her; she had both of Jinadh's exchanges by heart, and called the Anadh apartment first.

«Addas residence,» said the majordomo.

«Hello,» she said, «this is Lillian DePaul, the press attaché with the Geddan embassy. Is Mr. Addas in?»

He was, and very shortly she had him on the line. After he'd said «Hello» but before he could ask any questions, she said, «I wanted to let you know I would be free this evening to finish that interview.»

There was a brief pause on the other end of the line. Then, «Of course. My schedule is open. I should be able to get to Myazbah by half eight. Will that do?»

«Perfectly well, yes. The Aktanand at nine?» He would want time to freshen up and dress after the drive. And the Aktanand was close to the river walk, with its dark, quiet corners and winding paths.

«I look forward to it,» he said, and even if he had been a worse liar, she might not have been able to tell it from the truth.

The Aktanand was an old palace that had been turned into a

bathhouse and social club when its owner died bankrupt, without heirs. The architecture was no less opulent for a change in ownership. The front of the building faced a round plaza crowned by a fountain, home to hundreds of small glimmering fish that drew egrets from the river. Floodlights flared up the delicately carved façade of the building, picking out bright filigree and precious inlays.

She was early—she was always early—and he was already there, perched at the copper bar beneath low-hanging gilded lanterns. Brilliantine held waves of hair back from his face, and the high collar of his white tunic parted around his throat like the petals of a calla lily.

«Ms. DePaul,» he said, rising from his seat.

When they shook hands, his palm was dry and smooth, like fine linen. «Do you mind if we talk while walking? I've been behind a desk all day.»

«Not at all. May I offer you my arm?»

«No, thank you,» she said, and he dipped his head in polite assent.

He left without paying his tab. No doubt he had an account, which the treasury dutifully settled each month on his aunt's orders.

Most of their affair had been conducted out of the major cities, and Lillian had paid their way in cash. Circumstance made their schemes seem thrilling, rather than tedious. The thought of it, in retrospect, exhausted her.

«A beautiful night,» he said, «for this time of year.» Then, as they left the street behind and took the first curve of the river walk, he said in an altogether different tone, «What's going on?»

She shook her head and indicated they should walk a little farther, until the path branched. To the left it declined steeply, breaking into stair steps. Lillian had worn flat shoes, anticipating a ramble, and led Jinadh down to a small overlook on the bank, nearly hidden by a tangle of milkweed plants and jasmine.

«You said you visit your cousin's estate sometimes,» she said. «How about now? Could you go there for me?»

«I assume you mean the obvious cousin. I have a lot of them.»

«Yes.»

«I've been known to drop in on her, but she isn't usually pleased. What do you need?»

«Two things. My . . . companion, from the premiere. I think he's there now, and I want to prove it. Catch him at something if I can. Second, I need to know if the studio has hired anyone new, especially if they came on a recommendation from . . . » Damnation, she didn't know what to say, to avoid his name. «Her director. The Geddan.»

He nodded as she spoke. «I can do that.»

«And she won't suspect anything?»

He plucked a milkweed pod from one of the bushes and peeled its segments back so that the downy seeds caught the moonlight and the breeze. «Like most of my family—and, if we're honest, most of the country—she suspects me of nothing except vapidity.»

«I almost envy that,» she said, watching the white sylphs spread on the air. Some of them fell, settling on the river. Others rose and disappeared. «Underestimation might be a welcome change.»

He looked up from the milkweed pod and met her eyes. «It would suffocate you.»

«And it doesn't do the same to you?»

«I grew up in a vacuum,» he said. «I'm used to it.»

There was nothing she could say to that.

«How is he?» asked Jinadh, when the silence was just beginning to stretch thin.

«He's doing well; I had a letter this week. His bowling team won their end-of-term match. In victory, he's about as modest as you.»

That finally coaxed a smile out of him. Not his dazzling public one, but a smaller, one-sided quirk of his lips. «I've never claimed that I was perfect.»

«Oh no,» said Lillian, «I'm fairly certain that you have.» She was smiling now, too, and Jinadh even laughed. Jasmine scent caught in the eddies of air around them. Their shoulders touched.

Lillian caught her breath and shifted her weight, breaking the contact. Jinadh's laughter faded into a sigh.

«I won't be able to get down to Hadhariti for a day or two,» he said. «I'm supposed to lunch with Auntie tomorrow, and—»

«You can't reschedule on the queen. I understand.» She gathered up her abandoned professionalism. «Thank you, Jinadh.»

He shook his head. «I have entirely selfish motivations, as you know.»

«Stephen,» she said, which came out as a question even though she hadn't realized she was asking one.

«Of course,» he said, and threw the empty milkweed pod into the river.

CHAPTER

SEVEN

"How'd you end up working for this lady again?" asked Cordelia, as they left the picture palaces and aqueducts of Anadh behind them. "You said she was an old friend, but . . ."

"I knew her father. We did a little work together, though that would've been . . . oh, twenty years ago?"

"When you say 'work,' are you talking about walking the boards? Or are you talking about running the alleys?"

"Nadar was a punter, to his belly."

"Did he have money? He coulda put in for a show."

"You know he didn't."

"So are you still doing that kind of thing?"

He couldn't look away from the road for long, but he felt the upholstery shift beneath him as Cordelia's spine went stiff. Tension seeped from the passenger's side.

"It's just," she added, "I remember how my last stint working for you ended."

"You needn't twist the knife."

"I ain't twisting. I'm asking a question. You still got your fingers in the pie?"

He lifted one hand from the wheel and splayed it for her. "Do you see any mincemeat?"

She didn't answer, but the leather squeaked again as she relaxed.

They'd cut their stay in the city a few days short, at his suggestion. He could tell his charity grated on Cordelia, though he had the money and loved to spend it on beautiful things. Yesterday, he'd taken her to the harbor parade to be fussed over in elegant salons and ateliers. The awful dye job had been dealt with, colored a beautiful chestnut brown, clipped and curled and set in waves. It looked almost natural, now. She had refused a manicure, but he couldn't blame her for being self-conscious about those hands.

In the trunk of the car was a new set of cream-white leather luggage, stuffed with linen and silk and summer-weight wool. She'd been ambivalent about Porachin fashion—tunics, dhoti, tight trousers, abi, et cetera—but equally reluctant about the revealing turn most Geddan fashions had taken faced with such blistering heat.

"I don't know if I can pull it off anymore," she'd said, staring at her reflection in a low-backed jersey dress with a steep décolletage. "Not until I get a little better fed. And even then."

So it was mostly trousers and cambric shirts, culottes and modest jumpsuits. All of them, he noted, with deep pockets.

Aristide had reason to be glad his career had given him a lifetime of experience in sublimating guilt.

In addition to the physical marks, Cordelia had adopted a number of curious habits he recognized as the symptoms of paranoia.

Triple-checking doors once she had locked them, a tilt of the head that allowed her to glance over her shoulder without appearing to. She jumped at sudden noises: loud voices, backfiring cars. She sat with her back to walls.

It made him wonder what she had *really* been doing all this time, or if Gedda had actually gotten that bad. He knew there had been a few bombings, and wished for once he'd paid some attention to the news.

They rounded a sharp turn where the cliffs fell back to form a shallow cove. Across the inlet, a rambling white mansion perched on the lip of the steep red rocks. Late-afternoon light struck the clay tiles of the roof and the colored glass of windows thrown open to the breeze. The house's veranda hugged the edge of the cliffs, except for a narrow sparkling strip of water: a swimming pool, cantilevered over the empty space above the ocean. A second, smaller terrace perched above the first: earthy green flagstones and pergolas covered in flowers. A trim yacht sat at anchor far below. Where the grand house's estate stretched inland, Aristide could just make out the Lisoan village, the Cestinian villa, the pirate encampment. A series of low-roofed dormitories and office buildings bracketed the sets on one side, and on the other the open-air commissary. Beyond that, horses grazed in a pasture, along with two elephants and several zebra. Pulan kept the big cats caged, largely.

"Hadhariti," he said, pronouncing it as he had been taught: the soft fricative of the *dh,* the tip of his tongue lingering behind his teeth. It was the one Porashtu word he could reliably get right, besides his curses.

Cordelia whistled low. "I thought we were going to a studio."

"It *is* the studio. We prefer to film outside the city, but close enough to get into town for business."

"Yeah, but that's a house, too. Who lives *there*?"

The wheel slipped beneath his palm as the car came out of a curve, pointed toward the winding driveway. "I do."

There were other autos in the turnaround. Two of them.

Aristide let the car crunch to a stop on the white chips of gravel, with a good distance between his bumper and the spit-shining chrome grille of a low red racer, its seats upholstered in spotted animal hide.

That one he knew. The Kingdom of Liso was lucky Asiyah was so far down the line of succession. He'd be an embarrassment on the throne.

The second car was smaller, black, dustily innocuous. Of the two, it worried him more. Pulan wasn't expecting him home from Anadh for another day at least, and given what she'd gotten up to at the film premiere . . .

He wondered if this guest was someone she didn't want him to see, or someone she didn't want to see him.

Cordelia was, of course, unaware of anything out of the ordinary. He wondered if he should tell her. She hopped down from the running board and cocked her head back to take in the house's façade: arched double doors studded in brass, tall windows of colored glass in tiled frames. Two mosaic peacocks—the studio emblem and Pulan's family crest—perched at the apex of the entranceway, their tails trailing nearly two stories to the ground.

"Not too shabby," she said. Then, kicking one of Asiyah's tires, "This hers too?"

"No," said Aristide.

"Huh. Got company then." Her eyes were wary when she added, "Wonder who."

He didn't even need to come up with an explanation, because by then he could hear voices behind the massive double doors, growing louder, and then the echoing metallic *chunk* of the latch.

Cordelia had a hand out of one pocket—the left, and from her face it pained her—flexed as if she was prepared to grab ahold of something swiftly. From its position, just off her hip, he guessed a knife or a gun. She wasn't wearing one now, but that didn't mean she hadn't gotten used to it.

From her bare explanation, he'd thought she was whoring or doing a little black-market trade. He hadn't asked questions because he'd been afraid the answers might hurt. Now he wished he had—it seemed like ignorance might have held off the blow only to let it fall more heavily at a less opportune time.

Daoud saw them first, and put a hand to Pulan's arm. Her ringing laughter cut off abruptly when she saw Aristide in the drive. It took her guests a moment longer to catch on.

"Aristide," she said, venomously cheerful. "What a surprise. We did not expect you for another day at least. You did not call to say you were coming."

"I didn't know I had to." Asiyah stood behind her, with Inaz. And that man from the premiere, the one who had come with Lillian . . . Memmediv, that was it, looking like he'd swallowed a tack and could feel it scraping all the way down.

That would be the black car, then. Interesting.

"Satri," said Memmediv, staring straight at Aristide. Pulan held up a hand to silence him. The sleeve of her tunic fell back, and her bangles clinked in the hush.

The gravel moved beneath Aristide's feet and it felt like the earth shifting, the crumbling of his foundation. His hands might be clean, but had he been standing on a midden heap this whole time? "Am I such sour milk that you can only have your friends over when I'm away?"

"Well, you are not getting any sweeter, standing there in the heat. Daoud, please show Mr. Makricosta and his friend to the terrace."

"I can get there quite easily myself." Aristide half-turned and took a breath to call Cordelia, almost letting the name fly before he remembered. "Nellie. Shall we?"

As they passed by, he caught Memmediv's glare full on and flung it back, unsure exactly what was passing between them, but unwilling to take it without giving back just as good.

Cordelia didn't know exactly what had just happened, but she keystone-sure didn't like it.

She wasn't recognizable, not if she kept her hands hidden. And anyway, she didn't think her face had made the papers yet, nor her name the wireless. Put all of it together and there was no reason those folk on the steps should know her.

But she was still shaking when she followed Ari through the grand entrance hall. Didn't take much of it in—tall ceilings, a million tiny tile swirls, a staircase and gallery twined with an intricately carved stone railing. The heels of Ari's brogues slammed the marble floors. Cordelia, in sandals, slapped after him more quietly, up a set of shallow steps and out another pair of peaked and studded doors.

She wasn't prepared for the sea, and stopped dead on the threshold.

Born in the city, raised in the city, hardly ever having left, she was used to the ocean hemmed in by boats and boards and Spits. Flat and filmed with oil. Stinking. Her old squeeze Malcolm—in the Queen's arms now, face likely buried in her tits—had always said they'd go to the shore, one summer, but he gave too much time to the theatre and she gave too much time to other men, and it never quite worked out.

Seeing all that water, open to the horizon and breaking on the sand, she didn't think he would have liked it. Too big, where his world had been so small.

She took a deep breath of the clean air: fragrant heat mingling with brine and spray. For the space of that breath, she was glad of everything that had happened, if it gave her this view of the sea.

Then Aristide said "Damnation," and kicked a chair.

There was a group of them under the shade of the covered veranda, gathered around a table filled with the remains of a meal. Five, one for each of the folk they'd run into at the door.

Cordelia collapsed into one of them, picked up a piece of flatbread from a platter, and asked, "Something the matter?" with her mouth full. Something obviously was, but even more reason to eat while she could, if she was going to get booted out on her rear.

Aristide sat across from her and tilted the wine bottle to check its contents. When he realized it was empty, he got back out of his chair and started pacing. She watched him until he came to rest between two pillars, staring over the sunny terrace a few steps below, and the sea stretching to the edge of the sky.

"Ari," she said, and when he didn't turn, she said it again in the voice she'd learned to make folk listen. "Who are those people? What's got such a pin in your rear?"

He shook his head and let it hang, still not looking at her. "I think I may have lied to you."

"What do you mean?"

Before he could answer, an engine turned over and roared to life at the front of the house. Aristide put the curve of his palm to his forehead, pushed it to the edge of his carefully waxed curls.

"That *car*," he spat, and from the vehemence, Cordelia guessed it wasn't really the red auto his fury was aimed at.

"Who were they?" she asked again.

He pulled his cigarette case from his pocket, roughly, and flicked it open. "That was Asiyah Sekibou. Lisoan royalty, barely. Friends with their defense minister. He's been having an affair with Inaz for ages. That's the woman who was with him. She's an actress, works for Pulan." He still had those stageman instincts, and made her watch a whole burlesque as she sat in suspense: the jeweled latch snapping as his case closed, the flash of the gold band and teal-green paper as he tapped a straight on the snowy leather: once, twice.

A second motor rumbled away, and Aristide exhaled smoke.

"I thought that's why he was always around. Because of Inaz. Now, though, with Memmediv popping up like garlic mustard . . ." He took a drag, flicked ash onto the pristine tile. "That's the other man, the Tatien. He was at Pulan's premiere. Came with . . . with Cyril's sister."

"You think they're a pair?"

"Oh, how should I know?" Savagely, he jettisoned his butt over the terrace railing. "What matters is Pulan's father used to sell Lisoan guns to the Tatien militia, and he schooled her in the trade."

"Yeah?" Apprehension crawled up Cordelia's spine.

"You asked if I'd gone licit, Cordelia, and I have. But—"

"She hasn't?"

"Stupid," he said. "I should have known."

And *she* should have known it was a bad idea to pitch her horseshoes in with Ari one more time. All she had to do was hold her own hands in front of her face to see why. But here she rotten was, back in the midden, wondering if she should get out before she got stuck any deeper.

"I apologize for interrupting," said a soft voice from the doorway. Cordelia turned, too fast, and saw the boy's eyes widen. She *had* to learn easiness again, or folk were going to clock her, even if they didn't know what for. "But Pulan would like to know how long your guest will be staying."

"That's an extortionate exchange rate," spat Aristide. "She didn't tell me *anything* about hers."

"Do not be snippy," said the boy. "This is her house, anyway. You don't *have* to live here."

"It's convenient," Ari snapped, harsher than the situation called for.

The boy crossed thin arms over his chest and sneered. "I am sure it is."

Ari got that chastened look Cordelia used to pride herself on bringing out on men's faces when they carped about her stripping, or her late nights, or her knocking other fellows. So *that* was how it was with these two.

"Anyway," said Ari, as though there hadn't been a spat, "she isn't a guest. I'm bringing her on as an assistant choreographer. Chitra could use the help."

The boy said nothing except "Hm," but he cast a look at Cordelia that settled onto her shoulders with the weight of judgment.

"I can dance," she said, defensive. Mother's tits, but pride could stuff her head up her rear sometimes. "And I got a lot of experience working up routines."

"Before any final decisions are made," said the boy, "I'm sure Ms. Satri would like to speak with you, Miz . . . I apologize, your name?"

"Nellie Hanes," she said, like she'd practiced a thousand times on the way over.

Aristide rolled his eyes. "She'll say yes, Daoud."

"Sometimes," said the boy, "I wish the gods had blessed me with such confidence."

That brought Ari's smile back, until Daoud tacked on, "Then I think about how you arrived here, and I remember it is completely unwarranted." He turned on his heel and went back into the house.

Aristide's fingertips tightened around the lip of the ashtray until his nails turned white. Cordelia worried he was going to throw it.

"It really was that bad?" she asked, looking at the tendons in the back of his hand instead of meeting his eyes. "The shell game and all?"

"Well, I didn't show up in a limousine." He let the ashtray go. Cordelia heard a faint clink of glass on tile as it settled.

"Ari," she said.

He gave her a poisonous look she didn't feel like she deserved. "What?"

"If she gets caught at whatever she's doing . . ."

"It won't go well for us, I assure you."

"You gonna stay, now you know?"

"I don't *know*," he said. "I *suspect*."

"Still," said Cordelia, figuring she could benchmark her own plans based on his. It was comforting, somehow, to know he was balancing on the same rope she was. Or at least one between the blades of the same shears. "How much you stand to lose, if she does get scratched?"

He tapped his fingers on the tabletop, then pinched another cigarette from his case. "My job and my credibility. And I doubt they'll let me stay in the country, without either of those." Then he cocked his head behind his lighter and stabbed her straight through with a keen expression she hadn't seen on him since Amberlough. "But I'm beginning to get a feeling that it's more serious for you. Isn't it, *Nellie Hanes*? Is there somebody who you're hiding from?"

"Why?" she asked. "You afraid they're gonna pick up the wrong rock and find you instead?"

He opened his mouth to reply, but over the sound of the surf Cordelia made out the roar of an approaching engine. From Aristide's suspended retort, she figured he heard it, too.

"Lady's name. It's getting to be like a livery garage around here." He pursed his lips and stared at her, eyes narrowed, the pad of his thumb making considering circles around the base of his cigarette. "I suppose we'd better go see who it is. Unless you're afraid they're turning over stones."

She followed him, at a little distance, not liking the tack his attitude had taken. In the city, he'd been fun and games, dinner and drinks, money over the spillway. All his, of course, which she could hardly stomach. She tried to look on it as reparations, but there wasn't a set of swags in the world that would set her hands to rights again. He'd put his hackles up whenever she mentioned old times.

Now he was coming too close to asking questions, and there was a brimstone curl of the old Ari's wickedness rising off him, trailing in his wake, even in the way he walked across the hall. It came on stronger when he caught sight of the new arrival.

"Mr. Addas," he said, pitching his voice for the stage. "I didn't know you were coming."

The man stood backlit on the threshold, a loose white tunic billowing around his legs in the breeze. Even as she spotted him, a couple of domestics were coming to take his bags and close the doors behind him.

"Neither did I." His voice hit the same false note that Ari's had, and rang as brightly. "But I had several days free, and after a successful premiere my cousin is always a generous host. Is that correct?" Without the sun glare, she could see his face, and its angle: He was looking up at the gallery that ran around three sides of the hall. Cordelia followed his eyes and saw the older woman from the front steps: the one who'd pinned Ari so hard when they arrived. Must be Pulan Satri, the boss of the operation.

Jinadh said something in Porashtu—fast and musical, coming out of a grinning face. Pulan's answer came in Porashtu also, sharper and shorter, ending on an up note like a question. Jinadh came back a little wheedling, and Cordelia watched Pulan's expression change from harried to sly. Then, it bloomed like a bursting four o'clock into over-the-top delight.

Mother and sons, she was hemmed in on all fronts by stagefolk. And they didn't turn it off when the curtains came down. They didn't *have* curtains. They walked their *lives* on the boards.

Pulan swept down the stairs, now chattering sweetly as a mockingbird. Jinadh laughed and opened his arms for an embrace. When they parted, Cordelia saw the camera hanging around his neck, just in time for him to lift it and snap a photograph of Pulan, who flirted and mugged at the camera.

At the click of the shutter, Cordelia's stomach clenched.

"How long will you be staying?" Aristide thrust his question into their pantomime like a greenhorn busting onto the scene too early, and it was about as jarring. Cordelia caught the moment of irritation on both their faces, and wondered if they were in some kind of racket together or headed for two different ends and just playing off each other to get there.

"A few days, I think. If Pulan will have me?" Jinadh had got his grin back on by now. He was good-looking, she'd give him that, and his smile had her about ready to join in. Catching, like measles, and probably as dangerous. She read him as the kind of man who could get you to go along with his schemes.

"Of course," she said. "Go get settled in. Cocktails on the terrace around half seven. Aristide, you and . . ." Pulan's outstretched hand paused, gesturing faintly to Cordelia.

"Nellie," Ari answered for her.

"Nellie," repeated Pulan, rolling the *l*s luxuriously over her tongue, as if to test their sound. "You are of course welcome to join us. There might even be music if we can persuade Djihar to bring out the gramophone. Perhaps dancing?" Then she turned to Jinadh and started speaking in Porashtu again, following him up the stairs and down the hall.

That left Cordelia alone with Aristide again.

"Who in the holy stones is that?" she asked.

Aristide rolled his eyes. "Pulan's horrible cousin. Nobody you need to worry about."

The echo of the camera's shutter still ringing in her ears, she wasn't so sure about that.

Straight away, Cordelia didn't trust Jinadh, though Ari had dismissed him out of hand, and Pulan seemed pleased to use him as a distraction. The way sparks flew every time she and Ari spoke to each other, they were pinning each other sharp.

There was something too slick about him. Something too silly. Like he *wanted* them to think he was just there for a song and some snaps. He drank like an actor, gossiped like a grandmother, and all the time had a chip of flint in his eye whenever Cordelia caught it.

She couldn't understand why nobody else noticed. If they'd been on easier terms, she might have asked Aristide. But he'd turned into a hot ball of needles and if she brought it up with him he'd only use it as another avenue to pick at the wide weave of her story. And she didn't know Pulan well enough to approach her, didn't have any kind of trust to trade on there.

So after enduring a day on the run from that camera and those casual, too-keen questions, she cornered Pulan's tiny secretary, Daoud. The one Ari might be knocking. Speaking of sparks, he'd been flint on steel with Ari since they arrived. Apparently, where went Pulan, he went after. If he and Ari were keeping each other up, it wasn't worth as much to him as his position in this organization, whether it really was a film studio, or something less legitimate.

She was up late, looking for something to eat down in the cavernous kitchen of the servants' quarters, which she'd mostly found by luck and sense of smell. The halls all around carried traces of garlic and onions and spice, and the scent had gotten stronger as she got closer. She'd been skipping most meals to avoid socializing and the hard squeeze that Jinadh brought to it, and wasn't pleased to find a few days of good eating had broken her down. She couldn't go hungry so long anymore.

As she was pouring herself a cup of some kind of kefir out of a glass pitcher from the refrigerator—she'd never even seen one, only heard of 'em—the overhead light snapped on and she froze. A few spatters of thick yogurt struck the countertop, shaken loose by the sudden clench of her grip on the pitcher handle.

"Ms. Hanes," said Daoud. "You are awake late."

Carefully, she set down the pitcher. "Couldn't sleep."

"Ah." He stepped into the room. "I wish that I could say the same, but I have not even tried yet."

"Business?" she asked.

"Yes." But he didn't give details. "May I?"

She put the pitcher into his outstretched hand, and he took a glass from a shelf above the massive basin of a sink.

"Can't you just call a domestic for something like that?" she asked.

"At this hour? I would not think of it." He tipped his head back and drank. "I grew up with good manners and few advantages. While I have gained the latter, I retain the former."

"Your Geddan's good," she said.

"Ms. Satri saw to that, as she did to many other things. Though, I have a gift for languages. Perhaps because I learned two early. My parents are from the Belqat tribes; we spoke Belqati at home, though I rarely use it now."

"The who now?"

"Caravaners." He took a long drink of his kefir, and licked it carefully from his lips, which were full as bee stings. "Bad enough to be a man, and turned; no one needs to know I am a dust heel as well."

"Ari's a man," she said. "He seems to do all right here."

"He is foreign. It is different." There was a note of longing in his voice.

"And . . . what, turned? That mean what I think?"

He raised a meaningful eyebrow.

"Mother's tits," she said, to the expression. "You deserve each other. So they don't like that kind of thing here?"

"Among women, it is expected at certain times." He shrugged. "Men? It is mostly not talked about. Lots of things men do are not talked about, except among ourselves. Women do not often care to know."

"Is that why nobody in this pile seems to give three dried shits about Jinadh and his rotten questions? 'Cause he's got hanging tackle?"

Daoud cocked his head. A cowlick had come loose from his pomade and stuck up on the back of his head, so the gesture gave him the look of a fancy parakeet. "Mr. Addas is a journalist," he said. "Well, a gossip columnist. His curiosity is annoying, but not unusual. Does he disturb you? I could speak to Pulan."

"No," she said, too fast. "That's all right."

"Perhaps you should talk to him," said Daoud. "Publicity has helped to secure Aristide's position here. It might be good to show your face."

She snorted at that, and said goodnight.

CHAPTER

EIGHT

Early in the morning—just as she was coming from the washroom with her teeth freshly cleaned, ready to do her morning dhusha routine—Lillian got a call from a car service.

«Amil would have taken you,» said Waleeda, when she relayed the message. «You should have said.»

«I didn't want to get him out of bed so early,» said Lillian, wondering where she was headed, and who wanted her there.

She forewent dhusha, and her sports clothes, changing directly into the suit Waleeda had laid out for the office. By the time she had packed her last paper into her briefcase, a black car was idling at the curb.

«Don't tell Amil,» she said to Waleeda, smiling conspiratorially. The smile expired as the door shut behind her.

Curtains were drawn down over the windows in the rear of the car. Lillian felt a stab of apprehension. When she touched the door handle, her hand slipped against the metal and she realized her palms had begun to sweat.

«Good morning,» said Jinadh, once she opened the door.

She let out a breath that had sat too long in her lungs, and slipped into the seat beside him. «You kept me from my dhusha.»

«You still practice?»

«Every morning. Just like my teacher.»

«Then you know I skipped mine as well, to be here so early.»

«It was very neatly done. Is this your car?»

"No," he said, switching languages. "It is a regular cab. And the driver is a regular citizen. As far as I know, he does not speak Geddan."

"You won't drop me at the chancery, will you?"

"I thought we would play at being regular citizens ourselves," he said. "The driver is under the impression we are attending a meeting together, in the Sheerwolla Complex."

"So we're stockbrokers today?"

"Or some other variety of remora, yes. *Chii bhale.*" This last was a Porashtu exhortation to the driver, who pulled into the empty early-morning street.

"What do you have for me?" she asked, nodding to the satchel between them on the seat.

"I developed them myself," he said, taking out an envelope. "In the master bathroom. And I cleaned up well enough I don't think the housekeeper will suspect anything. Can you picture me on hands and knees scrubbing the tile?"

"Yes," she said, and closed her eyes as if savoring the image. It was too easy to do this with him—to relax, and joke, and take full breaths.

"Then I wish you were less imaginative." Jinadh tapped her knee with the envelope. "Here, look at them."

The photographs tipped out into her hand, slipping against each other and threatening to spill across the leather upholstery. There weren't many of them.

"I only made prints of the relevant ones," he said.

There were three, to be exact. "He isn't in any of these."

"I missed him by half an hour, maybe. I passed Sekibou leaving on my way in, and a black car, closed. I did not see the driver, but he is my best guess."

"So what are these?" She spread them like playing cards. In one photograph, Satri posed for the camera with a cocktail shaker. There was a gramophone behind her, and Makricosta had just slid a record from its sleeve to play. They were both out of focus, in favor of a woman mostly hidden by the gramophone horn. She was shorter than Makricosta, by a significant margin, but that was all Lillian could tell from the image.

In the next, taken from above and behind, the same woman stood at the railing of a terrace, looking over the sea. Jinadh had tried for an angle that captured her profile, but he had come just short. A curl of dark hair had fallen into her eyes, further obscuring her face. She wore a loose collared shirt—white, or some light color—and pleated trousers over bare feet.

The third photograph showed her behind several other people again, this time sitting in a rattan chair, holding a highball. Blurry shoulders and heads blocked most of the view, but Jinadh had managed to catch her eyes over the rim of her glass, and she had seen him do it. She stared straight into the camera, brows lifted, expression the blank mask that preceded panic.

"After I took that," he said, "she got up and left. She avoided me very neatly most of the time."

"Who is she?"

"Pulan's new assistant choreographer. An old friend of Makricosta; definitely Geddan. She did not speak Porashtu, and had an awful accent—very nasal. And when I say new, I mean that she showed up the same day I did. I was not able to get him for you, but I was able to get her."

"Thank you," she said, and put the photos back into their envelope, which she placed in her briefcase.

"Will they be useful?" he asked.

"I hope so."

"Good."

She turned to look out the window, away from his hopeful eyes.

The car crossed the Hilazi Bridge, over the waters of the Shadha. Above the upper cataract, the river ran unobstructed; there were no rocks or sandbars to churn it into whitewater. It was deceptively placid before it reached the struts of the bridge, green and sparkling in the rising sun. She felt a moment of kinship with the river, whose untroubled surface was a thin glaze over the brutal current beneath. Foreign anglers had a habit of dying in its clutches, mistaking its outward countenance for a truthful representation of its internal workings.

"If I need you again," she said, to the window glass and the bridge and the precipitous drop beyond its railings, "should I call the house? And who am I, if I do?"

"You can be a new source on Inaz Iligba. Everyone wants stories on her now, after Pulan's film. It would be credible enough to fool my staff." They were drawing close to the Sheerwolla buildings now, a banking complex as arched, frescoed, and gilded as a temple. Which, Lillian supposed, it was: dedicated to the pan-denominational god of commerce.

The cab pulled up at the main entrance, a lapis-tiled arch framed by potted palms. Jinadh got out and came around, held the door for Lillian. She let him, faintly vexed at the absurdity of ritual in a way her job didn't often allow for. That was the moment she realized she'd forgotten she was working.

"Will you?" asked Jinadh, as they entered the gate.

The question, without context, threw her. "What?"

"Need me again?"

She almost said *I hope so,* but she had caught herself earlier and now managed to say, "I'll know soon."

They parted in the foyer, him to the left and her to the right, from the center of a mosaic chrysanthemum the color of sunrise. Outside, the sky had turned the same. Lillian blinked away the glare and hailed another cab, this one empty of old lovers and conspiracy.

"He couldn't get quite what you wanted," she said, and put the envelope square in the center of Flagg's desk.

He raised an eyebrow. "But he got something."

Lillian nodded, and didn't avail herself of the chair until Flagg said, "Sit, please."

The leather stuck to the backs of her legs, and she wished state secrecy allowed for open windows. In the corner of the office, a fan whirred valiantly behind its metal cage, but it didn't accomplish much beyond riffling the occasional paper.

"The original subject of your interest," said Lillian, tipping her head toward the door of Flagg's office to indicate Memmediv, seated just outside, "left just as my source arrived. I have reason to believe they passed one another in the drive."

Flagg paused in opening the envelope, and the quiet in the absence of crinkling paper pressed on Lillian's ears. He was staring at her.

"You're not joking," he said.

The muscles of her face were sore when she tried to smile for him. "I rarely do."

Flagg shook his head, eyes cast heavenward.

"The photographs," said Lillian, and he brought his gaze to the envelope again.

They slid into his hands as treacherously as they had hers, but he caught them more firmly and laid them out one by one across the black leather of his desktop. The terrace, the ocean, the cocktail glass.

"Is it her?" asked Lillian. "From what he said, I thought it might be, but—"

"What's the story?"

"New choreographer. Assistant choreographer, sorry. She has some connection to Makricosta, though it's unclear exactly what. Geddan, definitely, and from the description of her speaking voice I'd say urban Amberlinian. *Very* urban."

He took the photograph from Lehane's file and placed it above the three Lillian had brought him. "I'm not sure. I'd like to say yes. It seems probable."

"Even if we don't have solid facts," said Lillian, "I can announce in a press conference that we suspect Satri is harboring a terrorist. We may be on shaky ground with Porachis, politically, but the queen will still need to save face. We can demand an investigation of Satri's activities and business interests, and—"

"—end up with our faces in the midden. If Memmediv is involved in Satri's conspiracy and we ask the Porachin government to investigate her, we've as good as cut our own switch."

Damnation. "Well, what do you want me to do?"

"Have you arranged to meet with Memmediv again?"

"Yes," she said. "We're seeing one another this evening."

"Good. If possible, I'd like your . . . *associate* to be our eyes at Hadhariti. Between the two of you, I want to find out what's going on here and put a stop to it before it scratches me. This"—he tapped the photographs—"is a good start. Funny, that. Your old lover spying for you, while you spy on a new one."

Her urge was to snap at him; instead she spoke softly, with a half-raised hand to ward off what he had said. "I wouldn't call him my lover."

"Which one?" asked Flagg, snake-smiling.

Lillian bit the inside of her cheek and tasted blood.

"I honestly don't care what you call either of them." Flagg crisply straightened the stack of photos and clipped them inside Lehane's file. "As long as you wrestle some information out of one or the other, and soon."

She rose from her seat, too quickly. "I have a meeting."

Flagg's short exhalation might have been a chuckle, in a more emotive man. "No, you don't. But you have a job to do. And a son, who I know you'd like to see again. I'm sure he wants to see you."

Lillian's wrath was usually a cold thing, channeled into implacable action like a glacier. But occasionally—such as now—it rose like a molten geyser. She capped it only by the grace of practice, but steam still leaked out when she said, "Have a care, Counselor."

If she had not been so angry, the look of surprise on his normally expressionless face would have frightened her. Instead she pushed just a little further. "You ought to be wary of alienating your assets. I'd have thought this whole affair would have driven that home."

He blinked and tilted his head, like a lizard focusing on something larger than itself. "Are you threatening me, Ms. DePaul?"

"I wouldn't dare," she said, hand on the doorknob. "As you're well aware, I have far too much at risk for that."

She knew very little about Memmediv, except that he was clever enough to have fooled Flagg for this long. That meant he was clever indeed, and far less likely to fall for this ploy than Flagg thought.

How, then, to gain his confidence, if that was possible at all?

What *did* she know about him? That he was a little older than her, but new to the foreign service. That he had been a fox far longer than he had been a diplomat. That he had betrayed his country for the Ospies. That he was ready to betray the Ospies now for Tatié.

That he was a man with a single goal, for which he would compromise all other loyalties.

Perhaps they were not as dissimilar as they seemed.

Myriad small crises kept her in the office until after dark. This close to the equator it came at the same time no matter what the season, which meant she rarely saw the sun. Not, given the temperature, that she minded.

Despite handling several bouts of bad publicity over the course of the day—military exercises on the Lisoan border, a confirmed outbreak of typhus in the Cultham internment camps, and half the Geddan delegation walking out of the Tzietan peace talks—a small piston had been firing in the back of her mind, so that by the time she left the chancery she had begun to formulate a plan.

If she had told Flagg what she planned to do he might have thrown her in a cell. She was fairly certain he had the power to do so, without the inconvenience of a warrant. Luckily, he hadn't asked her how she planned to gain Memmediv's confidence, only demanded that she deliver it.

He cared about one thing, and one thing only? Well, so did she. She wasn't a fox but she knew people; she knew narratives, and how emotional connections could be leveraged in service of a goal.

Things would go one of two ways this evening. Either Flagg was right, and Memmediv was not as clever as she estimated, and she would end up doing just as Flagg wished. Or *she* was right, and she could play on the suspicion she had sensed in Anadh, after the premiere. If Memmediv had picked up on the false note in her amorous advance, she would hammer on it as loudly as she could, and show her cards. One often learned more about a new game playing with an open hand in the first round. The trick was to apply those lessons later when the stakes were high.

Upon arriving home, she peeled off her blouse and skirt and even her slip. The dress she had in mind would not hide it, and in fact, the purposes it served were counter to her own.

The neckline of this gown alone had earned it a place in the back of her clothespress. That, and its color. Lillian was partial to neutrals and, when an occasion called for something more lively, to any shade of blue bar the truly garish. This dress was dark red, reminiscent of an uncut garnet. The deep décolletage, embellished with a line of seed pearls, left the wings of her collarbones bare, and the flat plane of her sternum, hinting at the inner curves of her breasts. A drape of superfluous satin swept low across her back, showing the groove of her spine in its entirety. Against the black-scarlet fabric, the stretch of her exposed skin shone, luminous.

She had bought the dress in an imprudent moment, nearly a decade ago, and worn it once to meet Jinadh in a hotel bar. She had felt nervous, then, and awkward, as she did now, but the dress had more than served its purpose. She didn't hope to take things quite so far tonight, but she aimed to *look* as though she did.

Before sitting at her vanity, she pulled the bell rope. Waleeda arrived as she was uncapping her lipstick—rarely used, and nearly full.

«Yes, ma'am?»

«Will you ask Amil to bring the car around?» The heat made the pigment soft, so that it swept slippery across her lips and left a thick coat of color. «I'm dining out this evening.»

«Of course,» said Waleeda. And then, lingering a moment, «You look very beautiful, ma'am. May I ask, what's the occasion?»

«Just meeting a friend,» she said.

Waleeda made a disbelieving sound through her nose, but let Lillian keep her secrets. When this incident got back to Flagg—Lillian was fairly certain that it would—he would know who she was bound to see.

Across the river, some miles east of the cliff's edge, the night market was smaller and shabbier than in the middle of the city or down on the floodplain. Hookahs and liquor were cheap, and of no outstanding quality. Most of the storefronts—largely laundries, lunch counters, and bookies—were grated and dark by the time Lillian stepped from her car and sent Amil off on his own recognizance for the next hour or so.

They had agreed on this place because it was discreet and out of the way. Though Flagg approved of their liaison, Lillian hoped to convince Memmediv he didn't, or at least make a show of doing so.

This time, when she arrived early, she was not preceded. She asked the proprietress for a corner table in the back, a shot of cheap whiskey, and a hookah, and she got them, in that order, in a relatively timely fashion.

Tobacco haze hovered at head height, twisting and curling in the draft from the ceiling fans. Sinking into the cushioned bench, she kept well below it, where the air was more easily breathed. Women sat around the place, and a few men of dubious moral character, tucked into nooks much like Lillian's, or at small round tables woven from reeds. These were liberally scorched where ashes had fallen on them. The patrons laughed and cursed, drinking beer and sorghum whiskey and small, strong cups of coffee.

That had never been her, boasting in the bars and buying drinks for prostitutes—temple bells, she'd been raised by a lawyer and a diplomat. She had no reason to feel kinship with these women, no reason to feel so melancholy at their freedom. But her heart hurt, all the same. If not for a personal loss, for the general loss of a way of life. She remembered her school friends sneaking away to drink unchaperoned during holidays in the city; the sight of razors congregating on bar stoops, wreathed in cigarette smoke and swearing.

She hadn't been back to Gedda since things changed. She wasn't sure she wanted to go. It was easier to ignore, so far away. Easier to do the job they'd dragged her back for.

Besides, how much more would it hurt her heart to return to Carmody, or the house on Coral Street, to be that much closer to Stephen and still unable to see him? How much would it hurt him, if he found out she had been nearby and hadn't come to visit?

She took a deep drag on the hookah's hose, and the nicotine rush pushed the thoughts from her head for just a moment. Exhaling slowly, she let the smoke wreath her head.

When it cleared, Memmediv stood in the doorway, squinting into the haze. He was already getting some dirty looks from the other clientele. Lillian put a hand on a passing coal-girl's arm. «That man,» she said. «He's with me. Bring him over?»

The girl hesitated, looking Lillian's clothes and complexion up and down with a critical eye until she took a coin from her clutch and offered it. The girl—who couldn't be more than twelve or thirteen—made the money disappear between her abi and her skin, then hurried to Memmediv's side and thwacked his arm with the back of her knuckles. He started at the blow and Lillian laughed, smoke trickling from her nose. When the girl gestured toward her, she let the laughter settle into a small, coy smile.

"A hard place to find," he said, sitting not across from her but perpendicular, against the other half of the corner bench. Positioned this way, their knees were close enough to touch, so she closed the extra few inches.

"You don't come across the river much?"

"Not in six months, no." He took the hookah hose when she offered it, and she let it trail between her fingers. "I didn't realize there was anything over here I might be interested in."

"Hm," she said. "So this is new territory." It was easier to flirt with him when she was furious with Flagg. Anger made her predatory. She put a hand on his thigh, echoing her advance of a few nights before, and slid it across the fine linen of his trousers. "Are you feeling adventurous?"

He tilted his head back and she saw the angle of his jaw shift. Muscles in his throat contracted. As he exhaled, he made a soft sound and expelled a perfect smoke ring. Then he dropped his chin, blew the rest of the smoke out of his lungs, and shook his head.

"Ms. DePaul, what are you doing?"

She pressed a little harder on his leg, moved her hand a little higher. "It's not obvious?" The smoke had made her voice deep; she sounded like a femme fatale from a pulpy wireless drama. It made her blush, though that wouldn't be noticeable under the rouge.

His laughter fell like ashes, soft and acrid. "Please. I have more practice at seductions like this than you do. Though you weren't bad out of the gate."

The feeling that twinged in her stomach was akin to the shame of a lover truly spurned. Which was absurd, and disgusting, but this was a kind of hubris that kept little company with reason.

"You might even have caught someone less astute," Memmediv went on, "if you hadn't pushed it so hard the second time around."

She let her wounded pride show in her posture, and pulled her hand from his leg. "But you asked to meet again."

"Because I have some questions," he said. "Who put you up to it? Flagg? That stings. I thought he trusted me."

"Perhaps he shouldn't," said Lillian, and hoped it was the right thing. At least it wasn't a full admission of guilt.

"He certainly doesn't wield the same amount of power over my actions as he seems to over yours. A honeypot? I thought you had more class."

This part was too easy to play, and almost rewarding. She let the cap off of her anger and spat it at him, sizzling. "You have *no idea* what you're talking about."

"I have some. What hold does he have over you, to make you do this?"

It was easy, also, to let tears prick the inner corners of her eyes. But she didn't speak, not until Memmediv's expression softened into pity. "I'm sorry," he said. "I should not have put it quite so cruelly."

Then she did let her eyes close, her lips compress. "My son." It came out hushed, trembling. She almost thought she'd overdone it, but Memmediv pressed a glass into her hand—the cheap whiskey she had ordered and never drunk. She did so now. It burned on the way down, lingering painfully behind her ribs.

"My son," she said again, clearing her throat. "He's at school, in Gedda. Flagg wants me to . . . I don't know when I'll see him again, if I don't . . ." She put her fingers to her lips, to stop the words from coming out. She wasn't sure she was acting anymore.

"Don't what?" asked Memmediv.

"He thinks . . . I don't know what exactly. That you're up to something."

Thoughtfully, Memmediv tapped the hookah hose against his chin. "And what do *you* think?"

"I hardly know you. And honestly, I don't care. I only want to see my son again. I'd agree to anything. I already have done." She turned her face down, counterfeiting shame.

"Understandable," he said, and there was something in that single word that confirmed her suspicion, validated this mad plan.

He sucked on the hose, drawing deeply. The flare of the coal illuminated his eyes, so she could see he was smiling even before he exhaled. "So Flagg has threatened your son."

"He has." She clasped her hands around the empty shooter, and they slipped slightly in liquor that had dripped down to coat the outside of the glass.

"And what incentive," he asked, his consonants soft with smoke, "might mitigate that ultimatum?"

"I don't know," she said. "Why don't you tell me what you're prepared to give?"

CHAPTER

NINE

As Aristide had suspected she would, Pulan used her cousin as
an excuse. He'd never seen her so solicitous.

Jinadh was, by all accounts, a particular favorite of the queen
in much the same way a small dog or precocious child might be,
and therefore worth a certain amount of flattery. Besides, he had
a sharp pen when it came to his society columns. All of the brown-
nosing his presence required usually put Pulan in a foul temper,
as he was younger than her and a man besides. Under normal
circumstances, Aristide was happy to pick loose threads with her
behind Jinadh's back, having too often read speculations about
himself beneath the latter's byline.

This time when Jinadh left, Aristide didn't feel much like
gossiping. Pulan had used the long visit to put off whatever confrontation Aristide would have liked to bring to the forefront.

Which meant it festered and turned rancid, worsened by Jinadh's prodding.

He tried to wheedle stories about Gedda out of Aristide, and chased Cordelia around half the estate until she snapped at him, in fine form rife with the curses of Kipler's Mew, and locked herself in her room.

After perhaps forty-eight hours, he finally left them alone. Aristide might have aged ten years in that time. He felt tired. He felt stupid and extraneous, faintly ill, and wholly disgusted with himself. He had *trusted* Pulan when she told him she was done. Since when had trust become a habit with him?

Perhaps when he burned his old life, he'd burned his old habits, too. If this development was any indication, he'd better start combing through the ashes for useful fragments the flames had missed.

A knock on the door brought him back to his coffee, his crumbs, himself. He had taken his afternoon meal alone, barricaded inside his rooms. "What?" he barked, sinking more deeply into his chair.

"The post." It was Daoud. "You received a letter." He had a sour expression on his face, as if he was not pleased to be yoked with this duty. Usually when he brought Aristide's mail it meant a little naughtiness before afternoon meetings, but he had stuck close by Pulan behind the suppressing fire of Jinadh's militant socializing.

He held the letter out, but Aristide hesitated. He was used to business correspondence, which in the film world meant too-familiar invitations to lunch, desperately cheerful pleas, or gushing praise with a crumb of a request buried deep within it. Beyond that, it was bills and the occasional interview request. Nothing he wanted to deal with now.

But this, when he looked at it more closely, didn't resemble any of the things he wanted to avoid. It was a thin envelope, cheap paper wrinkled from its rough passage in a mail sack. The handwritten address, slanting gently upward, was in Geddan script.

The few letters he'd gotten from Geddan acquaintances, he had not been happy to read.

"It is not a snake," said Daoud, flapping it at him. "It will not bite you."

"Unlike some other creatures of my acquaintance." He couldn't quite make it flirtatious; it mostly came out accusatory.

«You usually deserve it.» Pitched at a low grumble, in Porashtu, it wasn't meant for Aristide. "When you are done with that, Pulan wants to see you." Then he was gone, closing the door none too gently.

Aristide held the envelope at arm's length and squinted until the letters grew sharp, then gave up and scrabbled behind his back for his spectacles, which he'd left lying on his desk amidst the dirty dishes.

By the slant and curl of the penmanship, he guessed the author had been schooled in the art; likely they came from wealth. By the slight smear of the ink, they were left-handed. Aristide ran quickly through a list of Geddan acquaintances he could call up at short notice. None seemed likely, and he didn't recognize the handwriting.

Inside was a single sheet of paper bearing a few lines of the same. The message gave him nothing but an address in Anadh, a time, and an imperative:

> *We must speak.*
> *-Sofie Cattayim*

At least it didn't say *I need your help*, though he imagined that was what it meant.

He knew the name. Cattayim. A Chuli name, unusual out-side Farbourgh, let alone in Porachis. More than that, it was familiar. Why did he know that name? Then it struck him.

In Geddan tradition, spouses took the surname of the eldest person in the union, whether that union was between two or more. And Mab Cattayim was the eldest spouse of those three hapless newlyweds he'd sent packing to Porachis in the failing days of regionalist Gedda. The letter was from Sofie Keeler.

He balled it up and threw it, hard.

Pulan's office took up prime real estate within the walls of Hadhariti: Just off the upper terrace, its row of arched windows opened onto a view of the ocean and caught the breeze. Sunset flooded the room each evening just as the temperature began to drop, giving it the benefit of natural light without turning it into a sauna.

It was at the apex of perfection when Daoud answered Aris-tide's knock and stepped back to let him in. He was impeccably polite, in front of Pulan, but coldness rolled off of him like fog.

The scent of the potted frangipani on the terrace mingled with the smell of coffee, carried on a gentle current of salt air. Golden light spilled across the polished floor and made dust motes glow. It caught in the fine hair on Pulan's arms, in the fly-aways that had escaped from her pomade, making a halo that moved with her. She looked like some sort of blameless celestial being. Which is why, he suspected, she had agreed to see him at exactly this time of day. Perhaps, in fact, the entire reason she had situated her office just so. Anyone other than Aristide, who knew how the trick was accomplished, might have a hard time accusing her of subterfuge.

As it was, he had a hard time *seeing* her, once he was sat opposite and staring into the sun. He felt as though *he* were the one being interrogated. Smugly, Daoud stationed himself at his own desk, tucked into a corner and shaded by a delicate teak screen. From the plates and coffee detritus on Pulan's desk, and the stool tucked behind her chair, it was clear he'd been perched at her elbow until Aristide entered. Discreetly—he hoped—Aristide scanned the papers on Pulan's desk but found nothing beyond correspondence and invoices. He wished he could do the same for the sheaf of documents Daoud was straightening into a pile across the room.

"Well," said Pulan, sweet as treacle. "What can I do for you this evening?"

"I'm just curious." He plucked a sugar cube from the coffee tray and turned it in his fingers so the crystals caught the light.

"About?"

"What kind of business are you running, exactly? A film studio? Something else? A little bit of both?"

"Aristide, you work on my films. You know what we do here."

"And is Asiyah financing your next one, in partnership with the Geddan government? Or perhaps Memmediv represents some splinter group in Tatié. Though why they'd spend their money on a picture when they could spend it on machine guns, I don't know."

"I thought you were not interested in this kind of thing anymore."

"Because I didn't want it in my *life*, Pulan. But it seems to have crept in without my looking for it."

"You would not be asking questions if you did not want to know."

"If I want to know," he growled, "it's because I'm frightened."

That caught her off guard, as he'd meant it to. She tried to cover with a smile. "Aristide Makricosta, frightened of a little arms deal?"

"So you admit it. Mother's *tit*, Pulan, of *course* I'm frightened, and you know what it costs me to say that. You are my *bulwark*. If you're caught at this it could mean my neck in the noose."

"The queen abolished capital punishment ten years ago."

"Idiom," he snapped. "And it isn't the queen I'm worried about."

Much to his chagrin she laughed, bell-bright. Too bright, so he knew it was a front. "I am cautious, *duladhush*. I will not be caught. And if I am, you may claim ignorance. But only if you stop asking questions and demanding answers."

"Nobody will believe that. Not given my past."

"Ah yes," said Pulan, changing tacks. "Your past. It seems to have made a sudden reappearance. What can you tell me about this Nellie Hanes? Because I made several calls to people who should know. There were any number of Nellie Haneses in Amberlough at the time, but none of them ever danced with you."

"Of course not," he said evenly. "Nellie Hanes is an awful stage name. Malcolm never would have allowed it."

"Then what name *did* she go by?"

"Why don't you ask her?"

"Because I do not think she will tell me."

"And you think I will? After the secrets *you've* kept?"

She went on as if she hadn't heard him. "Maybe you will not say because you do not know."

He sneered. "I know who she is."

"But what is she running *from*?"

"I should think that's obvious."

At that, she only raised an eyebrow and said, "Mm."

A knock on the door kept things from escalating. «Enter,» said Pulan, dropping back into her seat and back into Porashtu.

Djihar, her steward, stepped softly into the room. «Mistress, a telegram from Myazbah.»

She held her hand out for the onionskin and snapped her fingers. Djihar slipped past Aristide to place it in her palm, then bowed and backed out of the room.

Perhaps she was less a celestial being, and more a wrathful god.

Pulan slit the seal on the telegram and read. He watched her thinly plucked, darkly penciled eyebrows rise by degrees.

"What does it say?" Even he could hear the sharp edge on his voice. There was a rustle of papers, and when Aristide looked over, Daoud had lifted his head from writing to watch Pulan's face.

"Nothing important."

"You're usually a better liar."

"Usually I am *trying*," she said. "You can go. Find your friend Nellie and send her up. If I am putting her on my payroll, I want to ask some questions."

An awful pettiness in his heart whispered that he shouldn't warn Cordelia. That if everyone else was going to keep secrets from him, he ought to turn their tactics back on them, let them fend for themselves in this whispering garden of poison and thorns. But she had lost her fingers for him, and almost her life, and who knew what else besides. And now he'd gotten her into another mess.

So he would go and find her, and send her up, with a warning that Pulan had caught an inconvenient case of suspicion. But after that . . .

Something in him, crabby at having been woken, was beginning to stretch. If everyone around him had their secrets, if he was already in the thick of something nasty, why shouldn't he pursue an avenue of his own? Nobody had to know—he could storm off in a huff, and Pulan would put it down to masculine volatility or artistic temperament. He'd be leaving Cordelia to her own devices, but Queen's sake, she'd more than proved she preferred them to anyone else's.

From what Ari told her, Cordelia didn't think this meeting with Pulan was going to go her way. But her choices were run for the road and hitch up to the city, or see what Satri had to say. She didn't think a gunrunning Porachin was going to tip her into the Ospies' open palm, at any rate.

Cordelia had to ask a couple domestics—a young boy dusting light shades, and a woman in a hurry down the hall—where to find Pulan's office. By the time she got there, evening was rolling in and the freshly dusted electric lights had come on underneath their decorative silk tassels.

The doors were closed. She had to knock. And when they opened, she had to blink.

The eastern half of the house might have been cast into gloom, but this room looked west and was soaked in red light like someone had put a color gel over the spot, then aimed it straight into Cordelia's eyes.

"I apologize," said Pulan, from somewhere in the glare. "The sun will set in a few minutes. Daoud, could you perhaps slide the screen?"

Cordelia heard casters roll. The light dimmed and she could see her way clear to an empty chair in front of Pulan's desk.

"Can I offer you some wine, Ms. Hanes? Or perhaps coffee?"

There was an ironic kind of weight on the name. But there were manners in it, too: Pulan got the game and she was going to play it. For now.

"I'll take the wine," said Cordelia, and sat on the edge of her seat.

There was a bottle by the desk, in a bucket on a stand. Pulan pulled it free. Cordelia heard ice clatter, and saw drips land on the floor. By the time she looked up from the spatter of water on wood, her glass was full and Pulan was pouring for herself. The same pale green wine she and Ari had drunk in the city. She reminded herself to go slowly—no good to jaw with Pulan like she had with him.

"I understand you are looking for a position with my studio. You are a choreographer?"

"Yeah," said Cordelia. "Yes. I dance, and I can put together a solid routine, even on short notice. Did it for years."

Daoud tapped away at his typewriter at a smaller desk in the corner. Pulan ignored the metallic thwack of keys, the crank of the platen knobs. "You used to work with Aristide."

"We walked the boards together a couple of times. Stage work pays swineshit, but there were other perks."

"Selling tar?" asked Pulan, face prim and perfect as a doll's. "Or something else?"

Cordelia snorted into her wineglass, fogging the inside of the globe. "A lot of something elses, most of 'em good-looking and keen to get between a girl's thighs. But yeah, I ran a little for Ari. Why? Didn't seem like it stopped you hiring him."

Pulan lifted her wineglass but didn't drink. "Aristide is an old friend, and I have a debt to him. I will risk things for him that I will not risk for you, if you require them."

"You," said Cordelia, one eyebrow canted high. "You have a debt to *him*?"

"Family business."

"Uh-huh." Cordelia twisted her wineglass on the table, watching the liquid slip against the crystal. "He said he did some work with your dad."

"Did he?"

"Don't worry. He didn't tell me what kind. I guessed."

"You are clever. That is good."

"It's a little more than just mush and raisins up here," she said, and tapped her forehead.

"Then you will understand the danger when I tell you the Ospies are looking into my affairs very closely at the moment."

Cold swamped her gut and her hands went numb, but she kept her teeth together. The sun had finally sunk below the horizon, and suddenly she felt the shadows like a smothering weight.

Daoud clicked on his desk light, and she jumped.

"Depending upon your level of involvement with Aristide's . . . enterprises, you may or may not be aware that they went beyond simple smuggling. Things that made him very interesting to the Geddan government. But nothing that surprised me, and nothing outside my ability to protect him." This time when she paused, she did drink. Her lipstick left a smutch on the glass, which she examined closely as she said, "I like to know what I am hiding. And I am certainly hiding something, if I put you on my payroll."

"Why are the Ospies prying into your business? You got something going on in your dad's line, maybe?"

Pulan tapped her wineglass pensively. Her fingernails, Cordelia noticed, were varnished beetle-green.

"Drugs?" asked Cordelia. "Whores?" Then, thinking about the Lisoan prince on Pulan's doorstep, about the reports of border skirmishes she'd gotten just before she ducked and ran, she added, "Or maybe guns?"

Daoud's typewriter bell dinged. This time it was Pulan who jumped, though barely.

"It's guns," said Cordelia, "ain't it?" Then, thinking back to earlier in the day, to Aristide's careful identification of the strangers on the steps, "From Liso, to Tatié. You're some kind of broker."

Pulan leveled a stare over the wineglass. Her words, when she spoke, were crisp and sharp as creased paper. "If you pose a threat to me, I will not hesitate to throw you to the sharks."

Well, that was nothing new; how else did folk live their lives?

"Y'know," said Cordelia, an electric crackle of excitement growing in her chest, "I'm getting an idea."

When Opal had shaken her hand and stuck her in the Cattayims' truck bed, the last thing she'd said was maybe Cordelia could work from Porachis. Find them money, backers, weapons, anything. It felt, then, like a petty task, the kind of thing you told a kid to do to keep them out from underfoot. Where was she supposed to find that kind of thing, in a country where she didn't speak the language?

Well, she wasn't a rotten kid, was she? And now she'd found somebody who spoke *her* tongue, and might have some words she wanted to hear.

Squaring her shoulders, Cordelia shed her doubts and let her chin come up. "If I was looking to buy from you," she said, "how much would I have to spend before you forgot I was dangerous to keep around?"

A small curl at the corner of Pulan's generous mouth was the only indication she'd been caught off guard. "And are you? Looking to buy?"

"I represent some people who are. Maybe you've heard of us. We're called the Catwalk."

"Oh," said Pulan. "Yes, I think we have heard of them. Have we not, Daoud?"

The little secretary laughed politely at her joke, and Cordelia realized she'd forgotten he was there.

"We have also heard that you are penniless"—when Cordelia opened her mouth to tell some kind of lie, Pulan put a hand up and ran over her—"but very well organized." She plucked a telegram from amidst the papers on her desk. "And right now, I have a problem that money cannot solve."

PART

2

CHAPTER

TEN

Aristide didn't stay at the Abna Bhangri this time, but at a much smaller hotel in a less shimmering part of town. They had a garage at least, so he could park his car off the street after making several roundabout diversions through the tangled avenues of old Anadh that had grown up before the queen's mother's-mother's-however-many-back had imposed a grid system. The first in the world, Porachin historians liked to claim.

He got in late and slept badly, but he didn't like the idea of being spotted around town, so he stayed in the stifling confines of his room until dawn broke.

Breakfast was a potato turnover, purchased hastily from a cart on the street. The steam burned his mouth, and the peas burst scalding on his tongue. It hurt on the way down, but he swallowed it anyway.

He caught an omnibus heading into the center of the city, got off before they crossed Noonaplati, caught a second bus into the garment district, and then finally boarded a third headed east. The first two had been crowded, full of commuters on their way into the city's heart. This one, aimed uphill at the desert, was nearly empty.

Well, it was hardly desert *now*. More like slums. Porachis's famous aqueducts had watered a dusty hollow around a natural harbor until the city of Anadh grew from the parched earth, and spread like creeping ground cover. Over the lip of the rise, out of sight of the sea, shanty towns straggled into the rocks and sand.

One could measure desperation by distance from the cliff's edge. The address Sofie had given him clung to the margins of the lower middle class. He waited two stops past the most convenient and meandered back along a convoluted path, casually catching reflections in what glass he could find, and listening for footsteps. He hated that he'd come; hated that he'd returned to dodging around corners, laying false tracks. No one followed him, and his suspicion felt ridiculous.

He'd been largely insulated from surveillance, under Pulan's protection. She hired staff rarely and with great care. Yes, there were spies in her house and company, but she knew who they were and knew the strength of their loyalty to the last gram. Daoud, for instance, had been approached by the Ospies at one point early on, and promptly informed Pulan of the offer. For a while he had made a handy conduit for falsehoods, until they clocked he was feeding them spoiled meat and cut the connection.

Besides, Pulan could out-bribe any government, and Aristide hardly ever gave them anything to report. This adventure would certainly be an exception, if the story made it back to anyone who cared what he got up to. But he didn't intend that it should.

Eventually, just a little after noon, he arrived unmolested and—

as far as he knew—unobserved, at his destination: a low, dark coffeehouse cloudy with the exhalations of multiple hookahs.

He didn't see her, even once he'd blinked away the smoke. He *did* see half a dozen women in foreman's hats and cheap wool tunics having their lunch-hour smoke and coffee. A few of them shot sharp glances his way as he crossed the room to the counter, asked for his own pipe and cup, and settled into a corner booth to wait. He didn't shoot back—it was no good to *ask* for trouble, and he'd learned the hard way that returning a glare from a certain kind of woman in Porachis meant exactly that, especially if one talked back with a Geddan accent.

Sofie arrived ten minutes late, hair escaping from its pins, dusty to the knees. She wore a shapeless tunic over tight trousers and cheap rope sandals. He might not have recognized her—they'd only met for what, ten minutes in an attic, once?—but she was the only foreigner in the coffeehouse, and her pale face was drawn into a searching squint. Her eyes passed him once, as she scanned the room, but snapped back when she realized there were no other men present.

No other pale women, either. Which wouldn't matter too much until she opened her mouth. She could've been Enselmese, Hellican, Ibetian at a stretch.

Her approach was tentative. She stood several feet back from his table when she asked, "Mr. Makricosta?" Her voice faded toward the end of his name, and she looked over her shoulder when she said it. A couple of women at the bar had overheard and sent some nasty looks her way. He hoped they would get out of here without a memorable incident.

"Sit." He held out the hookah's hose. "You don't speak Porashtu, do you?"

She collapsed with an alacrity that might have alarmed him, if she hadn't then snatched the hose and taken an ambitious drag. The cloud of smoke that issued from her mouth when she exhaled engulfed her head, so that when she spoke her voice came from within. "Blessed Queen. You came."

"I almost didn't."

She waved away the smoke, and with it, his qualification. "Badly. Porashtu, I mean. I know it's not ideal." She looked around again, nerves plain on her sunburnt face.

"Stop that," he said. "Be still or you'll make it worse."

She swallowed hard and folded her hands in her lap with stern intent. "I'm terribly sorry I was late," she said, as if restarting a scene that had gone badly. "But after traveling down I didn't have bus fare and I—"

"Is it money?"

"Pardon me?" Lady's name, she still had it. Despite the dust and the dark circles under her eyes, her mended hems and ragged nails, she could still call on the imperiousness of inherited money, the manner of Nuesklan high society before the OSP.

Aristide was not cowed. "Is it money, that you need? Your letter didn't say."

Sofie's mouth rearranged itself a few times before finally settling into a smile that failed to hide insult. "No, Mr. Makricosta. It isn't money."

"Pity." He held out his hand for the hose and she smacked it into his palm. After a long breath of sweet, cool smoke, he said, "That might have been easier than whatever else it is you need."

"I'm sure it would have." The ice in her voice did not freeze him. In such a hot place as Porachis, it was welcome.

"What is it, then? Because I'd rather get this over with."

"I didn't mean," she said, with the precision of a lancing needle, "to place an undue burden on you. I am simply trying to find my wife."

He let her talk at him, absorbing the story of her woe through an insulating layer of scented smoke.

Taphir, the young husband, had left them both as soon as he hit home soil. In Porachis, Aristide couldn't imagine a marriage in which two women shared one husband would have been easy to sell to Taphir's matriarchal, and no doubt massive, family. And his own security would probably have been paramount, having come straight out of prison and across the sea as the Ospies ate his homeland.

"It was hard," said Sofie. "Especially since I had just realized I was pregnant. Mab was my pylon. But then we started getting news about the seizure of Chuli pastureland, the railroad bombings and the reprisals, and now the prison camps, and the typhus . . ."

Aristide didn't keep up with the news from home, but as Sofie talked he heard echoes of half-remembered conversations, mostly in Porashtu, poorly translated thanks to his disinterest and mediocre skill.

"She wanted to help," said Sofie, staring at the smoldering hookah coals. "Can you imagine? Her family disowned her, for marrying outside, but she still wanted to help."

"If she's gone to Gedda," said Aristide, "I hate to say it, but all the alleys where *I* did business have likely been bricked over." Perhaps "hate" was a strong word, but he did find as he said it that something pinched in his chest: a kind of grudging regret.

"Not Gedda," said Sofie. "I wouldn't let her. Not if it left me alone here with Nadia. But I . . . she found a way. She was sending money—money we couldn't afford—and letters to a cousin. I didn't know she kept in contact with them, or maybe it was recent, since the Ospies. Mother knows we've all made some interesting decisions in the intervening years."

There was a freighted pause. Aristide brushed some ash into the hookah's tray, and declined to comment.

Sofie cleared her throat. "At any rate. There was money going missing, and then one day, a woman shows up on a cargo ship and Mab says we're meant to take her in."

"A Chuli woman?"

Sofie shook her head—a pin dropped to the table—and leaned closer. Her eyes cut side to side before she said, "Catwalk," in a low voice. "This was just after they found a passel of them hiding with the Chuli, in the mountains."

"Oh," said Aristide, who comprehended about half of what she'd said. "The Catwalk. They . . . bombed a few things? Rail lines, or something like that?"

"You're going to make *me* tell *you*?"

"I don't pay attention to the news from Gedda."

Her laugh could have flensed flesh from bone. It certainly set him back a few inches in his chair.

"So you were harboring a fugitive?" he asked, feeling his steps blindly. Suddenly it seemed Sofie was holding up the opposite end of a very different conversation than the one he thought they had been having.

"Only for a night," said Sofie. "I was livid. We fought, and finally agreed she couldn't stay. And that was that, until . . ."

"She disappeared," he finished, picking up the bitter fact she'd dropped in front of him at the beginning of this interview. "And you sent me a letter. Why should I know where she is?"

"You helped us once before," said Sofie.

"I had the means."

"You have means now."

"Not the ones that you require. I have no credit with the Ospies or the queen, and my employer's protection only extends so far."

Sofie's eyelashes fell across her broad cheeks, and he saw the delicate skin of her eyelids was stained red-purple with fatigue and broken blood vessels. "It isn't just the money, or the connections. I want to know why they took my wife. It might help me, to prove her innocent or . . ."

"How on earth should I know?" he asked, and sucked—perhaps a trifle petulantly—on the hose.

"Because this woman we sheltered, she knows you."

He forgot to exhale the breath he had drawn. A small dribble of smoke curled over his lower lip, disappearing in a flood as he said, "Oh. Does she?"

"She saw your photograph in the roto. When Mab asked if she knew you, I remember her words exactly."

"Which were?"

"'He's why I'm here, if you go about it the long way.'" Sofie's slum whine was surprisingly accurate.

"What did she look like, this woman?" Aristide braced himself, because he could feel the tension in the air that came before a painful revelation.

"Very skinny, rather small. She had freckles, and her hair was cut like a razor's. Dark brown, poorly dyed."

"I don't suppose she gave you a name?"

Sofie shook her head. "Do you have something to do with the Catwalk?"

This time *he* laughed, so caustic it nearly burnt his lips on the way past. But she didn't flinch. Her body just collapsed further into itself, exhausted.

"Not in the way you hope I do," he said. "Though now, the imprudence of arranging this meeting via post, without any subterfuge, smacks of a suicide attempt, rather than an amateur mistake."

"I am past prudence. I have not eaten anything but gruel this week. My wife is gone, only the Eyes of the Arches see where, and I don't know what to tell my daughter when she asks me where her mumma is." Sofie's face curdled, and she sucked hard on the hose to save herself continuing. When she had blown out her breath full of smoke, she said, "Please. You must know someone."

He finally heard a note of supplication in her voice. Admirable, how long she'd held it in check. He imagined her hoarding pride like precious coins. It hadn't been enough; she'd spent it all on this encounter, and she was playing on credit now.

"Isn't there a name you can give me? Just one name. Somebody sympathetic, in the police, or . . . ?" Her knuckles turned white, she gripped the hookah's hose so tightly. "I took a bus down all the way from Berer. Please."

"Porachin police can't help you," he said. "I'd wager she hasn't even been arrested. Not by them, not officially."

"The government then."

"The palace won't want to get involved, not for your wife. The only reason I'm safe is that I'm famous, and so is my employer. It isn't fair, but it's the truth. They can't afford to let me disappear."

"What about our people?" she said. "Gedda."

He started to scoff. Then, he stopped.

He knew at least two people in the Geddan embassy, if passing acquaintance counted. And he knew at least one of them was mixed up in something nasty, likely counter to the Ospies' aims. That didn't mean Memmediv would help Sofie, not unless she could give him something. Or potentially ruin something for him.

Oh, and this was pettiness, but Aristide wanted to put that fear in him: the fear of ruination. The same fear Memmediv had brought back into his life. And what would it cost him, if Sofie did the work?

"Just one name?" he asked.

"Yes," said Sofie, and her eyes grew wide. The bones of her face, which he remembered as strong, not pretty but handsome, were slightly too prominent now. They cast shadows beneath her eyes.

"All right. But this never crossed my lips—you heard it somewhere else. And please, when you contact this man, *don't* send him a letter anything like you did me."

It turned out Pulan was in deep with a couple of branches of the Lisoan government, most importantly the defense ministry. And she assured Cordelia her contacts had an interest in stirring any Geddan pot that threatened to boil over.

"If they are busy mopping their own floors," she said, "they will not have the time to build another house on their neighbor's land. And if it all leads to a regime change in the process, I do not think his Majesty will mind."

They had a stockpile of weapons left over from the Spice War— stuff Gedda and their allies had sold to republican rebels in hopes of scratching palace rule, which had been confiscated everywhere south of the partition. The stuff was a few decades old by now, but it had been stored well and still worked.

"I have tested the chain guns myself," said Pulan, and her smile made Cordelia's heart kick—the same way a leopard's snarl might have. "Though it seems likely that your interests lie more with TNT, and mines, and blasting caps."

That was true, but it made her dream: What if they could use a chain gun? What if they brought the whole creeping, grinding conflict out into the open, instead of tearing up rail lines and chucking homemade bombs into office buildings?

"I might like to look at a gun or two," she said. "For a laugh."

"I'm sure Asiyah would be more than happy to supply you," said Pulan, refilling her wineglass.

But as dinner went on and they got into the gritty details of the plan, Cordelia started to understand what Pulan expected her to do. She wasn't exactly thrilled about it, and said so.

First of all: Cyril's sister had a kid.

Why should that matter so much? Why did it get her behind the ribs, to know this woman she had never met had popped out a baby boy DePaul? Why was she wondering if Cyril had ever met him? Why should she care at all about Cyril, who had ruined everything she ever knew?

Second of all: She wanted to go back to Gedda, but the prospect of really doing it, with a price on her head probably, caught cold and sharp in her gut like she'd swallowed an icicle.

Third and final: She didn't really understand why this kid was so important.

At the outset, Pulan had asked her to contact her people in Gedda, but given the tatters of her network and the difficulties of reaching back into their communications from so far away, not knowing how things had gone after she left . . . it came out pretty clear there was no easy way to arrange this at a distance. She regretted selling the Catwalk to Pulan as a solid organization, because now that she was going to be flinging herself off a cliff and hoping it caught her, she wasn't sure it would hold.

"I did not think, anyway, that you were the kind of general who gave her commands from far away," said Pulan. "Surely you wish to return to your people." Her smile, over her slice of cocoa sesame cake, struck Cordelia like a blowdart and stung like poison.

"Well yeah, but . . ." There wasn't a "but," not really. She'd been ready to crawl back across the border before the CIS started scooping people up. Now she wanted to make sure she had her feet under her before she went home; make sure she had a plan and firepower.

"Are you afraid?" Pulan asked sweetly.

Cordelia leveled an iron stare across the remains of their meal. "Tell me why."

"You need to know? I thought that this was commerce."

"Courtesy," said Cordelia. "Trust. They're valuable. So tell me."

Pulan tapped her fork against her chocolate-smeared plate, making the silver and porcelain chime as she considered. "The child," she said at last, "is leverage. They use him to control her. And now, they have asked her to . . ." She rubbed the tips of her fingers together thoughtfully and said a few Porashtu words. "To break my plans. To snare Mr. Memmediv. I cannot afford this. So we must win her for ourselves. This is the cost."

It didn't surprise her, the Ospies leveraging a kid. What it did was make her mad as a snared rat. "Tell me more."

Pulan smiled, probably because she knew her hooks were in. "He is at school in Cantrell. Term ends in two weeks. I think that would be the ideal time to take him. Things will be in . . . uproar? Routines broken. Good cover."

There had been, at one point, a small network in Cantrell, headed up by the station agent who had scouted cargos for them and flagged trains that made good targets. Code name: Greasepaint.

It'd be ideal if Cordelia could get some kind of message to him before showing up on the back stoop, but that was fraught with all kinds of risk. And anyway, he might have got drug in. Cordelia'd been reading the papers, and getting Daoud to translate the wireless for her when she could. They must have rounded up half her networks by now, not to mention some poor folk named no doubt out of desperation. It seemed like her scrappers were having a hard time keeping their jaws locked against the Ospie pry bar.

She didn't blame any of them. She knew the weight and pressure of that jemmy: It broke teeth and bones.

But to make it to Cantrell she'd have to get into Gedda at all. "And how am I supposed to cross the border? It was hard enough getting out. I don't think they'll let me sail through without any papers."

"I could get you some. Very easily."

"There are too many details I don't have," said Cordelia, still leery. "Things like this you have to do right. Who usually picks the kid up? Does it need some kind of letter? Permission slip? Kidnapping's risky—the easiest thing, safest thing, would be to do this like it normally goes off, close as we can. Folk get sore when kids go missing and I don't want my people tarred with that reputation. If we make it *look* tabletop, less chance people will start checking under the board."

"I will get you what information I can," said Pulan, "but I cannot promise much of it, or very quickly. My source is under too much scrutiny. I understand it is a difficult job, but I am offering a substantial payment. So if you want your guns, you will find a way."

CHAPTER

ELEVEN

"He knows you're onto him," said Lillian as she shut the door behind her. She hadn't heard from Flagg since their last meeting, which had ended poorly. But his car had been waiting for her this evening at the bottom of the chancery steps. She took some pleasure in dropping this unpleasant news in his lap.

Flagg pinched the bridge of his nose. "If he knows, Satri will too. And who knows who else."

"I have a plan," she said.

Palm up, he swept his hand through the air: an invitation to continue.

"He offered me a deal, when he realized I was working for you." She omitted the part of the interaction in which she had deliberately blown her own cover with overdone makeup and overt sexuality.

"So you're serving two masters now?" Flagg picked a piece of lint from his cuff, then casually said, "Must run in the family."

"With all respect," she said, speaking past the ligature of anger and grief that had tightened suddenly around her throat, "I'm cannier than my brother ever was. I know where to put my feet."

"And is he offering you firm ground?"

Lillian smoothed the flap of her briefcase, fingertips lingering on the metal clasp but not quite fidgeting. "Counselor, you needn't worry about where my loyalties lie."

"That isn't an answer, DePaul. What is he offering you?"

"Nothing he can deliver on," she said, a little too tightly.

Flagg didn't look convinced.

"You have my son," said Lillian. "Whose orders do you think I'll follow?"

"Speaking of your son." Flagg laced his fingers. "Have you been in touch with your royal contact?"

"He's been busy. Lady Suhaila's birthday, you know. The party lasted several days. He had to put in an appearance, as family, and for his column."

"Of course," said Flagg, though he looked unsatisfied with her explanation. "But the Cattayim woman is proving to be rather more ignorant than we'd hoped, or more reticent, so I'd like any source of information I can get about our likely fugitive."

"You arrested her? Cattayim, I mean."

"Please." Flagg picked some minuscule piece of dust from his lapel. "We have no jurisdiction off the chancery grounds."

Lillian imagined a black bag over the head at night, a swift blow, awakening disoriented in a cell. She hoped the reality had been less dramatic. "I'll speak with him this evening."

When she finally got home, she dropped her briefcase on the floor, shed her jacket and pumps, and made it to her study before Waleeda had finished collecting her detritus from the floor.

«Long day?» the majordomo asked.

«I'm sorry!» Lillian called, and leaned back to look out the door. Waleeda had an arm full of shoes, satchel, and linen, and she was shaking her head.

Shutting the door to her study, Lillian pulled the screen across the open window and turned on her fan. Under cover of the electric whirr, she unlocked her desk and pulled out a bottle of whiskey. Not sorghum, but pure Enselmese barley dried over peat. Prohibitively expensive, imported to Porachis, so she'd been making this bottle last. The cork came out with a soft *whoop*, releasing the scents of brine, smoke, and fennel. As her portion sat in the tumbler, airing out, she collapsed into her chair and peeled away her stockings.

Stockings. In Porachis. This never would have happened when Van Kappel was ambassador.

She didn't usually let herself dwell on what-ifs. The Ospies were the reality and it wasn't safe or productive to imagine otherwise. But ever since her meeting with Memmediv, her mind had been peeking down shadowy paths she wouldn't have otherwise allowed herself to notice.

It was unlikely he could do what he said he could. Retrieve Stephen from Gedda? What would she do then? She would have to leave Porachis, and her position in the embassy, under a cloud of chaos and shame. She would need to run, and tear her eight-year-old son away from everything familiar.

Familiarity didn't necessarily connote worth or safety. But she had seen the Ospies in action, and knew they could deliver on a threat. If Memmediv tried but couldn't execute his promise, the careful détente Lillian had built with the current regime would be destroyed, and the consequences unbearable.

Meeting Flagg's demands meant she would at least see her son.

And then, she would have to figure out her own bargain with

his father. His father, who had asked her to do all the things she hardly dared consider now, when doing them would have been safe, but scared her.

One step at a time. First his father had to help her catch a fugitive.

Jinadh looked tired when they met the next day, on a park bench along the river. He sat slumped low, one ankle over one knee, rather slovenly for a Porachin gentleman in public. But this close to midday the park was nearly empty, so there was no one to see.

«Palace living took its toll on you, I see.» She sat beside him and snuck a look at his face from behind the dark, round lenses of her sunglasses. He wore a pair as well, though they didn't do much to hide the pouches beneath his eyes.

«Don't tell,» he said. «I would lose my playboy reputation. But keeping up with Lady Suhaila and her set is a marathon. I'm thirty-seven, not seventeen.»

«I'm sure you were just as bad as her, when you were that young. She should hope to age half as well.»

He cupped his chin and rubbed at his beard, considering the compliment. In Geddan, no doubt to foil potential eavesdroppers, he asked, "Are you flirting with me?"

"No." She turned away, stared at the river and the egrets on its bank. One of them dipped to stab at a fish. "Yes. I'm sorry. You make it easy."

That made him laugh, with a note of bitterness. «The hill up from habits is slippery.»

«A pretty boy is the fruit peel beneath a woman's shoe,» she said, pleased to hold her own in the volley of Porachin aphorisms.

"What do you need?" he said, dropping out. He looked, perhaps, a trifle stung. She regretted her display of wit.

"How soon can you go back to your cousin's house?" She was cagey about naming names, though the path was empty in either direction and the sun beat down on the pavement like a foundry hammer.

"A week, perhaps? It would help to have an excuse. She cannot exactly throw me out, but I am not her favorite relative."

"Could you go sooner?"

"Why?" He straightened slightly, finally turned to face her fully. "Did he find something in the pictures?"

"We need more information about that choreographer. Flagg thinks she might be . . . important."

"You can tell me," he said. "It might help to know. And to whom would I reveal the truth? Telling anyone how I found out would require a complicated explanation."

She cast her eyes from side to side, hidden behind their lenses. Still alone. Nevertheless she spoke softly, and he had to lean closer to hear. She could smell the musk of his sweat, faintly, beneath limewater and hair tonic.

"He thinks it's Cordelia Lehane. The founder of the Catwalk."

His eyebrows puckered above his sunglasses. "What is she doing in Porachis?"

"Well, she's at your cousin's house. What do you think?"

He shook his head and said, "Pulan," with such resignation Lillian felt as if the bench sagged beneath them. "Is that what she and Memmediv talked about at the premiere, with the Lisoans?"

Lillian pushed her sunglasses back up her nose; they had begun to slip as she perspired. "I don't think so. That's something else entirely, and he's quite nervous."

"Oh?" A line of mirth cut a curve around the corner of his mouth. "He told you that?"

"Yes." She must have said it too curtly, because he turned more fully to face her.

"He did." Jinadh cocked one elbow onto the back of the bench. "When?"

"Flagg has me . . . watching his slate carefully, as it were. Keeping an eye on him," she amended, when Jinadh's brow furrowed at the idiom.

But the wrinkle remained, even following her clarification. "Beyond asking for my help?"

"Yes."

"How far beyond?"

She did not like the angle he seemed to be taking; if he tacked any closer he might start to suspect her original intent. "He offered me a deal to double-agent for him. To pass false information to Flagg."

"What can he offer you that could possibly . . . ?"

She watched realization kindle in his eyes, watched it spread across his expression like flames catching in a dry wood gone too long without a burn. Or, not a wood: a grassland. His face was wide and open for miles, unshadowed by guile or suspicion. He had always had such a beautiful smile. "And you said yes."

"Of course I said yes."

He put a hand to her upper arm, his grip thoughtlessly tight with elation. It was not just the strength of his hold that made him difficult to shake off; a host of inconvenient emotions made her reluctant to move.

But she did, in the end, pushing him away so his palm slipped against her skin, moving to her elbow before falling away. "It was the only way to get close to him, to find out what he was really doing with Satri."

"What." It wasn't truly a request for clarification: Devoid of all inflection, it was more like a blink, a breath, than it was a word.

"He can't *do* it, Jinadh. They're onto him; they're about to fold his operation up."

"What was his plan?" Jinadh's hand had tightened on the bench, and the one she had pushed from her arm was fisted now, suspended several inches above his thigh. Not quite as if he meant to throw a punch, but more as if he didn't know what to do with his limbs. Or perhaps more that he had forgotten he had them.

"I didn't ask," she snapped. "Because I knew it would be implausible. And that asking might smack of canniness. I am supposed to be desperate for his help, not shrewd."

"I do not believe you."

She sighed. "Yes, you do."

"Well, I do not *want* to!" He stood from the bench, shoulders hunched, and spoke to the river. To her horror, she caught the echo of his words bouncing from the water.

"Calm down." She stood, too, and went to him. "We're very close to scratching this whole scheme, and as soon as we do, when the Solstice holidays begin—"

Arm raised, he whirled around and she startled, though he did not touch her.

"If he can do what he promised you, he is offering us something we gave up years ago. No, I apologize. Something *you* gave up. And now, you are giving it up again. What for, this time? What reason can you possibly have to stay?"

"It isn't worth the risk," she insisted, and this time she was the one to put a hand on him, to hold him tightly with their faces close so he might listen to at least half the words she said, she hoped. "If he fails, I . . ."

"You'll never see Stephen again?" he asked, and if he had not been raised according to Porachin standards of masculinity, she believed he would have shoved her away. Instead he took a step back, yanking himself out of her grasp. "So what do *I* have to lose?"

She had not expected him to react this way, and now she was furious with herself for failing to predict it. What *did* he have to lose? He had already offered to leave everything for her, once: his home, his title, his family, his work. What would keep him from seeking out Memmediv and his conspirators and spilling all these secrets in a bid to see the son who had been kept from him?

"Me," she said, only now fully grasping the truth of it.

Because she had never truly considered Memmediv's offer, the inherent dangers had never seemed relevant. Now that Jinadh demanded an explanation, she found one she hoped might convince him. "If he fails, neither of us sees Stephen, and I go to prison. Maybe—probably—to the scaffold. Or wherever Cyril went."

She rarely spoke of her brother, and hoped his name would lend weight to her fear, her threat. She hated herself for using him as a tool, but imagined he would have done much the same.

Proud chin raised and nostrils flared, Jinadh stared at her for a long moment. The silence between them broke with the splash of a stabbing egret and the creak of its wings as it rose from the bank. Jinadh, likewise, turned and flew.

CHAPTER

TWELVE

"This oughta be turned back into pulp," said Cordelia, slapping the Geddan translation of *Song of the Sky* onto the table in front of Pulan. "I can't feature shooting any kind of picture in the middle of such a rumpus, but *this*? It's so sappy it's an insult."

"It is entertainment," said Pulan, and shrugged. "Is there not a phrase for this in Geddan, that stage people use?" She tapped her lip with a varnished fingertip, all campy confusion. "Oh yes. 'The show must go on.'"

"You're crazy as a busted tile," said Cordelia.

"Am I?" Pulan shuffled through a stack of invoices and correspondence at her elbow, some of them on Hadhariti's peacock letterhead. "This," she said, picking a shipping manifest from the bunch, "says that a cargo ship will carry my lights and cameras and properties to Tzieta. And this"—another bit of paper, with an official seal at the head—"says that I may bring them into the country freely. And this"—yet another manifest—"is the train on which I will take them north and east, into the steppe, very close to the Geddan border."

It clicked for her then. "You're moving the guns with the picture. So we've got to make the picture to move the guns."

That got her a smile like a twist of sugar candy. "Very good."

"I don't see why I gotta read the script, if I'm gonna be off kidnapping."

"Because Chitra is preoccupied with the big numbers, so Inaz needs choreography and coaching. If Aristide brought you on to dance, why not use you?"

Cordelia sighed in resignation and hauled a magazine into her lap from the stack beside the breakfast tray. It was all in Porashtu, but there were heaps of pictures—stars and producers and royalty, laughing and gleaming in the bright light of the camera flash. Flipping through, she landed on a spread from last week's premiere: Aristide, and Pulan, and a blond woman with pale eyes who couldn't have been anyone other than Cyril DePaul's sister. Cordelia didn't need a caption to tell her that.

She spent a long time staring at that picture, at the bright crescent of Lillian's smile and the angle of her jaw, and wondering. Was she anything like him? Would she make the same mistakes, trample on the same principles? The Ospies had a hold on her and they were using it, and how was that any different than what had happened to Cyril?

Did Lillian know about that? Did Aristide know what had happened to him? Did anyone?

She almost wished Ari were here, so she could grill him. Feeling like she had an upper hand, she might press him harder this time. But he'd run out on them pretty suddenly, no explanation. Just left a note with Djihar that said he'd gone back up to Anadh, and that he'd be back in a day or two.

Pulan didn't seem worried. "He will return when he is done sulking and can behave like an adult again. Men," she added, and gave a roll of her eyes that said more than any insult would have.

As if Cordelia's thoughts had conjured it, a car roared up the drive outside. Pulan looked up from the schedule she had laid out on the veranda table, weighted down with dishes of pistachios and green almonds still in their shells.

"Ari?" asked Cordelia.

"Perhaps," said Pulan, freeing her bare feet from the voluminous folds of her kaftan and stepping down from the chaise.

Before she had quite straightened, before Cordelia had quite risen to follow her, a *bang* echoed through the hall and out onto the terrace. Cordelia could make out the scurry of footsteps— Djihar's slippers slapping on the tile, the sharper ring of running leather soles—then Daoud's high, clear voice, though she didn't understand the Porashtu words.

A wrinkle appeared between Pulan's dramatic eyebrows, in the small triangle where they almost met above her nose.

Cordelia didn't like that wrinkle. That wrinkle meant Pulan didn't know who was charging through her own house, trailing staff after them like tumbling trash in a strong storm wind.

She sat lower in her chair, put her hands between her knees where they were hidden but easy to raise if she had to . . . what, throw a punch? She wasn't armed. She thought Pulan might be— that kaftan could hide a multitude of nasty pieces. There was a team of bruisers, too, but too far off right now to do much good if it came to something ugly on the terrace.

Unless there were keen snipers, stationed up above. She wouldn't put that past Pulan. Best thing was to keep low, try to stay out of the way. Her heart slammed against her ribs. She got ready for a freight train, or a battalion, or whatever came through that door, open from the terrace onto the entrance hall.

But it wasn't a train that nearly ran them down, bursting from the house into the open air.

"Jinadh," said Pulan, and the wrinkle finally went, replaced by an eye roll. "What are you doing back so soon?"

But Pulan's cousin had lost all that oily swell veneer that had coated him so thick last time he'd been at Hadhariti. He looked wild, almost. He looked the way Cordelia's heart felt: frantic, ready to beat against whatever bars held him back.

And it only took Pulan a second longer to clock the difference, because the frown lines came back and she said something in Porashtu that sounded serious, concerned. The way you'd talk to a pregnant lady clutching her belly, an old man in a faint. Jinadh snapped something at her, then shook his head and said, more softly, «I'm sorry,» which Cordelia could pick out.

Maybe she perked up at that, or made some movement that caught his attention, because suddenly those wide, hungry eyes were on her. He reminded her a little of a half-feral street dog: the type that remembered humans could be kind, but was ready to bite at any fast movement, any slight, or for no reason at all.

"How's it turning?" she asked, voice low and steady. Like the way you talked to that kind of dog, to get it to come close enough to eat a scrap.

"You," he said, "are in terrible danger. And it is all my fault."

"Do you care to explain?" Pulan settled back into the chair she'd so recently left. "Did you publish something unwise, and bring a horde of admirers down on us?"

"Ms. Hanes," he said, his voice rising like a question on the name, "would not tell me anything to print. In the end, it likely gained her time."

Queen's cunt. He knew.

Her heart had not slowed down. The ramekins and coffee cups on the table pulsed in time with its beat, or rather: her whole body pulsed, even her eyes, and so nothing around her would stay still. To steady herself, she clutched the arm of her chair with her right hand, because there was no point hiding it now. "Who did you tell?"

"I did not tell anyone," he said. "They already suspected. But I did give them some photographs."

"That rotten camera," she said. "I knew it."

Pulan's feet had not left the tile, and now they flexed, as though she might stand again. She asked him something in Porashtu, grave as an undertaker.

Jinadh's eyes flickered to Cordelia and he said, "To the Geddans."

Pulan's eyes followed the same track his had, and then went narrow. "Why?"

"Because . . ." He dropped his gaze to the tile. Cordelia, who had only ever seen him glittering and proud and grinning too hard, thought solemnity looked better on him. Made him less ridiculous. He took a breath, shoulders rising, and then went on. "They have my son."

There was a tight, brief silence Cordelia couldn't parse—surprise, maybe, but with an edge of sulfur, a sear to it.

"Your son," Pulan repeated. And then something more, in Porashtu again. As if Jinadh's words had shocked her Geddan vocabulary straight out of her head.

"We both know she never bore a child. Do not make this more difficult than it needs to be," said Jinadh. Then, "This story concerns Nellie. She should understand it."

Pulan's eyes went narrow and shiny with malice, and this time she didn't look at Cordelia after Jinadh did. She did switch to

Geddan though, her voice pulled tight over a searing bed of angry coals, curling crisp at the edges. "Who was it? Who did you . . . who is the mother?"

"A Geddan diplomat," he said.

"*What?*" This time she did stand, and it brought her very close to him. He was not much taller, and she thrust her face into his. Cordelia shrank more deeply into her chair, but Jinadh didn't flinch. "Who?"

"Lillian DePaul," he said, and Pulan burst into the kind of laughter Cordelia had spilled so many times, the last few years. The kind you let loose when it was that or scream.

"I loved her," said Jinadh. "I know it was foolish. But I did, and both of us always wanted children, so when she . . . What other chance would I have, in this country?"

"Sorry," said Cordelia, scrambling to keep up. "I still don't—you were knocking Cyril's sister?"

"Yes," he said.

"How old's the kid?"

"Eight," said Jinadh, and she saw his smile start, then die.

"*Eight?*" Pulan's voice climbed through an octave, incredulous. She put a hand over her mouth and rolled her eyes. Something that sounded suspiciously like a curse leaked out between her fingers.

"You been carrying on this whole time?" asked Cordelia. "And nobody knew?"

He shook his head. "It was always too . . . not dangerous, but . . . it was never a good idea. When she had the baby, she needed a story people would believe. If anyone entertained suspicions about us, it would be a strain upon her fiction."

"But you couldn't just . . . she ain't got a husband, does she?"

"No," said Jinadh. "But there is a taboo against widowers remarrying. Stephen could not be made legitimate, and I very likely would have been disowned. And I would have let Auntie do it, too." Here he sliced a sideways glance at Pulan, like a street magician flashing a card face-out between two fingers. "I did not care. But Lillian would not part with her career. She would never have gotten another posting if the story came out, she said."

Cordelia shook her head. DePauls. Seemed like they could blow a spark into a scorching fire, but they couldn't tend the coals.

"You . . . you . . ." Pulan's hands came down between the bowls and cups, rattling ceramic against mosaic tile, splashing coffee into saucers. Elbows stiff, she plunged her weight through her palms so the table legs squealed. "Did you never consider the risk to . . . all of us? The danger . . ." Here, Geddan apparently failed her, and her rage vented forth in Porashtu so liquid and blistering that it flowed together like a stream of molten lava.

Jinadh almost looked amused. To Cordelia, he said, "I made myself a liability: that is what she is saying. To the royal family, the government, the entire country. That I made it possible for a hostile foreign power to peer into the entrails of palace life: gossip and strategy and politics. It is true."

"And all for the sake of a woman who was not your wife!" Pulan spat it out; it was the first time Cordelia had seen her less than elegant. She looked not just furious but disgusted, as if Jinadh had squatted to take a shit on the terrace.

"My wife is *dead*." Jinadh was fighting now, Cordelia realized. There was an anger in him that struggled against hobbles, and it made him shake, but his voice didn't rise. Cordelia was amazed, and thought—for just a moment—of the few times she'd seen Ari really pinned. That kind of fury wasn't anything you wanted aimed your way. "I loved Lulita, and I respected her very much. But she has been gone for thirteen years and I am *still here*."

They faced each other across the table, across Pulan's bills and scripts and business correspondence, breathing hard.

It was Cordelia who finally said, surprised at her own meekness: "So they got your son."

They both startled at the sound of her voice, their breath catching in unison, and then they turned to stare at her.

"Why are you here, telling us?" she went on, wishing she had stood already, but unwilling to get up in the middle of what she had to say. "And what does it have to do with me?"

Jinadh nodded, once, then looked back at Pulan.

"Are you selling guns to Vasily Memmediv?" he asked.

Her plush lips pulled into a painted slash.

"This is not the time for pettiness," he said.

"He is the representative of a larger group."

Jinadh tucked his chin. "Lillian has been set up by a man in the embassy to catch him, because they know their traditional networks to be compromised. When Memmediv realized—"

"He offered her son," said Cordelia. "Your son. He's in Gedda."

The fact that she already knew seemed to knock him back for a moment. He sat, heavily, in one of the iron chairs at the table, and stared unseeing at a bowl of broken pistachio shells.

"She accepted his offer," said Pulan. "Which, I might add, he made without consulting me. Luckily, Ms. Lehane revealed herself in time to take up that snarl in the thread."

"I think I know some people who could help me get him," she said, which was just this side of a lie; she *hoped* she knew some people who she *hoped* could help her get him. "Catwalk folk, in Amberlough. If they ain't got drug in yet. It'll be tricky but it'll be worth it, if Pulan makes good on her offer. We grab him after school is out, and once the kid's across the border, I bring home a load of goods."

He looked like she'd stuck a boot hook in his gut and torn his liver out. Making a soft sound, he put his face into his hand.

"What," she said, "that ain't a song you want to hear?"

The breath he hauled in came out ragged. "She did not do it."

"Did not what?" Pulan looked ready to strike him.

"The offer. She did not think he could deliver, and took it straight back to her handler in the chancery. It was, she said, the only way that Memmediv would trust her: if she appeared to join his conspiracy."

Pulan sat opposite him, just as heavy, and swore. Cordelia didn't know the word, but she knew the tone. "And the photographs?"

"Lillian asked for my help. She knew Memmediv was here but she needed to prove it."

"But you gave them *my* picture," said Cordelia.

"Yes." He wiped his hand across his face, pushing damp curls back from his forehead. "She asked me to . . . investigate any new hires at the studio, especially if they were Mr. Makricosta's friends."

Cordelia made fists, and her left hand ached. "Somebody screeched on me." Well, it had only been a matter of time. Opal or Luca, one of them had been drug in, or both, and broken under the blows. She didn't blame them. If she had, the pain in her wrist would have been a harsh reproach. "So what are you doing here now? Come to say you're sorry?"

"Lillian did not believe Memmediv could fulfill his promise," said Jinadh. "She was not willing to take a risk."

"But you are." A little flame of admiration lit in Cordelia's chest, like a lighter, or a wavering match. "You're brave."

"Or reckless," said Pulan, but even she looked impressed.

"I am neither," said Jinadh. "I only want to see my son."

Pulan sent Djihar down to tell the cook it was four for dinner, rather than three, and they passed a tense hour or so on the terrace as they waited for the meal. Pulan called Daoud in to take notes. Cordelia was starting to get used to the idea this kid knew everything Pulan did, and kept track of the details better. It was a little strange, to trust her secrets to somebody she wasn't dealing with directly, but Pulan obviously thought he could keep his jaw clamped if it came to it, so she made her peace.

Cordelia quizzed Jinadh about details of Stephen's schedule, who usually picked him up from school at the end of term. "You know anything about how they handle this?"

But he had about as many details as she did. Broke her heart. And every time she said Lillian's name, or called Stephen Jinadh's son, she saw Pulan tense, or flinch, or give one of those skin shudders like a horse shedding flies. Jinadh noticed, too, and the longer he tried to pretend he didn't, the tighter his smile got, the more pinched the skin around his eyes.

She couldn't think of anything that bent her nails back like this did Pulan's. The woman had coolly discussed dynamiting office buildings, destroying railroad junctions, shipping tons of ammunition and explosives. Now her cousin had a kid, and it wasn't even *who* he had a kid *with* that seemed to really pin her, but the fact he had the kid at all, with somebody who wasn't his long-dead wife.

Djihar finally came to call them in to dinner. The dining room windows were thrown open onto the night, and a wind had picked up so that the tassels on the lanterns shivered. A silver tureen rested over a spirit lamp. Fragrant steam rose from the thick brown stew: tender goat, slippery sweet onions; cloves, cumin, coriander. A bowl of delicate white rice sat by, studded with nuts and golden raisins. Tall pitchers of water, filled with ice and slices of lime, sweated onto the tiled tabletop. Wine cooled in buckets between tall candles of lapis-colored wax.

Cordelia's stomach, tied in knots, wasn't sold on eating. Still she sat, and drank her wine.

As they were all settling in, a footman Cordelia didn't recognize—there were dozens of them around the place, running soiled clothes and sheets from bedrooms to the laundry, fetching food and misplaced pens and pairs of shoes—slipped into the dining room and put his hand to Djihar's elbow. The majordomo bent his head to listen to the boy. Cordelia scanned her companions, but no one else seemed to have noticed the minor interruption. Just her nerves, like catgut, plucked by every little thing.

Djihar cleared his throat.

«Yes?» It was one of the few Porashtu words Cordelia could reliably make out, and Pulan spoke it loudly, imperious.

Djihar said something, something, and then *Vasily Memmediv*.

Pulan nodded curtly and curled her hand in a "come here" sort of gesture. Djihar disappeared from the dining room. He returned with a telephone on a gold tray, and brought it to Pulan's elbow. He handled the trailing cord with expert dexterity.

"Excuse me," she said, dropping a sickly sweet smile on Cordelia, and then on Daoud. She still couldn't quite look at Jinadh, not straight on.

The telephone call was conducted in Geddan. Unfortunately, Pulan's end of it didn't exactly give her much to go on.

"Hello, sweet one," she said, wrapping the receiver in deliberate fingers tipped in flame-blue varnish. "I was not expecting a call. You caught me during dinner. No, no, it is no trouble."

Then, a long pause.

"Oh," she said. "Really? Who?"

And then, "Well, that is unfortunate. And what did you tell her?"

Jinadh looked up at that, fixing Pulan with a gaze so hard and sharp she must have felt it like the edge of a newly whetted knife, because she finally met his eyes. When she did, a strange sort of smile flared and died on her painted lips.

"Do not worry," she said. "I am confident we can smooth things over." Then, "No, not yet." And, a little tartly, "*Please*. Be calm."

Jinadh's fist closed on his napkin, bunching the fabric. Cordelia looked from him to Pulan, leery of making assumptions when she only had half of the information available.

"We will be in touch," said Pulan finally, and dropped the receiver back into its cradle. The impact jostled the ringer, producing a cheerful little bell tone.

"What was that?" asked Jinadh.

"That," said Pulan, dabbing at a curry stain on the tablecloth, "was a complication."

"If you do what you're proposing," said Cordelia, slum whine bursting into full feather, "I swear on my mother's two tits that Sofie rotten Keeler'll be the *least* of your troubles!"

"Ms. Hanes," said Pulan, who was sticking to the fake name either for safety or convenience, "please lower your voice, and be reasonable."

The argument had run through dessert, but Cordelia had ignored the black rice pudding and fried cheese in syrup, too pinned to do much besides shoot back chemically strong coffee. "I ain't gonna be reasonable about this," she said. "You leave that woman's wife with the Ospies, this is what happens. Or worse." She held up her broken hands. "And I'm guessing worse, since she's Chuli and goes in for pears."

Turning to Daoud, who was perched at her elbow, Pulan asked, "Can you understand anything she is saying?"

"The general idea, yes." He nibbled delicately at the lip of his wineglass, teeth clicking on the crystal. "Ms. Hanes, we have established a way of operating that is very . . . efficient. Pulan has years of experience in this type of matter. Decades. The cleanest solution is the one she has proposed."

"Those women helped me," said Cordelia. "We ain't killing one outright and leave the other to die."

"And anyway," said Jinadh, who had so far remained quiet, "if we kill her, the story may still run."

"That can be dealt with too," she said. "No newspaper in this country wants to cross me."

Speaking into his coffee cup, Jinadh said, "I can think of a few."

Cordelia was overwriting her first impression of Jinadh. Now that he wasn't trying to put one over on her, and please all parties with his grin, greasy as spilled fry-oil. Now, apparently, that he didn't care what any of them thought, as long as they could truly get his kid.

Lillian's kid.

"Hang on," she said.

All three of them turned to look at her, and she realized she'd dropped her volume, and her eyes, and generally stopped acting like a welterweight boxer taking on a bull-neck. Funny, how that made them pay attention, when all her shouting hadn't.

"Lillian," she said. "She's still singing for this Flagg character, right?" She angled her chin at Jinadh. "And he trusts her. So why don't we use that?"

She saw a muscle move in Jinadh's jaw; his nostrils flared with a breath. "I do not want to put her in any danger, if she has not agreed to the risk. Any more than I already have."

"All we need is a little information, at first." Now Cordelia did take some cheese. It left her fingers sticky, smelling like cheap perfume. Rosewater. "Something to keep Sofie quiet for a while.

We just gotta buy time. Once the deal is done, when the guns are in the right hands, none of us cares what the papers print about Memmediv. Right? And then the Ospies get embarrassed, maybe they release Mab." It was a big maybe, but that was better than the death of two good women on her conscience.

"What do you propose?" asked Pulan, eyes narrow as a cat squinting in the sun.

"So we all know that she never took Memmediv's offer seriously. But she doesn't know *we* know. Anything he tells her, she'll take back to Flagg thinking it's some big secret. So Memmediv drops this sack of crabs in her lap, asks her to fix it. Flagg ain't gonna want any of this in the papers."

"And?" Pulan skewered a piece of mango with her fork. She looked, suddenly, much more interested in what Cordelia had to say.

Cordelia shrugged. "We see what he gives up. Might be nothing, might be gold."

CHAPTER

THIRTEEN

Aristide couldn't face Hadhariti, not before he worked out some kind of strategy. The thought made him ill—or perhaps it was that last martini—but he wasn't sure that he should stay much longer with Pulan if she was . . . not just dabbling, but well and truly sunk in the murky waters of international intrigue.

Reza's was not the worst of the cheap bars catering to the extras, roustabouts, and general dogsbodies who haunted the backlots of Charaplati, but by last call it still turned into a midden. Aristide was no exception: He couldn't have driven himself to his hotel even if he had one. An obliging cabbie got him to the Pukkari, where a capable bellhop got him to a suite. He didn't remember much of it, and imagined she might have had to use a luggage trolley.

He'd gotten very good at gauging his hangovers; this nausea would clear up shortly and then it would be a headache and the spins. Those were easily dealt with, if unpleasant, and a sip of something to settle it all wouldn't hurt, either.

He needed to pick the car up from Charaplati. And then he needed to decide where to go. Back to Hadhariti? He was due to start production on *Galatar ul Walibi* in a few days' time. Inaz, in another career shift, was playing the sorceress villain. She had taken a small holiday in Liso but would be back in Porachis today or tomorrow; he should be at the studio to meet her. They'd do some work on the lot in the next week or so, and the rest of the thing on location in Tzieta.

But returning to Pulan's estate meant planting himself in the center of whatever scheme was going on there. And now that he had raised his eyes long enough to notice that everyone around him had their hands in several different pies up to the elbows, he couldn't pretend it wasn't happening.

Everything was clearer now, the edges and subtleties defined; as if cataracts had been cut from his eyes. He'd rendered himself blind through force of will, and hadn't realized how the charade exhausted him until he began to see again.

Perhaps a little independent investigation was required. If he could find out what sort of risks Pulan had exposed him to, perhaps he could mitigate them, or at least craft more accurate defenses.

Pulan and Daoud might be shut up as tight as cockles, but they were miles down the coast. Aristide was here, in Anadh, where Hadhariti Studios kept offices on the Silver Street. Very close, incidentally, to where Aristide had parked his car.

It was one thing, of course, to show up unexpected to his own office. It was quite another to break into Pulan's. Hadhariti's suite in the Olukarta Building was quiet at the weekend, but there were still people working. Yasullah, buried under a pile of scripts, barely raised her head when he walked by. Oomin was on a call, and whoever was on the other end of the line was so angry Aristide could hear the reverberations of their voice even in the hallway. Apparently desperate for any kind of distraction, Oomin caught sight of him and gave a sad little wave. But she was tied to her telephone, so he was safe from any interference there.

Still, out of habit he unlocked his own door first, and settled into the comfortable embrace of his linen-upholstered chair. He'd been very picky about it—uprooting his life and settling in a new country hadn't performed any miracles on his stubborn spine—and now took a minute to enjoy this one small thing he had done right.

And in that minute, he heard the distant chime of the lift. He didn't sit up straighter in his chair, but he sharpened his attention to the sounds in the corridor. Footsteps, and then a man's voice: deep, good-natured, flirting a little with Yasullah.

«Your Highness,» she said, then scolded him and laughed.

Asiyah Sekibou walked straight past Aristide's open office door, and went to Pulan's. Holding his breath, Aristide listened to the key turn in the lock, and the faint sigh of well-oiled hinges. Then the door shut, and the hall fell quiet again except for the murmur of Oomin's soothing telephone voice.

If only Aristide had a key! If only he could so casually walk into the office he wanted to search. Then again, why did Asiyah have such a thing, and the confidence to use it?

A few words from Pulan—*Prince Sekibou will be by this afternoon to pick up some things from my office*—and Aristide could see the thing accomplished easily, unsuspiciously. And nobody need know that whatever he was picking up might have nothing to do with the pictures at all.

Perhaps, then, Aristide didn't need to go through Pulan's papers on his own. Perhaps Asiyah was plucking exactly what he needed from the stack, and it would just be a matter of charm and a little social lubricant to ease it out. These skills, at least, he had not let grow rusty.

The door to Pulan's office opened and shut again, and Asiyah's footsteps and whistling filled the corridor.

«Your Highness,» he said, mocking Yasullah's pouty tone.

Asiyah started like he'd stepped on something sharp, and paused in the doorway. Once he'd shaken off his shock he grinned and leaned on the frame. «Aristide! Inaz is already headed to Hadhariti. If she gets there before you she'll never let you forget it.»

«I had a little work to do,» he said.

«I will let you get back to it, then.» Asiyah made to leave, but Aristide flapped one hand and took off his sunglasses, which up to this point he had not removed.

«No, no,» he said. «I am finished, almost. Do you want to have a drink with me? Reza's is quiet, at this time.»

Asiyah cocked his head, not quite succeeding in masking his quizzical expression with an air of consideration. «All right. I have an hour or so.»

Aristide gauged the remnants of his own hangover, calculated how many cocktails it would take for Asiyah to grow indiscreet, and thought he might last at least that long.

Three drinks in, they had exhausted their small talk and industry gossip. Aristide had bought the first round and the most recent, which meant he'd had three tonics, only one of them with gin, while Asiyah thought he'd had three whiskey cocktails but had really drunk one single bracketed by double pours.

It was time to make a move.

He slipped his cigarette case from his pocket—ugly scuff on the leather; this was the problem with white, but it looked so *chic*—and flipped it open.

"Straight?" he asked Asiyah, offering.

"Thank you, yes." He deliberated a moment in choosing, and fumbled the straight as he withdrew it from the band. Perfect.

Aristide lit Asiyah's cigarette with a match from a book he'd taken from the bar—his blue enamel lighter had disappeared at some point during the previous night, probably into the bellhop's pocket, along with the generous tip she had taken for herself—then put the flame to his own.

In the silence as they both drew, Aristide heard someone open the piano lid, and the first jangling notes of some popular song he wouldn't know. Asiyah hummed a few bars, then lost the thread and took another drag on his borrowed cigarette.

«So,» said Aristide, gingerly stepping back into Porashtu. When Asiyah spoke, Aristide didn't want him to think too hard, which if he was forced into his third language, he certainly would. «Inaz is going to Pulan's house. There are more things at Hadhariti than pictures, these days. She is a part of that, or no?»

Asiyah exhaled a thin stream of smoke, considering the curls and tendrils as they rose toward the ceiling. When he'd blown it all out, he took a clean breath and said, «Pulan told me you didn't know about it.»

«I am not an idiot.» Aristide tilted his glass so the ice clinked. «Princes and picture stars? Fine. But Geddans? No.»

«There is a Geddan sitting right here.»

«I do not work with the . . . the . . . » He flicked his fingers in frustration and said "embassy," in Geddan. «I am not so dangerous, for her.»

«And you would not believe me,» asked Asiyah, «if I told you Memmediv was a fan?»

At that, Aristide only smiled, and ashed his cigarette. Too bemused to convey his sentiments properly in Porashtu, he said, "She didn't invite Lillian for the papers, did she?"

Asiyah snorted; smoke came from his nostrils. «Heavens' eyes, of course she did. Though she only had the idea after I asked to meet Memmediv in person.»

«The idea was yours?»

«I like to see a person's face before the deal is done,» said Asiyah. «Maybe that's old-fashioned, but . . . » His straight had burned down to his fingers, and he paused to bury the smoldering butt in the ashtray. «I had heard some things about him, and I wanted to look into his eyes.»

«So you trust him now?»

«Hell's breath, no. He's a tree viper, hanging over all our heads. The trick will be to do a deal before he decides someone else is better worth his time. Do you know how many people he has—»

Aristide didn't catch the word, and shook his head. Asiyah took it for an answer to his question, and went on.

«I had the whole story from an old FOCIS agent, who ended up in Liso after the Ospies took over and did a bit of counter-intelligence work for us.»

«Was it Merrilee Cross?» Aristide asked. He'd heard from her once—a letter, sent shortly after his name began to crop up in Porachin papers, feeling him out on renewing their trade in tar. He'd responded, curtly, that she had the wrong address, and never received another note on that subject or any other.

«No,» said Asiyah. «Though I do know her. Talking about tree vipers, that woman is a dragon among snakes. You have met?»

«We worked together, in Gedda.»

«Ah well, she's causing some problems for the port authority in Mbarada. But it's not my . . . oh, in Porashtu, not my peas to shell? Is that what they say?»

Aristide shrugged. «But Memmediv. You heard bad things?»

«Just that he is as likely to shake your hand as stab you; whichever will get him what he wants. No . . . » Asiyah thumped his chest with his hand. «No *center*. For instance—oh, this is *delicious*—» He had begun, ever so slightly, to slur his words, and Aristide had to work hard to follow him. «The man who told me all this, Memmediv had blown his cover, gotten him arrested, nearly killed. Knew he'd done it, too; proud of his work. And just last week, after Pulan's premiere, you know what happens? This fellow's sister tries to drop down on him.»

Aristide, who had been just raising the last of his cigarette to his lips, felt it beginning to burn the skin of his knuckles. Still, he did not move. "His sister," he repeated. The pain of the ember against his flesh was distant, some other man's petty problem.

"Lillian DePaul, yes." Asiyah's eyebrows furrowed, and he fell back into Porashtu. «Memmediv thought it was funny. She was trying to . . . we call it an ant trap? I think the word in Geddan is . . . » He snapped his fingers and said, "Ah, *honeypot*." Then, «Something sweet, you know, to draw the vermin close. She was not very good at it. He thought it was hysterical, and turned it right around on her.»

«You knew Lillian's brother?»

«He never gave us his real name; called himself Paul Darling. But we figured it out eventually, and anyway, they look like twins.»

What Aristide should be gathering from this information was that Asiyah was more deeply enmeshed in the Lisoan intelligence operation than he had heretofore realized. Instead, he had forgotten to breathe for so long that his last drag of tobacco was beginning to ache in his lungs. He let it out and asked, voice just on the verge of shaking, "And where is he now?"

Asiyah shrugged, then glanced down. "Your straight, Aristide, it's—"

Aristide cast the butt of his cigarette thoughtlessly into the ashtray, scattering sparks. "DePaul," he snapped, too loud. "Where is he *now*?"

"No—I do not know. I—" He shook his head, as if the Geddan words were distracting flies. «We think he was captured, or maybe killed, running an operation on the border about a year ago. Why? Did you have ties to him as well?»

Aristide could feel the burnt flesh on his fingers, now, stinging and insistent and painful out of proportion to its size.

"Just one." He struck his knees, getting up from the table. He didn't even remember deciding to stand.

"Aristide?" Asiyah half-rose, but Aristide waved him away.

"No," he said. "No, it's fine. I simply . . . please excuse me."

And then he was out the door, blinking in the sunlight, and suddenly in the seat of his car. He was less capable of driving now than he had been the night before, yet he punched the starter, and laid down a layer of rubber squealing away from the curb.

CHAPTER

FOURTEEN

There was a breath of rain-smell on the air: the scorching end of the dry season about to break, perhaps, or perhaps just teasing. Lillian savored a sneaky cigarette on the balcony of the Agaz, listening to the murmur of diners around her, the bubbling of hookahs and drunken laughter.

She had bought the pack of straights at a tobacconist on the way here. The craving had struck her as she passed the shop, and she'd put it down swiftly, as she did most cravings that might get her into trouble.

But then, at the end of the block, she'd had to pause at a streetlight. And there, waiting for traffic, she thought, *Oh after all, why not?* She was meeting Memmediv for yet another faux-clandestine exchange, at his behest. He wouldn't give three bits if she smoked.

The cigarettes were not particularly good. Not as good as she remembered cigarettes being, when she smoked more regularly. And that would have been . . . oh, before Stephen was born. But it was less the quality of the tobacco that made her shiver with delight, and more the transgression.

And that, she knew, was dangerous. She'd been treading an edge for some time now. She had thought, after her last tear-up with Jinadh, that she was back on steady ground. But she found herself wondering where he'd gone afterward, what he planned to do. Part of this was worry—surely he wouldn't scratch her, would he? Not after what she'd said?—but part of it was just wistfulness. She felt a little like she had . . . Lady's name, was it almost ten years ago now? When she'd look at the cut of a man's tunic and think, *That would look good on Jinadh.* When the play of sun on a fountain made her wish Jinadh was there to admire it with her. When she used to rearrange the puzzle pieces of their affair and hope that she could make it all fit neatly, somehow. Make it *work.*

She hadn't found a way in time. Jinadh had been ready to leave for Gedda the day she told him she was pregnant. He'd been, quite honestly, ready to leave long before that. She sometimes wondered if it wasn't her foreignness, the fact that she came from a place that might not strangle him, that had attracted him to her.

But, at the time, Porachis hadn't strangled *her.* She had loved her job; she remembered what that felt like, and almost wished she didn't. She had hoped, perhaps, to move up the ladder, maybe to an ambassadorship someday, in Porachis—she had plenty of experience—or in her father's old post in the Niori peninsula. If she was clever, and skilled, because she didn't believe in luck, maybe she would be assigned to Cestina, or Ibet. One of the plum postings.

At the time, the thought of *leaving* made her heart leap to her throat; the thought of partnership, of interdependence. She was not used to any check upon her actions, to seeking a second opinion.

Deep down, in dark moments, she sneered at her own cowardice; Jinadh had been safe, as a lover, because their affair could never end in commitment. Could never strangle *her*.

So instead of eloping, she plucked a convenient father from the rumor mill: a foreign affairs correspondent of whom she'd been fond, but who had always hoped for more from her than she quite wanted to give. She'd let him have it finally, just once, before she started to show.

He was killed in a pipe bomb explosion in a Dastyan café a few months later. She hated to be grateful for that, but it did make things simple.

Stones, if she kept in this line of thought much longer she was going to need a drink to go with the straight. Luckily, when she pushed away from the balcony railing, she spotted Memmediv coming through the dining room and toward the double doors, a glass in each hand.

"A gin gimlet," he said. "I remembered, from the premiere. Or if you'd prefer whiskey . . ." He tilted the other glass.

"I'll take the gin," she said. "Thank you."

Memmediv handed the glass over, then freed his own cigarette case from his pocket. He deftly maneuvered it open one-handed, pushed a straight free with his thumb, and caught it in his lips. "Light?" he asked, around the paper.

Lillian leaned in to touch the ember of her cigarette to the end of his. He took a deep breath, and then let it out in an uneven shudder. The raggedness of his breath was the only sign she had of an upset before he said, low-voiced, "We have a serious problem."

She tried to look nervous instead of relieved. "Sit down at least. Standing here isn't making us inconspicuous."

They took a pair of tall chairs in the corner by the railing, so that the roar of the lower cataract cloaked their conversation. Mist settled on the fine hairs of Lillian's arms and cooled the back of her neck. It glistened on the black and silver of Memmediv's hair, beading on his pomade. Now that she was facing him head-on, and he had shed the last of the mask he'd worn in, she could see the worry lines between his strong, dark brows.

"All right," she said, putting out the butt of her straight in the ashtray. "What kind of problem?"

"It is so prosaic, I am almost ashamed to admit. But, blackmail."

"Well." Lillian lifted her glass. Before she drank, she spoke to the slice of lime: "There's something to be said for tradition, I suppose."

"There's a woman we have in custody," he said, unsmiling. "Mab Cattayim. Here, in Porachis. There might have been questions about jurisdiction, but it was done very quietly."

"What? That's madness." Let him think this was fresh news to her.

"I was completely ignorant of all of this. Flagg has frozen me out, it seems. But not you. He trusts you."

"You want me to do something for you."

"I *need* you to," he said. He finally did drink his whiskey, in one swallow. "Cattayim has a wife, in Berer. Sofie. I don't know how she found my name, but she did, and now she's leaning on me."

"And what did she have to say?"

"She wanted to know what had happened to Mab. Wanted her freed, really. And she knew about Satri."

"How much?" asked Lillian, who still didn't have details about the arms deal, or all of its participants, and sensed an opening.

"Enough to ruin everything," he said, dashing her hopes. "She told me the story was with a friend of hers, a journalist. If I don't help her, the whole country finds out the CIS has arrested a Geddan political refugee outside of their jurisdiction. Chaos in the chancery. Close scrutiny from here and from home. Scrutiny my current position will not bear. I will lose all of my progress. I'll probably be recalled, with Flagg, and who knows what you'll be left with. A press nightmare. Certainly not your son."

"Which paper?"

"The *Call*," he said. "Out of Berer."

"Nobody reads that rag," said Lillian, with false bravado. As if bravery could make it true.

"Somebody will," he said. "A story like that will break in the bigger papers eventually, and make it to the wireless. You know it will."

Flagg was not going to be pleased.

"Find me something," said Memmediv. "Anything Flagg will tell you. I just need a scrap or two, to keep her happy until things wrap up with Satri. Then I couldn't care less what the papers print. Buy me some time."

"All right," she said. "I'll see what I can do."

"This," said Flagg, "is not ideal."

Lillian pulled minutely on the hem of her skirt, fussing with it in order to avoid looking at Flagg's bloodless face. "No. It certainly isn't."

"And he has no idea how she connected him with this government's activities on foreign soil?"

"Or, he knows and he isn't saying." The thought had entered her mind in the dead hours she should have spent sleeping, and had instead spent sitting in the garden, hoping for a breeze and divine inspiration.

"Do you have someone in mind?" he asked, too sharply.

She sighed. "No. I'm only chasing a runaway spool, which I can hardly afford to do." She looked pointedly at the clock on Flagg's desk. "This entire assignment is eating up time and resources I should be spending making sure Gedda doesn't look like a midden heap in front of hostile foreign powers. *Especially* if something like this is ripening on the branch and ready to fall."

"It can't," he said flatly. "This story *cannot* break. Do you understand?"

"Well then you'd better release this woman from wherever you've got her locked away. Unless you've already killed her?" She hadn't meant to say it with such pique, but it was too late to haul the words back in.

Flagg's lip curled. "Out of the question. She'll go back to Gedda to stand trial. She and Sofie Keeler are both here illegally. Porachis would have deported them years ago if they had merited a second glance."

"They'll merit a second glance now," she said. "Look at Makricosta. The worse we treat people, the softer they land in our enemies' beds."

"Not if this is handled correctly," said Flagg.

"And how *do* you plan to handle Keeler, if you aren't acceding to her demands?" Flagg had never once called Sofie "Cattayim," and she didn't know if he would acknowledge the name, or even realize which of the women she was referring to.

"*I'm* not handling her," said Flagg. "You are. You're the press attaché; she's talking to the papers."

"With all due respect." It did not *sound* as though she had any respect left in her. When had she grown so *irritated* with him? So vexed that it almost drowned her fear? "This is clearly a matter for your department. You got yourselves into it. What am I meant to do to get you out?"

"Kill the story," Flagg snarled. "I don't care how, but *kill it*. I can't afford something like this right now."

That was new: Flagg admitting fallibility. It might have scared her, once. Now, she saw soft belly where his armor had come askew and wondered if a pike might strike that spot; if the dragon could perhaps be slain. If there was some way out of this, after all.

"Counselor," she said, "does home know that you've taken Cattayim into custody?"

A tic in his lower eyelid made it twitch: once, twice. "Of course not. It is completely against policy."

She almost didn't catch the irony. "I see. This is white work." That was what her brother had done—the things between the lines, the orders never written down. "If it comes out, it's your neck in the noose. And if they haul you out of the chancery, your replacement will have a nasty surprise waiting for him, with Memmediv's rotten networks and an arms deal percolating under his nose, ready to explode the Tzietan armistice. Nobody will thank you for that."

"Astute." His sourness verged on hydrochloric.

"You thought you had it all under your control," she said, "but now it's slipping."

"It will not slip," he said, diction clipped. "Not if you do as you're told. And you will, or I will personally guarantee that your son forgets he ever had a mother."

The creeping frost of fear killed her excitement.

"You couldn't," she said. "This story would destroy your career, your credibility."

Flagg blinked, once, lizard-like. "I said *personally*. I do not require the government's backing to make good on my threats."

This was new, too, and far more worrying. Lillian had counted on Flagg's promises because he valued order over chaos. He kept his pens in neat rows, his blotter at a right angle to his desk. He so valued order that he had gotten himself into this awful snarl to avoid any appearance of a mistake or misstep, any evidence of broken rules.

He was not a man from whom she would have expected that particular threat. He was becoming unpredictable, which meant that she could no longer rely on him to fulfill his end of their bargain. Flagg might not give her Stephen, no matter what she did.

But Memmediv claimed he could.

Now it was merely a matter of playing the odds.

"I'll do whatever you want me to, Counselor." She stood, knees threatening to give way as though she bore a great weight. "Just tell me what that is."

He considered her for a moment with narrow, silver nitrate eyes. This time, his regard did freeze her. Did he know what she was considering?

Then he made a small sound with his tongue against the backs of his teeth and said, "You tell good stories, and you know the papers. Talk to her, make her think we're considering. Find out who she gave the story to, at the *Call*, and give them something else. Discredit her. I don't care what you tell them; just make it nasty. You know what journalists like." The ghost of a leer hung about the angle of his eyebrow and the slight sideways pull of his lips.

It haunted her throughout her catch-up meeting with her staff, who had reams of dispatches, piles of newspapers, and shorthand notes on the week's wireless broadcasts. The delegations in Dastya were on their third draft of a peace resolution; each side had walked out at least once. She didn't envy the mediators. A family on the Lisoan border had been murdered in something the north painted as a blood feud and the south insisted was an act of republican aggression. Two children had died of dehydration in the Chuli internment camps. Gedda did not look good right now on the global stage.

Lillian had let things slip a little too far, playing these games, and now found she could hardly keep up. It was tempting not to try. Why struggle to put a good face on such hideousness? Especially given a stubborn bit of her brain insisted on replaying the conversation with Flagg, the flash of vulnerability he had shown her, the possibilities it opened up.

The fact that she was even considering them terrified her.

When the undersecretaries and assistants cleared out, she reached two fingers into the inner pocket of her jacket and felt the softening edges of Stephen's letter. The paper, carried against the curve of her breast where she had held him when he was small, had lost its crisp folds and starchy stiffness and become more like cloth. A little like the ribbons Wind Worshippers carried pinned beneath their clothes. She certainly reached to it for comfort as often.

This time, though, she reached to it for courage.

Cordelia had heard the name Inaz Iligba bandied around, and seen a few of the posters framed in Pulan's office. But the artists had softened her face, given her a halo of light she didn't carry with her off the printed page or the screen.

She came by speedboat around dinnertime the day after Jinadh arrived, sweeping onto the terrace in a low-cut jumpsuit of palm-patterned satin, waving a cigarette in a long jet holder. She put it out when she saw the lit hookah, and held her hand out for a hose.

Under a jaunty captain's hat—clever piece of costuming—her hair was tied into braids along her scalp. They were done up so tight they seemed to draw the skin of her face up, turn it haughty. Or, haughtier than it already was. Her eyebrows were plucked into razor arches above the dark mirrors of her sunglasses, and her lips—painted persimmon orange—seemed caught in a secret, side-heavy smirk.

She reminded Cordelia, strangely, of working on Temple Street. This was someone who hadn't been born beautiful but had learned it to make tips. She wouldn't be surprised to hear this peach had earned a living onstage before she went into the pictures, probably out of her clothes.

"Inaz," said Pulan, blasting center-stage delight, and then went on in Porashtu. Inaz laughed and kissed her cheek, then did the same for Jinadh, leaning against the balustrade. Cordelia thought they might have met before, from the familiar way she touched his arm, the falsely modest smile Jinadh conjured up. It made sense: an actress, a writer for the gossip rags.

So she was the only stranger here.

"I have just told Ms. Iligba you will be choreographing her dances," said Pulan, passing the hookah hose from Inaz to Cordelia.

"I see at least one problem here," said Cordelia, plugging the pipe with her thumb. "I don't speak Porashtu, and it don't look like she speaks Geddan."

"Jinadh can translate for you," Pulan said. "It will get him out from under my shoe."

Jinadh started, then shot Pulan a nasty little smile that flirted with a sneer. Inaz patted his rear end, kissed his cheek again, and said something that made him turn and simper.

Cordelia felt a pang of kinship. She'd turned that look on folk she had to please, who'd put their hands where she'd rather they hadn't.

Pulan had a whole setup down the hill from her house: soundstages and recording rooms and anything you might need for shooting a picture. A whole passel of people, too—camerafolk and makeup artists and everything in between that walked on two legs and four. Despite her supposed job as assistant choreographer, Cordelia hadn't been down until now.

The company was running something the morning she started with Inaz—she heard the music in the first studio she passed, the big one, and recognized it. Her feet went into the steps before she realized she'd auditioned on this number. What would that peach Chitra say if she poked her head in now? But she'd had enough trouble in the last day to fill her for a lifetime, and didn't feel a powerful urge to find out.

Jinadh and Inaz had arrived before her and thrown the windows in the smaller dance studio open to catch the sea breeze. Gulls cried, barely audible over the whirring of fans.

"All right," Cordelia said, surprising them both as she entered. "Let's turn this heap of swineshit Pulan calls a picture into something passable."

Jinadh turned to Inaz and said something in Porashtu, presumably repeating what Cordelia had just said. Inaz snorted, not particularly elegant, and replied.

Jinadh looked taken aback, and didn't translate. Inaz rapped his arm with her knuckles and said something sharp.

"She says 'It doesn't have to be good, it only has to get us into Tzieta.'" He cocked his head at Cordelia. "You need to get to Tzieta?"

She wondered how much he knew about the picture, and its true purpose. "It'll be better than this steam bath, by a mile."

Inaz bent forward in her chair, leaning to adjust the laces of her dance slippers. Her skimpy sports clothes showed surprisingly muscular legs, but then, hadn't Cordelia wondered if she'd ever been onstage? This might not be too painful, if the lady could actually move.

"She know what she's doing?" Cordelia asked Jinadh. He repeated it to Inaz, who laughed: a loud, single bark. She stretched out a hand, asked something, and Jinadh answered by producing a cigarette case and a sleek gold lighter inlaid with tiger's eye. He sparked it to Inaz's straight, and she inhaled, then said something he translated to Cordelia with a wry tone that perfectly matched Inaz's harsh laughter.

"She's been dancing since she was fourteen," he said, "and the only difference now is nobody throws coins at her or tries to tug off her panties."

"She ever try spirit gum?" Cordelia didn't really mean for Jinadh to relate this, but he did, and this time Inaz's laugh was less caustic. When she looked up from adjusting her shoes, there was a new light in her eyes: maybe respect, maybe just fellowship.

"You are a real dancer," Jinadh translated.

"What did you think I was rotten doing here?" She was talking straight to Inaz now.

"You're not one of—" Jinadh faltered, then asked Inaz a question. She opened her hands, palms up, and repeated whatever she'd told him.

"She says, 'You're not one of Memmediv's people?'" He shook his head. "I didn't know she was . . ." He looked at her, eyes narrow, and then turned back to Cordelia. "I didn't know Inaz was mixed up in it."

"Well, we're just all learning loads about each other this week, aren't we? Want to hear about my indigestion next?" Cordelia bent into a hamstring stretch, felt the muscles on either side of her spine pull tight straight to the base of her skull. "If she means a Tatien scrapper," she told her kneecaps, "you can tell her that ain't my bag. I got other birds to pluck." Queen's cunt, she hadn't so much as tapped her feet since that ill-fated audition. And before that . . .

It had been a while. This would be some kind of toil. "How's she know about all this, anyhow? She in on the deal somehow?"

He turned back and asked her a question, which she answered with a pout and a heap of false modesty. Then, just as Jinadh had started to smile, she flung him another sentence with enough sass that Cordelia felt it on her skin like the sting of a wet rag snapped at speed. "What was *that*?"

Jinadh shook his head, but Cordelia leveled a glare at him. "She says she is charming and pretty and only a film star; she is invited to all the parties and people tell her stories that they shouldn't. Asiyah often finds her useful." He raised an eyebrow and added, "She says, also, I must know all about that sort of thing."

"She's in on it all right." Cordelia said. "She's some kind of fox. She know about the kid, too? Pulan tell her that?"

His eyes slid toward Inaz, but he said, "I think not. Pulan would not want to be embarrassed." He took out a cigarette for himself, and lit it in the height of a sulk.

Cordelia went to flip through the records on the shelf by the turntable. Pulan had said there was a demo of the picture waiting for them, but all the labels were handwritten in Porashtu. Inaz rose from her chair, stretched, and sashayed to Cordelia's side. She plucked a record from the shelf and slipped it from its sleeve. Looking straight at Cordelia, as if she were saying something comprehensible, carrying on a regular chat, she rattled off an airy string of words and dropped the record onto the spindle.

"She wants to know," Jinadh said, "how under heaven they are supposed to get guns to *your* people, so deep in Ospie territory."

"Holy stones, word travels fast around here." She flexed her foot against the wall, stretching one screeching calf muscle.

Inaz's smile made a pretty orange curve, lips full and lush, pink at the inner edges where the lipstick wouldn't adhere to spit-slick skin. She said something else, still smiling. Cordelia heard Caleb Acherby's name, in the midst of it.

Jinadh took a moment too long, and Inaz's smile collapsed into a sneer. She rattled out an order, and a shadow of apprehension scudded across his face. "She says Asiyah will be happy to give you whatever you need. The more slop in Acherby's bowl, the better. But she wants to know, also, what your . . . ah, *Orodha*? Your strays? What they hope to do with it all."

"Blow things up," said Cordelia. "What in damnation does she think we're going to do with that much dynamite?"

As Jinadh translated, Inaz set the needle onto the record. Her smile tightened, as if she could tell Cordelia's answer from her tone. Her reply was light, precise, in the same way a very sharp pin or a piece of glass might be.

"A few piddling bombs?" Jinadh's translation was business-like. "That is all? What do you hope that will accomplish?" He watched Cordelia over his cigarette, brows drawn together and eyes bright with worried concentration.

The first few bars of the opening number started to play: chimes and drums under a maddening nasal reed.

"Well, right now," said Cordelia, cranking the valve shut on her steaming head of anger, bottling it up for later, "I aim to come up with some dance routines."

FIFTEEN

Lillian did not have the time to go up to Berer. And yet, she found herself on a train, working through a series of reports from her deputies on the increasing number of anti-Ospie columns in Porachis's conservative media, and the royalist Lisoan sentiment cropping up to accompany them. There were several separate documents gauging the bellicosity of various journalists, talking heads, politicians, and publications, all flagged with analysis and notes on a suggested response.

The impression she got, once she had collated the reports, was not encouraging. As if she had expected anything different.

It was a longer ride from Myazbah to Berer than to Anadh, but because she had work to do, it went quickly. And, because she traveled alone this time, without Memmediv's presence putting her on edge, or the looming onus of an unpleasant duty, she breathed a little more easily.

The meeting, arranged via discreet but official channels, was not nearly as cloak-and-dagger as any she had recently been a party to. Sofie Cattayim met her in the restaurant of her hotel, wearing a Geddan-style dress that Lillian suspected might be the only nice thing she owned. It was completely incorrect for the season and locale: black rayon unsuitable for Porachin heat. But it was cut very well, which made Lillian suspect it might have been something she owned when she was still a Keeler. Her shoes wanted a shine, but she had wound her hair into a neat chignon and wore small pearls in her ears that were likely also left over from better days. She had not put on any paint: her naked lips stood out pale in her suntanned face, stippled at the edges with freckles.

Lillian rose as she approached, and offered a hand. Sofie's skin was burned several shades darker than hers, and though her nails had been scrubbed clean they had not been manicured, whereas Lillian's were filed smooth and buffed so they shone like glass. Lillian's fingers were bare. Sofie wore a wedding band, in the old style: a puzzle ring. One of the pieces had been removed, so that its pattern set unevenly below her knuckle, missing the whorls from one-third of its design.

They shook, then broke apart. Sofie settled into her chair with only the faintest air of self-consciousness, and took up the glass of water by her plate. She held the crystal without reverence.

She had been wealthy, once. Flagg had given Lillian a dossier to read. But she had fallen in love with the wrong people, at the worst time, and not had the sense to pinch the wick before the flame caught.

One sympathized. One felt slightly superior. But perhaps one also quashed the smallest twinge of envy.

"It's very nice to meet you," said Lillian. "I hope you had an easy time getting here."

Sofie's smile wasn't exactly sad. Nor was it genuine. It was a smile that wanted very much to be some other expression entirely: one that communicated disdain and disappointment born of misery, and fear. "You know," she said, "the omnibus doesn't stop anywhere *near* this neighborhood. But I suppose that wasn't a consideration, for you."

"I do apologize."

Sofie shrugged, and took another sip of water. "I wouldn't have considered it either, once."

"They tell me the lamb shank is excellent." Lillian raised her menu. "But I've just noticed there's green fish curry, too, and that kind of thing is always so much better on the coast."

Sofie's eyes flickered down toward the embossed card laid across her plate, then back up to Lillian. "I really didn't come to—"

"Order something," said Lillian. "Please." Because she knew Sofie couldn't afford to eat here, and she was angling for a little goodwill. Or at least plates on the table; it would look odd to spend any amount of time in the restaurant without eating.

So when the waitress came and nodded at Lillian's request for green fish curry, *hot,* Sofie asked for seared squab and okra. She managed it crisply, as though she had never considered going hungry, and then bestowed a tight, closed-lip smile on Lillian when she translated for the waitress.

"Now," said Lillian, when the wine and olives had arrived. "This story you're telling, the one about your wife—"

Ice clattered in Sofie's glass—her grip had tightened, changing the angle of the water. "A story. Is that what you're calling it?"

"May I ask, how did you come to contact Mr. Memmediv? And why him?"

"It is my understanding," said Sofie, carefully placing her glass back onto the table, in the wet ring it had left on the linen, "that he works within a part of the embassy which is involved in . . ."

Here, she turned the crystal with her fingertips, a precise ninety degrees. "Extralegal activities."

"As the press attaché," said Lillian, channeling the irony Flagg had turned on her the day before, "I must insist that none of the embassy's activities are extralegal."

In the ice bucket, the wine bottle shifted.

"And off the record?" asked Sofie, who had caught her sarcasm a moment late.

"Off the record," said Lillian, "whoever told you Memmediv could free your wife was incorrect."

What little color there was in Sofie's peaked face drained away below the collar of her dress. She opened her mouth, but the waitress arrived with their plates before she could speak and set down first one charger, then the other. She poured the wine as well, which neither woman had touched.

It took Sofie a moment to recover from the interruption, and when she did, she had collapsed from within. She looked hollowed out, without an armature to hold her head up or keep her shoulders back.

"I could tell you," said Sofie, "that I will only say this once. But that would be a lie. I will say it as many times as I need to, until I am hoarse. *Please*. If you know *anything*. Mab and I—we have a child. A daughter. She asks me every morning when her mumma is coming back. She has already lost her father. I cannot bear for her to lose another one of us."

Lillian laced her fingers together over her plate and put the smooth tips of her manicured first fingers to her lips. "And you aren't afraid that leaking this story will lead to retribution? Leave your daughter an orphan, or a ward of the Porachin state?"

In truth, if both the Cattayims were here illegally, even the success of Sofie's plan might lead to deportation for the parents, and a foster family or orphanage for the girl. Or laurels and residency. Maybe citizenship. It would depend on how useful the queen thought they could be.

But Sofie was already shaking her head. "I swore to spin Mab into my life, like plies in a woolen thread. Those vows are not just breath, Ms. DePaul. Not to her, and not to me. I'll do whatever I must to keep our family together."

Lillian did not bring up the broken puzzle ring, the absent husband. She wasn't trying to talk Sofie *out* of this scheme, though personally she thought it ill-conceived. It only had to serve *her* needs.

She hated herself for thinking that, but self-hatred was an emotion with which she had long ago made peace. She was glad she could still feel it.

She wished she didn't have cause to feel it quite so often.

"What should I do?" asked Sofie, face turned down toward her squab. Hope and anger had both fled from her face, leaving her limp. She didn't sound like she expected an answer, and she certainly looked surprised when Lillian gave her one.

"Ask me who can." Lillian's fork hovered over her curry. It was true that the dish was one of her favorites, and that seafood was never quite as fresh in Myazbah as it was on the coast. But her appetite had retreated in the face of the step she was about to take.

"What?"

Lillian set the fork beside her plate. "I said, ask me who *can* free your wife."

Sofie looked like she was waiting for rocks to fall, or a trap to close its teeth on her leg. "All right. Who?"

Once she said it, she was committed. Her heart beat hard beneath her lapel, under the folded paper of Stephen's last letter.

"Me," she said. "Or, I'm nearly certain that I can. But I need your friend at the *Call* to hold off on the story for a little while."

"How long, exactly?"

"A week," she said, "maybe two." Term would be over then. If Memmediv could do what he promised—get her Stephen—it wouldn't matter what happened after that.

"Two *weeks*?" If Sofie hadn't come from Keeler stock, been raised by boarding schools and business tycoons, Lillian imagined her mouth might have fallen open. As it was, her nostrils flared and the skin around her lips turned white beneath the freckles. "Do you understand what they might do to her in that time?"

"More than I would like to." Hands hidden below the table-cloth, Lillian made a fist. Her nails bit into the skin of her palm. "But trust me. Please."

Sofie narrowed her bloodshot eyes. "Why should I?"

Lillian took a breath, met Sofie's stare, and said, "I am not asking as the Geddan press attaché. Not as someone associated with the . . . the administration. I'm asking as a mother trying to help her son. Someone who made a different decision than you did, a long time ago, who regrets it now."

Sofie stared at her for too long, and Lillian almost looked away. What she had said was the truth, but not the whole of it. Lillian pretended she was at the podium, facing down a difficult journalist, and the panicked itch between her eyes that made her desperate to glance down became a challenge not to.

"You aren't lying," said Sofie. It had the air of a question but not the intonation.

Lillian shook her head once, with the stiffness of certainty. "No."

"Two weeks?" Sofie's fingertips were pale where they pressed against the tablecloth.

"Probably less. Is there an exchange where I can reach you?"

"We don't have a telephone," said Sofie. Her voice had lost its edge and become tremulous, deeply tired. "But you could leave a message, with the shop downstairs."

Lillian handed over a pen and one of her cards. Sofie scribbled an exchange and handed it back, smutching the ink in her haste.

"Promise me," she said, "that this isn't some kind of setup."

"If it was," said Lillian, "I would still make that promise."

Sofie grimaced. "I know. But I just want to hear the words."

Lillian gave her driver the afternoon free to avoid him finding out where she was headed. The omnibus took its dear time in arriving, and in picking its way through traffic. She got off at a random stop and walked in circles until she found a lunch counter tucked between a telegraph office and a dry cleaner's. Arriving an hour or so before the after-work rush, she sat at the counter to order coffee and some flatbread. She sipped the former and asked for the pot to be refilled twice, but only picked at the bread and chutney.

As she sat and fiddled with scraps of soggy dough, biding her time, the flow of customers ticked up markedly. She watched women on their way home drop in to eat a quick meal of lamb kebab and spicy peas, or just to down a coffee: half-standing at the counter and chatting with the staff. Husbands, sometimes with children in tow, picked up orders wrapped in greasy paper, tied with twine. A few families piled into chairs around the woven reed tables and ate an early dinner from communal platters.

It was all so domestic, cheerful, pleasant even in its tenser moments: crying babies, squabbling spouses. Lillian granted herself a moment's respite, to imagine what it might be like if this was her neighborhood. If her largest concern was dabbing at a turmeric stain on her blouse, or settling an argument between two cranky children. The scenario was almost inconceivable, which she found horrible and gratifying in equal measure.

She had just pulled the runner from beneath her own career: a career she had spent her life building up, for which she had sacrificed so many things. Or, looked at from another angle, a career that had allowed her to avoid the things that frightened her. What would she do with herself, when she ran? Because she *would* need to run.

A fence to jump when she came to it, but worth keeping in the back of her mind. At least she was practiced at balancing a thousand anxious calculations simultaneously.

When the commuter hubbub died down, she paid and asked if she might use the telephone. The grill-boy shrugged and waved her back behind the register.

The receiver clattered on the other end as it was raised from its cradle. "Hello?"

"Vasily Memmediv?" she asked.

Paper crackled in the background. "Yes."

"I'd like to speak to your supervisor. And the rest of your team, if they're available."

This time in the pause she heard nothing. "I am afraid you've used my home exchange."

"I'm aware of that," she said, willing him to recognize her voice. "It's just that I've been thinking about our conversation last week, about your generous offer."

As if her urging had traveled through the cables, he said, "Oh." And then, "You haven't reconsidered, have you?" The calm with which he asked impressed her.

"I told you. I'd like to speak to the person in charge of your operation." She didn't mean Flagg, or Regional Affairs, and was fairly certain that he knew it.

"I'm afraid that won't be possible."

"Make it possible," she said. "It's now a condition of the agreement."

"But I—"

She hung up on him before he could go on.

CHAPTER

SIXTEEN

Memmediv came through for Lillian. It took him two days, during which she must have lost half a stone sweating, but he got her a memo through interdepartmental mail. Its origin in Regional Affairs excused its vagueness to prying eyes, but Lillian read it and knew she was in.

"Rinda," she said, and her secretary appeared. "I'll be leaving early tomorrow afternoon. Mr. Odell will be acting as my deputy. Will you send him in, please, so that I can brief him?"

Odell was competent enough she wouldn't have to worry about anything but the worst public relations disaster. And she suspected, with Tzietan peace negotiations stalled and most of Porachis flat on its back at the dragging end of the dry season, that it would be a slow weekend for news.

She could have simply sent Odell a memo of his own. But a

little show had been necessary, to draw Flagg's eyes, and Rinda was prompt in her reporting. Less than an hour later Flagg called her to his office. Memmediv was conspicuously absent.

"I've sent him on an errand," Flagg said, when Lillian's eyes strayed to his empty desk. "The rewards of caution may not always be obvious, but they can certainly be vital at times like these." He held his office door for her, and she reluctantly stepped into the stuffy inner sanctum of the foxes' den.

"Memmediv has asked for some time off. Apparently he's taking a long weekend. With a mistress, he implied. It was a rather vulgar conversation, so I didn't ask too many questions."

"That seems counter to your profession," said Lillian.

"Rest assured that I would have pried, if I hadn't already heard that you are also leaving at the end of the week, and that you won't be in at all over the weekend, or even available by phone. I had a hunch that your holiday plans might intersect."

"How astute of you," she said. "Almost as if *this* is your job, and not Regional Affairs at all, whatever that might be."

Flagg's eyes narrowed, and she regretted her piquancy. She needed to play along for a little while yet.

"Where is he taking you?" Flagg asked.

Her regret evaporated at the expression on his face when she told him, replaced by an ember's glow of satisfaction behind her ribs. Not because she had exceeded his expectations for her, wiling her way into Memmediv's confidence and Pulan's inner sanctum, but because now, it was all for her, and he had no idea.

"Into the heart of the bramble," he said. Lillian could very easily imagine him rubbing his hands together, a melodramatic stage villain, but he kept them laced in front of him on his desk. "Very good. I take it this means things have been cleared up with Sofie Keeler?"

"For the time being. She wouldn't give me much information, but I bought us a week or two. Then we'll have to do something more drastic." Likely more drastic than he conceived of.

"Well," he said, unlacing his hands to straighten a stack of papers that had not needed it. "One problem at a time. Have you had any word from your . . . associate? The one who got us those photographs? Has he been back to Hadhariti? It might be good to know what to expect when you arrive."

"You mean Jinadh."

His nod was almost imperceptible.

"That connection," she said carefully, "has been severed. Rather finally, I think." Jinadh's face flickered briefly behind her eyes, an old reel of film over a faint projector bulb. In her memory, he wore the expression of betrayal from that conversation by the river, and she felt regret douse the glow her successful deception had kindled.

"A pity." He did not sound as if he meant it. He sounded as if he wanted to crush something. "But not, in the end, a crippling loss. Not with you in Satri's stronghold."

"It is only a weekend," she said.

"Well, do whatever you have to, to get yourself invited back." He laced his fingers again, but she saw his eyes stray—so briefly— to the stack of papers he had just needlessly straightened. The fan had blown one of the sheaves slightly out of alignment. "Where have you told your office that you're going?"

"Cruising up the river to the spa at Rainab." She and Jinadh had done that once. It had been a lovely trip.

"Ah," said Flagg, "what a funny coincidence. Memmediv is supposed to be on a boat as well. He's told me he's taking the steamer down to Charasoor. Had a pair of tickets and everything."

He was trying to lay a false trail for Flagg to follow, and doing a good job of it. She didn't look forward to peeling back her layers of deception for him. It would be rather more like flaying than it would be a burlesque.

At the end of the week, Lillian found herself at the rail of the *Yaima II*, watching the casino town of Charasoor draw closer to the prow. Coastal golden-hour light burnished the fort battlements and turned the water into bronze.

Memmediv, returning from the bar, brought her something pale and sparkling, poured over ice and scented with anise.

"Arrack spritz," he said. "I didn't want to opt for anything stronger, on an empty stomach. Our hostess has said she'll feed us."

She sipped at it, and sweetness coated the inside of her mouth. She hoped it would honey the words she needed to say. Words she'd been tiptoeing around since they boarded the *Yaima* early in the afternoon.

"How do we proceed from here?" she asked, nodding to the city ahead and its sprawling harbor. Charasoor was miles down the coast from Hadhariti, and Satri's estate wasn't convenient to any rail line. They had overshot on purpose, and now would wend their way back, she assumed, by some untraceable means yet to be revealed.

"Someone will be waiting," he said unhelpfully. A few days ago, she would have cursed the lack of detail for the sake of her obligation to Flagg. Now she cursed it because it did not provide a distraction, a separate conversation to the one she knew they needed to have.

"Mr. Memmediv," she said, stepping away from him so he would follow her to the rail. The deck was far from empty, but no one would pay them attention if they didn't look like it ought to be paid, and the churn of engines and shriek of gulls would cover stray words snatched by the wind.

He came after her, wearing an expression of intrigue above the rim of his glass.

She put her forearms on the rail. The cold flute hanging between her fingers threatened to slip from her hand and fall into the water sliding past the hull. She imagined the small splash it would make before disappearing into the sea. "I need to discuss something with you before we arrive at our destination."

The intrigue took on a distinct shade of alarm. "What's wrong?"

"Nothing's wrong. I only . . . damnation, you aren't going to like this."

"I already don't like it." His voice dropped into a growl, and she would have been frightened if she hadn't reached her capacity for fear some time ago and pushed past it. "Put me out of my misery."

"You've been under the impression that I'm on your side, in this." She freed one hand from the lattice around her flute to pass palm up in front of her, indicating the nebulous constellation of conspiracies that "this" encompassed.

"And aren't you?" He said it lightly, but she heard the quaver.

"I am," she said. "*Now*. But Flagg knows more than either of us might like him to, and I had to tell him where we were going or he would have been suspicious at our little vacations coinciding."

There was a beat in which he did not move. Molten sunlight caught in his eyes, so they turned to narrow burning slits like the vents in a hot stove. If she touched him, she half-imagined she might be burnt. She felt her heart seize.

Then his somber expression broke and he began to laugh. "You think I didn't know?"

"But you're . . . you're bringing me to Satri's house. With her permission, I assume. And you knew all the time I was Flagg's informant?"

"She wouldn't have invited you if she didn't think you were a string she could pull. We knew you were passing information, and we wanted you to pass the information we wanted him to hear. If you have well and truly turned you will be even more useful to us."

"How long have you known?"

"Since you pinned Addas. He came straight to Hadhariti, poured all your secrets onto the table. Once Satri knew, she told me I could use you to solve my problem with Sofie Cattayim. I haven't heard from her again, or seen the story run, so I assume you did."

"I bought us a week or two," she said, defeated even in victory; she had been doubly used and now felt limp and helpless.

Memmediv, however, smiled. "That should be enough time."

"So close to finishing up?"

The smile stayed, but he said nothing. Smart. He didn't trust her, still.

She sipped her drink. The bubbles burnt her nose.

"Tell me why you changed your mind," he said.

She thought of Sofie's broken wedding ring, her dusty shoes. The distance she had walked and the danger she had courted, so that her daughter might feel her mother's arms around her shoulders, so that her wife might kiss the top of their little girl's head.

"There is one thing in the world that matters to me more than any other," she said. "And I got tired of waiting for other people to give it to me."

The cruel humor faded from his face, and the lines around his deep-set eyes grew deeper still. The flattering light of sunset made his expression cinematic. "I know the feeling."

The ship shuddered to a halt and they both grasped the rail to keep from stumbling. Lillian recovered first, smoothed a loose strand of hair behind her ear, and said, "Well, don't I feel like a fool."

"You aren't," said Memmediv. "You were just one smart woman alone, with a conspiracy arrayed against you. I should let them know about this before we arrive, so that we don't spring any surprises on them."

"Of course," she said. "I can't imagine Lehane was pleased at the prospect of hosting an Ospie agent for dinner."

Memmediv's eyebrows puckered. "What?"

"Lehane, the Spotlight. Founder of the Catwalk? She's working for Satri under an alias. Flagg wants to bring her in."

"*Cordelia* Lehane? Who used to strip at the Bee?"

"That wouldn't be most people's first association with her name." Lillian picked up her valise, which she had not checked, and headed for the gangway. "I didn't know you had been an aficionado of Amberlough's nightclub scene, Mr. Memmediv."

"I was in the foxhole," he said. "She was moving fraudulent documents for Aristide Makricosta to sell on the black market. We knew about it. That's all. The next time I heard her name was in an intelligence briefing on terrorist activity in Ospie Gedda."

"Official policy is Unified Gedda," she reminded him, one eyebrow cocked hard in irony.

He ignored it. "So she's here? In Porachis?"

"If Flagg is right, and I'm fairly certain that he is, we'll be seeing her in an hour or two." She dropped the conversation as they passed between the crew members at the head of the gangplank, who thanked them both for traveling on the *Yaima*. Lillian's smile and nod came so naturally she didn't realize she'd done either until she stepped onto dry land. She had to shake like a dog to drop the persona.

Perpetually smirking Memmediv didn't have the same problem. "She's at Hadhariti?"

"Working for the studio; Makricosta got her a job as assistant choreographer, but Flagg thought you might know about anything else. He wants to find out if she's a part of the deal."

"Not as far as I know," said Memmediv. "But I will have some questions for Pulan when we arrive."

"Yes, how *are* we getting back up north? And in time for dinner, too?"

"This way," he said, and led her along the dock. Not toward the taxi rank but toward a herd of cigarette boats bobbing gently at their moorings. "It's good you packed lightly."

"Well, it was only a weekend," she said. "But why?"

He inclined his head toward a low, sleek craft at the end of the pier, with a woman waiting behind the wheel. "I don't think it would bear anything larger than a valise without sinking."

CHAPTER

SEVENTEEN

Aristide timed his return to Hadhariti for the late afternoon, when the studio would be getting back to work after the midday break. The house would be quiet, and he could retreat to his rooms and begin to make arrangements in peace. For one thing, he needed to write a resignation letter. That would be a good start.

Bringing the car around the drive, he hopped out and tossed the keys to Pramit, who had come running at the sound of the engine and the tires on the gravel.

Djihar arrived next, his white hair still mussed slightly from an afternoon nap. «Welcome back, Mr. Makricosta. Did you have a good trip?»

«No,» he said. «And if Pulan asks for me, I am busy. I have some work to do.»

«Ms. Satri herself has work to do,» said Djihar. «But I will ask the others to avoid the halls around your rooms.»

«How many people are staying here?» he asked. «Has Pulan gone into the hotel business as well?»

«His Highness Prince Asiyah, and Inaz. Mr. Addas is here as well. And I understand we are expecting a few more guests for dinner.»

"The rotten queen herself, likely as not." Aristide stripped his driving gloves from his hands and flung them back into the front seat of his car. Pramit stacked them carefully and placed them on the dashboard. Aristide caught the small shake of the chauffeur's head, imagined it came with an eye roll, and ignored it. «You can tell her I will come to dinner.»

Djihar ducked his chin in a small reference to a bow, and swept Aristide into the house.

In his parlor, he dropped his bag, yanked off his jacket, and kicked his basket-weave loafers into a corner. Standing barefoot on the cool marble floor, just at the rug's edge, he looked around at the room: its flowering potted plants, its tall windows thrown open to the dusty, salty breeze. The mirrors sewn into the brocade upholstery. The gauzy curtains, the angle of the light, the lingering presence of a maid in the regimented positioning of his personal effects.

There weren't, he realized now, so many of them. Effects. A few books. No photographs. Some pill bottles and tinctures, pots of lotion and cold cream. Things you might find in the rooms of any old man. Nothing . . . curated. Nothing he could point to, or lay his hand on, and say that it was *his* in more than simply the sense that he had paid for it. And even things for which he had footed the bill were rather thin on the ground.

Had he really spent almost three years in this house, in this country? He could hardly remember the time passing.

He didn't think that he would miss it, much.

Softly, someone knocked on his door, despite his plea for privacy. He sighed and called out, «Enter.»

"Djihar told me you were home." Daoud hovered in the doorway, cradling a datebook in one hand and a stack of scripts under his arm.

The word "home" struck an odder chord with Aristide than it might have yesterday, a week ago. He wondered if Daoud meant to imply all the emotional subtext of the word, or if it was just a poor translation. "He wasn't supposed to. I have work to finish."

"If you were so concerned about work," said Daoud, "you would have been here when Inaz arrived."

"You needn't tear me up," spat Aristide, and immediately regretted it. "I'm sorry. I didn't mean it to come out *quite* so sharp."

Daoud's expression did not tighten. He didn't snap back, or even roll his eyes. Instead he stepped across the threshold, set down his book and scripts, and said, "Aristide, what is the matter? You have been behaving . . . strangely. Rushing around, bringing strangers back to the house, disappearing."

"What's wrong? A fine question to ask. Though I suppose Pulan's secret cabal isn't so secret to you. You've known all this time, haven't you? Since I showed up like a foundling on the doorstep."

Daoud didn't even have the decency to look down in shame. "What I do not know about Pulan, I do not think she knows about herself."

"But you didn't tell me." Aristide went to the bar by the window and poured a significant glass of brandy. "And *don't* say I drink too much."

"Well, you do." There was a little of the sting Aristide expected, in that. But the edges softened when he went on, "I make love with you, Aristide, but she is my employer. I keep her secrets by contract."

Turning his glass in his hands, Aristide felt the weight of the liquor shift against the crystal and change the balance of the globe against his palm. "And what if *I* had secrets?"

Daoud's tart expression softened into ruefulness. "I do not think that you would tell me."

Aristide put his nose to the snifter and drew a deep, burning breath. "Would you want to know?"

"Maybe." Daoud stepped up to the empty place beside him. "I cannot say until I know them, can I?"

"Didi . . ."

"Oh no, pet names." Daoud took the bottle of brandy from the sideboard and scanned the label, then poured for himself—maybe half the volume Aristide had put into his own glass. "What horrible thing are you going to tell me?" His dark eyes were focused on the bar-top accoutrements, his motions controlled and careful. So much of his attention was dedicated to flippancy, to corking the brandy bottle and casually replacing it amongst its fellows. He was being too bright, too irreverent. His manner broke the light into shards like cut glass, and had an edge as sharp.

Aristide felt suddenly guilty—horribly so, as if withholding his story from Daoud had been a betrayal. He hadn't used to mind betraying so much. He wished he didn't mind it now.

To distract himself—to stop himself thinking too hard—he pulled Daoud close and kissed him. The taste of fennel seeds and stale smoke lingered behind his teeth. Sneaking straights—maybe even Aristide's. Pulan kept a hookah for company, but hated the perpetual haze of casual cigarette smokers.

That lingering flavor of insubordination made Aristide kiss him the harder. When they broke from each other, Daoud's lashes fluttered down and he spoke to Aristide's chest.

"We were working well enough without honesty," he said. "Weren't we?"

"Until recently," said Aristide, stroking the high curve of his cheek, "we didn't need it."

"Do we need it now?"

"Perhaps not for the next hour or so," he said, and caught Daoud's mouth again with his.

The sex was good. The sex had always been *good*, with Daoud, though sometimes it felt a little too much like a game, or a giggling concession to Aristide's odd whims.

Not this afternoon, though. Aristide brooked no laughter, no small smirk or amused flash of the eyes. He couldn't have borne it, not with Asiyah's words echoing in the base of his skull.

He never gave us his real name; called himself Paul Darling.

A stupid risk, to use the work name from papers someone must have seen, before his arrest, and certainly after.

If there had even *been* an arrest. Aristide knew nothing about what had happened. Only that his oranges had never come.

"You are all right?" Daoud reached up to touch the edge of his jaw, and Aristide shook him off. As if he could hold his thoughts under and drown them, he sank himself more deeply into the warmth of the body beneath him.

The sex was good, but never exactly what he wanted.

This was partly because Daoud held strong convictions about what was proper for someone of his own age, and someone of Aristide's age, in a situation such as this. Convictions Aristide found frankly ridiculous. But truth be told, the things he would have liked to do, he would never have wanted to do with Daoud.

His pride would not have borne it. There was something about fighting for what he wanted, something about earning the ache, and the hipbone bruises in the soft flesh of his thighs . . . something necessary to his satisfaction. Daoud would not have wanted it badly enough, nor begged for it with quite the desperation Aristide desired. He would have raised an eyebrow, said a cursory "please," and then put it in when asked.

But he had a clever tongue, and made pained and tender noises at the perfect times. It wasn't his fault that he wasn't . . .

Aristide wished he didn't hear the name in his own stage voice, curling theatrically off the tongue. The memory was nearly a physical sensation.

"We do not have to keep going," said Daoud. "I think you are distracted."

Shame warmed Aristide's face and made him irritable, so that he had to quash a sour remark. Still, he wasn't too proud to know when he needed a graceful exit. He pulled out, too quickly—so much for graceful—and fell onto his side. Daoud made a small sound of surprise, or possibly pain. Ironically, the sound went straight to the core of Aristide's arousal. He quashed that, too, and wiped sweat from his eyes. Bending his elbows made his tired triceps burn.

When he blinked away the sting of salt, he was surprised to see it had grown dark. Equatorial dusk always descended earlier than he felt it should; like many things in Porachis, he had never quite got used to it, and always felt off balance when the sun began to set.

Dinner would be soon. Likely, Daoud had already been missed. Nothing had yet been explained. Drawing a breath, he intended to speak but found he could not assemble satisfactory words. He let the breath out in a sigh.

Daoud didn't let him get away with it. He untwisted from his postcoital disarray like a house cat waking and put one hand on Aristide's chest, cautiously. Only his fingertips touched skin, pressed into the patch of curling hairs between Aristide's pectorals—half gray, half dark—which he no longer bothered to wax.

"All right," said Daoud. "Is it time for honesty now?"

Aristide closed his eyes, and covered Daoud's hand with his so both were flat against the plane of his sternum. "I'm going away."

"Again? You just got back."

"For good, I mean." Aristide stared up at the mosquito netting drifting on the breeze. "I'm leaving the studio. And Porachis."

Daoud said nothing; only flexed his feet so the sheets rustled beneath him.

"Are you all right?" Aristide squeezed his hand in an imitation of reassurance.

Daoud pulled away, and shifted slightly so they were no longer touching. "I am fine," he said, and he sounded more irritated than anything. "I do not think I am as delicate as you imagine."

"I'm sorry," he said, for want of anything better. He was not good at this kind of thing, and Daoud was not reacting quite as he'd imagined.

"Sorry?" Daoud sat now, so that he had the advantage of height he often lacked. It was disconcerting for Aristide, to look up into a face that had so often looked up into his. "For what?"

"Leaving?" ventured Aristide.

"The studio? Porachis? Me?"

"I thought you would be upset. I thought we had . . . well, something, anyway." He shook his head, felt the strands of his hair tangle and snap where they caught between his skin and the pillowcase. The tiny pains felt sharper than their scale warranted.

There was a trace of pity in Daoud's smile. "You don't *love* me, Aristide. I was only ever a . . . a *convenience*."

It was true. There was nothing he could say to that.

Daoud seemed to take his silence for agreement, which it was. "So, now you owe me. Now you are *my* convenience."

He should have seen this coming. It had just been a distraction, at first, this dalliance. It helped him forget what he had hoped for. But then he had kept on, because Daoud reminded him somehow of himself: hungry young Erikh Prosser, down from the mountains and on the make. Fierce, prickly, bad family background, blessed with fey beauty that Daoud—unlike Erikh—was loath to use to climb the ladder.

In those days, as he left Erikh behind to be Ari, he had his own older lovers and paid in sex for good meals. For well-cut clothes and introductions, fine jewelry, a new name, hands to help him toward the top.

He should have known the ask was coming, when Daoud's mouth first closed around his cock.

"What do you want?" he asked. "Money? There isn't much else I can offer."

Daoud snorted. "That is because you cannot imagine what it is like to be anyone other than Aristide Makricosta, with Aristide Makricosta's problems."

"Well, this certainly isn't how I'd ask for a favor," Aristide snapped, shoving himself upright in bed. "Just tell me what you rotten want."

"When you leave," said Daoud, "take me with you."

"It won't be any kind of honeymoon," said Aristide. "If that's what you're angling for."

"I do not want a honeymoon with you." The pitch of his voice rose, though not the volume. So careful, always, even in fury. "I want a life of my own. I cannot rise, here, any further than I have, and that by Pulan's charity. I have no opportunities in Porachis as a turned Belqati man. So take me, wherever you are going."

"Liso," he said, and was gratified to wipe the anger off of Daoud's face and replace it with confusion.

"What for?" Daoud asked. "Asiyah?"

"No. Nothing to do with Asiyah, or the pictures, or Pulan's business there." He paused, stared down at his own body and the softening lines of muscle, the curling hair on his thighs and chest which he had let grow, the fine lines where his skin caught in the creases of his joints. So much had changed, on the surface of things. "I'm looking for something I used to have. Something I lost when the Ospies . . ." He waved one hand, barely, to sweep away the trailing end of the sentence. "Tell me something."

"Will you take me with you, if I do?"

«Only tell me, please.»

Daoud scowled. "You always use Porashtu when you want something."

«Didi,» he said, half pleading, half exasperated.

"I am not wrong." The angle of Daoud's chin rose, and he dared Aristide with his eyes to contradict him.

«Pulan is using the picture to bring guns to Memmediv,» he said. «I am not wrong, either.»

«No,» said Daoud. «You're not.»

«Is Memmediv coming to Hadhariti anytime soon?»

«Why does it matter? Do you have questions for him, too?»

Aristide closed his eyes, which ached with weariness and strain and perhaps something less concrete.

«Honesty,» said Daoud, and made it sound like a scolding.

«No,» said Aristide. «I want to see him for personal reasons.»

Daoud raised his wrist—he was still wearing that awful watch. Aristide allowed himself a moment of imagination, conjuring a world in which his holiday had not been interrupted, in which he and Daoud got their vacation filled with lackluster sex and false relaxation. Retroactive panic choked him, stifling. He was almost grateful to Asiyah for the awful revelations he had bestowed.

«Lucky you,» said Daoud, and initially Aristide thought he

meant it for the painful truth, the peeling back of illusion. But then he went on. «He should be here now. I heard he was coming for dinner.»

The sun was starting to slant into Pulan's office, so Cordelia had to squint. It wasn't doing her growing headache any favors.

She'd been packing up, last minute, ready to go lay low in a little town a couple miles off while Hadhariti hosted a party she wanted no part of. Pulan wanted to pass false information to the Ospies through Lillian, and Jinadh thought he could get Cordelia some specs on Stephen's school, make it a little easier for her once she got to Gedda. Cordelia couldn't afford to be seen. But just as she was ready to hop into the car behind Pramit, Pulan called an emergency meeting and announced a piece of news that had Cordelia all twisted around again.

"Why are we supposed to trust her this time?" she asked. "She's making me dizzy, the way she turns."

"Memmediv was quite clear over the wireless," said Pulan. "Would you like to hear his message again?"

"All I'm saying is what if she clocked us and this is how she gets her hooks in?"

Prince Asiyah gave her a look that said to shut her teeth. If she'd been on firmer ground she might not have heeded him, but this whole enterprise seemed to be skipping from dinghy to dinghy in rough surf. Things moved faster here than she was used to, greased by money: private security, keep-quiet bribes, fancy radios so you could switch sides every five minutes and keep your cronies up to date. Memmediv had buzzed them from the rotten boat.

"Fine," she said. "But how do we know for sure?"

She was not encouraged by the general shifting and mutters of the rest of the crowd around the desk in Pulan's office. Inaz was there, and Prince Asiyah. Jinadh, too, had maneuvered his way into the inner circle, and sat quiet at one corner of Pulan's desk, a small coffee cup cradled in his hands. The skin was tight across his knuckles, but otherwise he was keeping it together. He didn't say much except to translate for Inaz and for Cordelia, when the conversation required it.

The only person in the know who hadn't showed was Daoud, Pulan's secretary. Every so often, Pulan would turn as if to ask him for something, and realize anew he wasn't there. Each time, her eyes flicked to the clock on her desk, and she gave a little shrug, as if reassuring herself. She had a pen in her own hand, and took her own notes. Cordelia had only known her for a week or so, but even so: the sight of Pulan holding her own pen struck her as odd. She wondered where Daoud had gotten off to.

"We have already reviewed this," said Pulan. There was a burnt curl of annoyance coming off the words like acrid smoke. "I apologize. I understand your reservations. But we must make the decision to let her in. She is our best hope at keeping our activities covered. And you yourself said you need more information about Stephen's school. Who better to give you that information than his mother?"

It was a good reason. It didn't make her feel better. "All I'm saying is we already know she hauled a sack over Memmediv's head. What's to say she isn't running some scheme now?"

Silence hung over them all.

"You," she said, leveling a severe, straight-knuckled finger at Jinadh. "She pushed your kid's head out. You trust her?"

He stared into the dregs of his coffee, and worked his jaw.

"Don't suck on your plug," she snapped. "Answer me."

The rest of the cohort turned to stare, hanging on the indrawn breath that came before his words.

"I want to," he said finally.

Cordelia killed an urge to spit. "Wanting ain't the same as doing."

"Well," said Pulan, putting her palms decisively to her thighs. "It is, in the end, only dinner. We do not need to talk business over the nuts and cheese."

"For you it's only dinner," said Cordelia. "But this mummer here"—her finger, still outstretched, jabbed hard in Jinadh's direction—"gave Lillian some photographs of my sad cast and I'll wager she's keeping one sharp eye out for wanted Geddans stuffing their faces at your board. So I ain't so sure I should show."

There was a moment while they all worked out what exactly she'd said. But could she help the way she talked? She wasn't a rotten grammar book.

"You have nothing to fear if she is telling the truth," said Jinadh.

"And everything to fear if she's lying. You can't tell me which it is, so I know which side of this scale is safer."

"You have it in your power to rescue her son," said Jinadh. "Prove that to her and she will fall firmly in your favor."

"I *can't* prove it to her." Cordelia could feel her face turning pink with frustration. "I don't even know if I'll get out of there with my skin, all right? If she's in, she can help me, but if she isn't in, I don't want to see her."

He opened his mouth to sling something back at her, but they all heard a door slam at the same time and jumped, so he was left hanging there with his jaw slack as a dead eel's.

Pulan said something in Porashtu, her tweezed eyebrows drawing tight in the center as she cast her eyes up. For a minute, Cordelia believed she could see through the walls to whatever commotion was occurring.

And there was one. Down the hall, from the same direction as the slamming door: raised voices and the strike of footsteps on the floor, growing louder.

Before any of them could react, the handles on Pulan's double office doors began to rattle. Finding them locked, the assailant outside crashed an insistent fist against the wood.

"Aristide!" That was Daoud's voice. "What in the eyes of heaven—"

"Open the rotten door." And that was Ari. "I know you have a key."

"Come in." Pulan's voice, pitched level, miraculously carried over the chaos. Cordelia would have liked to get the hang of that skill.

Silence in the corridor, and then the quiet rattle of teeth on tumblers. The door swung open on silent hinges.

"Aristide. You're back." Pulan folded her hands demurely in front of her chest, like a Hearther celibate. "And Daoud." Then she said something in Porashtu that had a little bit of a leer to it, a little lard spread over the words.

Daoud's cheeks darkened and his chin came up at a smart angle. He answered her crisply, businesslike.

"He isn't here," said Ari, his eyes flicking from left to right and back again, taking in the schemers staggered around Pulan's desk.

"Who is not, *duladhush*?" Pulan released her clasped hands and spread them, perfectly timed and level as Aristide had ever managed it behind the mic. "Our leading lady, her dance instructor. Our most important backer. And now, our talented director."

"Don't you dare," he said. "I won't play that game anymore."

"There is a picture, Ari. Honest." But when Cordelia turned

to face him and saw the look in his eyes full on, she knew nothing was as serious to him in that moment as finding whoever it was he didn't see here.

"Where is Vasily Memmediv?" he asked. There was murder in his voice.

Behind him, the bell rang in the hall.

"Aristide, wait." But before Pulan could get out of her chair, before she could begin to navigate the seats surrounding her, he had turned and left them all staring after.

Daoud had the least ground to make up, and Pulan barked an order at him. He was a little too slow on the uptake, to Cordelia's eye, but he gave chase eventually. Prince Asiyah was on his heels, and he looked less baffled than the rest of them, but certainly more worried. Cordelia got out after him and grabbed the sleeve of his robe.

"What's he want with Memmediv?" she asked, trailing in his wake as he made for the gallery that ran around the front hall. She could already hear voices.

The prince quickened his pace. "Nothing good, I think."

"You know something?"

"I think I told him a story he should not have heard."

And then they were standing at the head of the stairway, staring down at something that looked like the climax of a stage drama. Or maybe more like a frame from a picture. Cordelia wouldn't know; she'd never actually seen one. Like the wireless, they hadn't been big in Gedda before the Ospies with their catchy tunes and propaganda flicks.

Djihar, hunched and placating, stood right in the center. He'd apparently been caught by Ari in the act of opening the door for

Pulan's dinner guests: Vasily Memmediv and, with him, Lillian DePaul.

Cordelia had never met her. Only heard her name, and looked at her photograph, which had been hard enough. Seeing her stand there, blond hair wind-mussed, brows drawn down in confusion, lit the fuse of Cordelia's hottest anger, and put a shank straight through her gut.

She couldn't imagine what it must be like for Ari. And yet all of his attention was aimed straight at Memmediv, sharp and narrow as an augur.

"Mr. Makricosta," said Memmediv. "Good evening."

Ari spoke with a tight jaw. "I've had better."

"Aristide," called Pulan, from halfway down the stairs. "Why don't you invite our guests in?"

"That man," said Aristide, "will not come any further into this house."

"It is not your house," she said. "Come away."

"I don't care. If he takes one more step I'll knock him flat. And I've killed people with my hands, Pulan."

Watching Aristide fight to keep his anger in check, watching his face twist against a mad-dog snarl, Cordelia suddenly understood he was capable of many more and much worse things than she had realized. She wondered how many of them he'd done, to get to where he was today. She wondered if she'd see one now, and what it might be for.

"I'm afraid I don't understand," said Lillian, like she was trying to step between shards of broken glass. "Have we done something to upset you?"

"I *hope* you don't know what he's done," said Ari. "Or I should hate you too, for standing next to him. I suppose Asiyah's had neither time nor reason to tell you."

"Aristide." It was the prince this time, all the charm gone out of him. He didn't even sound like a swell; he sounded like the worst kind of hound walking the slum streets: the scared kind. They always hit the hardest.

"None of us are exactly blameless," said Lillian, but Memmediv put a hand on her arm and she shut up quick, definitely confused and starting to look scared on top of it. Cordelia didn't blame her, and bet her own face looked about the same.

"We all did questionable things in those days." Memmediv's stare had taken on the same rebar quality as Aristide's: iron straight and totally unwavering, liable to kill you if it struck home.

"Questionable?" Cordelia had never heard Ari's voice so low or rough. His breath came hard and uneven between clenched teeth, and the fine finish on his accent had chipped off so that traces of the north showed through. She'd forgotten that about him: that he had the same burr to his voice that Tory'd had, but hid it so much better. "You have no *idea* what you've cost me. Not the faintest trace of an understanding."

It was then Cordelia started to get an idea what this was all about.

"I would like to think we can come to an accord," said Memmediv, "as men with deep coffers willing to pay dearly for the things we want."

There was a beat in which it seemed almost possible. And then, before anybody could move to stop him, Aristide was on Memmediv. Djihar, to Cordelia's middling surprise, pulled a small revolver from one sleeve and aimed it true. But Memmediv's skull had already cracked against the floor, so loudly that Cordelia flinched. Ari wrapped one hand in Memmediv's thick hair and pulled back, hard, so the other man's larynx cut sharply beneath the skin of his throat.

"I have *paid*," spat Ari, "and paid double again, and I've seen no return. I am living on *credit*, so don't you *dare* speak to me like that. Do you understand?"

Djihar said something in his gentle butler voice, but the barrel of his pistol didn't waver. Neither man heeded him.

Memmediv swallowed, his eyes closed tight. Aristide hauled his head up from the tile as if to strike it down again. "I said *do you understand*?"

He grunted. The pain on his lean, dark face was a mirror to Ari's. Cordelia waited for the last blow, the one that would knock him out for sure, and maybe end him. If not right away, a couple of hours from now. She'd seen folk die that way, brains swelling in their skulls until the fits started and they shook themselves into the grave.

"You cannot kill him, Aristide." Pulan's voice broke the silence like scissors snipping cleanly through a taut thread. "Unless you no longer fear extradition? I can shelter a political fugitive. I cannot protect a murderer."

His body shuddered finely all over: not dread or anguish, but fury, hot as a skillet and barely contained. Still, he lowered Memmediv's head to the floor this time, instead of slamming it back, and untangled his fingers from the other man's hair.

Pulan said Djihar's name, and he put the gun away. Cordelia let out a breath that had turned sour in her lungs.

"Will someone *please* explain what's going on?" Lillian crossed her arms and stared down her knife blade of a nose and looked so much like her brother. Even the way she said the words was him all over: indignant, with a thread of fear buried so deep you wouldn't find it unless you knew to listen.

"This man," said Ari.

He got no further before Prince Asiyah started trying to talk over him. "Aristide, this is not the time or the place—"

But Ari, still straddling Memmediv on the tile of the hall, raised his voice over Asiyah's and said, "This man as good as murdered your brother."

Lillian's breath wouldn't come. The arches and inlays of Satri's entrance hall telescoped strangely around the tableau of Makricosta sneering down at Memmediv. His words did not echo, but the memory of them felt numb, like flesh upon which a blow had landed that had not yet begun to ache.

"What do you mean," she said, "'as good as'?"

"I think that is enough drama in the front hall for one evening," said Pulan, sweeping down the stairs. "Aristide, get up or I shall call Pramit to pry you from the floor."

"What did you *mean*," demanded Lillian, and to her mortification, her voice cracked on the last word.

"*Aristide*." Satri was perilously close to shouting, and a flush had risen on her cheeks. "Get *up*."

Not taking his eyes from Memmediv's face, he rose slowly, moving as if his joints pained him. As if he were old—though he must only be what, ten years her senior? Fifteen?—and immeasurably tired.

When Memmediv started to sit, Makricosta feinted toward him and snorted disdainfully when he flinched. Satri put a stiff arm between them, pressing Makricosta back.

"Perhaps we can discuss this over dinner," she said.

"If you think I'm sitting at a table with that . . ." Makricosta struggled for a noun. "I'll take bread and cheese in the rotten stables first."

"I will put you there if you insist on behaving like an animal.

Now—" She turned to Lillian. "I apologize for your poor welcome into my home. How can I amend this? Would you like to be taken to your rooms? Some refreshments?"

"I—" She felt as though railroad spikes had been pounded through her feet, straight into the marble floor. She could not move forward, and her knees threatened to give way. "Vasily, what did you *do*?"

"Nothing," he said: the first words he had spoken since falling. Struggling up from the floor, he stood slowly, one hand on his knee for leverage. Head hanging, he paused before he straightened. Pain seamed his forehead and puckered the corners of his eyes. "Not what he says, anyway."

"That isn't what I heard from your friend Sekibou," spat Makricosta, who bit off further remarks when Satri lost patience and rapped him with her knuckles.

Memmediv laughed: one hoarse, bitter sound. "And how would Asiyah know anything about me?" Then he flung up one hand and said, "Sacred arches, *please* don't answer. Ms. Satri, if you have some ice?"

"Absolutely," said their hostess. «Djihar, please take Mr. Memmediv to the blue bedroom and see that Aza brings him a cool cloth and a pack of ice for his head. And some Aceto powder, for the swelling.» Then, in Geddan, "Mr. Memmediv, I do apologize. Please let the staff know if you need anything. We are all at your disposal."

Lillian took a step after Memmediv as Djihar ushered him away, tearing one of her hammered-down feet from the floor. "Wait," she said. "What did he mean—"

"Ms. DePaul," said Pulan, "I think if you just—"

"He blew Cyril's cover."

Lillian twisted to stare at Makricosta over her shoulder, but he wouldn't meet her eyes. "During the election?"

He cast a caustic glance up the stairs. "Asiyah didn't give specifics."

Something tore in her chest; not a muscle or a ligament but something less tangible, more important. "Does *everyone* know what happened to him but me?"

"No."

The word fell from above her, from the landing that ran around the hall. She looked up and saw the heart-shaped face of the woman from Jinadh's photographs hovering in the gloaming, wide-eyed.

He had caught her unawares and unhappy, or on edge. Now, pale with alarm, her complexion grew brighter as evening leached light from the room. She looked like an apparition, a haunting. Everyone, not only Lillian, turned at the sound of her voice. The moment deserved the slam of a spotlight striking her features.

Spotlight. Well, now the code name made sense. Though she was small, and at the moment rather drab, she had a kind of magnetism. One that made Lillian open her mouth to say, *Ms. Lehane*, which might have spooked her, and which changed, halfway out, into, "My brother. You knew him?"

"Oh, sweetness," she said, and the way she shook her head was not a negation, but pity. "You two could have been twins."

The laugh that broke from Lillian's chest sounded like a gasp, a dry heave. "You wouldn't believe the number of times we heard that."

"I wager I would," said Lehane. "It's like seeing a ghost."

The squeal of leather on stone tore Lillian from her bespelled stillness, snuffed the small glow behind her sternum that had kindled hearing someone speak that way about her brother. About her. She blinked, looked down, and saw Makricosta's back retreating. The young man Lillian remembered from the premiere—Satri's assistant, or secretary—looked back and forth between his employer and her temperamental director, and then went after the latter. Satri watched them both go with mingled apprehension and relief.

Lillian looked up again, scanned the faces watching her: Lehane was still pale, but half-smiling now. Sekibou wore a glower so thunderous it ought to have been shooting lightning bolts. Beside him, Inaz Iligba, looking skeptical. And beside *her*—horribly, incredibly—

"*Jinadh?*"

Tendons in his throat stood out as he inhaled and lifted his chin, the proud look he used in the face of slights. It was not an expression she had ever wanted to see aimed at her.

«Heaven's eyes,» said Pulan. «What a snarl. If you put this all on-screen, no one would believe it.»

CHAPTER

EIGHTEEN

"Leave me be," said Aristide to the incoming tide. He meant it, of course, for Daoud, who had followed him all the way along the terrace, and even out to the edge of the cantilevered swimming pool. "I'm not planning to jump."

"I did not think you were."

"Oh? How could you tell?"

"Someone so angry at another man would rather see him dead first, I think. If you had killed him just now, I would maybe worry." Daoud collapsed into one of the wicker chairs at the corner of the deck, slouching the way he never did in Pulan's presence. Aristide wondered if insouciance was really his natural state, rather than a flirtatious persona he wore for afternoon trysts. If so, he dissembled very well. "May I have a cigarette?"

Aristide, who had removed his case from his breast pocket, flipped it open and let Daoud pick one from the row. His lighter had cropped up in the hotel bedclothes when the valet turned down his sheets. After holding the flame to his own straight, he cast the device onto the table, heedless of the enamel against the tile top. Daoud flinched at the impact, then inspected the lighter for damage before he put it to the tip of his cigarette.

The tide advanced notably up the beach before Daoud said, "Will you tell me what that was about?"

Aristide exhaled blue smoke into the dusk, and pretended to contemplate its trajectory for a long moment to buy time. Finally he said, "This is one of those secrets you said you might not want to know."

"I said," Daoud corrected him, "that I would not know unless I heard them. And after that"—he jabbed the ember of his straight back at the house—"I think I would like to. It seems safer."

"Well then," said Aristide. "What do you *think* it was?"

"You knew Ms. DePaul's brother," he said. "You were lovers?"

Chagrined, Aristide ashed his cigarette into the void above the ocean. Cinders glimmered and burnt up on the breeze.

"And he died," Daoud went on. "The Ospies?"

"I really don't know," said Aristide. "I never heard from him, after I left Amberlough. I didn't, honestly, hear from him in the last several weeks I was there. He just . . . disappeared." The butt of his straight followed its spent ashes into the ocean. The wind caught it and sent it spinning, so he didn't see where it landed.

He wondered if he ought to tell Daoud what Asiyah had related, that Cyril had made it out of Gedda and been working in Liso for at least a little while. That there was some slender chance he might be living yet, deep undercover, buried in obscurity.

In the end he kept silent, because he couldn't bear the thought that Daoud might laugh.

"He was very important to you." Daoud's voice was so soft Aristide could barely make out his words over the crash and hiss of waves, the moan of wind along the cliffs.

When he did parse what Daoud had said, he only shrugged. Any hard-hearted adage he might roll out about attachment being apt to cause one trouble, he had already thoroughly belied through his actions.

Daoud had been dealing with his straight less aggressively than Aristide, and had several drags left on it. When he opened his mouth to speak, a thin shear of smoke escaped over his upper lip. But he was interrupted before he got the words out.

«Ms. Satri would like you both to come in for dinner,» called Djihar, voice raised over the sound of the ocean and the wind.

Daoud flicked his straight to the ground and stubbed it out with his toe, then rose to the summons. Between extinguishing his straight and standing, he reassembled his demure, subservient persona and donned it like a jacket, right down to a slight shrug of the shoulders as if he were shooting his cuffs.

Still hunched over the balustrade, Aristide settled his weight more deeply onto his elbows, sank his head further. "Tell her I meant what I said about bread and cheese."

"She will not like that."

"I don't care." He bit off the consonants and placed a full stop between each word, then slid back into his customary clipped sourness. "Tell her anyway."

But when Daoud went alone up the cantilever toward Djihar, the steward said, «Ms. Satri was quite clear that Mr. Makricosta should come to the table.»

«Ms. Satri can eat shit,» snapped Aristide, who at least knew his rudimentary swears.

There was only expectant silence behind him. Djihar was trying to wait him out, as one might a recalcitrant child. Playing into it gave him the same kind of sickening satisfaction as eating a sticky tart or a trifle past the point of enjoyment.

But Djihar waited and said nothing, and neither did Daoud, and pressure built in the vertebrae of Aristide's neck as though someone were cranking a winch to force him to turn his head. He lasted perhaps another thirty seconds before he thrust himself from the balustrade and whirled too quickly, torqueing his back. "Lady's sake, why does she want me there? Haven't I smashed enough crockery for one evening?"

When Djihar puzzled over that for a moment too long, Daoud slipped in with a swift—likely idiomatic—translation.

«Ah,» said Djihar, when he understood. «Yes. But at dinner we're going to put together the pieces.»

«What does that mean?» he asked, and for once managed to inject a satisfactory amount of snarl into his Porashtu without mangling the accent.

«No polite dinner conversation,» said Djihar. «At Ms. De-Paul's request, since so many people with parts of her brother's story are at the house this evening, we are going to hear the whole of it.»

Aristide felt himself blanch, and hoped it didn't show. "Mother and sons, I want no part of that tent show."

"Aristide," said Daoud, "I think that you may *be* a part of it."

Aristide had taken naturally to law-breaking out of the gate, and as such had never had occasion to enter a court for sentencing. But he imagined it might feel similar to entering the grand dining room at Hadhariti under the stares of seven pairs of eyes whose expressions varied on a spectrum between wrath and pity.

Pulan took the head of the table, and Lillian and Memmediv sat to her right and left, the former looking slightly less shaken and more determined than she had earlier in the evening, the latter rather more and less, respectively. Asiyah and Inaz came next, and then Cordelia, across from Jinadh. Daoud took the spot at Cordelia's elbow, leaving Aristide to sit beside Pulan's cousin, who for once in his entire life, perhaps, did not smile with his teeth. Or, in fact, at all.

Wine had already been poured, and the assembled guests had been picking at the olives, as evidenced by the pits on their plates. Even as Aristide sat, Asiyah plucked one from his mouth and dropped it to the porcelain with a faint but discernible *plink*, which echoed in the silence Aristide's arrival occasioned. Or which had, perhaps, hung over the table even before.

Pulan broke it, and though her tone was sweet enough to rot teeth, it cut through the quiet. Candy, licked to a wicked edge. "Thank you for joining us. At last. Perhaps now we can begin the meal?"

Inaz tapped Jinadh's arm, and he leaned close to translate. Aristide was pleased there was someone at the table *he* could pity; relaying this debacle would no doubt make tiring work.

"I wasn't hungry," he said, dipping his fingers into the brass bowl of rose-scented water by his plate. They weren't dirty, but he did like to stand on ceremony, and anyway it gave him something insouciant to do with his hands. "But then Djihar told me this is less a meal than it is some kind of storytellers' circle, and I was expected to perform."

"You never pass up a chance for that, do you?" Cordelia lifted her eyes from her plate and pinned him.

Anyone less hardened by life, less accustomed to other people's censure, might have withered. As it was, Aristide had to collect himself before he could smile and say, "It's in my nature. Now, will you tell me what I've done to offend *you* today?"

"You knew what happened to him and you wouldn't say." Her grip on the edge of the table tightened, threatening to bunch the immaculate, freshly ironed tablecloth. "What did you think, I didn't care? Or you just weren't brave enough?"

By the time she finished speaking, his molars were clenched so tightly he could feel the pressure against the bones of his jaw. A bolt of nerve pain through his face startled him almost to gasping, but he caught himself and only said, "I would have told you, if I had known when you asked."

"I'm sorry." Lillian put one hand on the table, her movements excruciatingly poised. "Can we please tell this in order?"

"And what order is that?" Aristide failed to rein in his frustration, though of the people at this table she deserved it least. Still, she did not flinch. "In my version of things, I find out that my— that *Cyril* had been crawling around the Lisoan jungle for months after I'd assumed he was dead. In your version, you cozy up to his murderer before you ever find out what he's done. I don't think any of us have things in their proper order."

What little color there was in Lillian's face had begun to drain when Aristide said "assumed," and by the time he wrapped up and crossed his arms tightly over his chest, her mouth had opened slightly—as close as she probably got to slack-jawed.

Memmediv looked as incredulous as Aristide imagined someone with a concussion could.

"He's alive?" Lillian's voice whispered like salt spilled across pale stone, spreading into invisibility as she reached the end of her question.

"No," said Asiyah, sliding a quelling glance down the table.

Aristide bounced it right back, unwilling to be cowed. "But it was not the Ospies who killed him. Not directly, anyway."

Lillian shook her head. "I don't understand. I saw the file—it was redacted, heavily, but I . . . he *did* die in Amberlough."

"Or the idea of him did," said Memmediv, voice hoarse, eyes closed. "Sometimes that's all you need to kill, to save face."

Aristide could feel the heat under his anger rise, so that it threatened to spill over in a froth. He half-stood from his seat but before he could speak he felt a hand on his wrist, beneath the table—a silent, invisible admonition.

Jinadh did not hold him down by force. Did not even glance at him. But the intent was unmistakable and the manner and source so surprising that Aristide sat back down without saying anything.

When Jinadh spoke, it was with an air of unfamiliar authority. "Perhaps this situation requires an impartial view."

Pulan's derisive snort felt out of place in the fraught atmosphere. "*You* are impartial?"

"I do not like to see Ms. DePaul in such distress," he said. There was a little of his old charm back in it, except that he still didn't smile, and the words weren't coated in oil. He sounded, bizarrely, as if he meant something for a change.

The DePaul in question sent a sharp look in his direction, which Aristide didn't understand.

"But," Jinadh went on, "my partiality ends there. And no one has yet lied to me about whatever events we are trying to parse. If it suits all parties, I will conduct this as a kind of interview. You will answer whatever questions I ask, and I hope we will create some kind of sense from the answers."

The food arrived before anyone could voice approval or dissent; Djihar supervised the arrangement of tureens of curry—fish, chicken, lamb—the lighting of spirit lamps, the placement of cellars of lemon salt and pots of garlic yogurt in the midst of a silence born of suspense. Eyes flicked back and forth above the silver filigree of chafing dishes, through the rising steam.

Aristide did not feel like being interviewed; he had no interest in scraping bare the painful events he had long ago buried underneath banality.

But he had a powerful hunger to know whatever the other people at this table were hiding, or had simply never thought to share. And if he had to dredge up his own piece of the story for it, he would keep it minimal and hope for a good exchange rate.

Cordelia's evening had begun with fear: of the new developments in their conspiracy, of Lillian's arrival, of what that might mean for her own safety. It had descended into confusion and shock with the scene in the front hall, and now she felt like everything was happening behind a scrim. A haze hung between her senses and reality, so that words and actions seemed unreal, a dream sequence in a ballet or tableau.

First Cyril was dead, and Memmediv to blame. Then alive, then dead again, somewhere in a jungle, far past any hope of saving him or even leveling some kind of revenge. If it wasn't the Ospies who'd killed him . . .

Well, she still had plenty of reasons to tear them down. But she felt a little like one of her claws had been pulled out, or some of the breeze had slacked from her sails.

Jinadh broke in on her tail-chasing with a plate full of black rice, red curry, and a seared skewer of goat and small green peppers, placed gently back in the spot from which he had taken it, empty, moments ago. She had missed that, still trying to untangle everything that had come before.

"I hope it is to your taste," he said, and then began to serve himself.

Cordelia had the sense to look up the table, and saw everyone was staring at him, and at her, their own plates empty. He'd have been at home on the boards, with this kind of showmanship.

"Now," he began. "From what I understand, Lillian's brother meant a great deal to Mr. Makricosta. So, let us begin there."

Cordelia watched Ari's face and saw him bite back his first response, which she could tell from his hard swallow had been a real scorcher.

"Cyril and I were lovers for some time." He had to pause after that, and while his expression didn't waver, Cordelia could see him reset his spine and straighten up. "He started working with the Ospies to save his skin, so I found him a girl to prove good faith." Here he cast a heavy glance at Cordelia.

"That was me," she said, as if it wasn't obvious. But hey, they wanted the truth.

"All of that," said Lillian, "I know. His associates weren't blacked out, in the file. Only the names of the . . . only Ospie names." She raised her eyes and stared pointedly across the table. "Your name, perhaps, Mr. Memmediv."

"Wait. We will get to that." Jinadh held up a hand. "Mr. Makricosta, Ms. Lehane, I am curious. You knew that Cyril had turned to the Ospies, and you aided him?"

Cordelia looked to Ari for her cue, but he was only sneering down his nose. When Jinadh turned his regard on her, with nosy tabloid intensity, all she could say was, "I didn't realize what he'd do. And I might not have cared, straight off. But I care now. If he was standing here in front of me I'd slap his teeth out." She poked a potato chunk with a torn piece of flatbread. "But he ain't, so I wanna know why. Ask Memmediv what he did."

Rather than speak, Jinadh opened his palm in Memmediv's

direction. The other man closed his eyes and his face sagged. He looked older than he had that afternoon: pouches under his eyes, and new, deep wrinkles carved by agony. "Did you know, Makricosta: He did it for you."

Aristide scoffed. "He did not."

"Ari," Cordelia said, and wished she were close enough to touch him under the table. To stomp on his foot, or put a hand on his knee. "Let him talk. Or don't you want to know?"

The look on his face shook her own certainty.

"He did," said Memmediv. "But it seems he didn't tell you."

"Cyril was as selfish as I am," Ari snapped. "Don't try to sell me this cut."

"And the false papers he had on him when he was arrested? Where did he get them? They were new—he couldn't have forged them before he was placed in custody."

Ari's nose went up, but a faint blush colored his cheeks.

"You were working toward the same goal with different methods, and you both failed. *You* came close, but they never would have given him the second passport that he asked for, the way out for his 'friend.' Not even if he had personally put a bullet in Hebrides's brain. But oh, how he *did* hope."

On either side of his still-empty plate, Ari's hands lay flat on the table, motionless. Or, no: not quite. A fine tremor ran through the left, so that the shadow of his fingers shuddered on the cloth.

Cordelia wished she could reach out and take that shaking hand in hers. He would hate her for it. She would still hold on.

"Mr. Memmediv," said Jinadh, reeling them all back. "Do you care to explain why Mr. Makricosta thinks you are responsible for Cyril's death?"

Memmediv dredged up a smile Cordelia wanted to peel from his face and salt like a slug. "From what I've heard at this table," he said, "DePaul didn't die at the hands of the Ospies."

"We are telling this in order," said Jinadh, matching Mem-mediv's smarm but sliding some iron underneath it. "So for now, let us forget anything His Highness may add when you are finished."

"I was a mole, inside the FOCIS. Cyril was assigned to infiltrate the Ospies in Nuesklend and turn over information that could be used to expose electoral fraud. I sang about it and then we turned him, under some duress. I had no part in anything that happened to him after that, except to help him, once, in snaring Ada Culpepper. That is all." He put his hand to his bowed head, hiding his eyes.

Pulan poured him a glass of wine and put a hand on his forearm. Eyebrows went up on the Porachin men around the table—Cordelia had started to get a sense of how things went around here, and understood Pulan had just stooped pretty low by her country's standards.

Memmediv drank the wine, and didn't even thank her.

"Why?" Cordelia asked. "I mean, Cyril turned to save himself, and try for Ari, but why were you with them? The Ospies, I mean. 'Cause I figure if you're here now, it wasn't 'cause you were on their wagon."

He lifted his chin long enough to throw a chagrined look at Lillian, then lowered it again, wincing. "As Ms. DePaul said to me not too long ago, 'There is one thing in the world that matters to me more than any other.' Unlike her, I had not yet ceased to believe that I could win it through alliances, or toadying."

"He means Dastya," said Lillian, though she addressed him rather than Cordelia. "You betrayed my brother for a harbor town."

"I betrayed your brother for *my* brother," he said. "For my father and my mother, my sister, my nieces and nephew. For my entire family and what we lost." He paused abruptly, looking a little green, and for a moment Cordelia wondered if he'd be sick. Then he reined it in and added, more softly, "For the thousands of other families who have lost as much, or more."

Cordelia wanted to hate him. But she thought of the trains derailed, the depots and government offices burned. Practical and symbolic targets, but trains had conductors, coal-folk. People worked in those offices, and would have gone home to their families.

So instead of hate, she had to understand, and that put a bitter taste at the back of her throat.

"Your Highness," said Jinadh, a little more softly than he'd been breaking in so far. "Perhaps now you can tell us what you know?"

Asiyah had been translating for Inaz, murmuring beneath the conversation, half a beat behind. Now he cleared his throat and took a long drink of wine. An expectant hush fell.

Hang 'em all. Cordelia felt right back on the stage, and for once, didn't want to. Couldn't these folk just say outright what they meant without making it into a show nobody was paying to see?

"Maybe six months after Acherby took power," said Asiyah, "one of my case officers got a call from her contact in the police. They had arrested a man for drunk and disorderly conduct in a slum on the edge of Orriba. Not unusual, except that he was Geddan, without a visa."

"I thought you were just a playboy," said Aristide, so bristlingly snide Cordelia pinned him for uncertain, probably embarrassed, maybe scared. "But mother's tits, they've really put you in charge of people."

Asiyah's tight little smile said more than any cruel comeback might have.

"She went to question him, in jail. He called himself Paul

Darling. He had no papers. He would not say how he arrived in Liso, let alone harassing strangers on the street in Orriba. But when she asked if he had fled the Ospies, he laughed, and said that they had thrown him out.

"That made her interested. She alerted her superiors. Darling was very useful; he told us everything he knew about their methods, ideologies. But never anything about himself. And we needed to verify that what he said was true."

"And how did you find out?" asked Jinadh, wineglass cradled delicately in his fingers.

"Mm," said the prince, hastily swallowing a mouthful of rice. He was one of the few of them who had made inroads on his food. Cordelia certainly hadn't touched a bite. "In fact, an old friend of Makricosta's. Merrilee Cross. We had rumors she fled the Ospies after, um . . . she pulled too many runners from them? *Diwe*, she used to sell our secrets to old Gedda, so we decided to collect a debt. She recognized the photo, and after some . . . *strong* encouragement, she said he was Cyril DePaul."

"She *knew*?" Aristide looked like he wanted to spit. "That sculler knew he was alive and she said *nothing*?"

"He didn't die?" Lillian, who had been quiet, finally lowered her hands from her mouth. There were pale marks on her cheeks where her fingers had pressed, starting to fill in pink. "They said he died. How could he not have died?"

"At a guess," said Memmediv, "somebody didn't want to get in trouble."

Prince Asiyah shrugged. "He never told us how he escaped, or how he got to Liso. He started to run a network for us, right on the border. He was painfully careful with his agents—he hated to leave any of them . . . oh, how do you say . . . on a rock in the rising tide? But with himself? Never so much. He had a few near escapes, and then, we stopped hearing from him. Many people wanted him dead, I am sure, and no doubt one of them succeeded. There was evidence of a break-in at his home, a disturbance. No body, but there are bad stories about what the militants in the north do with the corpses of their enemies. Not fit for the dinner table."

Cordelia waited for the next part of the story, but Asiyah only wrapped a bite of curry in flatbread and pushed it into his mouth.

"That's it?" she asked.

He looked down at her, still chewing, and shrugged.

"Nobody's gonna say it?" she asked. "But everybody's thinking it, right?"

"Cordelia," said Aristide, and the *o* was too cramped, the *r* edging into furry, back-of-the-teeth territory. Like Tory, when he was pinned, talking like he'd never left the hills.

"Ari," she said. "Disappeared ain't dead."

Before she got the last word out, he shoved his chair back from the table and turned tail.

Aristide wrote his resignation the minute he had the door locked behind him.

Well, not strictly true. He locked the door, uncorked a bottle of sorghum whiskey from the bar, and drank too much straight from the neck. He left the bottle open as he wrote.

His handwriting scrawled across the page—he had no patience for a typewriter—and the ink blotted hideously wherever his anger got the better of him. He tore the embossed peacock stationery from its pad and stuck it to his desk with a letter opener, then hauled his small valise from where he'd flung it earlier and started to throw in whatever came to hand.

Cross had known for ages. She had written to him and said

nothing. But why should she have told him? Maybe Asiyah hadn't approached her yet. And he'd certainly clipped the threads that connected them. Torn them apart with his teeth, more like. Just as he had every avenue that might have brought this news to him much sooner, in some less sensational way.

A pot of cold cream popped open on impact and spattered the inside of his case. He swore, tossed it out, and then sat down heavily on the chaise, head in his hands.

Someone knocked, very softly. He didn't answer, or even call out to them to go away. He was too busy holding in his breath, crushing the heels of his palms to his eyes.

Stupid. He was so, so stupid.

Another knock. He hardly even heard it.

What finally got him to look up, stand up, was the gentle rasp of metal in the keyhole, and the click of the latch. He was half-way across the room, stumbling in a fury, when Daoud opened the door.

"You have the *key* to my *rooms*?"

"I have the keys to every room," he said, pocketing the offending objects.

In some way, Aristide had known he had no true privacy at Hadhariti. He was in someone else's home, living largely on forbearance. Until lately, he had not minded; it had been numb surrender, almost pleasant. Now it all caught up with him. It cost him mightily not to break something.

"Did you come to *console* me?" he snarled, catching on the *s* like an angry snake. "I don't want a piece of it. *Leave.*"

"I will not," said Daoud. He looked around at the spilled cold cream staining the carpet, the letter opener stabbed through Aristide's hastily tendered resignation. The pill bottles and spectacles case resting crookedly at the bottom of an otherwise empty valise. "You are too drunk to drive anywhere, and besides, you will forget your toothbrush and underthings if someone does not calm you down." Neatly, he corked the whiskey bottle and set it back among its fellows.

"I said leave." Aristide's voice sounded thick to his own ears, but he couldn't tell if it was drink or emotion.

"No. Do not make me bully you."

"You," said Aristide, pointing a vicious finger at him, "overstep yourself. If you tried to bully me in earnest I would—"

"Kill me with your hands?" It wasn't mocking, but it carried too much pity.

Aristide made fists that put spasms in his forearms, then collapsed in despair onto the chaise beside his pathetic half-filled bag. "What do you *want*?"

"To see if you are well," he said, sitting down beside Aristide.

"I'm not. Will you go now?"

"And to ask you when you planned to leave."

He gauged his balance, his bravado. "As soon as I'm sober."

"In that case," Daoud said, "I am also here to ask you to postpone."

"Never."

"We will talk about it in the morning."

"I'll be gone by then."

Daoud's eyebrows quirked in poorly concealed amusement. "You will be hungover then."

"Why stay?" demanded Aristide. The liquor was settling in by now, and he hardly cared what he said or did. "I'm superfluous to Pulan's real business." "Superfluous" did not come out quite as he meant it to.

"You are not. The studio cannot afford to draw publicity now. If you resign so suddenly the tabloids will get ahold of it, and all eyes will turn to us. For the next week, things must run very smoothly."

"I will not make this easy for her," he said. "And especially not for *him*. I'm going, and they can't tell me when."

Daoud sighed. "You really think that he is still alive?"

"I know that I need to see for myself," said Aristide, staring at the white blots of cold cream on the carpet between his shoes. "Or I will live the rest of my life like a man with a toothache he cannot leave alone, and I will poke at it until it grows into an abscess, bursts, and kills me."

CHAPTER

NINETEEN

Lillian excused herself shortly after Makricosta made his exit, though she parted company less dramatically. She felt eyes linger on her as she left, and even without turning she knew whose they were. She was not surprised when, shortly after she fled to the upper terrace, she heard footsteps on the flagstone stairs.

"Not particularly subtle," she said. "How long did you wait before you followed me?"

«We don't need to be subtle anymore,» he said, and took her hand.

She had reached her capacity of shock for the day, so the impact of this blow was muted, diffuse. She pulled her hand away and curled it against her chest as if that might protect her heart from any further abuse. "You told them?"

He hung his head. «Pulan knows. And Ms. Lehane.»

"You shouldn't have." It came out as a sigh.

«How else could I explain myself, showing up here and demanding *your* son?»

She shook her head. "And if I hadn't changed my mind, what were you planning to do? Take my child from me?"

«He is my child too. Better he should have one parent than none.»

She had thought the evening's events had inured her to emotion, or emptied her reserves, but the deep volcanic well of her fury spat up a surge of magma. Her own growling voice surprised her. "He *did* have me. Just because he's at school doesn't mean I'm not his *mother*."

Jinadh's anger cracked back at her. «You aren't his mother, you're a *pawn*. He isn't just at school, Lillian, he's . . . dangling from a string in front of your face. You were never going to get him back.»

"So you were going to get him for yourself instead? That isn't your decision."

«More mine than most people's. I'm his father. Who is Maddox Flagg to Stephen?»

"He doesn't even know you!"

«And whose fault is that?»

It wasn't until the echo reached her, bouncing from the walls and windows, that Lillian realized he was shouting. They both were. A light flicked on inside the house, silhouetting a curious head. Lillian took a steadying breath and let it out in time with the rush of the receding tide.

«Walk with me,» she said, tilting her head toward the window. Saying it in Porashtu leant her poise, a ghost of diplomacy.

Jinadh gave a fractional nod, and motioned for her to descend the stairs ahead of him.

«I will not apologize for that,» he said to her back.

"Did I ask you to?"

They proceeded in silence to the lower terrace, at which point Lillian looked around helplessly for an exit. She felt backed against the cliff, trapped by the walls of Pulan's house.

Abandoning the Geddan that had so far only been a vent for her frustration, she asked, «Is there some way to get down to the beach? It will be quiet.»

«There's a lift,» he said. «Here.»

It was tucked into an alcove on the lower terrace, and they stood beside each other in silence as it fell. It let out into a dark antechamber, and when Jinadh opened the door, the room flooded with moonlight, reflected from the sand and water so it struck mirrors set into the walls. As the tide moved, the light moved, wavering across the tile floor, across the pale skin of Lillian's arms, across the white cambric of Jinadh's tunic and dhoti.

The soles of her pumps scraped; a fine layer of sand dusted the floor. She bent to remove her shoes, and left them by the door. Jinadh was already barefoot.

Between her toes, the dunes were still hot with the remains of the day's sunlight. The breeze off the water was warm, too, but it cooled sweat on Lillian's skin and she shivered.

«Here.» Jinadh took the fine white scarf from his shoulders and offered it to her.

«No, thank you.»

«At least allow me to be kind.» It almost came out a snap. If he had been any less strangled by societal convention, it would have.

Lillian gritted her teeth and held her hand out for the shawl, rather than let him wrap it around her. The fabric fell softly, almost imperceptible. Cashmere, still warm from his body heat. It smelled of him, too: sweat, of course, and his cologne of leather, figs, and sandalwood. Under it all, the particular smell that was just . . . Jinadh.

She did not raise the fabric to her face, but it was a very near thing.

«I told you I would go to prison,» she said, as much to remind herself as him. «That I would face retribution if Memmediv miscalculated. And you still went to him.» She should have been shocked, or angry. Instead, a chasm of sadness cracked open in her chest. «Did that mean nothing to you?»

«It meant everything to me,» he said. «But in the end, Stephen meant more. As I'm sure he does to you.»

The truth of it settled onto her shoulders, and she wondered she didn't sink into the sand. She felt as heavy and exhausted as she had late in her pregnancy, with so many of the same dreads she had carried then and none of the anticipatory joy.

There was a flat stone at the high-tide mark, seaweed caught around its base. Breaking away from Jinadh, she lowered herself to its warm surface. Grit and salt clung to her palms, and the tense ache in the large muscles along her spine settled into a steady gentle pain that was almost comforting in its familiarity. The only familiar thing she had, tonight, and she clung to it.

Jinadh picked a stone from the sand and pitched it out to sea. He stared after it for a long time, as if searching in vain for ripples.

«Can I trust you?»

He spoke softly, but in the stillness filled only with waves and night birds and soughing dune grass, the sound of his voice still jarred her. She had been, she realized, half asleep. «What?»

«Casting in with Memmediv,» he said. «Are you in earnest? Or is it just another ruse?»

«It isn't a ruse,» she said. «I just can't manage it anymore.»

«*You* can't manage it? I have *had* to manage it.»

She closed her eyes. On the backs of her lids she could still see the long rollers spreading into white foam. The water rose to her ankles at the foot of the rock, and receded. «I'm sorry.»

The warmth of him was her first indication he had sat beside her, not quite touching. «Lillian,» he said. «May I ask you something?»

She snorted, clinging too precariously to composure for polish. «As if I could stop you.»

«Did you begin this affair because . . . because a handler asked you to? Am I a target? Was I some kind of bargaining chip?»

It turned out she was quite able to feel shock, after all. Only this time there was no anger: just a deep, aching sorrow. «Oh, Jinadh. How long have you been wondering about *that*?»

He was angry, though. «It doesn't seem so implausible, now that I've seen what you're capable of.»

That stung, especially since he hadn't been privy to Flagg's original plans for her, and that she had been prepared to undertake them. Perversely, she wanted to tell him. Instead, she said, «If our affair had been some kind of operation, I would not have kept the baby. You never would have known. *They* never would have known. I would never have had Stephen with the *intention* of using him like he's being used now. Even if I . . . »

He tried to wait her out. She saw him try. But he broke a moment too soon and said, «Even if what?»

Damnation. She should have stopped before she let out that ellipsis.

«Lillian,» he said, and she felt him move on the rock but couldn't look at him if she had to say the thing he wanted her to. She stared at the tops of the cliffs, instead—first at the scattered lights still burning in the studio buildings to the south, and then the lights in the upper floors of the house: other people with other awful secrets. She wondered how many of them would sleep peacefully tonight.

He said her name again, this time not so steadily.

"I wouldn't have done it," she said, in her native tongue for certainty of meaning, speaking to the walls of sandstone, the echoing crash of the surf. "Even if I hadn't felt the way I did, about you."

Rage had been leaking from him since she said she had never intended their affair to yield assets. The last of it trickled away now. "Did?" he asked, also in Geddan. He was too fluent to question the tense, which meant the question was weightier than that.

Here she had to laugh, to keep back tears. Her body demanded one or the other, and the first gave less ground. "Things are a little different now, aren't they? Than when we started, I mean." As she said it, she realized that it wasn't true as she intended, but in a much more frightening way: Now, she had every reason to leave with him, and—fate willing—the ability to do so. She had no excuses left. She wasn't sure she wanted them.

"They do not have to be," he said. "Not now."

She felt his palm over the back of her hand. This time she let him take it, and did not pull away. Some reticence lingered in her wrist, her elbow, but he was patient.

«This is our chance,» said Jinadh. «I believe Ms. Lehane can do what she says—snatch Stephen from Gedda. We can take him and go somewhere new. We can make a life without all this, without politics and intrigue.»

"I wouldn't know what to do with myself," she said, lingering in jocular territory to save herself a cliff dive into something more significant. "I've spent my entire life dedicated to precisely that. I'm a very specialized piece of machinery." *She* had never shared her workload, shared her worries, shared herself.

He cradled her face and she let the urge to flinch pass through her and shatter on her will. It wasn't that his touch repelled her; she had simply spent too long afraid someone might see him do this and draw the correct conclusions. Too long afraid that if she let her weight fall into his arms, she would not be able to stand again under her own strength.

The pads of his fingers were warm against her skin. "You are not a machine. And you will kill yourself if you continue to act like one."

"Like my father," she said, and laughed. "How many times did Mother say that to me? 'You're just like your father.'"

"You do not *have* to be."

She lifted her cheek from his hand, and finally looked him fully in the face. "But I would *like* to be. That's what you didn't understand, when I wouldn't leave with you." She meant it professionally, but as the words came out she remembered her father's cursory kisses on the top of her mother's head, the way their marriage seemed to function like a business or alliance between foreign powers. In her memory, there was no instance in which they leaned on each other.

Now she wondered if they had only hid it from her, and the world. Holding up under strain alone took a steep toll; in a geopolitical alliance, didn't one power support another in a crisis?

He lifted her knuckles to his lips. When he spoke, she felt his lips move, saw his jaw shift beneath his closely trimmed beard. "You so rarely spoke about your family. I knew you had a brother, but . . ."

Her fingers twitched, unbidden, and he smoothed them with his own. "I wish you hadn't heard all that. It was . . ." She squeezed his hand. "Thank you, for getting them all in order like you did. I couldn't have stood the scramble much longer."

"I am glad I did hear it," he said. "I want to share these things with you. I want to help you bear them." She could feel his breath on the sensitive skin.

Her breath hitched, but she steadied it.

"Jinadh," she said, putting one foot over the precipice.

He made a small noise of assent, mouth opening against the divot between her knuckles so she felt the warm inner edge of his lips.

"If we run—"

The movement of his breath ceased against her hand. She imagined she could feel even his blood pause in its beating.

"If we run," she repeated, leaping into open water from the crumbling headland of her certainty, "we have to think about money. I won't have anything beyond what I can carry—they aren't going to let me access any of my accounts once they realize what I've done." She should pull her hand away from him; he had turned it over and laid his face in her palm, rubbing his beard against it like a cat, and kissing the pulse point on her wrist. Then she realized that she didn't have to; that she could take small comfort in his touch and still forge ahead. "And forgive me, but *you* are a very charming sponge. You live on your aunt's generosity, and that won't last if—Are you even listening to me?"

His laughter was almost too low to hear, but she felt his body move and the exhalation against her skin. When he spoke, it was in Porashtu, and the sensuality of the language in his mouth caught her by surprise. She had forgotten how it could sound, when it wasn't being used as a tool of diplomacy, a lever against an opponent.

«Enough to know you should put it all aside for now,» he said. «Tonight, my love, have faith.»

After *that* dinner, Cordelia was ready to walk back to the city and start auditioning for any other studio that would have her, with or without references or an understanding of the local language.

But that wouldn't get guns for her scrappers, so she took herself in hand and dragged her rear out of the dining room. Asiyah invited her to smoke hookah with him, and she knew she ought to do it to build some kind of fellow feeling, but she just couldn't face another minute of conversation.

Out the back door the terrace was quiet and shadowy. Cordelia sank into one of the woven divans and put her face in her hands.

Cyril had been alive this whole time. Mother's tits. And now he was . . . well. Who knew? Ari's face hung in her mind's eyes, slack as a death mask.

And Vasily Memmediv had done it all. Or at least, enough of it to get eyeball-deep in rancid shit with Ari.

And her? Well, she was wading in there, too, if she was honest with herself. And it was too late to get out, even if she wanted to.

Under the sound of the waves, she heard the sharp ring of hard leather shoes on marble. Faint light from the inner rooms of the house showed the edge of a silhouette against a darkened archway.

Geddan shoes, and not tall enough to be Ari or small enough to be Daoud. Asiyah had been wearing slippers.

"You can find somewhere else to feel sorry for yourself," she told Memmediv. "I don't want to watch."

He didn't quite laugh—it was a sort of loud sigh, pushed out at speed. "Are you going to knock me down if I don't go?"

"Nah," she said. "Too easy."

"Indeed." He struck a match, startling her, and held it to the straight between his lips. "From what I hear, you like your tasks impossible."

"Yeah?" She cocked her head, inviting more despite herself.

"Pulan says you're going back to Gedda. I don't like your chances."

"What else you hear? And where from?"

"Where do you think?" he asked. "I know what I look like, but the CIS doesn't just push papers."

"I listen to the wireless," she said. "And read the papers when I can. I know what you've been doing to my people."

"Not me," he said, and she was surprised by the softness of it.

"That pity I hear?"

"I was aiming for sympathy."

She shook her head. "I don't want it from you."

"Too late," he said. "I admire what the Catwalk has done, with so little."

"You calling us cheap?"

"Thrifty. Inventive. Determined."

"Yeah, well." She pulled her feet up off the tile and tucked them under her rear. "Look what all it's done for us. Acherby's still sitting in the Cliff House and parliament ain't sitting anywhere. Decent folk are getting drug in to inform on their neighbors, and their neighbors are getting penned up under armed guard to die of dysentery."

"Your people aren't decent folk," he said. "They're soldiers."

"They're idiots," she said, meaning it hard when the word came out and feeling sorry about it before she took her next breath. "I'm an idiot." He didn't try to reassure her. She was grateful for that, but a little pinned, too. "Inaz asked me what I thought I was doing, and I got to admit, I ain't fighting a war right now. I'm spitting at a fire."

He finally left the doorway and came to the patio furniture, walking slow, putting down one foot before he picked up the next. When he sat, he took a shaky breath and hung his head before he spoke.

"Since we're sharing," he said, "I will admit that on our own, we have little hope of making a dent. Popular opinion has turned from us; not because Tatiens don't *want* their land, but because they have given up hope of ever taking it back. These peace talks with Tzieta? Would not have happened five years ago, when our pride was starving and savage."

"Why now, then? The Ospies lifted the state tariffs, and you all felt grateful for the bone?"

He snorted. "What they gave us was a mercy killing. There is no more desperation now, because there is no more pride. A fight like mine, pride is the only thing that will keep you bleeding. Now Dastya is becoming a tired cause; if Tatié is not roused soon, it will swallow this armistice without complaint."

Tired. That was for sure. *We need more phosphorus, more copper pipes, more food. We can't afford that and still pay bribes. Can we hold out another week, another month, another year?*

Victory had never seemed like a possibility. Only spiteful, grinding opposition.

She stared into Memmediv's dark eyes, caught in a web of pained lines and tired shadows. He stared back from deep beneath hard eyebrows; he had bones you could bruise yourself on if you got too close.

But getting in with him might be worth the black and blue, if they could offer each other something. She hated to think of throwing in with the man who'd done for Cyril, but a lot of the bitter things she'd swallowed in the last few years had helped her on her way.

"Sounds to me like we got similar problems," she said.

Memmediv cocked his head, and the ember on his straight flared before he pulled it from his lips to say, all smoky, "And?"

"You think this might be one of those times when two left turns'll take you right?"

He squinted at her through his cigarette haze, and she could feel him hesitating at the edge of a cliff, casing a narrow bridge across, no railings. Gauging what might be worth the risk of crossing to the other side.

She knew the feeling.

There was a hard irony in fighting back against the Ospies: It required blind trust on an order Cordelia would not have countenanced before. You had to trust everyone to do their jobs, to look one way while you looked the other. But on the flip side of the coin, you couldn't really trust anyone, not all the way.

The Catwalk was good at what it did, or had been until this latest spate of roundups. Still, you couldn't trust every board of it; there were paths she didn't care to walk for fear of dry rot that still did their job enough she left them alone.

Hammering down another moldy board, holding her breath when she stepped across it—if it would get her where she wanted to be, she'd take the risk.

"You got money, right?" she asked. "And old soldiers. Folk who know their way around real war. And you got some way to get your guns over the border from the drop point in Tzieta."

That got her a grudging nod: hardly more than a dip of his chin and the gleam of changing light across his eye.

"All right. So we got folk inside Gedda proper. Not just Tatié. We got 'em in all four states, but they're hanging on by their little fingers and they're scared because they don't know from beans. We made up most of what we did as we went along."

"I think that we have very different goals," he said. "My people want to break away from Gedda—federal policy has never aligned with the needs of Tatié. It has made us check our blows for too long. Even under the Ospies, who promised otherwise."

"Well, there you go," said Cordelia. "We want the Ospies gone. After that, I don't care what you do."

"You misunderstand me," he said. "I don't care about the Ospies. They can keep the rest of Gedda if they want, as long as they cede my state to its own independent government."

Cordelia closed her eyes and blew out a breath. She was ready to hit him, but it might put him under, or do worse, the state he was in. Maybe he'd forget the whole thing that way. But those bright black eyes were a pitch trap and she knew he wouldn't. Which meant she had to convince him now, or he'd be laughing at her as long as they both breathed above the dirt.

"Look, you rotten cockle." She let her feet down, put her elbows on her knees, and leaned in close to his face. Bruising distance. He winced as he tried to focus. "I didn't open up this line of conversation so we could argue over millet seeds. You're losing ground to folk who don't see an end in this for them. They're ready to sign away the thing you've been chewing your own leg off for because they think you chewed it off for nothing."

"You think I don't dwell on that every night before I go to sleep?" he said, weary as a cart horse.

She put a hand up to stop him. "I say, you're on the eastern front of this and we're on all the others. The Ospies won't let you go 'cause you poke them with a stick; you've got to land a mortar where it hurts them. Throw in with me, this won't be the same old worn-out scrabble about Dastya. It'll be civil war. The Ospies ain't ready for that, and they'll crumble like dried-up swineshit. Plus, you show a little strength, flex your muscles, prove yourselves. Give your people's pride a meal. Do this with me, you get what you want, we get what we want, and then we shake hands and get back to our own business. Do you clock me or are you still standing there blowing air up your own asshole?"

He looked a little shocked. Good. If she was going to swallow all the hate she felt toward him and shake his hand, she needed him to look a little less like he knew better than her. Even if it might be true.

CHAPTER

TWENTY

The sheet was cool on Lillian's skin when she woke up and stretched, sore as if from vigorous exercise. But she hadn't—

Her flexing foot struck a calf, slipped to a hairy ankle.

That pulled her fully out of sleep, into a bedroom that was not hers, nor even the bedroom Satri had given her. This one was larger, airier, with a balcony at the southwest corner, open onto an ocean view and the cliffs marching down the coast. Royal falcons stooped from every curl of the bed frame, burned in the brightly painted frescos, glittered in the mosaic of the floor. Somewhere on the grounds, outside the open window, a peacock bawled.

She craned her neck to look above her head, and sure enough: the royal crest hung above, vaguely threatening with its curved scimitar and flail, its growling hyena and screaming bird of prey.

Reflexive anxiety spread through her body like a fever, making her flush. She used to have *dreams* like this: waking up in a room like this one, next to Jinadh. She would open her eyes, convinced everything was real, and then the door would burst open and—

But it didn't. Distantly, she heard someone else open theirs, the rattle of a tray, the murmur of voices. No one disturbed the peace of the royal suite.

Still shaken, Lillian turned carefully onto her side. She had never made it this far, in her dreams. She had *known* he was beside her but never seen his face.

In sleep his lips parted slightly, and the permanent small furrow between his eyebrows smoothed flat. Someone breathing more easily, without so many misgivings, would have leaned in to kiss that small patch of skin, dusted with fine, dark hair. She used to wake him like that.

This morning she only ghosted the tips of her fingers across it, barely touching, and then pressed them to her lips. She did not want to rouse him, though she wasn't sure why. Some combination of rational fears—they would have to *talk*, to make *decisions*—and irrational. If he opened his eyes, perhaps she would find they were in *his* dream, and might still be disturbed, discovered.

He must have sensed her wakefulness. Though he did not quite open his eyes or speak, he made a sound that was half a word and moved closer, curling into the line of her body. The touch of his skin felt like a vivid memory, but it was in the present and very real: dry and cool like the coarse back side of charmeuse. When she—cautiously—put her nose into the tangle of his hair, she smelled nutty argan oil, stale tobacco smoke, and the last heart notes of his cologne.

"Lillian?" This time he *was* awake, and she had to gather herself before she could afford to pull her head back and face him. Her eyes stung and her heart fought to escape its cage.

«Are you well?» he asked, blinking sleepily. The divot between his eyebrows returned.

«No,» she said, which made him laugh until he woke fully and got a look at her face.

«You're frightened,» he said. «About what?»

She laughed, then. "Reach in the hat and choose one."

Sliding one arm through the space between the mattress and her ribs, he put the other in the divot of her waist and pulled them closer together.

"I'm a traitor to my government—a crime for which my brother was killed."

"Or not," said Jinadh, into the crease of her neck.

"Might as well have been," she amended. "And the man who drew him into treachery has drawn me just as surely, using my son as bait. Not to mention that a secret I've rigorously kept for a decade has abruptly come into the open."

He moved away, so she could see his face if she worked to focus on it. "The last one. Why does that frighten you?"

"I don't—" She closed her eyes and caught the raw inside of her lip in her teeth, trying to sort out the strands of thought snarled in her skull. "No, I do know. It's . . . I worry if I let this one thing go, if I give myself that much leave . . . that it will feel so good that I forget to—oh."

His hand had slipped between her thighs.

«Moon-eyes,» he said, «fire of my heart. Please breathe.»

She did, shuddering.

His next words were spoken against the curve of her throat, barely audible, more felt than heard. «You will not forget, because of who you are.»

"Wound tight?" she gasped. Sweat prickled between her breasts.

He smiled against her skin, then licked the place beneath her jaw that always ached with tension. «As a watch spring. But, too, you are careful, and patient, and circumspect.» He licked the other side of her neck, nipped her earlobe. «Graceful, poised. A diplomat.»

By now she could not speak, only bite down on whimpers and wrap her fingers in Jinadh's hair until he hissed with pain. But when she tried to let him go he pressed the curve of his skull into her palm and said, «It's fine, it's fine,» so she tore at him, put her teeth into the meat of his shoulder to stifle a cry.

«So quiet,» he said, breath in her ear. «You don't need to be. Not now.»

The muscles in her back and the curve below her belly tightened, and she heard Jinadh make a small sound of surprise, felt his hand flex. She could taste blood in her mouth, and realized she had bitten the inside of her cheek—the same place she found with her teeth each time she wanted to talk back, to snap or snark or say something unwise.

«Lillian,» said Jinadh. «Please. I want to hear you scream.»

And like water pouring from a shattered dam, she did.

No sooner had she caught her breath than someone knocked on the door. Lillian froze, heart pounding. A timid footman's voice called in from the hallway. «Coffee?»

Jinadh took one look at her face and burst into helpless laughter. At first, she was chagrined, but then she found it was infectious, and surrendered.

Cordelia could say one thing about Pulan, which was no matter what dust and thunder got kicked up around her house, she always put food on the table.

Not, necessarily, that folk showed up to meals on time.

Breakfast had been laid out on the terrace, but so far only Asiyah and Inaz had staggered out, bleary-eyed, to drain small cups of coffee and retreat to the cool interior of the house. They must have got up to more than smoking hookah last night, and she was glad she hadn't joined them—better to have a clear head around this house.

Memmediv, understandably, had stayed in bed. Daoud was missing again. Pulan looked almost naked without him, and now each time she turned to ask him for something—write down a date, check her calendar—and found him missing, annoyance flashed in her eyes.

Ari was missing, too. But given his mood last night, Cordelia didn't think he was up to shucking any oysters.

When Jinadh and Lillian showed up at breakfast, though, Cordelia had to shove a piece of pastry in her mouth to keep from saying something off-color. She choked on it, too, so she ended up coughing and pounding on her chest.

Lillian had a blush on her cheek, and couldn't quite raise her eyes. Jinadh looked pleased with himself. A love bite bloomed just inside the collar of his tunic, a mottled shadow on his brown-black skin.

Pulan pursed her lips and picked up her coffee, ignoring their entrance.

She must be croup-serious about this taboo thing. And she could see the strain starting to ratchet tighter on Lillian's face, and anger evaporating the sleepy, sated look Jinadh had been wearing so well.

So Cordelia swallowed down the dry lump of flaky dough that had choked her, and managed a hoarse "Glad to see you two ain't been getting up to nothing."

That broke the awkwardness that had started to pile up like a thunderhead. Lillian turned even pinker.

"Ms. DePaul," said Pulan, without a spare glance for Jinadh or a spare second for small talk, "I understand you came to Hadhariti for an explanation."

Lillian lowered herself into an empty chair, embarrassment fading from her cheeks. "It wouldn't go amiss."

"Ms. Lehane agreed to help us with your problem," said Pulan. "Long before, I now understand, you truly agreed to help with ours."

"I apologize," said Lillian. "But you must see—."

"She is only trying to raise your guilt," said Jinadh. "Do not let her."

Lillian shot him a sharp look, all her tenderness replaced with rue. "And I was only trying to be polite."

He shrugged and sank back into the wicker divan, giving Lillian the stage. But he didn't stop staring at Cordelia, hunger and hope bright in his eyes.

"They tell me you can get my son," said Lillian. Then, at the press of Jinadh's hand over hers, she added, "*Our* son. What *is* your plan?"

"I got a lot of people still roaming around Gedda," said Cordelia, which was sort of true. For accuracy, she should probably have dropped "a lot."

"The Catwalk," said Lillian. "We can be frank. It isn't a secret any longer."

"Right. So, I've got—or should have—a pair of hands in Cantrell who can set me up with something. Except communications are rough. We used to use a radio channel, but we'd change the codes and frequencies pretty often, and the broadcast time. Miss one call, you can't pick up the next one." It had been a good system. Nobody had ever got drug in off a tip from the wireless. Only once folk started talking in person. "There are safe houses and drop points all over the country but what good does that do me if I'm in Porachis?"

"*You* are going back to Gedda?" Lillian's flush evaporated. "I can't say I like your odds."

"I'm clever and keen," she said, defensive. Memmediv had said the same thing, and other people's doubt always made her cocky. "And I can keep my head down. But I do have a problem."

"Which is?"

"Once I get there, I don't know what things are supposed to look like. Figured you could help with that. What's the steps to this dance? Who picks your kid up at the end of term? What kind of car do they drive? What kind of papers they carry?"

"I don't know. I've never gone along. My guess is a black car, government plates. Maybe flags on the bonnet. That's how the diplomats' children went when I was young, but that was years ago. Someone at the school could tell you, probably."

Greasepaint might know somebody, if he was still in place. Mother's tits, too many ifs.

"They'd carry credentials, too," said Lillian. "And there's always a letter, saying who's to take him, and where. Flagg usually writes the letters," she added. "I only sign them."

That cruelty had an outsize sting. It was funny, how the small insults really made her gorge rise, when the Ospies stood for much larger things, and worse.

"This time," said Cordelia, "you're gonna write it. We can get a car easy enough, and the flags. Plates'll be tough but we might be able to fake that with some spit and polish." She was lying, a little, maybe. But even if her folk were all drug in to the last pair of boots, surely she could scrounge a car. For Queen's sake.

"You'll have to get there before the people they actually send," she cautioned. "Otherwise I'm fairly certain they'll be able to tell the difference."

"Have you signed Flagg's letter yet?" asked Cordelia.

Lillian nodded. "Last week. What about the government credentials?"

Yeah, she was stuck on that one, too.

"I have some."

They all looked up at the new voice. Memmediv leaned heavily on one of the pillars, wearing dark glasses and holding a cup of steaming coffee.

"Mr. Memmediv," said Pulan, a little too brightly. "How are you feeling this morning?"

"Unwell," he said, and staggered toward an empty chair. By the time he sat down there was a fine white line around his lips.

"Perhaps," Jinadh suggested frostily, "you should have stayed in bed."

"And miss the explanation that I promised to Ms. DePaul? Especially when it seems I might be useful. Permit me one suggestion?"

Cordelia looked to Lillian. Her jaw was stiff and where Jinadh's hand was on her knee she covered it with her own. She didn't clench her fist, but the pads of her fingers were pale from the pressure. Still, she gave a single, curt nod.

"Let me get the boy."

For a tense moment, Lillian said nothing and Jinadh watched her. Cordelia prayed this living DePaul could step over the dead (or resurrected) one. She needed Memmediv to stay on her good side.

"What are you thinking?" Lillian asked, after a pause that taught Cordelia the scripture by heart.

"I need a way out of Porachis that will take me close to the border, and my people, once the guns come through. Flagg is already suspicious, and Lillian can only put him off for so long. When things crumble, which they will, I want to be safely out from under his boot. I can bring the boy across the border to Asiyah, on the film set. He can fly Stephen wherever you need him to be. Which, I think, should be outside of Porachis."

"You're too high profile," said Lillian.

"No," he said. "I'm just high enough. Nobody at Cantrell will question me, not with my credentials. Not the way I will wield them."

"And Flagg?" She was bearing down on him now, like a sleek hound over a rat or a weasel. "How am I supposed to distract him from your absence? What am I supposed to say?"

"You don't have to say anything," he said. "As long as we have a good diversion. Ideally, one that puts the spotlight where Flagg doesn't want it, and keeps the press attaché far too busy for intrigue."

The coin hit the pavement half a second later for Cordelia than it did for Lillian, who was already saying, "You're talking about Sofie Keeler, aren't you? Breaking the story about her wife in jail?"

Memmediv touched the frames of his sunglasses, moving them a fussy fraction of an inch up his nose. He didn't say yes, but he didn't have to: His smile crept across his face at quarter-speed.

"It . . . isn't a bad plan."

Cordelia wondered what it cost Lillian to say that. Her face gave nothing away.

"It is an excellent plan," said Pulan, "and puts Vasily where I would prefer him, without bringing my name into the . . . oh, fiasco? Yes. Does it suit you, Ms. Lehane? You could travel together. It would give you good cover, moving with an Ospie diplomat."

She liked it. She *hated* that she liked it, but Pulan was right. She could pose as Memmediv's secretary, maybe. Wear a skirt suit and gloves with the fingers stuffed and not say much at all. Just nod and smile and get him sandwiches, like Daoud did for Pulan. And how many times had she forgotten Daoud was even in the room? She would be invisible.

Lillian looked like she was working up to say something, but before she could get it out, the ring of leather on marble echoed from inside the house, and Daoud came skidding onto the terrace, out of breath.

He gasped something in Porashtu, which got him a swear out of Pulan, and a name.

"*Aristide*," she said, with the same kind of long-suffering venom Cordelia had heard out of people married to drunks who just wouldn't die.

"Please excuse me." Pulan rose from her chair and set her coffee by. "A small problem has arisen."

And while Lillian and Jinadh seemed content to let her handle it, and Memmediv had turned even paler than before, Cordelia got up to follow.

He was actually in the rotten car before Pulan came after him. But she caught him cursing at a flooded engine, trapped in the turnaround.

He'd meant to get an earlier start, but slept through sunrise and woken with a pounding head that wouldn't permit any sudden movements. He hadn't managed to pack the night before, and while he didn't need many things, he did need *some*. He was so ill-prepared he felt trapped in a parody of his flight from Amberlough. Even the outcomes were reversed.

Stones, he *hoped* the outcomes would be reversed.

"Aristide," said Pulan, "where are you rushing to, so soon after your return?"

Cordelia trailed after her, narrow-eyed and silent. He resented her for looking so much better than she had when he scooped her from the gutter last week, and for slotting so easily into Pulan's subterfuge. The shadows under her eyes had faded, and she walked a little straighter—less like she expected a sniper's shot or a bomb blast. He suspected the latter had less to do with food and sleep and more to do with successful business dealings. She took to Pulan's lifestyle very well, with excellent effect, while all it had done for him was break his teeth, give him an ulcer, and turn him into an alcoholic.

Well. Perhaps the lifestyle wasn't entirely to blame.

"You were supposed to find my resignation letter after I'd gone," he said. "It's stuck to my desk. With a knife, and all my love."

"Well, I did not find it," she said. "I found you first. Which means I can tell you in person, I do not accept it."

"I don't care if you do or don't." He tried the ignition again, to no avail. Queen's cunt, if he had to *walk* to Anadh, he would. "I'm leaving."

"If this is about Mr. Memmediv—"

"It doesn't matter what it's about," he said. "Nothing you can say will keep me in this house a moment longer."

"If you go," said Pulan, "you put many of us in danger. Including—perhaps especially—Ms. Lehane."

He hoped he didn't look as startled as Cordelia did. He certainly felt it. "Explain that one to me."

She crossed the gravel of the drive and folded her arms on the side of his car, tucking her chin over her crossed wrists. Kitten-like, she smiled.

"Do you think it prudent," she said, "to stir up a storm of gossip in the glossies at this moment? Do you think it would be good, to have so many curious eyes watching the studio, as we begin to shoot in Tzieta?"

She had leaned into the last sentence a little too hard. "You don't want me tearing the lid off your little business deal."

"Nobody does," she said. "Am I right, Ms. Lehane?"

A flush turned her sunburned face blotchy under its freckles. "Pulan, I don't—"

"What did you do?" he asked, because this had become absurd: all of the elisions and evasions and the questions neither asked nor answered. The assumption that ignorance meant safety for both of them. "Who did you become, while my back was turned? Sofie Cattayim said you're some kind of terrorist."

"And what do *you* know of Sofie Cattayim?" Pulan's voice was sharp with curiosity, and maybe fear.

"I know our friend here got her into an awful bind," said Aristide, "and she wanted me to get her out."

"*You* gave her Memmediv's name," said Cordelia. "Tits, Ari. Like trouble wasn't tailing us close enough already."

"Us," he hissed, and shook his head. "She was right, then. What is it you're up to now? Planning some kind of fireworks display?"

"If I tell you," she said, "you promise you won't go haring off to Liso?"

His dignity bowed heavily under that assumption, but he shored it up and raised his chin. "You don't know *where* I'm going."

Her eye roll bore down heavily on his creaking sense of self-assurance. "Well, if all you're going to do is mock me," he said, and made as if to turn the useless key.

"Ari, wait." Cordelia took a step forward, dropping her attitude in favor of earnest insistence. "Stay. Just for a little while—a week or so. It wouldn't be great if you went right now and folk start looking our way. Especially not with Lillian—"

"Oh, are you going to twist that knife as well?" He wrenched the keys so hard they tore the skin in the crease of his knuckle. Hissing, he pulled back his hand. There was nothing for the engine but to let it drain. "You might as well fillet me."

"I ain't *twisting*," she said. "I ain't in that line. Never have been. Why do you always think other folk'll do what you would? We ain't all got your gears and springs behind our eyes."

"Perhaps," said Pulan, "we could discuss this indoors? The heat is coming up."

"I'm scared," said Cordelia, and he admired how she ran over Pulan in favor of him. Not many people would dare. "Not just for me. I'm scared for Lillian and her kid and that dope who'd lie down in front of a—"

"Kid?" he said, because he'd stopped listening after she said that. The other words had flowed over him while that one burrowed in and stuck, parasitic, leaching warmth from his limbs.

"Yeah," said Cordelia. "Mother's tits, I can't keep track of who knows what anymore. Her kid. Stephen. With Jinadh."

He blinked at his own hands on the useless steering wheel, wondering when his grip had grown so tight. "A son?"

"Aristide, please get out of the car."

Distantly, he could tell Pulan's voice had taken on an edge. She was still trying to be pleasant, but she was a hairsbreadth from calling for Pramit or one of the bigger footmen to manhandle him out of the driver's seat, if necessary.

Maybe they would have to. He wasn't sure his own limbs would obey him. He couldn't remember exactly how it felt to move under his own power.

Cyril would have been—or was?—an uncle. Why did that strike him as little else had? It did not hurt *worse* than Cyril's death, or his sudden resurrection so swiftly followed by news of his disappearance. It didn't have the same heft as any of those things. But like a sliver of glass, featherweight and nearly invisible, it slipped into him with agonizing precision and promised pain with every step, every brush of fabric on his skin.

"How old is he?" His own voice, wet and hoarse and caught deep in his chest, alarmed him. He did not sound like himself.

"I don't see—" Pulan started, but Cordelia cut her off.

"He's eight," she said. "Old enough to be away at school."

Another thing he had never known. Had never thought to ask. Not, he suspected, that Cyril would have told the whole truth. But he might have guessed something from the other man's evasions, if he'd bothered to elicit them in the first place.

How careful they had been with each other, despite the bruises, scratches, bite marks, blows.

He felt a sense of inevitability drawing close around him. There might have been resentment, too, but it was muffled, far away. All he felt now was the riptide of Cordelia's confession drawing him along: *I'm scared for Lillian and her kid.*

He could leave now and run headlong into the Lisoan jungle, but if he found Cyril, did he want to haul him out of the jungle to see Lillian's face on the front page of the paper, Cordelia in prison or worse, and all of it his fault for being in too much of a hurry?

He yanked the keys from the ignition so suddenly he caught Cordelia flinching from the corner of his eye. "All right," he said, "but from here on out, you tell me everything."

"You *what*?" He had expected something sinister, but not quite on this level. He was, quite honestly, impressed. Impressed and horrified.

"Yeah. The Bee, that was our first hit. Or, mine. Zelda Peronides put me in touch with a guy, and then he knew this peach—used to work the theatre district—it was her who said why didn't we go bigger, branch out. She was the brains behind it all. I was just kind of . . ."

"A figurehead." He shook his own, looked down into the glass of fig brandy warming in his palm. Pulan had left them alone, in the library: a dark room with narrow, high windows and deep shelves of books bound in jewel-toned leathers tooled with gold. It was also the home of the best-stocked bar in Hadhariti, where rows of fancifully shaped bottles nestled in terraced ranks before a three-sided mirror. He was even gladder of this now than he had been when Pulan first guided them inside and shut the door.

"We were doing all right for a year or two," she said. "I was pretty surprised you didn't clock me straight off, or even suspect. We weren't really low profile, until we started getting torn up in Amberlough and Nuesklend, and had to lay down in a ditch up north for a while. People started coming to us up there, even. The thinking was we'd go bigger when we'd gotten our feet under us again."

"And since I found you stumbling through Chitra's choreography in open auditions, I assume you never did?"

"Nah. We got word the CIS had our scent and they bundled me out first off. My right hand said . . ." *Folk look to you. If you get drug in, we fall flat.* "Said we'd all get back on track when it blew over, but it didn't. It got real bad."

"And how did you end up staying with the Cattayims?"

"Mab's family put some of us up, in the mountains," she said. "She was sending money. When I had to go, that's where they sent me. The two of them didn't clock my face—didn't remember ever meeting me."

"Well, they remembered *me*," he said. "And hauled me into this mess I only ever wanted to turn my back on."

"Hauled you?" she said. "How in damnation was Sofie Keeler gonna haul you anywhere? You got all this money, all these friends, and all she had was her wife and her kid and two rooms over a fry shop. Even if she had a juicy cut of gossip on you, the spatter wouldn't touch you when she slapped it down."

"Recent circumstances seem to have proved you wrong," he said, happy not to comment on the dubious strength of his friendships, and the distinct lack of heel marks in the dirt where he had gone to Sofie willingly.

"All right, I'll give you that one." Cordelia crossed her arms, which had been aggressively held akimbo until now. "Why'd you give her Memmediv's name? Because you were mad about Cyril?"

"No," he said. "I—I didn't know, yet. But I was certainly angry at all of this . . . *intrigue* cropping up when I thought I'd left it behind." He drank, swallowed, concentrated on the burn of the liquor down to his belly. He didn't notice he had closed his eyes until Cordelia spoke and he realized he couldn't see her.

"The way you get your creepers into every crack," she said, "I don't think you could get free of your own tangle even if you wanted to."

When he looked up, her arms were still crossed but their line had gone soft. She was shaking her head almost fondly.

"You know," she said, "it was Mab said I should look you up. That you might have some work for me."

"I didn't realize it would be quite so up your alley."

She snorted. "So far up it's against the wall."

"What's your plan, then? Or can't you tell me?"

"It's my job to get Lillian's kid out of Gedda safe," she said. "And then for gratitude, Pulan drops a heavy load of dynamite for me, some guns and ammunition. Plus good boots, tents, all the kind of stuff they give an army that we never managed to put together for ourselves. Rucksacks and blankets and things for living rough, out of sight. Take the load off the Chuli, if we can. See if we can do some good there. I'd wager they'll put their weight behind us if we get them out of the pens."

"And then what? You . . . kill Acherby? Blow up the Cliff House? How many of you are there? You can't possibly win."

She closed her eyes at that, and breathed deep through her nose. A flush crept up her neck. He had made her very angry, but she was mastering it for him. To keep from driving him off again. When she had herself in hand, she opened her eyes and stared straight into his. "I threw in with Memmediv."

Aristide felt his mouth drop open, but wasn't sure if any words were forthcoming. Cordelia cut them off if they were.

"He's got people with experience, and he can hold the east for me, or anyway keep the Ospies dancing fast over there while we sneak up to trip them from behind."

"You," he said. Then, lagging too long after it, "What?"

"Don't start in about Cyril. I swallowed that castor and now I'm moving on. He's got something I want. Don't tell me you never worked with somebody you hated before. Don't tell me you never bit your tongue and nodded."

The curve of the brandy glass filled his hand more snugly than it had before. He breathed into his grip, willing the muscles to loosen up, then set the glass aside to spare it further danger.

"Ari," she said. "I think if I use him, I can win."

"Win what?" he said. "Civil war?"

She shrugged, as if he'd asked her what time a train arrived, or if the post had come. "If it comes to that. And I think it will."

Her nonchalance changed something in the air between them, as if a gauzy scrim had lifted and he saw her clearly for the first time since she had arrived in Porachis. Cordelia Lehane was no longer the stripper from the Bee, but someone to be reckoned with, and feared.

«I'm not sure about this.» Pacing along the balustrade, Jinadh ran a nervous hand through his hair. Lillian noticed for the first time some shimmering threads of silver. «Putting our son in the hands of the man who—»

«Please don't,» she said. Memmediv had retired indoors once Cordelia and Pulan chased after Makricosta, citing the sun glare off the ocean, and his pounding head. It wasn't as if he were around to hear the insults. But Lillian was tired of the heightened emotions, the accusations, the surprises and shouting and conflict. She liked things to run smoothly. It was perhaps the only trait she had in common with Maddox Flagg. «You trusted him before last night.»

«I did,» he said. «But trust can be undermined. Your *brother*, Lillian.»

«In service to the same cause he's pursuing now.» It hurt her to say, like ripping out a tooth from the root, but it was the truth.

To that, Jinadh's only response was a significant look.

She sank back into the stiff wicker curve of the divan. «I don't like it either,» she said; an understatement. Grief wailed deep within her, but pragmatism kept it muffled. «However, it's convenient and clean and if I don't trust Memmediv at least I trust his sense of self-interest. He can't afford to alienate Satri right now, or the Lisoans.»

«How can you bring politics into this?» He turned to face her, and had to put his hand up to shade his eyes from the sun.

«How couldn't I? This entire situation hangs on politics.» She sighed, and switched to Geddan for the ease of jargon. "I've become a lynchpin in a multinational operation to undermine Ospie sovereignty. Memmediv needs me to keep Flagg's eyes off of him until the guns are safely with his people and he's off the map himself. If I don't succeed, the border conflict surrounding Dastya piddles on, no pin in the rear for anyone. Liso, and by extension Porachis, would rather have that pin in deep to bleed Gedda's resources heading into the Lisoan border conflict, and these guns are how they plan to do that. Memmediv can't afford to let anything happen to Stephen."

Jinadh shook his head. "Sometimes you are so cold, I am amazed."

She schooled her face to hide her hurt. He saw it anyway. The intricacies of alliance and mutually assured destruction were not his strong suit, but in this he was her equal, if not better. No matter what she sought to keep from her expression, he could always sense it.

"Ah, I apologize," he said. Then, in Porashtu, she assumed for the clarity he had failed to find in Geddan, «I didn't mean it as it sounded. It . . . it leaves me breathless, sometimes. I find it beautiful, like snow or the sweep of a glacier. But like ice it is alien to me; I wasn't born to it and had to learn.»

«You learned badly,» she said.

«And I'm glad of it.» He sat by her and touched her face. «I like to make you melt.»

She indulged in the warmth of his palm on her cheek for the space of one breath, two, before she straightened and said, "Yes. Well. That will have to wait a little while longer."

He pulled his hands into his lap. "Oh?"

"This will take planning, and time. I cannot risk a liaison with you in the interim."

She saw him build up his façade, brick by brick. "Of course."

Now she was the one who touched him with tenderness, cupping the curve of his elbow. "It's only a week, Jinadh. Maybe two. We went months sometimes. And then years."

«I know,» he said. «Only, it's so *hard*. Do you know how often I dreamed of . . . It's like you said. I let myself indulge and now it is that much harder to abstain.»

«Would you like to know my secret?»

He smirked, then turned his head so his ear came close to her mouth. Lips against the delicate curves of his sweat-salted skin, she said, «The ice is a shell to hold the fire in.»

CHAPTER

TWENTY-ONE

It took him too many tries, but Aristide finally swallowed enough of his pride and fear and embarrassment to knock on Asiyah's door.

The prince answered half dressed, looking hungover, but woke up a good deal when he realized who was on his threshold.

"Aristide," he said. "Ah. Come in?" He had a towel around his neck and his face was damp, as if he had been caught shaving. Indeed, the edges of his beard looked crisper than they had the night before, his neck more streamlined.

Aristide wondered briefly if he had someone else to shave him, when he was at home, or if this was a task his hand was trained to. Surely Pulan could have leant him a valet. Perhaps he preferred to wield the razor when it came so near his throat; one sympathized.

"Thank you," he said. "I didn't mean to interrupt."

Asiyah shook his head, flapped his hand, and stood back for Aristide to enter.

Inaz was still in bed, a tray across her lap. A bright wrap covered her hair and her face looked puffy with drink and lack of sleep. She watched him cross the room through slitted eyes and he imagined very few people saw her in this state and lived to tell the tale.

"I am glad to see you," said Asiyah. "I wanted to ask . . . I mean, I hope that I did not say anything that—"

He wasn't trying to apologize; he was fishing for information. But Aristide was good at playing ignorant when it suited him, and even better at simpering. "No, no," he said. "Thank you. I'd much rather have known. I apologize for my behavior last night. I was . . . overwhelmed."

"If I knew," Asiyah began, then shook his head. "But perhaps better I did not, and told you in ignorance."

"Perhaps." Aristide tried not to sound arch.

"Is this what you came to talk about?" Asiyah took a tunic from the foot of the bed and wrestled it over his head, covering the small, hard paunch of his stomach—muscles that would go to fat as he got older—and the tight curls of hair across his chest. Inaz watched him dress with a heavily lidded stare, and Aristide caught a spark of something between them that might have ignited if he hadn't been in the room.

He cleared his throat and Asiyah had the decency to look sheepish. "No, actually. Well. Partially. I wanted to ask you some questions."

Inaz shot him a crabby glance and said something to Asiyah in Shedengue. He answered her in the kind of soothing tone one used for highly bred horses and hysterical actors. Then, to Aristide, "Come. We will talk on the balcony and leave Inaz to her sleep."

They were at the northeast corner of the house, looking up the coast toward the rising red cliffs and the winding piece of road Aristide and Cordelia had driven in on—Lady's sake, was it only a week ago? The sun, well into the sky now, beat down on the small balcony. Asiyah did not seem to mind, though he put his back to it, which left Aristide blinking in the glare. Practical, but also a habit he might have learned in less innocuous circumstances.

"You're a slipperier fish than I thought," said Aristide. "I suppose it's no good asking what exactly you do for Lisoan intelligence?"

"Work," he said. "How do you say it? Odd jobs?"

"Of course," said Aristide, who didn't believe him.

"You did not come to ask questions about *me*," said Asiyah, stretching his arms above his head. "What do you want to know about DePaul?"

"Where was he living? And where did he disappear from?"

"He had a house—more a shack—in a little border village."

"Called?"

"Oyoti. You could perhaps find it, on the right map, if you looked closely. But you would not want to."

"I would," said Aristide. "Is that where he was, the last you heard?"

"Yes, but . . . you are not planning to go there?"

Aristide only looked at him, squinting hard in the sun.

"I do not think you will like it very much," said Asiyah. He leaned back on the balcony railing and tilted his head, as if to examine Aristide from a different angle. "No hot water, no cocktail bars. Two generators in the whole town: one for the whorehouse, one for the jail."

"You are under the mistaken impression," said Aristide, soft as the belly of a venomous snake, "that I am unused to hardship."

"Mistaken?" Asiyah snorted and waved a hand to encompass their surroundings. "And, besides the mud and poverty, there are the mercenaries waiting for war to start. And fighters from the north like . . . hm." He lapsed into Porashtu for the idiom: *Flies on a cow's ass*. "It is a violent place. People go missing, held for ransom, killed in the street. You will not survive your first week. Your first *day*." He dropped off and stared, as if waiting for Aristide to agree the idea was a foolish one, that of course he shouldn't go to this dangerous backwater.

But Aristide waited him out, silent and aloof, until he finally shrugged and said, "But what do I know? Maybe you are a sharp shot and a wrestler. You certainly gave Memmediv's head a knock last night."

"I have terrible aim, actually," said Aristide, in the conversational tone he reserved for tedious small talk and mild threats. "It's why I prefer not to shoot from any great distance. I like to put my pistol between the eyes, if I can manage it."

Asiyah blinked at him.

"Perhaps the LSI is less impressive than I thought," said Aristide, examining his nails. "Or perhaps your branch doesn't liaise very closely with the port authority. Otherwise, you might have some inkling who I am, and what I've done."

"You were a nightclub performer," said Asiyah. "And a political fugitive."

"Under one name, yes." He crooked his finger, happy to be standing on firm ground for the first time since sliding feet-first into this slop of intrigue.

Asiyah looked suspicious, but leaned in nonetheless. Aristide whispered a name in his ear, smiling as he did. Close to like this, he missed Asiyah's expression, but he heard the sharp intake of breath and felt the air move on his neck.

"So you see." He stepped back from Asiyah and tugged his lapels straight. "I'm quite capable of handling myself in a nasty situation."

Since he'd been wrangled into staying at Hadhariti for a little while longer, Aristide had time to consider his next moves carefully. To book passages and get papers in order. To contemplate the muddy, steamy, murderous sty he intended to stay in for as long as it took.

Sleep retreated in the face of *how much would it cost*, and *what to bring*, and *how long will it take?* Perhaps it was time to liquidate some of those assets he'd been ignoring; it felt less like betrayal, less like surrender, to pursue this end.

He began to write a ledger behind his eyelids, penciling in gains and losses, expenses, income, principle and interest. If he sold the property in Asu . . . no. No, he would keep that if he could. Successful or not, when he left Liso he wouldn't be coming back to work for Pulan.

He did not allow himself to hope for the former. Or, if he did, it was a feeling he sealed away deep within himself, so that it powered his actions like a quiet engine, unseen beneath chrome and steel. The purpose of his mission, he could not approach head-on. He could hardly bear to say the name of the man he hoped to find. Hardly admit he was looking for anyone at all.

When he opened his eyes, not having slept, the radium-painted hands of the clock on his bedside told him it was nearing dawn.

There were the pills, of course, but they would drop him into a cement-heavy slumber. Perhaps he was paranoid, but he would rather be alert in Pulan's house of falsehood and deception. If that meant going without sleep, well. He'd gone without much more than that.

He rose from bed and splashed some water on his face. The weather, he thought, might be turning. It was still difficult for him to tell. But there had been, of late, a clammy heaviness in the air, the tang of ozone, and a subtle chill when the sun was gone that slipped through skin and muscle like a fish knife. He was never *cold*, exactly, at this time of year: only uncomfortable. To hold off the damp, he donned a dressing gown of raw red silk, the same color as oxidizing iron.

Get out of bed, get out of his rooms. A little stroll around the house before the sun came up. Then maybe he could get an hour or so of sleep after breakfast.

He caught sight of Lillian as he passed the green parlor. She stood at the tall glass doors, open onto the upper terrace and the sea. Soft gray crept through the clouds from the eastern sky, over the house and toward the western horizon, striped with tentative fingers of pink and gold. The water lay untouched by light, dark and heavy as wet velvet.

She had her back to him, face turned toward the view. The edges of her silhouette blurred in the gloaming, but her carriage was unmistakable: the lift of the chin, the insolence in the crooked line of her shoulders.

"Do you often have trouble sleeping?" he asked, softly, so she would not startle.

He thought, for a moment, that he had succeeded. She did not jump or gasp. But it took her several seconds too long to turn and face him, and her reticence spoke of alarm: a need to collect herself before she spoke.

When she did look away from the black sea and fading sky, she crushed the air from his chest. Dawn made her features indistinct, enough that he forgot, again, and stepped toward her. When he remembered himself, he curled his hands into fists and froze, halfway across the parlor.

"Are you all right?" she asked.

He had to take a breath before he answered. "Certainly not."

"I'm sorry," she said, as if she had any reason to be. Ducking her head, she scrubbed at goosebumps on her arms.

Aristide crossed the rest of the room slowly, until he stood beside her in the doorway. The breeze off the water was cool, this early. It plucked at the silk of Lillian's nightdress, raising ripples across her belly and breasts.

"You're leaving today," he said.

"Yes."

"Back to Myazbah?"

"Unfortunately."

". . . And Memmediv?"

She only looked at him. Her eyes were blue like Cyril's, but her gaze was cold and anemic as thin air. He had never been so asphyxiated, staring into Cyril's eyes; Lillian's stare made him short of breath and dizzy.

"I apologize," he said. "You shouldn't have found out like that."

She lifted one shoulder, attempting to shrug. But as if the movement had broken some hold she held over her body, a shiver passed up her spine. "No one would have told me, otherwise."

Outside, a gull cried. In the potted plants on the terrace, a nightingale sang a few sweet notes. After some time in silence, listening to the birds, Aristide asked, "What are you going to do?"

She tilted her head and considered him peripherally, so that those blue eyes caught the growing light like chips of ice. Not tame ice, either: not the kind that sat politely in a cocktail glass. Not even the kind that coated branches in the winter, or crept across a pond. This was glacier ice, mountain ice. Remote. Forbidding. The kind of ice that turned sunlight into fire. He had heard stories of mountaineers gone blind from glare.

"You don't need to tell me," he said, ashamed of the way her sideways stare stirred fear in him.

"No," she said, and softened. "It's all right. I can't . . . I need to learn I cannot do this on my own. I've done so much on my own, for so long."

"Admirably," he said, for though he did not have a full understanding of the arc of her career, she was terrifying and she had survived. "Admirable" likely did not do her justice.

"I . . . we. We are going to Liso, I think."

That startled him. "Really?" He wasn't sure he wanted her to. Though she certainly had a right, it felt so much like *his* path to pursue.

She surprised him, though. "Not for long," she said. "And not far: just to Dadang. Only until . . . It's just that Asiyah can smooth things over for us there, and Pulan would like us out of Porachis. Away from . . . her, I suppose. Understandably. Mother and sons. This whole thing is such a mess."

"After Liso," he said, "what then?"

She shook her head, eyes closed, then opened them and looked out, searchingly, across the water. The diamond hardness had gone from her gaze and now, tear-shining, her eyes looked more like snowmelt. "Oh, how I wish I knew." She shivered again, and he wanted to offer her his robe, but had nothing underneath, and could not imagine the agony of seeing another DePaul in the early morning, wrapped in another one of his dressing gowns.

"Money is going to be a problem, I expect." She said it briskly, with the same sharp pain as a sticking plaster swiftly pulled. "And where we'll live I haven't a clue. All Jinadh's properties are entailed, and anyway, they're in Porachis. Mine are mostly

Geddan. There's the chalet in Ibet but that's the first place they would go looking, if they come after us." She put delicate fingers to her temple, pressing into the curve of skin and bone where the fine filaments of her hair began. "You've run before," she said. "How did you do it?"

"Better than you." He could hear the scorn sliding into his voice, and wasn't proud of it. "With significantly more planning."

"Don't be cruel," she said. "Please. I'm asking for your help."

"I'm sorry," he said, glad to accept her censure for his bad habits. "I . . . you have to want it, I think. To know that what is on the other side will be worth the bother of getting there."

"Was it, for you?"

The sun struck the water, finally. "No," he said. "But it will be, for you."

"Jinadh. Jinadh, wake up."

Lillian felt like she was playacting as a little girl on Solstice morning, badly. She was excited, yes, but also confused and not a little worried. Jinadh, still deeply asleep, mumbled something into his pillow as she shook him.

"Wake *up*," she said. "I need to talk to you about something."

He opened his eyes. Half awake, the muscles in his face slack, he seemed both older and younger—the tension had gone from his expression, but the lines at the corners of his eyes were more prominent, and the soft skin beneath them darker and more delicate without the animation of his mercurial expressions to make him look younger and less tired.

Then he went through the motions of waking—blinked, swallowed, tried to speak and had to clear his throat—and settled with each action into the wakeful version of himself.

The familiarity of the transition unsettled her—it was one that she had watched before, and forgotten about. How many more moments like this would there be, in which she remembered how to be in love?

«What's happening?» He sat up, unwinding himself from a sheet so fine it showed the shadows of his joints and moving muscles through the weave.

«I spoke to Makricosta about our plans.»

His thick brows wrinkled. «Was that wise?»

«In retrospect, one of the best . . . no . . . » She patted the bedspread with an impatient hand, trying to call up the word in Porashtu. When she failed, she shrugged and said, "'Canniest' is the word. One of the *canniest* things I could have done."

«And?»

«He has a house in Asu. Two, really, but the apartment in Sunho would suit us best, I think.»

«What?» he said. «Asu?»

«There are foreign language papers all over the city,» she said. «It's very cosmopolitan. We could both find work. The important thing is that it gives us a place to . . . go to the ground?» The idiom translated awkwardly. She knew there was a better phrase, but her vocabulary was flighty this morning, fighting a losing battle against anticipation.

Jinadh's face, under his tangled storm of hair, shifted from confusion to comprehension as he took in what she was saying. «How much does he want?»

«No,» she said, «he isn't selling it. Just offering it to us, to use. Until he needs it back, I suppose.»

«But that's perfect.»

«If there isn't a catch,» she said. «It seems that there should be, from what I know of him.»

«Admittedly,» said Jinadh, «I know less. But it is enough that

I can speculate. He isn't doing this for himself. He's doing it for your brother.»

«I had thought of that,» she said, picking at a bit of gold thread that had come loose from the embroidery on the coverlet.

«But?»

She sighed and smoothed the frayed bit of gold against the silk. «I don't know. What I read, about their affair . . . there were not many details. And they had a great deal to offer each other, in their work, so I assumed—»

But Jinadh was shaking his head. «Imagine how the dossier on *our* relationship might read.»

«But Makricosta—» she began.

«Is not a machine. Not any more than you are. Is it so impossible that he loved your brother?»

Lillian thought of Cyril. Not as she had last seen him—his charming veneer crazed with the craquelure of bitterness and pain—but as the boy he'd been before their father packed him off to train as a kit. Before the irregular letters and the sudden appearances at holidays with bruises, plasters, and half stories.

He had always been a little lazy, with a weakness for pleasure that often swamped his better judgment. As a child, he once made himself sick eating hard sauce with a spoon. But if he loved someone, he would lay down across a track for them, with the train oncoming. And he fell in love too easily: with causes, countries, people.

Someone like that, she knew, could be used cruelly. He had been, in her opinion, by many hands: their father, the Regionalist government, the Ospies. But by Makricosta?

You have no idea what you've cost me. Not the faintest trace of an understanding.

Perhaps it was not so impossible, after all.

CHAPTER

TWENTY-TWO

After the sun was over the horizon, things happened fast enough to make Cordelia's head turn on its stalk.

There were too many of them, by now, to fit in Pulan's office without banging elbows, and nobody wanted to sit around the dining room table again. Instead, Pulan got them all together in the library, around a large table with the air of having been swept clear of its usual debris.

And all of them included Aristide, who had asked to be let in on everything, and was working so hard to look prideful she got the feeling he'd rather hunch up like a vulture and glare. Maybe give a good peck at Memmediv's guts, if he'd really had a beak and talons.

Lillian's fair skin didn't hide the dark circles under her eyes. Beside her, Jinadh stared all haughty into the corner where the ceiling met the walls. From the angle of their arms, they were holding hands under the table. Lillian hid it better than he did.

Asiyah's eyes skimmed from face to face, as if looking for an in or a secret signal, and Inaz kept looking at *him*: a lieutenant ready for orders.

Cordelia had the unhappy position opposite Ari, at the head or foot or whatever end of the table she was supposed to be occupying. And at her left hand, just around the sharp edge of the table's corner: Memmediv. He kept his hands laced together in his lap, his eyes unfocused except when someone addressed him directly. Then she could see him wrangle his wits like elvers, hooking them through the lip and hauling them writhing to the surface.

Ari must hit pretty hard.

Satri doled out orders as if she were the general of a small and irregular army. "Mr. Memmediv, you and Ms. Hanes will depart from here this evening. Pramit will drive you to Anadh to catch your ship; first light tomorrow, an express liner to Amberlough City. You will be out of port before the ink on the first editions is dry. Once you make landfall, everything is up to you. Mr. Memmediv knows where we will meet, in the end."

She nodded to Daoud, who handed Cordelia an envelope. When she tipped it out onto the table, she got a spread of papers and documents for her trouble, complete with overlapping visa stamps that made it look like she'd been to a bunch of places she'd hardly even heard of.

"My properties department has many talents," Pulan told her, when she gawped at it. "You are now a Geddan diplomat."

"And when I've done *my* job?" Lillian's voice verged on hoarse. "How will I get out of Anadh?" Then, she caught herself and looked at Jinadh. "How will *we*?"

Some of the glee went out of Pulan's eyes, and her tone turned business-hard. "I understand you have some method of contacting Sofie Cattayim? Yes, good. When we adjourn here, you will call; her story runs tomorrow morning."

"And then?"

"You give us as many days as you can. I will send Jinadh on the *Umandir* up to Hoti, at the mouth of the Shadha. Take the ferry when you must leave Myazbah, and he will be there waiting for you. The *Umandir* will take you from Hoti to Dadang She is a fast little boat; you should arrive well ahead of Asiyah and the child."

Cordelia swallowed hard at the thought of that handoff. After that . . . well. It was a different set of logistics. After she and Memmediv passed Stephen to Asiyah, they'd be operating on a different timeline, with different goals. Everyone around this table would.

"And me?" asked Aristide.

"Ah," said Pulan. "Yes. You will of course be traveling to the shoot with the rest of us. You are, after all, our director."

"And then? We both know I won't be dawdling around making a musical. I can book my own passages."

The smile Pulan laid on him would have crisped the hairs on a softer man. "Of course not," she said. "I have arranged something very tidy for you."

It wasn't her smile that got him in the end. He held fast until she asked, "I do not think that you have ever flown?"

"In an airplane?" The fact that he didn't sass her, thought Cordelia, meant he knew she wasn't joking.

As the afternoon slipped toward evening, Lillian gathered her things and said a strange farewell to Jinadh—she would be separated from him for a fraction of the time they had been kept apart before this, but they both wept, overcome by fast-paced change. She felt embarrassed about it, after.

Red-eyed, she went down to wait for her car and, by some stroke of hideous luck, arrived in the foyer at the same time as Memmediv and his suitcase. Their gazes crossed, then strayed. Lillian pretended interest in a set of faïence figurines arrayed on a plinth. Memmediv whistled an abortive tune, then settled into a caned chair beside a potted palm.

Anyone else, Lillian reflected, would have happily let him sit there in silence. Anyone else would have been grateful for the fiction that they had nothing to say to each other, and were in fact unaware of each other's presence.

But Lillian wasn't good at leaving people to their own devices. She didn't like to sit in silence wondering what they thought— she wanted to put thoughts in their head, control the direction of the conversation.

"How's your head?" she asked, speaking to the faïence.

"Horrible," he said. "But better than it was."

"Oh." She didn't say *I'm glad*, because it wouldn't sound credible. "What shall I tell Flagg, if he asks about you?"

"You won't have time to tell him anything," said Memmediv. "Tomorrow morning, your job will be more important than his."

"He'll make me take the time," she said. She could not turn to look at him. "He'll want to know what happened here."

"Then tell him you don't know. Tell him we kept you well away from negotiations, sent you out on the boat or to the beach. It's too bad you didn't get a sunburn."

"DePauls don't burn," she said, and immediately regretted mentioning her family.

"Really? With your complexion?"

"No. Dark eyebrows. We brown and bleach." Then, because it

was hanging between them, "By the end of summer holidays, my brother and I always looked like film negatives."

She wasn't expecting an apology. If anything, she thought Memmediv might lapse back into silence. But she heard him shift on his chair and clear his throat.

"Do you miss them?" he asked, after too long a pause. "Your family, I mean."

The words were out before she even considered them: a tinned response, ready to deploy without any preparation. "Of course."

In truth, she'd hardly seen her family all together in her life. Her father had been abroad most of her childhood, and her mother in Gedda at the bench. She'd been sent away to school at six. She and Cyril overlapped by a few years, but then went on to different secondary schools and universities. At most it was those scant summer weeks on the lake, or holidays at Damesfort. Then *she'd* joined the corps and hadn't been back in Gedda beyond the odd month or two, stationed first in the Onyongo consulate, then the North Lisoan mission proper, then Yashtan, and finally Porachis. She'd been home for Mother and Daddy's funerals, and when Cyril was in the hospital, but beyond that . . . sometimes it felt like she was just waiting for their next letters. Cyril, especially, had been an erratic correspondent. Months could go by between . . .

Never three years, though. Stones, had it really been that long?

But now that she would never see any of them again, she did miss them, truly. Or, the possibility of them. She had taken their existence in the world for granted. Now she was no longer a node in a network stretched across the globe, but a single blinking buoy on a dark sea.

No. She had Stephen. She had brought him into this world, and would keep him safe. And now—terror and excitement burst in her chest and spread through her veins like someone had applied a soda siphon to her heart—she had Jinadh as well.

"Do you miss yours?" she asked, rounding on Memmediv finally, snagging control of the conversation before he could . . . apologize? Excuse his actions? She wouldn't be able to live with herself.

"Every day," he said, and there was no trace of anything tinned about it. There was blood in the words, and yearning.

"Your parents," she said, "are they—"

"They still live in Tatié. In Solnin, now."

"The capital?" It was a sounding rope.

"A rancid compromise." His accent came on more strongly, held in the front of his mouth like sour spit. "I wouldn't call it a capital city."

"Flagg said your father was an alderman, in Dastya." This was more like it. He had let his emotions take over; she controlled the conversation's course.

"Yes. And my mother's family dealt in dry goods. Now, he has a bad heart and a wrecked name, and she's been working as a typist. A waste—she was very good at playing commodities."

"The Solstice Riots?"

"The riots, yes."

"I'm sorry," she said, and apologizing to him gave her a small, cruel shiver of pleasure. To have accepted his apology would have been unconscionable. To dole out sympathy to him? That put her on higher ground.

But he wouldn't let her take it, not all the way. "Ah well," he said, relaxing into the curve of his chair and kicking his feet up to rest on his case. "I've seen more of the world working for this cause than I ever would have selling beans."

Cordelia tried to get a little sleep before she headed out—it was always good to snatch it in a soft bed if you could—but Pulan's coffee was strong as nails steeped in lye, and she only used the time to fret.

Aza, the maid, brought her a folded set of clothes and did her hair up nice. Pinned a little hat on top. She got a look in the mirror before she went downstairs: nylons, black pumps, a plain skirt suit. A sweep of curls across her forehead, finger-waved over one ear. A pair of white gloves, embroidered flowers at the wrists, disguised her battered hands. She looked boring. She looked safe.

Aza gave her a carpet bag, too, with her new papers inside, and a soft coat of black wool. "Amberlough is cold," she said, patting the fabric. "You need."

"Thanks," she said, and took the luggage. "You know where Ari is? Mr. Makricosta?"

Aza worked the words over for a minute, then said, "Ah," and led her to the library.

The table still stood empty at the center of the room, chair arrayed crookedly around it. Somewhere behind the shelves Cordelia heard the whoop of a cork, the small splash of liquor into a glass, and a dramatic sigh as familiar and far away as the smell of greasepaint and sound of applause.

In that spirit, she pitched her voice to the back of the room and put on a heavy slum whine straight out of Kipler's Mew. "Pour me one, why don't you?"

Something metal clashed—tongs on an ice bucket, a strainer against the rim of a glass—and there was a short silence before she heard Ari say, "Of course."

When he brought the glasses, his hands were steady. Still, his voice sounded odd, a little tight, when he said, "You gave me a fright. I didn't realize anyone else was here."

"Came to say goodbye," she told him, and hefted the carpet bag. "Clock you next in Tzieta, I guess."

He got a real look at her, in all her boring swags, and his eyes widened. "That bag is rather small for such a long trip."

She shrugged. "It ain't like I'm gonna be dressing for dinner."

"Did Pulan give you the clothes?"

"Who else? Mother's tit, she's a little sergeant. Orders, schedules, do this, do that. Worse than Malcolm ever was before a new show went up." She almost hadn't said it, but then wondered when she might ever get to say it again to somebody who'd understand.

It knocked him sideways, she could tell, but he recovered fast. The small smile he managed surprised her—not that smutchy one she wanted to scrub off, but a real one tucked into the corner of his mouth like he was ashamed of it. "What ever happened to Sailer?"

"Blew his brains out," she said. "First sign of trouble. Always had to make a big scene over nothing, Malcolm."

There was a beat, in which she watched Ari try to dredge up a response that fit. He failed. "Here," he said, and handed her the drink she'd asked for. A big balloon of a glass that rested in her palm, fragile as a soap bubble, the bottom holding just a swallow of some golden, syrupy stuff. It gave off a whiff of fruit—apricots, maybe—and it was so strong it crisped the inside of her nose when she inhaled.

When they'd been sniffing and sipping in silence for too long, she said, "Sometimes, when things were good between us, we talked about leaving the city together, getting a little cottage when we got old." She took a drink. "You two ever come up with something stupid like that?"

Ari's hands moved on his glass, one thumb sliding on the rim so the crystal gave a faint squeak. "Don't be ridiculous."

She knew, from his pause, from his bitterness. "I ain't. You wanted to get out with him, didn't you?"

When he spoke, every last ounce of pride was gone from his voice. No angry northern burr, but no Central City, either. "I tried," he said, and the words were empty and aching.

She held herself back from a hand on his knee only because she worried it would break him. "What happened?"

After a silence full of the second hand, his answer caught her off balance. "Do you remember that contortionist trumpeter? The one who could play all twisted up in knots? She was always running late, always drunk, sometimes didn't show at all."

"Portia Prine. Yeah, I remember her." So many times she'd tried to buy a plug of tar on credit. Mal hated her, would have liked to sack her, but the girl could bring in punters straight and true. Everybody liked a bendy bit of flesh dressed in next to nothing.

"It was always a gamble," said Aristide, "each night, whether she would make it to the stage. And I remember how, when we were coming up on the middle of the second act, I'd be watching over my shoulder for Malcolm to give the nod, or if I'd need to vamp while she wiggled into her costume, or if she wasn't there at all and we needed to bring on Tory for a third set while the next act rushed to get ready." He looked down, cheeks flushed, and pressed his lips tight like he regretted letting all that out.

"Yeah," she said. "You used to come off spitting mad."

"It was like those nights," he said, "when Prine was running late." The breath he took here was ragged, and he chased it with his booze. "Trying to catch Malcolm's eye in the wings, losing the punters with every eight bars. You can only wait so long before you have to go on with the show."

PART

3

CHAPTER

TWENTY-THREE

Lillian took the sleeper back to Anadh so she could return to the chancery straight off the train. The *Yaima II* spent nights in port. Memmediv had booked the ticket—a single. She wondered if that had been for the appearance of an intimate affair, or because he had never planned on returning to the chancery with her.

In the rocking darkness of the compartment, she imagined the bull pen where Odell and the undersecretaries worked, visualized their bowed heads and cluttered desks and imagined what the place would look like tomorrow after Sofie's story went to print.

And then she imagined what it might look like when she was gone for good. Odell in charge, maybe? They would fall behind on deadlines, would miss a story here and there to be scooped by local outlets, who would paint Gedda poorly. He would play a game of catch-up she had striven to avoid. Though she hated that she'd kept the Ospies' noses clean, she was proud of herself for a job well done.

She wondered what sort of work she might pick up in Asu. She'd always been in the foreign service, from the day she took her degree. Early on, one of her mentors—Rathbone, what a horsewhip!—had spotted an aptitude for public speaking, for twisting words that might have left a mark into statements bland and comforting as warm potato soup. She'd been funneled straight into wrangling public relations for the corps, and in the hardest places, too. The Lisoan press wasn't friendly to her country, but on the personal level, she made friends. It paid dividends in the papers. In Yashtan, her first weeks were spent battling the assumption she should be married and a mother. Then, proving she was right where she ought to be when a Yashtani senator's wife was caught in an affair with the daughter of a Geddan business consultant. The scale of the resultant scandal was much reduced thanks to her actions. She had been given a commendation, and a discreet financial bonus.

So a company spokesperson, perhaps, or personal secretary to somebody important. A cleaner-up of gaffes. Lady knew she'd spent enough time sweeping up after her own.

There would be some kind of work to do. She could prove herself again. And if it wasn't the straight shining road she had envisioned for her life, evenly laid and paved in granite, neither was what she did now. She doubted that any such path had ever existed in the first place.

Right now there was *no* road beneath her feet; she walked a tightrope every day. She didn't dare look down, or second-guess. Nor could she charge forward without delicate consideration.

There was cash in her safe, and her jewelry. It would never add up to quite enough to start a life without some struggle. She wouldn't have time to pack much of a bag—not under Waleeda's watchful eye. If the story ran tomorrow morning, she gave herself two to three days of damage control during which she could effectively avoid Flagg's questions.

She hoped it would be enough. It *had* to be.

It took him a day and a half to make it past her staff; she'd given them a list of names whose calls she wanted, and Flagg's wasn't on it. He didn't come up to the press offices in person, perhaps because he knew that with the bull pen in this state, he might be torn apart for food.

"Counselor Flagg on the line for you, ma'am." Rinda's hair was in some disarray, her skirt creased at the hips and knees. No one had gone home since yesterday, except for Lillian, who had begged an hour to prepare for the afternoon's press conference. She'd used the time to move cash and jewels from her safe to her briefcase, buried under papers and cables and mimeos.

She asked Waleeda to put several suits into a garment bag for her, and a few changes of underthings. After all, she'd said, who knew how long she'd be stuck at the chancery, with this mess ongoing?

It was the best she could manage, given the circumstances. It would have to be good enough.

"Is his name on the list?" she asked, glaring up from a pile of ticker tape.

"Please, ma'am, he has called seven times today. And he threatened to have me sacked."

"Oh, fine. Put him through."

The phone on her desk rang and she picked up before the hammer had quite left the bell. "DePaul."

He didn't waste time on pleasantries. "Where is Memmediv?"

"Sir, I don't have time—"

"You've been stonewalling me, DePaul."

"I've been *busy*," she said. "In case you haven't noticed."

"Answer the question and I'll let you get back to work."

She bit the inside of her cheek. The much-abused spot had begun to heal, and so the pain of her teeth tearing through flesh was more precise, more potent. "I'm not certain, sir. He wasn't feeling well at Hadhariti, and honestly, I haven't had much time to think about him since this story broke." As if he were there to see her emphasize her workload, she sifted through the drifts of paper on her desk: transcriptions of wireless broadcasts, copies of newspaper articles, requests for comment.

"Your driver tells me he didn't get off the train with you yesterday."

Damn Amil to perdition. "He wasn't feeling well," she repeated. "He said he was going straight home, and that he'd ring the office. Did he?"

Silence on the other end of the line.

"Sir," she said, "I really need to—"

"What happened down there?"

"Do you really want to talk about that on this line?" she asked. "Right now?"

"Tonight. My office."

"Tomorrow," she told him, firm. "Tonight I'm speaking to the press. Unless you want us to stay silent on this? I'm sure the palace would love that. Porachin journalists will keep slinging mud and I'll be too busy playing spies and soldiers to wipe it off our face." Frustration made her bold, and she took it a step further. "As the person tasked with keeping Gedda's nose clean in Porachis, I strongly urge you to let this woman go."

"Out of the question. She funded anti-Geddan terrorism. She should be transferred to domestic custody."

"That'll hold wine like a sieve. It's the initial arrest that's at issue."

"And the statements she gives when she's out of custody?"

She could have told him what she really hoped for: a blistering condemnation the papers would print for days. Something that would keep the entire mission busy, with their eyes to the ground in Porachis. Instead she said, "Cattayim and her wife are illegal immigrants, and Geddan to boot. If you're lucky, no one will listen to them except a few bleeding hearts."

"That doesn't seem to be what happened with *this* story."

"No," said Lillian, "because this story makes us look worse than that one will. She can call us poor humanitarians once we release her, but that will die fast in the papers as long as you didn't torture her." A word with a mutable definition. "If the focus stays on our violation of Porachin sovereignty, this story is going to plague us like carpet beetles, eating holes in our international standing. Let her *go*, sir."

When he rang off, his voice was flat and cold as steel in winter. "Thank you for your thoughts, Ms. DePaul. Goodnight."

She let the phone fall into the cradle and closed her eyes, imagining swift miles cut through water.

A part of her was on the deck of a ship bound for Amberlough, staring out from the prow and straining for sight of land. But the larger part was here, striving to make sure the liner's most important passengers got down the gangway unremarked.

TWENTY-FOUR

When you leave, take me with you, wherever you are going.

Daoud had not brought it up again. Did he still want to come, knowing Aristide's reasons? Would he still want to come, if he had heard Asiyah's warning about the filth and danger in Oyoti?

Though Daoud's striving and bootstrapping reminded Aristide of his young self, he knew the boy had never experienced the kind of poverty he had suffered in his own youth, both rural and urban. He very much doubted that Daoud had ever killed someone, or even knew how to fight. He could probably take a beating stoically, but that only worked if one's attackers intended the beating to end before the critical juncture.

Daoud was firmly a member of the middle class—shopkeeper's son or something, Aristide couldn't quite remember. But some kind of ethnic minority, and eager to eat prick besides, which didn't go over as easily in Porachis as it did in Gedda. Or used to.

Aristide thought about leaving it lie—if he didn't mention it, Daoud might not, until it was too late.

Traveling alone was often easier, except when it was not. And Oyoti might be the kind of place where it was best to arrive with allies. Someone to cover you while you took a piss or signed a paper. Someone to put their back to yours when you were surrounded.

Besides, at least some of the work he intended to do in Oyoti—placing calls, sending letters, scheduling interviews—might go easier with a secretary.

He wanted to have this conversation away from Pulan, though. Away from Hadhariti, which after the weekend felt like an airless room in which too many people had been breathing for too long: stale, sour, nauseating.

With the entourage preparing to depart for Tzieta tomorrow, there was no chance of truly getting away—not to Anadh, for the holiday they had missed what felt like a thousand years ago. But perhaps just for an afternoon drive.

Before he popped his head into Pulan's office, he took a moment to assemble himself: slightly harried, aloof, unflustered by recent events.

"Can I borrow Daoud for a moment?" he asked, only putting his head around the door once he'd knocked and she'd called for him to enter.

It got him an incredulous arch of one sculpted brow. At his desk in the corner, Daoud perked up like a peaky houseplant hit with the watering can.

"To help me work out my travel itinerary, post-airplane," he said. "Nothing salacious."

"So you are still determined to leave us for Liso," said Pulan. "It will be a great loss to the studio."

"You'll find yourself another talented monstrosity." Maybe

one who didn't mind what was going on behind the scenes. Or one with less to lose if the operation came to light.

"No one will ever drive me so . . ." She snapped her fingers, then shook her head and said «crazy,» in Porashtu, but the word she used had, if Aristide's limited fluency could be trusted, several layers implying fondness and familiarity—the word you might use with a little sibling, or a vexing but adorable dog.

«Daoud,» she said over one shoulder. «Go with him. But please come back by three o'clock—I want you for my telephone call.»

He nodded sharply and nearly scrambled from his desk. Pulan's expression sharpened and Aristide cringed, toes curling inside his shoes.

This was an awful idea.

But, just as he thought it, Daoud regained his composure, pulled his vest straight, and gave a tidy half bow. «Three o'clock,» he said. «Of course.» And his steps to the threshold were measured and soft.

When he shut the door behind him, though, he turned to Aristide and said, quietly enough to keep his voice on the safe side of the doors, "Liso?"

Aristide tucked his chin in assent, but said, "Not here. We'll take my car."

Daoud followed at his heels as he navigated the corridors, screened and shuttered into artificial twilight against the heat and sun glare. "Ask Pramit to bring it and she will know we were not planning for your travels."

"I'm not going to ask," said Aristide. "It's my rotten car. I'll take it when I want."

Pramit, thankfully, was availing himself of the Porachin tradition of a noon-hour sleep. This meant, of course, it might be an unpleasant time of day to go for a drive, but as Aristide had noted, the weather was changing: a wet breeze blew in off the ocean, and clouds occasionally occluded the sun.

As soon as they cleared the long driveway and started back toward the coast, Daoud said, "So you'll take me?"

Aristide paid more attention to the next curve than it truly warranted, and then said, "It won't be pleasant."

"I told you, I do not expect a honeymoon."

"That isn't what I mean. I mean it will be dirty and uncomfortable, and very possibly dangerous. The rocks I intend to overturn may be hiding some sizable scorpions."

"I grew up in Porachis," Daoud said. "I do not fear scorpions."

"These are metaphorical," said Aristide, "and therefore rather different and more worrisome. It's likely I will be seeking out warlords, mercenaries, and intelligence agents of dubious loyalty."

"As if I had never met these, working with Pulan?"

"Not, I imagine, in quite the same capacity as you're liable to meet them in Oyoti. Can you fire a gun?"

That, at least, turned the corners of his mouth down. "Will that be required?"

"I can't say for sure. But it would certainly be advisable to learn. Here." He reached inside the lapel of his jacket and removed a diminutive snub-nosed revolver from the interior pocket. Pearl-handled, very pretty, with a punishing recoil. He'd carried the thing all over Amberlough, kept it in his pocket as he picked his way through puddles in the Culthams. He'd pulled it on a man who tried to rob him in Erlsbord, and when the thief had laughed at the diminutive gun Aristide put a bullet into the wall beside his face, so the flying chips of stone stuck in his skin. The next one, he promised, would strike somewhere more vital.

"The kick is bad and it's hard to aim," said Aristide, letting the gun drag his hand back over his wrist. "But you will get five chances. If you can't hit whatever's coming for you by the time the chambers are empty . . . well."

Daoud took the gun, gingerly, and cradled it in his lap, lying flat on his upturned palms.

Just out of sight of the house, the road curved past a scenic overlook bounded by a crumbling stone wall. Aristide pulled the car into the dusty patch of dirt on the cliff's edge and killed the engine.

"If you come," he started, and Daoud opened his mouth to protest—probably the "if"—but Aristide talked over his indignant indrawn breath.

"If you come, I want you pulling in the yolk. This isn't charity. You'll work as my secretary. If you decide you can't stay in Oyoti, that's fine, but I won't help you get out."

Daoud nodded, still looking down at the revolver.

"And," added Aristide, then stalled. His falter finally brought Daoud's eyes up from the sheen of deadly metal and mother-of-pearl.

"Our . . . affair," said Aristide, speaking to the steering wheel.

Daoud nodded, in a resigned kind of way. "Of course. I understand if you wish to keep it secret from this . . . the lover you hope to find. I can be discreet."

"No, no. That isn't what I meant at all." Why was this so much worse than the stern warnings about death in the jungle?

Because it was awkward. Because it was a relief, and he felt guilty.

Daoud looked puzzled. "What, then?"

"I want to end it. It isn't fair to you." He knew his altruism was unconvincing, but couldn't bring himself to speak the whole truth: that the safe, unsatisfying dalliance made him feel disgusted with himself.

"Please do not . . ." Daoud struggled for a moment, then said a word in Porashtu Aristide didn't know. "It means . . . put your thoughts on me?"

"Presume?" asked Aristide.

Daoud nodded, passing one fingertip over the butt of the revolver. "I am perfectly capable of deciding for myself what is fair and what is not." He hefted the revolver. "Is it loaded?"

"It is."

"May I try it?"

Aristide shrugged and swept his hand through the air with a trace of his old emcee manner. Daoud opened the passenger door and stepped out into the dust. At the edge of the overlook, thighs nearly touching the precarious stone wall, he lifted the gun and held it two-handed in front of his chest, elbows at his side.

"No," said Aristide, and got out of the car as well. He went to Daoud's side and said, "Arm's length, and one-handed. In a pinch you'll pull it and shoot without a steadying palm."

Tentatively, Daoud stretched out his slender arm, stringy typist's muscles cording from elbow to wrist.

"Good. Now sight along the barrel." For this, he stepped in closer, bracketing Daoud's body with his own. An intimate position, but less erotic now than it was charged with some more focused, ferocious potential.

"Breathe," he said. "You needn't aim just now, but you've got to get used to what the world looks like over those two sights."

The short barrel allowed for less than a hairsbreadth of error, when aiming, but as Aristide had told Asiyah, he didn't like to shoot from far away. He didn't imagine Daoud would need accuracy at any great range, either. Not if the gun was just for protection, or for execution.

"All right," he said. "Pull the trigger. Remember what it feels like, when the gun goes off, so it doesn't surprise you next time."

Daoud's voluptuous lips tightened, pressing together. He closed one eye, and narrowed the other to such a fine slit that Aristide anticipated he would squeeze it shut when he fired.

He was wrong. Daoud didn't close his eye, and when the wind blew the smell of powder back to them, he took a deep breath and smiled.

Djihar met them at the door when they returned. «Ms. Satri's three o'clock call is postponed,» he said. «She asked for you to meet her in the library, when you returned.»

Daoud blanched. "She will know you lied," he said. "She will know we were not planning for your trip as we said we were."

Aristide shrugged. "You were going to need to give your notice anyway." Then, to Djihar, «What is in the library?»

«The radio,» he said. «And luncheon. There is something interesting on the wireless that you might like to listen to while you dine.»

Wrapped in a satin kaftan, Pulan had her bare feet up on the library divan and a slew of plates and glasses arranged on the low table that held the hookah. It was as yet unlit, but Aristide imagined that would change when the food was taken away.

«Ah,» she said. «My little schemers.»

«Pulan,» Daoud began, «I need to—»

But she held up a hand to stop him, and with her other—occupied by a skewer of chicken spiced scarlet red—she pointed to the radio.

It was a handsome machine: hardwood case carved in whorls and lacy gingerbread. A showpiece, appropriate for the show unfolding.

Aristide didn't understand all of the words—the newscaster was speaking too quickly, and there was a hefty amount of jargon thrown in. But he got the gist, which was all he really needed.

« . . . report that Geddan spies . . . outside the law . . . Her Resplendent Majesty Queen Yaima . . . push for information . . . full extent of their abilities.»

"That didn't take long," he said.

Pulan waved her skewer at him. "Sit. Eat."

"How long has it been on the wireless?"

"Since this morning. Yesterday it was published in a Geddan rag out of Berer—lampblack printed on lavatory paper, not very reputable. But somebody saw it and it made the afternoon editions. Then, this morning, the wireless. They are still saying . . . oh, bother . . . *ghahalamida*?"

Daoud tapped his lips with one finger. "Mm. Unsubstantiated?"

"This." She jabbed the chicken skewer in his direction. "But it hardly matters now that the story has spread so widely."

"Have the Ospies given a statement yet?" he asked.

"*That*," said Pulan, "is what I thought you would like to hear. They are going to give a statement; it comes on soon. So sit. Have wine, some curry."

As if he could eat. But he did pour himself a glass of the wine: a light red with weak legs, very spicy and tannic. He felt some kinship with the stuff, and it suited his mood perfectly. Taking up residence in the chair at a right angle to the sofa, he leaned into the deeply curved embrace of its elaborate teak frame and paisley satin upholstery. Cradling the wineglass in his lap kept his hands busy, though he almost dropped it when he heard a familiar name on the radio: Lillian DePaul.

Silence, for a breath: the crackle of airwaves intercepted by distance and clouds. Then, her voice. Her textbook-perfect Porashtu with its sibilance and stresses in all the right spots. "What's she saying?"

Pulan rolled her eyes. "That the woman Cattayim agreed to come to them. That it is an 'extended interview.'" She used finger quotes for that, though only managed to crook the fingers of one hand as the other was still occupied with its kebab.

"Nobody will believe it," said Daoud.

"Of course not," said Pulan. "We don't want them to. We want a fuss. After this there will be another round of articles, lots of suspicion. They will have to give another statement. Um . . . give themselves cramps? Is that it?" She shot off a Porashtu idiom and Daoud said, "Ah, knots. Tie knots."

"Tie themselves in knots," said Aristide, "yes. How long do you intend this to go on?"

"It is out of our hands now," said Pulan. "We *need* it to keep up for the rest of the week, until Memmediv crosses the border to Tzieta. And talking of that, are you ready to depart?"

"Yes," he said. "All packed."

"Good." She turned to Daoud, and something hard came into the line of her mouth. «Daoud, what about you?»

«Yes,» he said. «I'm ready. Only, I need to say something.»

Pulan glanced at the clock. «Make it quick; I need to call the office now that this is out of the way.» She waved her skewer at the radio once more.

«I'm giving my notice,» he told her. «I'm going to Liso with Aristide.»

She blinked at him, then turned slowly to face Aristide. "It is not enough to lose my director? You must take my right hand, too?"

"He asked to come. I didn't steal him. If it's any consolation, he'll probably hate working for me far more than he hates working for you."

Daoud glared at him, and he met it with a bland smile.

TWENTY-FIVE

Lillian didn't have time to meet Flagg. She had a long-distance phone call coming through shortly from the press office in the Cliff House, three separate briefs to read, and two dozen requests for comment she needed to gracefully turn down.

"Ask him if he can wait an hour," she told Rinda, when she ducked in to say the counselor was on the line asking for her again. "Maybe two." It wasn't hard to play for time; she really needed it.

Five minutes later, Flagg was standing in the doorway of her office, rigid and white-lipped. "You will come with me, please." It was not, in fact, a request.

He didn't speak another word as she followed him through the halls. Out the windows she could see night had fallen, and realized she hadn't yet eaten dinner. Lunch had been black coffee and a piece of pastry, half of which she had forgotten in her rush to get to a meeting.

She tried to attribute the screeching of her nerves to caffeine and hunger. But many of the nonessential staff at the chancery had gone home, and the halls were quiet except for the occasional swift—sometimes running—footsteps of an aide hurrying off with an armload of papers or a bit of food brought in from the city for diplomats who hadn't left their offices all day. Every time she heard the clatter of shoes on marble, her heart knocked the inside of her ribs.

Flagg locked the door of Regional Affairs behind them. Memmediv's desk was empty. She didn't look at it, but Flagg still said, "Not a trace, if you're curious. But I imagine that you aren't."

"What's that supposed to mean?"

Smiling tightly, he half-shook his head and waved toward his office. Another locked door. Stifling air she felt as if she'd breathed ten times already. She didn't want to sit; she felt as though she should be ready to run. But where to, with so many locks behind her?

She was on Geddan soil right now, under Geddan jurisdiction. And this was the same man who'd stowed Mab Cattayim somewhere without even official orders.

There was no reason to think he would smell her treachery, or see some mark on her. He would not know she had switched sides unless she gave herself away.

This was less comforting than it ought to have been.

"Sir," she began. Good manners wouldn't save her, ultimately, but they might give her room to maneuver.

He didn't let her get further than the honorific. "They're recalling me."

It wasn't what she had been expecting, especially after that remark about Memmediv. "Oh?"

"Yes. I've been relieved of my post and I'm going back to Gedda."

She realized that her mouth was open, and shut it.

"Thanks to this . . . *circus*"—with the back of his hand, he slapped at a pile of newspapers on his desk—"it has come to the attention of the CIS that not all my work here received appropriate review or approval before I carried it out. This did not sit well with my superiors."

"No," said Lillian. "I imagine that it didn't."

"If you remember," he said, force gathering behind the words like bitter wind, "this was exactly what I sought to avoid by bringing you into my confidence in this investigation of Memmediv's activities."

"Did you relate your suspicions?" she asked, trying to keep misgiving out of her voice. If the CIS knew what Memmediv was up to, and decided to pursue it, he was standing on their doorstep. Or maybe already in their house.

"Absolutely not," he said, and if she had been standing, relief would have knocked her knees out from under her.

"I will answer for the debacle over Cattayim," he said. "I have to, at this point. But so far they have no knowledge of our intriguing over Memmediv's deal with Satri, and I want to keep it that way."

"Your replacement will—"

"My replacement will fend for himself," snarled Flagg. "There are no records. I have plausible deniability."

"What about Lehane?" she asked. "Did you pass on the photographs? Do they know she was at Hadhariti?"

"They were impossible to bury," he said. "But never linked to Memmediv. Yours and Mr. Addas's value to the CIS increased immeasurably after you delivered those photographs. You can expect that my replacement will increasingly make use of both of you."

Mother and sons, they had to get out of this bramble or Jinadh would be trapped spying inside the palace forever. The more valuable his intelligence became, the more tightly controlled his movements would be. He would be truly strangled. And she would be the noose around his neck.

If Memmediv and Lehane didn't make it out of Gedda . . . she needed a fail-safe. Something that would break the Ospies' hold on her family forever.

"However," Flagg went on, drawing her attention away from the gears that had begun to turn in the back of her mind, "you are not to tell him anything about Memmediv."

"Him?"

"The man they're sending to take my place. You will not breathe a word of my investigation into Memmediv's arms dealing. One insubordination, I can paint as a misstep, an error in judgment. Two will ruin me."

Oh, how she *wanted* to ruin him. But this was not the way.

"Rest assured," he said, "if he learns anything about that area of inquiry, things will not go well for your son."

"That won't be your purview anymore," she said, striving for polite but only achieving affectless. At least her fear didn't make it through. Oh please, let Lehane make good on her promises.

"At this point," he said, eyes unforgiving as pewter, "my purview consists of nothing more than clearing my name."

"Is there anything else, sir?" she asked, pinching the hem of her skirt between thumb and forefinger until the seam left a divot in her skin. She was so close to slipping out from under his heel.

"Who did this to me?" he asked. "Is this the Catwalk? The Porachins? Memmediv? Was it you?"

"I think you did it to yourself," she said.

"I was doing my job!" His fists closed on the newspapers piled on his desk, crumpling the cheap paper until it tore. Lillian jumped, but Flagg didn't notice.

"There will be someone to blame," he said, voice dropping into eerie calm. He was staring at his own hands like he didn't understand how they had come to such violence. She was terrified of the leap he seemed about to make—that she had led him here on purpose and planned to run while his face was to the wall.

"Will there be anything else, *sir*." She came down heavily on the last word, and strove to keep any ounce of inquiry from the sentence. If there *was* anything else, she didn't want to hear it.

He peered at her from beneath thick eyebrows, lips so tight over his teeth she could almost count them. There were more red veins in his eyes than there had been, and she caught the thinnest edge of a gray ring at the fold of his collar.

If he had been anyone else, she would have pitied his unraveling. But Flagg, she suspected, would become more liable to lash out the more helpless he felt: a wild beast caught in a snare.

She did not dare step nearer, but nor would she give ground. Showing weakness would be just as dangerous as antagonizing him.

"You may go," he said finally, sagging into his chair when she failed to present a threat or an opening. The newspapers made a racket as he released them from his grip.

"Oh," he said, catching her at the threshold, "there's a bit of news for your next press conference: We're releasing Cattayim from custody."

"I can't say that," she told him coolly. "'Custody' isn't the term we've been using."

"Use whatever word you want," he said. "But we're letting the bitch go free."

Once she was out of his office, past Memmediv's empty desk—she didn't dare look at it, as though doing so would give Flagg an inkling of her continuing involvement with the man and his cause—once she had gained the tall marble arches of the corridor, she sagged into an alcove and took a long, shaky breath. Sweat had soaked the armpits of her blouse beneath her jacket, and her heart kept hammering despite the two locked doors that had shut between her and Flagg.

It wasn't over yet. It wouldn't be over until she crossed the border and had Stephen in her sights. But it was ending.

She only needed to break that last hold, the one no one had brought up in negotiations. Perhaps because Pulan found it too embarrassing. Perhaps because no one considered Stephen's paternity to be a problem, outside the borders of Porachis and the reach of its taboos.

Yours and Mr. Addas's value to the CIS increased immeasurably after you delivered those photographs.

As long as this secret remained so, they would be worth something to the CIS. And that was not a worth she wanted anyone to trade on. Even if they made it to Asu, with their son, she could envision scenarios in which their arms were twisted, in which Jinadh compromised himself in order to avoid compromising his family.

He would never have the strength to bare his shame; much as she knew he despised the strictures imposed upon him by society, he had still been raised within them. Someone else would have to do it for him.

She wouldn't have been able to reach him to ask for permission, anyway. That would make a convenient excuse later. He would forgive her. He always forgave her. She hoped this wasn't the step that took her beyond his generous capacity for reprieve.

Before she went back to her office, she stopped in the first-floor washroom to splash some water on her face and compose herself. When the flush had died back from her cheeks and her breath came regularly, she flashed a demure smile at the mirror and proceeded on her mission.

"Rinda," she said, when she returned to the mess of papers and ticker tape the press office had become, "did Odell take the call from the Cliff House, or did they reschedule?"

"They were happy to talk to Odell, ma'am. I have notes, if you'd like to see them."

"Yes, please. And Rinda?"

"Yes, ma'am?"

"You can go home."

That surprised her. So much so that she forgot to add a "ma'am" when she asked, "Really?"

"Really. I'll see you tomorrow." Not true, but she didn't need to know.

"Thank you, ma'am." She was already gathering her handbag, her calico wrap. "Have a good night."

Rinda's departure left the bull pen empty. Odell was still in his office—she could see the light over the transom—but his door was shut.

She closed her own door and locked it, then sat down at her typewriter and began to compose a press release on official letterhead.

It didn't take long to write: a few dates, a few names. A notice of her resignation. Which necessitated the composition of a resignation letter after the press release, effective immediately.

She sealed the latter in an envelope and put it into the outbox on Rinda's desk. The former, she clipped into a folder that she put into her briefcase, next to a sapphire collar, a diamond tiara, and a frightening sum in banded bills. This was not a release she trusted the press office to disseminate.

She took her garment bag from the supply closet where it had been hanging since yesterday. No one had thought it strange when she placed it there—after all, didn't she usually keep a spare suit in case work required her to stay at the office overnight? If this bag was slightly bulkier than usual, as though it contained three or four outfits, no one had noticed or remarked on it.

The offices of *Al Ayina Wireless* weren't that far out of her way. She caught a cab outside the chancery—the second one that came, but at this point no one could say her paranoia wasn't justified.

When she asked after her goal, the elderly woman at the night desk directed her to the fourth floor through a wide yawn. The lift came swiftly, untrafficked at this hour. When she stepped out into the corridor, it was empty.

The nameplate on Satya Amal's door had been freshly polished, probably by her own hand. Lillian had met the Foreign Affairs editor on numerous occasions and always found her impeccably well groomed. If she hadn't known the woman was such a vicious firebrand, she never would have inferred it from her outward appearance.

The other option had been Vadan Muthi-Amahn, who had the Royal beat. But Amal had always frightened Lillian more. She would break this story smiling.

Lillian stood before that shining brass nameplate and contemplated the small sliver of space between the door's bottom and the tiled floor.

If she did what she was about to do, it was the final leap. She would not be able to come crawling back to her office, to her complicity.

In one swift movement, she pulled the folder from her briefcase, knelt at the door, and slipped the press release faceup into Satya Amal's office, where it would be the first thing she saw in the morning.

After, she did not go home. It wasn't home anymore.

CHAPTER

TWENTY-SIX

It wasn't smart to make a spectacle when she was supposed to be Memmediv's sour peach of a secretary, but when the kid in his smart sailor uniform bawled out to the dining room that they'd sighted land, Cordelia couldn't help herself. She went to the prow of the ship and leaned over the railing into the wind.

She wasn't alone: a passel of other folk came along, all straining to make out the details of Amberlough's docks. A smutch of city smog colored the crisp blue sky, but beyond that not much stood out at this distance. A lot of the watchers peeled off, excitement draining as the smutch failed to get much closer within the hour. Cordelia plunked herself down on a deck chair to wait. Her eyes and heart were hungry for home, and she'd never seen it from this angle.

They were due to dock in the early evening, and as the sun took a header to the west it blinded her. She held up a hand until it got low enough to the horizon it didn't bother her so much. Then she started to shiver—she'd gotten used to sweating. But the chills were a small price to pay for the sight of Amberlough's lights flickering on. She could almost taste the reek of the docks in the back of her throat, the diesel smoke and rotting fish.

"A beautiful view, isn't it?"

"Mother's tit," she said. "Don't creep up on me like that."

"Don't wander off," said Memmediv, "and I won't have to. I didn't want to ask after you and turn it into some steward's little mission. The fewer people we make an impression upon, the better."

"I know," she said, not trying to rein up on the snappish sound of it. Stones, he was insufferable. He had this little smile he wore nearly all the time—she could tell when he was nervous, because that was the only time he lost it—and she would have slapped it off his face if there hadn't been so much riding on their cooperation. "I just wanted to . . . well." She flapped a hand at the horizon, where the harbor had become a glittering crescent against which the ragged curve of the Spits rose like fangs in silhouette. The lighthouse on Big Snag lit its beacon as she watched, and the beam cast out over the water in a searching arc.

"When we dock," he said, "there is a hotel on Wick Street, near a livery garage."

"We ain't hiring a car," she said. "Not under your name. We're gonna go under my name"—the one on her new papers—"and we're gonna pay cash, somewhere that won't be out of the ordinary."

"And you know a place?"

Folk had started coming back out on deck, for the pretty sight of the city lit up. For the excitement of pulling into the harbor.

"I got some ideas," she said. "But they mean I gotta go out. And *don't*," she said, looking at his face, "tell me to be careful."

There came that poxy little grin. "I didn't think I needed to."

There were so many things she wanted to see. So many places she wanted to go and people she wanted to look up, if they were still in town. But she and Memmediv took a cab straight to the stodgy hotel on Wick—Second Precinct, near Armament, not a neighborhood she'd spent a lot of time in. Her room smelled like mothballs, and the window looked out on an air shaft.

She got out as quickly as she could, taking just enough time to change into boots instead of pumps. The neighborhood she was headed to hadn't been clean the last time she'd walked there. Some things about Amberlough hadn't changed even under the Ospies.

Really not a lot had, for the folk who pinned gray-and-white cockades to their lapels and got on with their lives, since they could. And, peering from the back window of her cab across town, it made her skin crawl to see how familiar everything looked. Driving south on Baldwin, they passed the Klipstone Arch, the dark mass of Loendler Park beyond the streetlights. Bellamy's was still there, advertising "Coffee and Tea" on its windows. Closed at this hour, but freshly whitewashed and looking prim.

She hadn't told the driver to do it—that would have been asking for the midden heap—but he turned onto Temple Street. Truth be told, even if it had been safe, she wouldn't have chosen to come this way.

This was one part of the city that didn't look the same. Or, it did, the way a death mask looked like someone's face.

After she'd blown the Bee, a lot of other managers had put their tails between their legs. She hadn't thought it would go that way. Hadn't thought much at all. But nobody had known who set the blast, and a lot of people thought it might be the Ospies, or folk working in aid of them. By the time she got smart enough to put around rumors, most of the theatre folk had cleared out of Temple Street. A couple of picture palaces moved in, and some of the restaurants stayed, but it had turned pretty quiet. The cab didn't even come on any traffic until the corner of Seagate, where there was some kind of construction going on around the trolley transfer.

"Here's fine," she said, a couple blocks down Waxworks Road. She was never going to get used to paying cabbies. It never felt worth it to her, who'd always had to save her coins for bread and cheese and wouldn't have taken a cab if it was pissing rain and she bare-naked. But no respectable secretary was going to be catching streetcars this late, nor to this neighborhood.

It wasn't that bad, not by her standards, but it was dark, and nobody much was around on the streets. The place she wanted—a little pub that did some after-hours business—was shuttered tight and she was worried it had been closed up for good. A soft knock got her a cagey woman with a torch peering out the chain-locked door.

"Oats or barley?" she asked, which didn't make sense on the face of it. Cordelia bet there was some answer that would get her painless entry into the bar. She didn't have time to guess, but she'd spent the passage over planning this.

"Look," she said, "this sounds ripe, but I been out of town and I ain't up on the codes."

"I don't know what you're talking about." The woman started to shut the door on her, but Cordelia put a hand to the wood and braced herself. "I know what I look like in this suit, but that ain't what I am. I wanna talk to Roustabout."

"I don't know what you're going on about," she said.

"Kurt. Lemme talk to Kurt." The code name was more a signal to let them know she was in on things, anyway.

"He ain't here."

"Swineshit."

"Don't you swear at me." The woman gave the door an ineffective shove. She wasn't strong enough to close it all the way, but Cordelia didn't want to fight her way in if she didn't have to. Bad first impression.

"I got a business opportunity for him," she said, and flashed a couple of large bills. They'd brought a lot of cash over from Porachis. Geddan currency, and who knew where Pulan had gotten it. Cordelia hadn't asked.

But the money didn't sway the lady. It was inconvenient, but it nailed down Cordelia's suspicion that the place still did a little more than sell beer past midnight. If she could just get *in*!

"Listen," she said. "Don't you tell a rotten soul about this. But I got a message from Spotlight."

The woman's eyebrows lowered skeptically, bringing the brim of her cloche down. "Sure you do. And I'm a goat with golden teats."

Cordelia clenched her fists inside their fussy white gloves, sending a spark of pain up to her left elbow. Then she got an idea. It would have been a bad one, if this woman had been any less stubborn about keeping her secrets. But that was just a part of the game: trust-that-wasn't-trust, faith that hung on a rusty nail.

She put her foot in the door frame in case the lady slammed it shut when she let go of the door. Good thing she'd changed to work boots. Then she tore the glove off her right hand with her teeth and held up her fingers, spread, to show where they were missing.

"Let me through the rotten door," she said. And the woman, eyes wide, did.

"I still don't think it was a good idea to tell them who you were." Memmediv had been pouting in the backseat of the car since they left Amberlough, though he said he needed to lie down on account of his pounding head.

"These folk know when to keep quiet," Cordelia said, from the passenger's seat. "It's why they ain't been drug in yet. They got good judgment about who they can tell what."

And they had told her a lot. Kurt had gotten word from one of their people on the rails—a stoker on the Farbourgh-Amberlough express—that Opal had been scratched, which explained how they'd clocked she was in Porachis. No one had gotten word from Opal since; figured she was still locked up. Or worse.

Things weren't as dire as the news made it seem, though. People had got hauled into the pens, but the papers were painting it rougher for the Catwalk than it had been, and the rest of the networks had just hunkered down closer to the ground and cut all their communications except the ones that came into their laps at a chance. It was patchwork, but it held at the important seams because folk hadn't quite given up.

She could have kissed Kurt when he told her that. Didn't, though, 'cause his spark was staring at her from behind the bar with cold eyes and one hand on the butt of his pistol.

One thing they hadn't been able to tell her was whether Greasepaint was still in place.

"If he is, he ain't broadcasting," Kurt's sweetheart had said.

"Not like we've needed to know much about the trains, these last few months."

"We'll get our feet back under us," she told him. "Don't worry."

He'd looked doubtful about that, but she didn't care to give any of her people details until the supplies Pulan had promised were ready to be distributed. And that would mean cleaning up her act in the north, bringing the Chuli deeper in, shaking hands with Memmediv's folk, gaining safe ground in the north and east to work from . . .

One step at a time, though.

"It got us what we needed, right?" she said to Memmediv. "Complete with a chauffeur."

Loren, behind the wheel, tipped an imaginary cap. A stropped-keen razor, she passed easily for a man and had been living as one even before the Ospies got their claws in, working as a grease-knuckle in Kurt's garage. She'd come with the car, spit-shined up as cleanly as its running boards and chrome. The folk at the garage had even wrangled a couple of flags for the bonnet, which she'd opted not to fly on the drive up. She only wanted to go under Ospie false colors when it would undercut the real ones. In the trunk, tacked down to keep them from sliding or upending at a turn and ruining the paint, a pair of hastily doctored diplomatic license plates, done from a sketch Lillian had given them.

Loren checked the mirror and then indicated—she'd been following traffic laws to the fine print at every turning—to take them through a roundabout and out the right exit.

They'd left early in the morning and were still in the heart of the weald: farmland, pastures, and houses big as city halls. It was a part of the state that was strange to Cordelia. Stones, everything outside the city limits had been strange, at first. Most of it still was. Though now she had a close-up acquaintance with the Culthams, and a map of the whole country's railroads in her head.

This was Cyril's territory. She remembered that conversation like it was a record playing in her mind. His slippery, polished voice telling her he'd grown up in the country and come south too late to pick up a city drone.

The sweep of soft hills under chill, gray rain felt muffling, like cotton wool. Low clouds snagged on the trees, bare now. It made her sleepy. She wondered how anyone who grew up out here turned as sharp as Cyril and his sister, as slippery and keen and cutthroat.

It was Amberlough that had turned her into what she was. Her heart pulled her back down the road toward it, like it had pulled no matter where she traveled.

She'd never been a strict planner, never seen past the horizon of each evening. She'd been a day-to-day type, happy as long as she had enough for rent and a couple of meals, a date lined up every other night or so and somebody to call on if it fell through.

You couldn't fight the Ospies with a hairpin and prayers. Opal had been better at the logistics, a natural-born wrangler of people and places and plans. Cordelia had learned from her: Make a list in your head, have a backup.

But sometimes—often—it all went wrong anyway. You couldn't cleave too close to details or the whole thing would crack apart.

That's when all Cordelia's time skating over thin ice, all her flying without looking down, really came in handy. And it was going to get them through this action neat and tidy. At least, that was the idea.

They came into Cantrell as the sun finally sank below the bellies of the clouds. Everything was soaked in red, the shadows deep purple, the underside of the rainstorm colored gold and pink and orange. Whitewashed cottages on the outskirts of town lit up like gold, their windows blazing. It was gorgeous, but it didn't look natural.

"Drop me at the station and then drive around to the north side," she told Loren softly. Memmediv had fallen asleep in the backseat. "If there's trouble I'll run down the tracks to you."

"Sure thing, boss." Loren brought them down the main drag of the cute little town, peering at street signs until one cropped up reading *Station Street*. "You expecting any?"

"I ain't expecting anything. I'm trying to keep an open mind."

It was a bigger station than some of the small towns they'd passed through kept, but Cantrell had the school, and the school meant parents and kids coming and going with trunks and baggage. Plus it meant things brought in to feed them, teachers brought in to teach them, lecturers and guests and old graduates. The town had more money than its neighbors, too, if the pretty shops and streets were any indication.

She couldn't have said if it looked any different now than before, but suspected it didn't.

"All right," said Cordelia, climbing out. "See you soon, one way or the other."

And then Loren was gone with the car around the corner, and Cordelia was standing at the station staring up the stairs. She took them carefully, unused to heels, and went into the foyer.

After the elaborate interiors of Porachin buildings—tile, gilding, carved screens, and embroidered hangings—the austere white marble and dark wood looked stark as an overexposed photograph: nearly black and white, all straight lines and plain stone.

"Excuse me," she said to the young man in the ticket booth,

taking care to keep her words in order and her whine tamped down. "Is the station agent in?" She couldn't ask if it was still Greasepaint; she didn't know his real name. Didn't even know what he looked like.

"What's your business with him?"

Kidnapping? Sedition? "I'm a friend of his cousin Pearl's," she said, cousin Pearl being the fake family member all Catwalk members shared.

"Cousin Pearl?" The ticket boy didn't look convinced, and for an awful moment she was sure somebody'd sung about the code. Her mouth went dry as sawdust. Then the boy said, "I didn't know he had one."

"She lives down in the city," said Cordelia, trying to summon some spit so her tongue didn't cleave to the roof of her mouth. "I told her I was coming and she said I ought to drop by. Said she'd ring him up to let him know I was coming."

The boy shrugged. "I'll check for you."

Waiting was hard. There wasn't anybody in the station to pretend for—it was late, and between trains—but she tried to look normal anyhow, like she wasn't standing on tacks in stocking feet. Like she wasn't hoping the man who came down the stairs the ticket boy had disappeared up would recognize her for a friend.

If he didn't clock cousin Pearl, and didn't by some miracle have one of his own, she'd have to play it off as a misunderstanding. If he clocked cousin Pearl but knew her for a Catwalk signal in a way she didn't want?

Well, that was why she'd had Loren park down the tracks. She could see the doors to the platform from here. Provided a train didn't come through, she had a clear shot at an escape.

It took the ticket boy long enough to dig up the station agent. By the time she heard the office door and footsteps on the stairs, Cordelia could feel sweat gathering between her shoulder blades.

When the kid hit the floor, he was leading an older man in a neatly pressed black suit: a bland-faced sort of sculler with thinning dark hair neatly parted at the center. He looked like somebody's boring uncle. He sure didn't look like the kind of person who'd throw in against the Ospies. The sweat between her shoulders dripped to the waistband of her skirt.

"Hello," he said, offering his hand to shake. "Aldous Dyer."

"Pleased to meet you, Mr. Dyer." At least the gloves would keep him from feeling her damp palms. She hoped he wouldn't clock the stuffed false fingers. "Pearl said she rang you up? Let you know I was coming?"

His unreadable smile reminded her horribly of Van der Joost, his look of satisfaction while she sobbed into a spreading puddle of her own blood, swallowing bile as she told him everything he'd asked her to.

"Oh," said Dyer. "Yes. I know who you are."

At that, her stomach dropped three feet straight down; she almost fancied she could hear the smack of it on the marble floor.

CHAPTER
TWENTY-SEVEN

Lillian got the last ferry into Hoti, and only made it by the barest edge of her nails. In the dead hours of the night, she sat under a lamp in the lounge and tried to read the week-old gossip magazine. Not *Gelari*. Her already rampant heart would not have survived the sight of Jinadh's byline.

A cab across town took her to the harbor. Satri had given her the berth number for the yacht, and she had learned it by heart. This many hours before dawn, the part of the harbor dedicated to passenger crafts was nearly empty. Her heels echoed on the boardwalk.

A woman in white-and-gold livery stood at the bottom of the gangway, swaying sleepily. She straightened at the sound of Lillian's footsteps and gave a half bow.

"First Officer Sandeepa Karthi," she said. "You must be Lillian DePaul. Welcome aboard the *Umandir*."

The yacht was small—perhaps eighty-five feet—but luxuri-ously appointed. Officer Karthi led her up the gangway onto the deck, into a partially enclosed patio open at the stern to the breeze and the view, decorated with potted palms and strings of colorful lights lit against the predawn gloom. It had rained in the night, and the clouds lingered.

«There's coffee in the galley, if you'd like some,» said Officer Karthi. «And the cook could make you breakfast. Unless you'd prefer to retire to your cabin?»

«Where's Jinadh?» she asked, and saw a flicker of something unpleasant pass over Karthi's expression.

«He couldn't sleep,» said Karthi, «so he went out for a stroll. He should be back soon.»

But he was not.

They sat around the table under the colored lights and fin-ished the pot of coffee. The clouds burned off and the sky in the east over town began to glow pink. Lillian yawned, the back of her hand across her mouth, and felt like it belied her inner tur-moil. The clock ticked. The sky brightened by another degree. Jinadh still failed to show.

A woman came down from the wheelhouse and introduced her-self as Captain Amunpoor. «Your pardon,» she said, «but the tide will be turning soon. If we want to leave Hoti this morning—»

«Still waiting on Addas,» said Karthi.

Amunpoor's eyes drifted toward Lillian, then snapped smartly back to her first officer. «Come tell me as soon as he's aboard.»

«I don't understand,» said Lillian, alarmed that her own voice sounded so close to tears. It was the moment she realized exactly how tired she was, and exactly how much faith she had placed in this delicate, porcelain plan. «What's happened to him? He should be here.»

As if she had spoken an incantation, a shadow passed in front of the risen sun's glare.

«And I am,» said Jinadh. «Though it isn't thanks to you.»

«You had no right.» It was the fourth time he'd said it, and it wasn't getting any easier to hear.

«I did,» she said, speaking softly, evenly, using the voice she employed when speaking to angry or panicked diplomats after they saw their names in unflattering print. «It was as much my secret as yours.»

«Did you not think it might make things more difficult for me? People know my face, Lillian.»

The ship hit a swell and she put a hand out to brace herself, then settled gingerly onto the foot of the bed. They were closed into the master cabin at the prow, where they had retreated after Jinadh's arrival and a decided lack of pleasantries.

«They know mine too,» said Lillian.

«The *press* know your face.» He shook his head—not a negation, but disbelief. «The *people* know mine.»

«I apologize if it caused problems for you,» she said. «But I thought—»

«No,» he said, volume rising. «You didn't! I barely got back to the ship this morning. If you turn the radio on right now, parliament has probably declared a state of emergency. Auntie may have a heart attack. People tried to stop me in the street, Lillian. Someone spat on me. Who knows? The captain might even throw me overboard. I can never come back here, now.»

«It doesn't matter,» she said. «We were never going to come back. Not for years, at least.»

The blood went from his face, as though he were only just realizing what their flight meant. «That wasn't your choice to make.»

"I didn't make it!" Anger threw her back into her native language. "Not on my own. We made that choice together, eight years ago. And now we're accepting the consequences."

Anger, likewise, kept Jinadh in his. «You should have asked.»

"When was there time? Did you want me to ring you up from Flagg's office last night?"

«We've had years to do this!» he said. «And you refused, every time.»

"You didn't want to *tell*," she said. "You wanted to run! So here we are. We're running."

«I only wanted to be with you. To live normally.»

It drew a bitter laugh from her. Live normally. "This is the only way we can. With no more secrets to exploit."

He shut his eyes and fell against a patch of wall, head tipped back to expose the stubbled column of his throat. The skin around his eyes pinched tight, emphasizing his crow's-feet.

"I'm right," she said. "You can't tell me I'm not right."

When he swallowed, she could see the muscles slide beneath his skin, the sharp movement of his larynx. When he spoke, though, he didn't tell her she was wrong. He only said, «Please. Don't ever do this to me again.»

It was everything she'd feared, this push and pull of risk and responsibility. She was terrible at it: selfish, controlling, decisive. She had ruined it all before they even began, doing only what she felt was necessary.

Aiming for levity to break the tension, she said, «I don't think I'll have to. We only have one son.»

«That isn't what I meant.» He put a hand to his face, across his eyes, and from the movement of his lips she saw with some alarm that he was about to cry.

"Jinadh," she said, and stood to go to him. But he put out an arm to stop her coming closer.

«Listen to me,» he said. «I love you, and admire you. But I have spent my life subject to the whims of people who view me as an ornament, an afterthought. Someone whose opinion matters very little, if at all.» He dropped his shielding hand and met her gaze. «I want to spend my life with you, Lillian. But it *must* be mine to spend.»

Embarrassed heat crept across the bridge of her nose and spread over her cheeks, but she didn't break eye contact. She had done the necessary thing. He could not shame her about that.

«If you want this to work,» he said, «we have to make it work together.»

"I made an executive decision," she said. "I didn't have any other options."

«There are always other options.»

"There have never been any other options. Not for us."

«There might have been,» he said, «if you had let us try.»

She wanted to say, *How dare you.* She wanted to demand a list: *What options? Enumerate them for me now.* But she also wanted, desperately, not to have this fight again. Not now, when it was so close to becoming irrelevant.

She shifted her conversational weight to bear his heavy accusation more easily. A complimentary tack would change the tenor of their rhetoric, make it less confrontational. «You're such an optimist.»

It worked; her words conjured a wavering smile out of his distress. «One of my many flaws, I know.» She wanted to know if it was surrender or self-deprecation, but couldn't tell. She knew, though, that either way he had bent to her will. It turned her stomach that she had such power, and filled her with relief.

«What are mine?» She took the hand he had held up to keep her back and drew him closer to her, the bed behind her a suggestion, an offer, a distraction.

«You don't have any,» he said, and the shift in his weight was not a metaphor—it pushed her back against the footboard, so she fell. «Which is in itself the worst kind.»

Not for the first time, his opacity impressed her. Was he insulting her? Was it a compliment, or pity?

The next roll of the waves brought him down on top of her, and to her great relief neither of them spoke again, except to sigh and curse and say each other's names.

CHAPTER

TWENTY-EIGHT

Ten minutes later, Cordelia was still shaking. Her teacup rattled in its saucer so bad she had to set it down and clasp her hands together.

"I'm so sorry I gave you such a fright," said Aldous. Now that she knew he wasn't about to take the rest of her fingers off, his blandness had lost its terror and become kind of sweet. She could see why nobody had clocked him: How could you suspect this pudding-faced father-type of anything? He seemed about as sneaky as milk custard.

This man alone had helped her people derail or destroy nine freight trains last year. Five railway folk had died on account of him. And here he sat, stirring a lump of sugar into his tea.

"I'm pretty ready to jump at a squeak these days," she said.

"I'm very sorry to hear that. I've been on edge myself."

"Cousin Pearl says you ain't been real chatty lately." The hot tea, once she got it down her chute, settled her. She hadn't realized how numb she'd gone, from fear.

"Well, it's been . . . tense, hasn't it? The family situation. And, I've had other things on my mind. Politics, you know. People are very riled up about pushing over the border in Liso. I think it's a trifle . . . jingoistic, myself. Closer to home, those peace talks limping along in the east. And then, right in our own back gardens, there's the matter of Acherby."

"What about him?"

"His son started at the school this year. He's making a big show of coming to get the boy himself for Solstice, see the prize-giving and what have you. There are police all over town, and some militia folk too. It's been . . . twitchy around Cantrell the last week."

"Mother's tits," she said. The news hit her so fast she hardly felt it.

"I'd close my teeth on that kind of swear," he advised. "They boarded up our temple up a year or so ago, and at the Equinox someone lit a fire. We lost some beautiful stained glass, hundreds of years old."

"Acherby's *here*?" she asked, setting her cup down too hard. The spoon rattled in the saucer.

Aldous nodded. "He gave the commencement speech yesterday for the older boys, and his son was awarded . . . oh, a commendation for good sportsmanship, or something. I believe they're leaving tomorrow, with the general outpouring. Traffic will be a terror."

Damnation. Loren was still waiting on her. "Thanks for the warning. I gotta get out of here and get back to the folks I came with, so they know you ain't cut my throat or something."

His laugh came near to a giggle. "It's thrilling to think I might be so dangerous."

He'd been pretty damn dangerous to those five people on the trains they'd blown. She didn't mention it.

"Before I go," she said, "you know anything about how this pickup works? With the kids?"

Thoughtfully, eyes unfocused, he poured himself another cup of tea. "Most of the children take the train themselves—it's such a festive time of year around the station, I adore it. So is the beginning of fall term. But, some of the higher-profile students do have chauffeurs or something along those lines. Just another reason this Acherby situation is so absurd."

"Yeah, but . . . I don't know, do they check you against a list or anything? Do you have to talk to somebody, or can you just . . . grab the kid and stuff him in a car?"

Suspicion or distaste pinched the corners of his eyes. "I'm not sure I like where this line of questioning is headed."

"It ain't kidnapping," she said. "I'm picking up a kid for a friend; I got a letter from her and everything. I'm just nervous 'cause I never done it before, and I don't want to stand out too far, for obvious reasons."

"Right," he said, though he still didn't look convinced.

"Listen," she said, lowering her voice. "This kid's ma, she's been in a bad spot—under the Ospies' boot. They won't let her see him, even at holidays, and they been using him against her like a knife to her back. I'm getting them both out of a bad jam."

As she talked, she saw his expression settling, his soft brown eyes turning placid again. "There," he said when she was done. "I like the sound of that much better. How old is he?"

She had to cast back in her brain for that. "Eight, I think."

"All right. If he were an older boy you wouldn't have to interact much with the staff at all. As it is, you'll have to talk to the matron of his dormitory, and she'll double-check with the dean of students. Her name, I think, is Sarason. We've lunched to-gether on occasion."

"She liable to give me trouble?"

"It will all depend on the boy," he told her. "Does he know you're coming?"

"He knows somebody is. The way his mom tells it, he's used to strangers in black cars coming for him at the end of term, as long as they've got a letter from her."

"That's good," said Aldous. "Some of the children have family drivers they've known their whole lives. If they don't recognize the person who's come to fetch them, or make the slightest fuss, the school won't send them away until things are cleared up."

She hoped this kid was a quick one, and turned his cards up behind two hands if he turned them up at all. She couldn't afford a fuss.

"How do you know all this stuff?" she asked Aldous. "You got a kid in school?"

"Oh no," he said. "I'm a bachelor, and childless. But I've lived in this town my whole life, and I was a day boy at the school when I was young."

"Really? They let you in there with all those swell kids?"

Instead of taking offense, he chuckled. "The Dyers have al-ways been a well-regarded family in town, and well-to-do. My mother was the station agent before I was; it's a position with some social cachet, though the responsibilities are very real. I'm proud to bear the title, and proud of the work I've done."

That brought her up short. "Even now? I mean, with . . ."

"With what I did for cousin Pearl, you mean?"

"Yeah."

Still staring at his watch, he sighed. "My mother was a very wise woman. Not religious, but well versed in the scriptures. She said there was wisdom to be found there, even if one didn't sub-scribe to the beliefs."

"And?"

"She loved to receive gifts, but loved to give them even more. There was a passage she was fond of quoting, whenever the occa-sion arose: 'The bringer of joy must be given joy in return.'"

"I know it," said Cordelia.

"Most people do. But there are two more imperatives that fol-low it, less well known. I didn't learn them until after my mother died, and I was searching for something for her eulogy." He caught her before she asked the question. "Apoplexy, a month or so after the election."

"How's it go?"

Placing his watch back in his pocket, he smoothed the front of his waistcoat and composed himself like a boy reciting a lesson.

"'The bringer of joy must be given joy in return,'" he said, "'and the bringer of natural sorrows accepted with an open and steady heart. But the bringer of sorrows unnatural and cruel, who inflicts the pain we need not feel? As with the bringer of joy, turn back upon them what they carry. Let them feel as you do, that they may never endeavor to harm again.'"

The clock above his desk chimed, and Cordelia remembered to suck in a breath. "Thanks for that," she said. "Inspiring."

"I thought so, yes." He rose to see her out. "Rather like your visit. Thank you for coming to see me. Perhaps it's been too long since I looked up my cousin. We should be in touch more often."

She hugged him, when he offered. It'd been a long time since somebody had.

"Hey Aldous," she said, just before she left. "One last question."

"Yes?"

"Can you get me a gun?"

It shook him for a moment—she could see the hesitation flit across his face. Then he steadied and gave her that milk-custard smile one more time. "Of course. Anything for a friend of Pearl's."

"No," said Memmediv. "Absolutely not. Has your head flown off?"

They had taken a suite in a local hotel. It was a swell place, and Memmediv refused to pay in cash—too conspicuous. Instead, he cut a cheque from a government account, complete with a seal on the paper. It would take long enough for the transaction to clear, he said, that no one would clock where they were until long after they were gone.

And now *he* was mad that *she* wanted to take some risks.

"He's *here*," said Cordelia, stalking from wall to wall like the tiger used to in the menagerie at Loendler Park. "We're gonna walk straight rotten past him tomorrow."

"On our way to collect Ms. DePaul's son, and take him safely to Tzieta, fulfilling our end of the bargain we made with Satri. I still want those guns, Lehane. And I'm sure your people would want theirs, if they knew what choice you were about to make."

"But this is *Acherby*," she said. "This is the man who burned down Gedda. We kill him and—"

"And what? His second-in-command takes power, or there's a coup and some other Ospie rises. Maybe it would help my cause, but I can't think of any well-placed politicians who would give a horse's fart about Dastya when the Lisoan border has caught the imagination of the public. And for you, it would be even worse."

"Sell me that," she said, "'cause I ain't seeing how."

"So you shoot Acherby. You won't escape. It will be suicide;

you'll be arrested, barely tried, and executed. Who leads your people then? What happens to the Catwalk?"

"They been doing all right without me so far," she said.

"What, because they aren't all dead yet? Because some of them are still hiding, waiting for word on what to do? They'll piddle along, I'm sure. But tell me—when your contacts in Amberlough realized who you were, did their eyes light up?"

She crossed her arms, unwilling to give the answer she knew he wanted. He gleaned it anyway.

"I'm sure some people will still fight against the Ospies. But will they join forces with the Chuli, with the Tatien militia? Will they find some common cause they can hitch their buggies to? Diffuse revolutions fail, Lehane. And I did not enter into this alliance with intent toward failure."

"You're just afraid if I do this it'll come down on your head."

"Of course I am. If I think for one second you will try what you propose, I will personally stop you. By force, if necessary."

For the first time—stupid—it occurred to her that he might be carrying a gun.

Well, fine. She'd have one, too, once Aldous came through. Memmediv might not look bad with a hole between his eyes. Wherever Cyril was—Queen's arms, pauper's grave, up to his oysters in a poxy whore—she thought he might like it, too.

It was tempting. Almost as tempting as Acherby. But then she wouldn't get her Tatien contingent, her eastern thorn in Acherby's side. That civil war she wanted would fall through. Unless Acherby died tomorrow. Then, how much would it matter to lose Tatié?

What he'd said was maybe true—kill Acherby, and another Ospie would pop up to take his place. But how could he lay that out then turn around and tell her if she got drug in, the Catwalk would fall flat?

It was just what Opal had said, too.

But apply that logic to the Ospies . . . break off their figure-head, maybe their ship would lose its way.

"Go to bed," said Memmediv. "We have to get an early start." He had his fingers to his temples, pressing so hard the flesh around them had turned white. She hoped whatever damage Ari had done to his head stayed with him a long time.

Next morning, while Memmediv was busy puking in the wash-room, Cordelia went down to the front desk. She'd rung Aldous up the night before to let him know where they were staying—which, over the line, she framed as thanks for the recommendation—and now there was a package for her in the cubbies behind the clerk.

"Courier left it with the night manager," he said, handing it over.

Heavy, but not so much for its size you'd know what it was right off. She thanked him and put the padded envelope in her handbag. In her bedroom—separated from Memmediv by a locked door—she tore it open and tipped out a small-caliber revolver, its nickel plating tarnished. Flipping the cylinder out, she spun it to check the chambers. Five bullets, no extras in the envelope.

She shouldn't need more than one to do the job. Two if Memmediv came after her. She'd practiced on bottles and cans and rats and grackles in the last few years to make sure of her aim. Her right hand wouldn't close on a pistol sure enough, so she'd learned to shoot with her left, though the recoil sent eye-watering pain up her crooked wrist. She was a good shot. The other three rounds were just insurance.

The whole thing fit neatly into the inside breast pocket of her coat, and barely showed. If she left the coat unbuttoned, the lump wasn't noticeable and she had easy access to the gun. Its weight against her chest made her notice her heartbeat.

A knock on the door made her jump to clear away the wreckage of the envelope. "Yeah?"

"Time to go," said Memmediv. So she went.

Traffic, as Aldous had said, was awful. Loren, done up in her smart black jacket with a peaked cap she must have had in her satchel, cursed softly as the cars around them jostled for better position. Cordelia caught glimpses of other drivers dressed about the same, lips moving in the same litany of foul language as Loren's. Some of the cars were empty. Some had curtains pulled down around the rear windows. She settled deeper into her own seat beside Memmediv, angling her head so the brim of her hat shielded her face from anyone driving by too close.

They finally passed through the tall iron gates of the school, swinging from an ivy-wrapped brick wall. Frost had browned the leaves and crisped them with a fine rind of ice. A pristine white gravel drive shone under the pearly morning sky. They followed a line of cars down its straight path toward the square brick face of the school, and then wound around behind it to the two dormitories facing each other across a wide quad with a fountain at its center, dry for the season.

Barely controlled chaos roiled in front of each dormitory: cars and luggage, adults with clipboards running after kids ranging from ankle biters to whatever age they started getting pimples and stray hairs.

"Show me the photograph again," said Memmediv. There was an edge on the words that made him sound angry, but probably came from nerves. His smarmy little smile was long gone.

Lillian had given her a picture, the edges soft with wear. The little boy, dark skin rendered in pewter gray, gave the camera a cocky grin that showed one missing tooth. Dark hair flopped over his forehead: thick like his father's, but straight as a pin. Huge black eyes took up about a third of his narrow face, in all. His sharp nose was his mother's, and so was the haughty angle of his chin.

"I think the tooth has probably grown in by now," she said, and put the photograph back into her handbag. The joke didn't ease the tension.

Loren parked them at the edge of the quad and sat back in her seat to wait. Before either Memmediv or Cordelia could make a move to get out of the car, she looked out the window and saw a little boy dragging a big suitcase behind him. He did not look happy to be heading toward their car but he was coming anyway, a determined look on his thin face. Lillian had been dead-on about the flags and diplomatic plates; they must look like what he was used to.

"That's him," she said, softly resting her knuckles on the glass.

Memmediv nodded, winced, and got out to meet him. Cordelia followed at a little distance, trying to look small and boring. The kid cased them both with wary eyes, but didn't say a word.

"Stephen DePaul?" said Memmediv.

The boy nodded soberly and offered his small hand to shake. Memmediv took it and introduced himself, with his title.

"Very pleased to meet you," said Stephen, in a swell, slippery voice like his mother and his uncle had. "Has Mummy sent a letter?"

Memmediv produced the letter Lillian had given them, typed up on letterhead and slipped into a velvety, expensive envelope that Memmediv had sealed after he and Cordelia got a look at the contents.

Stephen took it gravely and slit the seal with the attitude of a much older man. It was a little creepy, watching this kid in a blazer and starched white shirt read from the official-looking correspondence on its official-looking paper. When he finished, he put it into the pocket of his jacket and said, very seriously, "I'll just go tell the matron that we're leaving."

When his back was turned, Cordelia caught Memmediv's eye. Neither of them said a word, or changed their faces much, but there was a taut sense of being on the verge of success. Cordelia didn't dare breathe, almost.

Then over Memmediv's shoulder she clocked a face she'd only ever seen in papers. She caught herself before she gasped, turning it into a hitch and then a sigh. Memmediv didn't notice, and when a moment had passed he turned and went off after Stephen. Cordelia stood with the heels of her pumps buried in the gravel like tent stakes, staring at Caleb Acherby: the leader and destroyer of the country.

He was surrounded by bruisers in black suits, guns bald-faced under open jackets. And inside the circle, he was chatting with a man in tweed beneath black robes, some kind of teacher. Headmaster, maybe.

Beside him, a little kid. Younger than Stephen, even—Aldous had told her he was in his first year. That'd make him what, six? Seven? He was stuck to Acherby's side, one hand hooked into the pocket of Acherby's trousers, the other holding a small satchel. The long gray ears of a stuffed rabbit stuck out from under the flap. Around the circle of bodyguards, dozens of kids scurried by, screeching and throwing gravel and pulling each other's hair, or sitting quietly with books, or hugging parents they hadn't seen since the end of August.

She could do it. He was right there, and the gun Aldous had given her was heavy on her chest. All she had to do was pull it out and point it between Acherby's eyes.

He'd even see her face when she pulled the trigger. Queen's cunt, she'd *dreamed* about this moment.

As she watched, Acherby put a hand on the boy's white-blond head with a fondness she'd never gotten from her own father.

Of course it would come to this: her with the revolver, and his rotten kid standing behind him. His kid, and his kid's little friends all around with their runny noses and chapped lips and scabs on their knees.

She tried to imagine it: sent away at six, maybe the farthest you'd ever been from your family, and the longest. And the first time you saw your dad again—your dad who was proud of you and patted your head and applauded when you got a prize at school—a stranger put a bullet in his head.

But she had never been sent away to school, and her dad had never been proud of her or clapped his hands. He'd cuffed her for no reason and gone from her life when she was maybe as old as this kid. Imagining was hard for her, and what Acherby had done to people she loved was all too real.

He ruffled his son's hair, and shook hands with the headmaster. The bodyguards began to shift and clear a path back toward a shining limousine.

Cordelia's heart beat hard, and every pulse pushed against the weight of the revolver in her pocket.

CHAPTER

TWENTY-NINE

Aristide and Pulan heard the news on the wireless the morning they disembarked in Dastya. By dinnertime, every paper had printed the story in every edition, and the pundits were already into their second round of analysis.

Police and military swarmed through the city like ants. On the way to meet Inaz and Asiyah for cocktails, their hired car took them through a few Tatien streets, all hung with Ospie banners, or in some cases with Regionalist blue and gold that sped Aristide's heart uncomfortably. He didn't like to think of himself as particularly political, at least when there was no monetary benefit, but the last time he'd seen those colors displayed anywhere was during the ill-fated election that brought Acherby to power.

There were more police, on the Tatien streets, and more graffiti, but far fewer pedestrians. On these blocks, the driver was generous with his accelerator.

According to the radio, peace talks with Tzieta were on hold while Gedda dealt with this latest crisis. Aristide thought that was imprudent—better to batten what hatches you could in a situation like this. Though, knowing what he did about Memmediv's deal with Pulan, he supposed the outcome of negotiations wouldn't matter one way or the other; the Tatien separatists had their own plans.

Inaz and Asiyah were already checked in at the Byeczic Hotel, waiting for them. The rest of the crew had gone ahead to set up camp, and the other actors were quartered in circumstances rather plainer than the Byeczic but palatial, Aristide was sure, by most actors' standards.

«We expected it,» said Asiyah, when they met for dinner. «Something like this was bound to happen eventually.»

«It may not lead to war,» said Inaz, but even she sounded doubtful. «Not immediately, and not outright.»

«Porachis will back Liso, whatever the outcome is.» Pulan pushed her sea urchin pasta around the plate. She hadn't touched it, and was drinking almost as heavily as Aristide. «I must say I prefer third-party conflicts. They're safe as well as profitable.»

"People love entertainment in a war," Aristide said, applying knife to pork chop with gusto. "You ought to do very well indeed off the licit side of your business."

Overall, he thought that he had taken the news of stockpiled Geddan weapons discovered just south of the Lisoan divide with considerably greater sanguinity than the rest of them. Possibly because he had very little personal stake in the fate of any of the countries involved.

Except, perhaps, that it might make things complicated in Oyoti. But that fence when he came to it.

This was one of those political developments that meant a great deal but wasn't particularly exciting to layfolk. Not quite sensational enough—no sex, murder, or broken taboos. But exactly the kind of thing that would tip two countries out of a proxy war and into open confrontation. There were people in the kingdom who had wanted democracy, or at least the appearance thereof, and were willing to attack their own countrymen if Gedda gave them money and weapons. Up until now, Gedda had just been a little more subtle about it, pushing strictly through its puppet ally, the northern republic. This development destroyed the illusion of neutrality.

It also meant Pulan had an opposite number: someone brokering deals between the Geddan government and republican fighters. He wasn't surprised: Unrest meant money. He'd benefited from the principle often enough to know it was true. In another life, he would have welcomed this news, because it would have meant a tidy profit.

Now, it was simply going to be an inconvenience.

«You're not still planning to go to Liso, are you?» Pulan reached out as though she would touch his wrist, but her fingertips hovered so she never quite made the connection.

He looked up from her extended hand, amused. "Of course I am."

Daoud, at Pulan's elbow, made a small sound. Aristide would have expected scorn from Pulan, but to his surprise, her eyes softened with concern.

«Staying there is going to become more difficult for you every day,» Asiyah cautioned him. «Even in a backwater. Perhaps *especially* in a backwater, and one so far north. If fighting begins in earnest you'll be at the heart of it. And loyalists will not take kindly to a Geddan in their midst.»

«He is saying you're an idiot,» said Inaz, her blunt phrasing at odds with her upswept braids and elegant black gown.

Aristide shrugged. "It will be a while yet, if it happens. And, in the event, I can hold my own." He gave Daoud his warmest smile. It didn't work as well as he'd hoped.

Asiyah's mouth turned down at the corners, but he said nothing.

"Everyone is so dour," said Aristide. If he was honest with himself, their misery put him in an excellent mood. He felt tolerant, a certain tension gone from his shoulders. He was finally on his way to do what he had to, but time and distance prevented him from doing it just yet. Liminal spaces and times—taxis, train compartments, waiting in the wings—had always made him feel a little dizzy. They were filled with freedom, and potential. Teetering on the eve of a big shoot, in the midst of a political crisis that had yet to completely shake out, had gone to his head like champagne.

Spur of the moment, he raised his wineglass and offered, "To present endeavors. May the good succeed, and all the rest fall flat."

The rest of the company lifted their drinks. Looking straight at Aristide, Pulan added, "And I hope we have the wisdom to choose between them."

They'd waited to tell Stephen what was going on until they were far beyond the bounds of Cantrell, out in the farmland among the huddled sheep and slumping stone boundary walls.

He hadn't believed them at first, and then once he clocked they weren't trying to put a bag on his head he dropped the old-man act and turned into an eight-year-old boy at last, crowing and bouncing in his seat and asking a long string of questions without any breaks for answers in between.

It would have been cute, if they'd only been stuck in the car with him for an hour or two. But the drive to the border wasn't a jaunt, and the novelty of having a little boy along for the ride had faded.

"I really need to use the toilet," Stephen said, for the third time in as many minutes. This was a reprise; he'd first mentioned it about an hour back, and when Cordelia told Memmediv to pull over the boy had stared at her in horror. She'd shrugged and told Memmediv to drive on.

"Then you gotta piss by the road," said Cordelia. "Like I told you. Are you ready to do that yet? 'Cause if you just give me that look again, we ain't stopping."

He *did* give her the look again, but this time she saw his eyes were turning wet. She wasn't ready to have him piss himself *and* cry. "All right, Vaz, pull over when you can."

Loren had taken the train back to Amberlough and left them with the car. Cordelia had ditched the flags and false plates and replaced them with some more innocuous ones Kurt had dug out of a scrap pile. Now Memmediv was driving—Cordelia couldn't, and getting stopped for failing to indicate or crossing a center line wasn't something they could afford right now.

Not that there was anybody to stop them out here. Memmediv pulled over to the verge in the middle of a wide stretch of prairie, mown down and gathered into hayricks. The vista was bordered far to the northwest by the foothills of the Culthams. Cordelia could just make them out, shrouded in tattered cloud and broken beams of sunshine.

A small hand tapped her knee.

"What?" she asked, eyes coming down from the mountains.

But Stephen didn't even squeak; just looked at her with a lip that trembled until he bit down to make it stop.

"Come on," she said, turning irritable, "we're in a hurry."

One of the tears escaped and rolled down his cheek. A flush

had crept across his nose, and he wouldn't meet her eyes. "I don't have to . . . to . . ."

"Oh, Lady's name," said Cordelia, and was about to tell Memmediv to keep driving, but then Stephen blurted out, "It's the *other* one," in a cracked little voice that Cordelia was sure would have broken his mother's heart. She busted into raucous laughter, clutching the car door to keep herself upright. Even Memmediv, in the driver's seat, had to work to keep his dour face from cracking.

Stephen's woeful expression twisted into anger. "Don't *laugh* at me!"

"I ain't, I ain't!" Struggling mightily, she sucked in a breath. "Mother's tits, I needed that." Her belly ached and her shoulders were free from tension for the first time since before she could remember. "Come on. You can do that by the side of the road too."

He stared at her, goggling, mouth open just wide enough she could see the tips of his too-big front teeth.

"I done it," she said. Because when you were living rough in the mountains, there wasn't always an outhouse. "You're lucky—you got a nice wall to lean against."

"But," he said, and didn't go on.

"Come on," she said. "This is how soldiers do it. Or . . . I dunno. It's how you'd do it if you were on an adventure."

"Like Captain Courageous?" he asked.

She cast a look at Memmediv, who said softly, "Comic strips." Full of surprises, this one.

"Sure," she said, "just like Captain Courageous."

At this, Stephen's jaw tightened up and he nodded stiffly. Cordelia got out of the car and walked over to the crumbly stone wall at the road's border. There were some goats in the field, but they were far off, standing around a pile of hay.

"All right," she said, "over the wall."

He scrambled over with the speed and gravity of a spy infiltrating an enemy camp.

"Bottoms down and squat," she said. "I'll watch your back."

While the kid did his business, she sat on the wall and stared off toward the mountains. The ache of laughter still lingered in her belly, but it settled there heavily now.

She hadn't had a quiet moment alone since Cantrell to think about the choice she'd made. This would have to do.

It wasn't just the kid. It wasn't just what Memmediv had said to her. It was some combination of the two, and not quite either of them.

Opal had told her if she got drug in, the Catwalk would crumble. But she'd vanished into thin air and when she'd come down again, her people were still there. Scared and scattered, maybe, but still ready to sneak and fight. If she had never shown up again she hoped they would have sorted themselves out, gotten their feet back under them. If she—Lady keep her—ended up scratched, she didn't think it would be the end of them.

Maybe it was superstition, but in the moment that it really counted, she found she couldn't believe that about her folk, and anything else about Acherby's. Or rather, if she killed Acherby, it would be admitting that a single person stood for any idea—hope or hate or progress—and that when the person died, the idea did, too.

She hadn't been able to hash it out in the split second circumstance gave her. Now, with nothing but the wind in her ears, she knew that's what it was. She couldn't bear to be the only hope her people had—because then what hope could she put in them? It didn't work like that. Maybe Acherby thought it did, but she didn't want to be like him in any way.

"Um," said Stephen, from behind the wall. "I . . . do you have . . ."

She reached into her handbag and pulled out a handkerchief. "Ditch it when you're done," she said. It was the only one she'd brought, but if her nose ran she'd just use her sleeve. It wasn't like she intended to keep the suit. Wouldn't do her much good crawling through the Culthams.

They reached the Tzietan border sometime after dark. It shouldn't have taken so long, but they were staying off the main highways to avoid notice. If Flagg's folk had come for Stephen after he was gone, the confusion was bound to get the hounds' noses to the earth. But they'd been lucky, and seen only three other cars in the whole time they'd been on the road.

Stephen was asleep in the back, lying down across the seat and making little noises every now and then as he dreamed.

Memmediv, who'd been driving nearly eight hours with a bad head, looked like he wanted to lie down in the backseat, too. His expression had grown more pinched as they got closer to the border, and Cordelia couldn't tell if it was pain or nerves.

"Really," she said, "I can drive."

"Don't offer again," he said, terse but quiet. "This close to the border I don't want anything to go wrong."

"How long 'til we ditch the car?"

He lifted one shoulder. "Fifteen minutes?"

"And the walk?"

"An hour to the rendezvous, maybe."

"You know this route pretty well, huh?"

In the moonlight, and the glow of the headlights bouncing

back from the road, the line bracketing his half smile cast a deep shadow. "I have been fighting this war for a long time."

"I thought it all mostly happened in the south, near the harbor."

"It's harder to get people and supplies across the border there; everything is watched more closely, more tightly controlled. Here, it is easier to bribe guards at the checkpoints, or avoid them altogether."

She made a small sound of understanding, and leaned her head against the window. The glass was cold on her forehead, the stars painfully clear.

"Did you know," he said, so quietly he could have been talking to himself. Then he didn't say anything for so long she started to think she had imagined it, or that some swelling in his head had finally burst and he'd lost the power of speech. Then, "This is what he was doing before he . . . before the Ospies." Another long pause, and then he said even more quietly—and rough, like the words were digging in their claws—"DePaul, I mean. Cyril."

At the name, she froze. She had almost forgotten. It was like the tide, ebbing and flowing: Sometimes she hated Memmediv for what he'd done, and other times—like just now, after hours in a quiet car with the countryside rolling past them—he was just a partner in this scheme, the getaway driver, the man who knew how to cross the Tzietan border without getting caught. The one who read the same comic strips as Stephen.

He hadn't talked about his time in the CIS that much, and certainly not since they left Porachis. Probably he knew it would get her hard beneath the ribs like this and stoke her anger.

But it had put an itch in her, too. "Yeah? Doing what?"

He shrugged. "I'm not entirely sure. My old boss, Ada Culpepper, she was his case officer for a while. The information he was gathering mostly had to do with the militia's capabilities. I was . . . angry when I found out Amberlough was spying on us, but not surprised."

"Is that why you turned him over to the Ospies?"

He didn't answer at first—they had been gaining altitude, and the road had grown potholed and treacherous. Their path wound between buttes and stony rises crusted with frost, saw grass growing in their crevices. Between each bit of scrabbly mountain bone that poked from the earth were narrow meadows of tall weeds, all turned brown by the cold. It was into one of these that Memmediv pulled the car. They rattled over the rocky ground until they were out of sight of the road. In the back, Stephen halfwoke and said, "What?"

"Shh." Memmediv cut the lights. "We're almost there."

"Mm." Stephen laid back down.

"I ain't carrying him," said Cordelia.

Memmediv ignored her quip. "Get out and stretch. Change into your boots."

The hills to either side cut most of the wind, but she could hear it whining and gibbering between the standing stones and hissing through the grass. Buttoning her coat against the chill, she felt the revolver bounce against her breastbone.

She unbuttoned her coat again.

Without the headlights shining into the meadow, the angle of the moon cast everything into deep shadow. Memmediv was a moving patch of darker black, who she could mostly keep track of by sound. He trudged through the grass, took a piss behind a clump of gorse, and came back to the car. There was a brief spark, a flame that wavered in the protective curl of his palm, and the flare of a straight.

"I'll take one," she said.

He sighed, brow weary in the light of the cigarette, and handed her the one he'd just lit.

"It didn't hurt," he said.

"What?" It was late, and she was tired; the thread of their conversation had slipped just out of reach.

"The fact that DePaul had been selling our military secrets to Amberlough's Foxhole. It was not endearing. It made him easier to turn over."

Cordelia took a long drag on the straight and let the breath out as slowly. The weight of the gun pressed the smoke from her lungs. "Don't tell me you regret it, 'cause it won't do any good."

"I wasn't going to." He held out his thumb and forefinger, and she passed the cigarette back. Her hands were free now, and even though the cold made her left wrist ache, and recoil would make it hurt worse, she knew she could squeeze a shot off pretty fast.

But then who would harry Acherby's eastern flank? What would she tell Pulan when she showed up with Stephen alone? And if she was going to spare Acherby's kid the sight of brains blown out across the ground, why should Stephen have to see it?

Like she'd said to Ari: Memmediv had something she wanted, and to get it she had to put aside history and make peace with him.

Bitterness coated her mouth. She reached for the straight and he handed it back, still wet from the inner edges of his lips.

Memmediv picked a fleck of tobacco from his tongue. "I don't regret much. I just wanted to say it. I'm not even sure Lillian knows what he was doing, or where he was. I wanted . . . it seemed right, that somebody should know. So much of what we do, nobody will ever hear about. Or, if they do, they will not know our names."

The truth of it struck home. How many of her own folk only knew her as Spotlight? How many of them had ever clapped eyes on her, or knew her for the stripper at the Bee? She was a stranger to most of them, and would be forever unless by some miracle they won this fight and . . . what, they put her name in a book, on a plaque? Made a sculpture and put it in Loendler Park?

Flicking the straight to the ground and grinding it under her heel, she said, "Enough jawing about that; it's over and done. Let's stroll."

Memmediv turned up his collar so she couldn't see his face except the shards of moonlight that caught in his eyes. "Right," he said, and opened the rear door of the car. Stephen drew his knees up at the cold air and made a grouchy sound of protest, but didn't wake. "I'll carry him."

"What about his stuff?" Cordelia asked, jerking her chin at the trunk of the car, where they'd shut Stephen's luggage.

There was a pause, and then—did he sound pained? Or was that her imagination?—"Bring the small case. The rest is just a sacrifice to the cause."

He cried. Oh, mother's tits did he cry. Cordelia sent up a string of thanks to the Queen if she was listening: his blankie and his stuffed dog, Dash, had been in the luggage they brought along, and from the worn edges and frayed hems they were his best-loved bits of stuff. If they'd left those on the Geddan side of the border, no power would have saved them from his wrath.

Luckily, he didn't wake until they were safe in the back of a truck, rumbling through the midnight steppe a mile or so inside of Tzieta. And he was so tired and confused that after sobbing hysterically for about ten minutes he fell asleep again with his snotty nose in Cordelia's lap.

This dynamite Pulan had promised her had better blow the Ospies' oysters off.

The murk of predawn found them drawing to a stop outside a ring of elaborate canvas tents: massive things, more like houses than any camping equipment Cordelia had ever seen. Not that she'd seen a lot of it until this latest episode in her life, sleeping under tarps in the paltry shelter of hillside lees. This was a lot nicer than any of that.

The driver, whose name was Nafaz, hopped out of the car and held her arms out for Stephen. Cordelia maneuvered his dead weight into them. Nafaz murmured something in Porashtu, and Stephen responded sleepily, then tucked his face into her neck.

Stiff and exhausted, Cordelia clambered out of the truck and almost fell over. Her legs were cramped with cold and bracing against the jolt and bounce of the moving vehicle. Memmediv followed her down with a grunt.

Nafaz took them to an empty tent at the edge of the circle, with two empty cots. For the second time in recent memory, Cordelia ended up with a snuffling kid tucked into her belly on a tiny bed. This time, though, she dropped off faster than a dead pigeon.

Noise woke her up not long after, unrested and unused to feeling it. It was too easy to turn soft.

Then she noticed Stephen was gone, and was off the cot and nearly out the tent flap before she realized Memmediv was gone, too, and that the noise that had woken her sounded a lot like breakfast.

The last of the fear-ice melted out of her veins when she got to the mess tent—did they call it that on picture sets?—and saw Stephen tucked up against who else but Inaz Iligba, stuffing syrup-slathered cheese dumplings into his face like he hadn't spent the wee hours howling over his comic book collection.

And there, across from Inaz, drinking coffee from a porcelain cup just as if he'd been in a fancy café or his own dining room, a man she'd never expected to see within twenty-five miles of a tent.

"Ari," she said.

He set his cup down in its saucer. "You sound surprised. Weren't you the one who said we'd see each other in Tzieta? Didn't you believe it, at the time?"

It was only then she realized: She hadn't really thought they would succeed.

Then it was *her* crying. When she wiped her face on her sleeve, and he gave her a napkin and said, "Don't you have a handkerchief?" her tears turned to laughter. Then she sat down to eat for the first time in a full turn of the clock, with a real appetite she hardly remembered having since her days onstage.

Pulan had put off shooting until later in the day, to get Aristide, Asiyah, and Stephen safely off without the entire cast of the film watching them go and wondering where.

After breakfast, Pulan kissed Aristide's cheek. "The film will suffer for your absence."

"And you will suffer for Daoud's, I'm sure."

She followed the kiss with a gentle slap and a quick, dirty admonition in Porashtu that he didn't quite catch. Daoud, clearing up his breakfast dishes, winced.

"Thief," said Pulan, pouting.

"Please," said Aristide. "I'm a legitimate businessman."

Memmediv, at the other end of the folding camp table, made an eloquent sound through his nostrils. Aristide ignored him, and did not say goodbye.

The plane—a yellow-and-white-striped three-seater with candy-red propellers—was parked on blocks in a field a quarter mile from the camp. Aristide was not looking forward to this part of their escapade.

Asiyah led the relevant parties through the high brown grass to the makeshift runway. Cordelia, Inaz, and Pulan came along to see them off. When Stephen saw the plane his eyes went wide: so large Aristide half-worried they would fall out of his face. Over breakfast, the boy had been charmingly rambunctious, but as they walked he had grown quiet and developed a furrow in his brow that put Aristide in mind—awfully—of his uncle.

"I've never flown in an airplane before," he said to Aristide.

"Neither have I." Aristide was unused to children and so spoke to him like a four-foot-tall adult.

"Are you frightened?"

He lied often to anyone, when there was utility in it, but saw none here. "Terrified."

"Holy stones, Ari." Cordelia rolled her eyes. "You were born to be a rotten nanny, weren't you?" Then, to Stephen, "Captain Courageous ever fly?"

He nodded slowly. "Yes. And once, he had to walk on the wing to shoot a baddie who wanted to blow up the airplane and kill him and Dash, his dog."

"Ah," she said. "Like your Dash. You got him?"

Stephen lifted his tiny suitcase.

"Well," she said, "I don't think you and Dash are gonna have to do any wing-walking. Just listen to what Asiyah tells you. I bet it'll be fun." This last bit—including the injunction to listen to Asiyah—she aimed rather pointedly at Aristide.

In the plane, Asiyah was arranging sheepskin across the seats. Inaz lingered nearby, watching him with a pleat of concern around one corner of her mouth that did nothing to settle Aristide's nerves.

If Inaz had flown with him before, and *she* had that look on her face . . .

"All right," Asiyah announced, shouldering into a sheepskin jacket that made him look less princely and even more like a rogue than usual. "Time to say goodbye. We have a nice wind and I do not want to lose it."

"Be good," Cordelia said to Stephen. "Piss now, 'cause he ain't gonna pull over for you."

"I don't have to," said Stephen. Cordelia cocked an eyebrow at him. He gave a heavy sigh and set down his suitcase.

"Good kid," she said. "There's a nice rock over there."

Pulan and Daoud stepped off from the group, to have whatever farewell they felt was necessary. Daoud had, Aristide supposed, worked with her for some time, doing all sorts of unsavory things; it was worth five minutes before they parted ways.

Inaz and Asiyah were occupied with an intimate and enthusiastic farewell against the fuselage, which left Aristide and Cordelia standing face-to-face in the middle of a field, about to part. Possibly for the last time.

"So you've never flown before?" She said it in the direction of the plane, rather than to him.

"No," he said. "Why, have you?"

She snorted and shook her head, messy curls falling out of their much-abused finger waves to cross her forehead. "Where would I have found a plane?"

"Well, you've gotten up to all sorts of other mischief while my back was turned. Can you blame me for asking?"

"No," she said, and the light in her eyes dimmed suddenly.

"Cordelia," he said, and she finally looked at him. "Are you . . . you're sure about this. About staying here. You aren't frightened?"

"Sure I am," she said. "But didn't you ever want something even though it scared your guts clean?"

"Will it be worth it?"

"I hope so."

"And you trust him. Memmediv."

He didn't like the way her jaw moved, or the way she shifted her weight from one side to the other. Before she spoke she gave a sharp nod, as though she wanted to convince both of them. "I trust he wants his as much as I want mine. And as long as those two paths run side by side, we'll do all right."

Aristide's nails bit the inside of his palm. "Promise me you'll put a bullet in his head the moment he crosses you."

It didn't make her laugh; he wasn't sure he'd wanted it to. "If he does. If I can."

"Aristide." Asiyah was hanging out of the cockpit. "I am ready." Daoud was buckled in at the rear, short enough to clear the narrowing fuselage. Stephen stood patiently as Inaz swaddled him in sheepskins.

Cordelia turned back to Aristide like she wanted to say something else, but couldn't think of exactly what. She shook it off, whatever it was, and said instead, "I'll . . . well, I'll . . ."

"Be seeing me?" Campy disdain curled off of it: the same tone he used to use with punters, when he picked on them from the stage. It had the desired effect: She smiled.

"I guess not," she said. "For a while, anyway."

He wished she hadn't tacked that last bit on. It felt like an assurance neither of them would make good on easily. He couldn't imagine going back to Amberlough. He couldn't imagine her getting out, not a second time. For one thing, he didn't think she wanted to. There was something in her bearing, on the verge of departure, that had been absent from it thus far. A lift to her spine, an angle to her shot-away chin. In profile, she looked a little like the airplane: small and scrappy, nose pointed to the sky. Like she might take off and defy all expectations of physics, logic, common sense.

It made her beautiful, and reminded him of how things had been. For once, he didn't jerk back from the thought. Her presence had begun to temper the pain of his memories. And now, she was leaving, and so was he.

He didn't know how to do this. He had spent his life not doing this.

On her small, round shoulders his hands looked huge. He tried to let them rest lightly, so that she need not bear his weight. When he squeezed, he could feel her collarbone beneath the wool and skin and muscle.

Aristide had known so many ferocious people in his life, himself included. But in the end they were all bones, barely shielded from the world and all too easy to break. He hated to be reminded.

"Cordelia," he said. "Be careful."

She snorted derisively, but there was a shadow in her eyes. "Yeah, all right, Ma. I'll do my best."

"Really," he said.

A dimple appeared in her chin, and her lips pressed together so firmly that a bloodless white halo formed at their edges. "Really," she said, and the word barely made it out. "But I ain't making any promises."

Asiyah called his name again. Aristide ignored him.

"If anything happens," she said, and had to swallow hard. "If anything happens to me, I want . . . I just want folk to know what I did. All the way from the Bee to now. I just been working so hard, Ari, and I'm stagefolk still, deep down. I miss the applause, you know?"

Her slum whine haunted the vowels, conjuring the swish of

velvet curtains, the clatter of backstage at the interval. The smells of street food, sawdust, greasepaint, sweat.

"I do," he said.

"Will you make sure?"

He didn't often make promises, and when he did, he rarely kept them. But this one felt like a folktale geis that would boil his blood if he broke it. "I will."

"Thanks," she said, and wiped roughly at her eyes.

"And . . ." He couldn't look at her, but he made himself do it, commit her to memory as she was and remember her as she had been.

"And?" she prompted.

He swallowed against the tightness in his throat that threatened to cut off the words. "Thank you."

"What for, you overgrown blush boy?"

He pressed her shoulders once more, reassuring himself that she was truly here, that this wasn't one of those dreams he'd had where he did something he'd failed to do in waking life. He'd had those too often, since leaving Gedda.

"For the chance," he said, "to say goodbye."

CHAPTER

THIRTY

In the Grand Ldotho Hotel in Dadang, northernmost port city in the Kingdom of Liso, Lillian had fallen asleep by the telephone. She half-woke to Jinadh standing beside her chair, towel around his waist, receiver tucked between shoulder and ear.

«Yes, we look forward to seeing him,» he said, and Lillian was instantly alert. «Thank you for telephoning. Mmhm. Yes. Thank you again. Goodbye.»

«They've left?» she asked.

«This morning, early. They'll stop to refuel in Hyrosia, and should be here by tonight if the weather holds.»

Suddenly, the day stretched ahead like an endurance trial. Jinadh took one look at her face and said, «Let's go find something to eat. And then perhaps see a film?»

They did exactly that. The concierge directed them to a restaurant overlooking the harbor, which served rich lamb stew thickened with ground peanuts. Neither of them ate much. Jinadh attempted to be cheerful, which only made Lillian snappish.

During the newsreel that played before the latest Porachin export, the audience shifted and murmured. Lillian's Shedengue was rough at best, but she made out half sentences and whispered speculations about how the king and queen would respond to the Geddan threat to their sovereignty.

Lillian pitied whatever poor press secretary would have to speak on the palace's behalf, and felt guilty and grateful to be leaving the whole mess behind for Asu.

Then, politics disguised as a fluff piece: Lady Suhaila, third heir to the Porachin throne, receiving two Geddan refugees at the palace. The Porashtu reporter called them Mab Cattayim and Sofie Keeler, "companions," and she could parse enough of the Shedengue subtitles to tell they were likewise evasive.

Still, the two women were together, and safe for now: replacing Makricosta as the queen's symbolic charity case. Something she could feel good about, at least.

When they came out of the air-conditioned movie palace, the temperature felt even more oppressive than before.

«I rarely admit to this,» said Lillian, squinting in the sunlight, «but I suppose it's all right if I'm not the face of the Ospies anymore. I could really use a drink.»

Jinadh's laugh cracked as it came out. «Of course.»

They returned to the hotel bar, because the afternoon was waning and neither of them wanted to be away when Stephen arrived. It was not crowded at this hour, and service was swift. Lillian, sinking into the luxury of being unobserved, unremarked, unaccountable, held her gimlet to her forehead for a long time before she sipped.

"We have to talk about this before he arrives," she said, when she was halfway through the cocktail.

"'This' what?" said Jinadh, running a finger around the edge of his glass. He was drinking arrack cut with seltzer, milky-pale and shimmering with effervescence.

"What we're going to tell him. About his father."

"I am his father. Is there more to tell?"

"You know it isn't that simple."

He sighed and tipped his glass back. A drop of condensation fell from its foot and splashed the bar. «No. Of course not.» He stared down at the water droplet on the polished brass, drew his finger through it, refused to look at her.

«You're afraid,» she said.

«Can you blame me?» Now he did lift his eyes. «He may have spent the last two years away at school, but he grew up Porachin. He knows exactly what I've done, and what he is.»

There was nothing she could say to that; it was true. She only hoped that Stephen wouldn't spit on his father like people in the streets.

"What should we tell him about Gedda?" she asked. "And Liso?"

Jinadh shook his head. "I do not think he needs to know about that. Not unless it leads to something he can understand. He will have to adjust to so much already."

It was difficult, even for Lillian, to conceive of the magnitude of the change Stephen would face. He wouldn't be going back to Cantrell, or even to Porachis; they were moving to Sunho: a city larger and louder than any he'd ever seen. Whatever friends he'd made at school he would never see again. Whatever he loved best about Porachis was lost to him, perhaps forever.

The temptation was so horribly strong to treat it like a press conference: delivering facts coolly, refusing to take questions. But this was her *son*; he deserved a compassionate truth.

She finished her gimlet in one long swallow, and flagged the bartender down for another.

Stephen grew quiet as they drove away from the airfield. He had been glued to the window throughout the flight. Daoud had slept most of the time, and Asiyah had been busy keeping them aloft. Aristide could barely look down, but Stephen—sitting in his lap, because the plane was small, and hadn't *that* been a novel experience—kept a running commentary on all the things he could see: farms, cities, dolphins, islands, flocks of birds, the shadows of clouds. And he had been chatty as a mockingbird at the stop in Hyrosia, too. Daoud had uncurled from the rear seat to stretch his legs, and taken Stephen into the airfield bar for almond candies and a seltzer. He'd come back sticky and sugar-mad.

That hadn't lasted, and the second leg of the flight he'd spoken less, and rather more curtly when he did. Now he was cranky, tired, and judging from his somber expression, nervous.

Daoud, to Aristide's chagrin, had begun to act roughly the same. He hunched in the front seat, tapping the upholstery with his fingers. Occasionally he let out a beleaguered sigh.

Aristide was not a comforter, by nature or by practice, so he talked to Asiyah and let his new secretary fret up front. Stephen was a silent, brooding presence between him and the prince, suitcase on his lap and stuffed dog clutched to his chest.

"What's the most expedient route to Oyoti from Dadang?" Aristide asked. The tense, hushed atmosphere in the car pushed his volume down to just above a whisper.

"Hire a driver," said Asiyah, matching his tone but not meeting his eyes. "The trains do not go all the way in. The nearest you can go by rail is Ul-Kisr, and then you need a car. You are still determined to do this?"

"Why?" asked Aristide. "This war we're supposed to have?"

Asiyah turned to glare at him, stiff-jawed, and raised his eyebrows in a question. Aristide didn't clock his meaning until he angled his eyes at Stephen.

The boy was staring up at Aristide, mouth ajar. "A war?" he said. "Where?"

"Nowhere you're going," Aristide said. Which was apparently the wrong thing, because Asiyah made a hopeless choked sound and Stephen got that Cyril-like furrow between his brows again. Aristide had to look away, out the window of the car.

He was in Liso now. One step closer to an impossible goal he would hardly let himself conceive of.

Stephen didn't leave him alone. "But you are. Going to the war. Are you a soldier?"

"Have I given that impression?" asked Aristide, glancing back. "Lady's name, I've let myself slide."

"So you aren't a soldier," said Stephen. "Why are you going to war?"

"He is not going to war," said Asiyah, sliding an irritated glance at Aristide from the corners of his eyes. "He is being an idiot."

Stephen turned to Asiyah. "You shouldn't call people names," he said gravely. "Even if you are a prince."

Slightly taken aback, Asiyah struggled for words. Aristide slid smoothly into the gap and said, "Very true, Your Highness. Very true."

"I apologize," said Asiyah, mock-grave. "I did not mean to say he is an idiot. Only that he is in love."

If not for Stephen in between them, Aristide might have struck him. In the front seat Daoud shifted, then froze when the leather creaked beneath his weight.

"With who?" asked Stephen.

Aristide scowled. "Ask your mother," he said, and put his back to the boy.

Undeterred, Stephen said, "Prince Asiyah, is there really going to be a war?"

"Ask your mother," said Asiyah, and they all sat in silence for the rest of the drive.

The gimlet had taken enough of the edge off Lillian's anxiety that she realized how tired she was. Jinadh suggested she try to sleep, but she kept him from doing the same by restlessly tangling herself in the sheets, unable to get comfortable. It was a relief when the telephone rang.

"He's downstairs," she said to Jinadh, after she hung up. She wondered if her face looked quite as apprehensive as his, and tried to raise her cheeks for a smile. It didn't feel quite right on her face, and judging from his reaction, didn't look right, either.

But when the lift doors opened and she saw Stephen sitting on one of the caned chairs, all the stiffness melted from her; she could feel the grin stretching across her teeth, cramping the muscles below her eyes.

Breeze from the ceiling fans ruffled his hair. He still wore his school uniform, horribly wrinkled, and he was eating a stick of peanut-honey candy. There was a crumb on his face, near the corner of his mouth. She could see all of this in minute detail, crisp and super-saturated.

She didn't realize she had said his name until he looked up. She stepped out of the lift and he jumped from the chair—so much taller than when she'd last seen him, limbs too long for the rest of his body. Running across the room, he pitched himself at her belly and wrapped his arms around her waist so tightly that the ridges of his knuckles made her bones ache where he clasped his hands. His cheek pressed into the arch of her stomach just below her ribs, and she could feel his breath through her shirt.

Words failed her. She might have said *I missed you,* or even just *Hello,* but she could only hold him more tightly, pressing his sharp cheekbone more deeply into her flesh, pushing her fingers through his hair—mother and sons, he needed a bath, his hair was *filthy*—and kissing the top of his head.

"I flew on an *airplane,*" he told her, and she burst into something not quite fully tears, but not quite laughter, either.

"It was *so* much fun," he went on, ignoring her hysteria with a child's innocent narcissism. "Prince Asiyah can *fly,* like Captain Courageous! And in Hyrosia when we stopped to refuel there were *goats* on the *runway* and a woman had to come with a stick and chase them away before we could take off again."

"How exciting," she said. His hair was wet now with her tears. "Did you thank Ms. Lehane and Mr. Memmediv for picking you up from school?"

He pushed back from her embrace and gaped up at her. "They left my comics in the car. And Ms. Lehane made me poo in a field!" When she burst into helpless, tearful laughter once again he said, "It wasn't funny. She said that's how soldiers do it."

"I'm sure it is," she said, voice wobbling, drawing him close again.

Face tucked against her chest, he said, "Mr. Makricosta told me that there would be a war."

The bottom dropped out of her stomach and she shot a very cold look indeed at Mr. Makricosta, where he was chatting with the concierge. He caught it and looked confused.

Just one more thing to explain to Stephen, then, in a long list of difficult subjects.

Over Stephen's tangles of dirty hair, she saw Jinadh watching them, weight pitched forward onto the balls of his feet, like he wanted to join but couldn't. Untangling one hand from the back of Stephen's head, she beckoned to him. He staggered slightly, like a drunk or a sleepwalker, then caught himself and walked on with more composure.

"Stephen," she said, when he was by her side. "Do you remember Mr. Addas?"

Wriggling from Lillian's arms, Stephen looked up. His eyebrows knit together in a frown so like Jinadh's she couldn't believe he didn't recognize the man who had made half of him; she would have thought it was like looking in a mirror.

"I think we met once," he said. "At a party?"

"Yes," she said. "He'd like to speak with you."

Jinadh added, «We have some exciting news.»

The wrinkle between Stephen's eyebrows deepened momentarily before he smoothed his expression into a mask of geniality. *That* talent he had from both of them, and she suspected it had gotten him out of lots of scrapes with authority at school.

She also suspected that right now, he was using it to put them at their ease, while gears turned inside his tousled head. How had he grown up so much like both of them, so far away, only knowing half the truth about himself?

It broke her heart that he had become so guarded, so soon, even as it choked her with pride.

«I've kept up my Porashtu,» he told Lillian. Then, to Jinadh, «Do you speak Geddan, Mr. Addas?»

"I do," said Jinadh. "And I suspect that soon I will have to learn Asunese."

"I know some!" said Stephen. "I had a friend at school who was from there."

"Maybe you can teach me," said Jinadh, and Lillian found that her heart wasn't broken after all—only aching with fear and hope and a thousand other things she finally allowed herself to feel.

«Come on,» she said, letting it all show in the tremor of her voice, her outstretched, shaking hands. «Let's go bend our knees and have a chat.»

This touching family drama was all very well, but Aristide had business to take care of.

Daoud had peeled off as soon as they struck the marble floor of the lobby, snatched a key from the concierge, and disappeared into the lift.

The concierge handed Aristide his own key and informed him of his suite number. When he arrived, he found Daoud nervously arranging piles of luggage.

"Did it all come through?" asked Aristide. "I'm sure they've lost something. They always do."

Daoud brushed his hands together as though they were dusty from some kind of rural labor. «You are not seriously planning to take all of this with you,» he said, a caricature of criticism so elaborate Aristide suspected it might be a cover. «It's folly even to go to Oyoti now. Folly to stay this far north. Perhaps we should go down to Rarom, take a house there, wait and see—»

"Where are you keeping that pistol I gave you?" Aristide asked, pouring himself a glass of fig brandy from the bar. He hadn't had a drink since the Byeczik, and had started to notice a fine tremor in his hands. Better to still that before anyone else saw it, too.

"In my valise," said Daoud, very quietly. As though he hoped Aristide wouldn't hear him.

"Get it out now." He lit a cigarette. "Put it in your pocket." Smoke poured from his mouth on the plosives.

"I do not think that I will need a gun in Dadang," said Daoud. It was not Aristide's imagination: The humor in his tone verged on hysteria. "There is not a war *yet*."

"And by the time you *do* need one, you ought to be comfortable carrying and drawing it."

Daoud paused in his frantic arrangement of luggage and stood above his own cases, staring down at the leather and latches like he didn't recognize what they were.

"Unless you don't want to carry it at all," said Aristide, giving him the out he so obviously, desperately wanted. "Are you having second thoughts? If that's the case, it would be better to decide now."

"I—" Knuckles to his lips, he glared at the top of his smallest suitcase.

"It's real to you now, isn't it?" said Aristide softly. The first effects of the brandy on his empty stomach made him charitable, empathetic.

«Do not shame me,» Daoud said, voice quavering. Surrounded by stacked trunks beneath a vaulted ceiling held aloft by columns, lit by rays from narrow windows tall as two men, he looked even more diminutive than usual: a slender figure surrounded by something so much larger than himself.

"I wasn't going to," said Aristide, which was as much pragmatism as it was kindness. He would rather Daoud falter now, and leave him to his own devices, than follow him into the jungle and fall apart. "Didi, this is like nothing you've ever done before. It's going to be terrifying, I won't lie to you. The only question is whether you're ready to try it."

"How can I possibly know a thing like that?"

Aristide, perched on the sofa with one ankle over his knee,

stared at the boy for a long moment, then patted the upholstery beside him, careful not to scatter ash. "Come here."

Daoud's eyes were suspicious.

"I'm not . . . oh, Lady's sake, I want to tell you something. It might help. But I don't want to shout across the room."

Daoud settled on the sofa with a safe six inches between their knees. Aristide turned toward him and said, keenly conscious of his own age and the absurdity of his gravitas, "You'll never know. I didn't. And I was younger than you by almost a decade when I made my decision."

Daoud had clocked Aristide's rare candid mood. "To do what?"

"Well, I didn't go into a war zone," said Aristide. "But I certainly flung myself off some kind of cliff. I spent my childhood chasing after sheep and chafing under my father's orders, and I hated it so much I dove headlong into Amberlough City without the slightest idea of how hard it would be. And believe me, it was worse than you imagine."

"You are not helping," said Daoud.

"Listen to me, you runty cade," said Aristide, loosening the jess he kept around the ankle of his burr. "I'm saying ye've got more than I ever had: Ye know what ye're about to do'll be hard, and you've got me to tell ye *how* hard, exactly. Ye've got somebody to snatch your braces and haul you back to standing and believe me, I will. I won't leave ye wailing in the mud; ye're no good to me there."

Daoud's expression had lost some of its terror. In its place, bemusement. "Your voice," he said. "Why did it—"

"To prove a point." Aristide fell back into the clotted cream of his Central City intonations. "This may be harder for you than it was for me—at least in my case I was used to hardship, of a different kind."

"Life has been cruel enough to me," said Daoud.

"Of course it has, according to your metrics. Are you ready for those metrics to change? They will, drastically. It might not be a bad thing. It wasn't, for me; it put things in perspective. But some people prefer to live without that particular asset. The only question is, are you one of them?"

Daoud's liquid eyes hardened to volcanic glass. "And if I'm not?"

"Then you'd better get that pistol out of your valise and put it in your pocket now."

His frown deepened, but he let out a long breath Aristide suspected he had been holding. Then he rose from the sofa and went to his luggage. Unerring, he chose the piece he needed and had the pistol out within a moment. He weighed it in his hand, then fit it neatly into the inner pocket of his jacket. The linen, already wrinkled, neatly hid the shape of the gun.

"Right," said Aristide. "Now, let's go hunting."